From science fiction to fantasy—and everything in between . . .

FULL
SPECTRUM

Richard Grant's "Magister Rudy"—A young boy living in a repressive police state of the future discovers the terrifying and liberating evidence that he can alter reality—with his mind.

T.L. Parkinson's "My Imaginary Parents"—Billy has undeniable evidence that his family is composed of ghosts—or does he?

Pat Murphy's "Dead Men on TV"—The flickering ghosts of Hollywood's past become a dangerous obsession for a young woman mourning the loss of her movie-star father.

Elissa Malcohn's "Moments of Clarity"—Two hospital patients lie near death: a woman who knows the future and a man who forgets the past.

James Morrow's "Bible Stories for Adults, No. 17: The Deluge"—An unexpected passenger on the Ark throws a chink into God's plan—and sets humanity off on an alternate course.

And Much More

FULL
SPECTRUM

EDITED BY
LOU ARONICA
AND
SHAWNA McCARTHY

BANTAM BOOKS

FULL SPECTRUM

A Bantam Spectra Book / September 1988

Bantam Books are published by Bantam Books, a division of Bantam Doubleday
Dell Publishing Group, Inc. Its trademark, consisting of the words "Bantam
Books" and the portrayal of a rooster, is Registered in U.S. Patent and Trademark
Office and in other countries. Marca Registrada. Bantam Books, 666 Fifth Avenue,
New York, New York 10103.

PRINTED IN THE UNITED STATES OF AMERICA

O   0 9 8 7 6 5 4 3 2 1

CONTENTS

INTRODUCTION

There's something that unites the editors, the writers, and you the readers in this project. We've all been touched by the liberating, exhilarating effects of fantastic fiction; we've felt the world come into a different focus as a result of the mind-opening prose of the genre. Sometimes, the experience changes us. Sometimes, it gives us a new perspective. But at its best, it always thrills us in a way that no other kind of fiction can.

There's true joy in loving fantastic fiction. One really does have the sense that we who love the genre have a distinct advantage over those who don't know it. It's like the feeling of being invited in on a delicious secret, and wishing you could share it with others (while at the same time guarding it jealously). And with that joy comes a desire. Because if one *really loves* fantastic fiction (as opposed to enjoying it for an occasional fling), then one can't get enough new interpretations, enough different ways of looking at the world, enough twists on reality.

Full Spectrum was born out of that desire. As Publisher and Senior Editor, respectively, of Bantam Spectra Books, we live for the charge that is created from the fantastic fiction reading experience. We know that there is no one area of science fiction and fantasy that can possibly satisfy our longing to have worlds opened, to have reality turned on its ear. So we are constantly searching (while ever thankful for what has already been given us) for writing that stretches the imagination just a bit further or entertains us in a slightly different way. In letters to writers and in our announcement to the general trade of this anthology, we requested stories in all of the traditional subgenres of science fiction and fantasy, as well as "the ever-popular 'unclassifiable.'" It was our hope that writers would send us not only their best new stories, but stories that opened frontiers for them, stories that would give us that feeling of falling in love all over again.

What you will find in the twenty-five stories included in this first *Full Spectrum* collection is a wide variety of reading experiences. The settings range from around the corner to around the universe. The moods range from pensive, to playful, to downright outrageous. There is carefully researched scientific extrapolation here. And there is complete irreverence for all physical laws. There is magic that comes from some barely imaginable power, there is magic that comes from the soul, and there is the magic that happens when hearts and minds touch in remarkable ways. What we have hopefully provided you with in this collection is a tapestry made from twenty-five different colors on the science fiction and fantasy spectrum.

We will also give you very, very fine writing. Writing quality was in fact the only prerequisite for inclusion in this anthology. You probably recognize many of the contributors' names in this book. If you know their work, then you know the standards we were working with.

If you can't get enough of the fantastic fiction reading experience, if no amount of imaginative input is ever enough for you, we welcome you to the first volume of *Full Spectrum*. We hope it satisfies your desire, just a little bit.

Lou Aronica and Shawna McCarthy

VOICES
OF THE KILL

THOMAS M. DISCH

Thomas M. Disch is one of the most highly revered writers of fantastic fiction. He has written a number of brilliant novels, including *On Wings of Song, 334,* and *Camp Concentration,* and his short fiction has been collected in a number of volumes. For the last year Tom has been the theater critic for *The Nation.* His most recent books are a deluxe limited edition of his story "The Silver Pillow," published by Mark Ziesing, and the children's book *The Brave Little Toaster Goes to Mars.*

"Voices of the Kill" begins *Full Spectrum* with a haunting, mystical, contemporary tale. It is absolutely vintage Disch—which means you should keep your eyes wide open.

He lay awake through much of his first night in the cabin listening to the stream. It was early June. The water was high and made a fair amount of noise. A smooth white noise it had seemed during the day, but now, listening more closely, surprisingly varied. There was a kind of pulse to it. Not like the plain two-beat alternation of tick and tock that the mind projects on the undifferentiated ratcheting of a clock, but a more inflected flow, like a foreign language being spoken far off, risings and fallings such as an infant must hear in its crib as its parents speak in whispers in another room. Soothing, very soothing, but even so he couldn't get to sleep for many hours, and when he did, he slept lightly and did not dream.

The next morning he opened the plastic bag containing the wading boots he'd bought at the hardware store in Otisville. *Tingley*, the bag said. *Tough Boots for Tough Customers*. They came up to just below his knees. The soles were like tire treads, but quite flexible. He tucked his jeans inside the tops of the boots and went wading up the stream.

He had no intention of fishing. He fished only to be sociable and had little luck at it. In any case, he didn't much like to eat fish, and hated cleaning them. He'd got the boots purely for the pleasure of walking up the stream, as his ticket to the natural history museum of Pine Kill. Not exactly the kind of tough customer Tingley usually catered to, but that was one of the pleasures of taking a vacation all by himself. There was no code to conform to, no expectations to meet, no timetables, no one to say, "Mr. Pierce, would you explain the assignment again?"

A hundred feet up the stream and he felt he had penetrated the mystique of trout fishing. It was simply a macho-compatible mode of meditation. Even with the help of rubber boots, you had to step carefully, for many stones were liable to tilt underfoot, and even the stablest could be treacherous in their smoothness. Moving along at this slower pace, the mind had to gear down too. The busy hum of its own purposes died away and nature slowly emerged from the mists. Nature. He'd almost forgotten what that was. No one had *decided* on any of this. The complications, the repetitions, the apparent patterning—all of it had come about willy-nilly. The beauty, for instance, of these lichens hadn't been intended to delight his eye. The placement of those boulders, which looked so much like a monument by Henry Moore, simply one of an infinite number of rolls of dice.

Another hour up the stream and these abstractions, too, had melted away, like the last lingering traces of ice in spring. The city was thawed out of his limbs. A joy in, a warmth for, the ubiquitous hemlocks bubbled up through his genes from some aboriginal arboreal ancestor.

Where the sunlight penetrated the ranks of the high pines, he stood entranced by the play of the jittering interference patterns across the glowing bed of the stream, the wilderness's own video arcade. And there, darting about through the shallows, were the game's protagonists, two nervous minnows who seemed to be trying to escape their own pursuing and inescapable shadows.

He moved to the stream's next subdivision, a brackish pool where water-skates patterned the silt below with spectral wing patterns, six concentric-banded ovals formed by the touch of their rowing limbs on the skin of the water. For as long as the sunlight held steady over the pool he watched the flights of these subaqueous butterflies, continually delighted at how the light and water had conjured up something so ethereal from such unpromising raw material, for in itself the water-skate was not a pretty sort of bug.

And then there were the flowers, high banks of them where the stream swerved near the parallel curves of Pine Kill Road and the slope was too steep for trees to take root; flowers he had never seen before and had no name for. Some grew stemless from the rot of fallen logs, pale green blossoms of orchidlike intricacy, yet thick and succulent at the same time, as though molded from porcelain. There were great masses of pale yellow blooms that drooped from tall hairy stems, and beyond these a stand of clustered purple trumpet-shaped flowers flamboyant as a lipstick ad.

He braved the bees to pick a large bouquet of both the purple and the yellow flowers, but by the time he'd got back to the cabin all of them had wilted and couldn't be revived. He decided, guiltily, to pick no more bouquets.

That night he heard the voices clearly. So perfect was the illusion that at first he supposed there were people walking along the road on the other side of the stream, taking advantage of the full moon for a midnight stroll. But that was unlikely. His was the farthest cabin up Pine Kill Road, his nearest neighbors half a mile away. What women (for they were surely women's voices) would go walking such a distance, after dark, on such a lonely road?

No, it was the stream he heard, beyond a doubt. When he listened intently he could catch its separate voices merging back into its more liquid murmurings, but only to become distinct again, if never entirely articulate. He could pick out their individual timbres, as he might have the voices in a canon. There were three: a brassy soprano, given to emphatic octave-wide swoops, with a wobble in her lower register; an alto, richer-throated and longer-breathed, but somehow wearier even so; a coloratura, who never spoke more than a few short phrases at a time, little limpid outbursts like the exclamations of flutes in a Mahler symphony. Strain as he might, he could not make out a single word in the flow of their talk, only the melodic line, sinuous and continuous as the flowing of the stream, interrupted from time to time by little hoots of surprise and ripples of laughter.

He dreamed that night—some kind of nightmare involving car crashes and fires in suburban backyards—and woke in a sweat. The alarm clock's digital dial read 1:30 A.M. The stream purled soothingly, voicelessly, outside the cabin, and the moonlight made ghosts of the clothing that hung from nails in the wall.

In the morning he felt as though he were already weeks away from the city. Purged by the nightmare, his spirit was clear as the sky. He set a pot of coffee on the stove to perk. Then, faithful to the promise he'd made to himself the day before, he went down the flagstone steps to the stream and waded out to the deepest part, where two boulders and a small log had formed a natural spillway, below which, under the force of the confluent flow, a hollow had been scooped out from the bed of the stream, large as a bathtub. He lay within it, listening, but from this closest vantage there was not the least whisper of the voices he had heard so plainly the night before. The water was cold, and his bath accordingly quick, but as he returned to where he'd left his towel on the grassy bank he felt a shock of pleasure that made him stop for breath, a neural starburst of delight starting in the center of his chest and lighting up every cell of his body in a quick chain reaction, like the lighting of a giant Christmas tree. *Too much!* he thought, but even with the thinking of that thought, the pleasure had faded to the merest afterimage of that first onslaught of well-being.

That day he went up the mountain—a very small mountain but a mountain for all that—that was coextensive with his back-yard, a low many-gapped fieldstone wall being the only bound-ary between his three-quarter acre and the woods' immensity. He bore due west up the steepest slopes, then north along the first, lowest ridge, and not once was there a house or a paved road or a power line to spoil the illusion that this was the primeval, pre-Yankee wilderness. To be sure, he encountered any number of No Trespassing signs, spoor of the local Rod & Gun Club, and once, at the first broadening of the ridge, he came upon a rough triangle of stacked logs intended for a hunting blind, complete with a detritus of bullet-riddled beer cans and shattered bottle glass. But none of that bulked large against the basic glory of the mountain. The grandeur, the profusion, the fundamentality of it.

On a slope of crumbling slate beyond the hunting blind the mountain revealed its crowning splendor to him, a grove, horizon-wide, of laurels in full bloom, each waist-high shrub so densely blossomed that the underbrush was lost to sight beneath the froth of flowers. Laurels: he knew them by the shape of the leaf. But he'd never seen a laurel in blossom, never understood the fitness of Daphne's metamorphosis. For surely if a man, or God, were to be doomed to love a tree, then it would have to be one of these. They were desire incarnate. You couldn't look at them without wanting . . .

Something.

There was something he wanted, but he could not think what. To faint away, to expire; to become a song or painting or column of stone that could somehow express . . . What? This inexpressible wonder. But no, that wasn't what he wanted at all. He wanted to feel this place, this mountain, in his own being. To be a bee, moving ineluctably from bloom to bloom; to be the swarm of them converging on their hive.

To be a part of it.

To belong, here, forever.

Sleep came to him that night at once, as automatic as the light that goes off inside a refrigerator when the door is closed. He woke in a wash of moonlight to hear the voice of the kill, one of its voices, whispering to him. Not clearly yet, but as though a message had been left on a tape many times erased, distant and blurred by static. Words. Two words, repeated at long intervals: "Come here . . . come here . . ."

"Where shall I come?" he asked aloud.

"Here," said the voice, already fading.

He knew that she meant beside the stream, and he went out of the cabin and down the flagstone steps, obedient as a lamb.

"That's better," she said, pleased. "Lie here, next to me. The night is cool."

He assumed a reclining position on the grass, trying to be unobtrusive as he displaced the small stones that dug into his hip and rib cage. When he lowered his gaze and bent toward her, the stream filled his entire field of vision, a film of blackness flecked with vanishing gleams of purple and pale yellow, neural relics of the flowers he'd seen on the banks upstream.

She did not speak again at once, nor did he feel any eagerness that she should. A strange contentment hovered about him, like a net of finest mesh, an Edenic happiness that did not yet know itself to be happy, a confidence that blessings were everywhere on hand.

"What is your name?" she asked, in the faintest of whispers, as though they spoke in a crowded room where they must not be seen speaking.

He was taken aback. "My name?" It seemed such a prosaic way to begin.

"How can we talk to each other if I don't know your name?"

"William," he said. "William Logan Pierce."

"Then, welcome, William Logan Pierce. Welcome to Pine Kill. To the waters of your new birth, welcome."

Now that was more like it. That was the language one expects from water sprites.

"What is *your* name?" he asked.

She laughed. "Must *I* have a name, too! Oh, very well, my name is Nixie. Will that do?"

He nodded. Then, uncertain whether she could see him in the darkness, he said, "I don't know how to speak to you, Nixie. I've never had a vision before."

"I am no 'vision,' William," she answered with dignity but no perceptible indignation. "I am like you, a spirit embodied in flesh. Only, as I am a Nereid, my flesh is immortal. But you may speak to me as you would to any mortal woman."

"Of what things shall we talk?"

"Why, we may begin with the elements, if you like. Your views on oxygen, your feelings about complex hydrocarbons."

"You're making fun of me."

"And you no less of me, to suppose that I am incapable of ordinary civil conversation. As though I were some nineteenth-century miss only just liberated from the nursery."

"Excuse me."

"It was nothing." Then, in a tone of mocking primness, as though she'd slipped into the role of that hypothetical young miss: "Tell me, Mr. Pierce, what did you think of today's weather?"

"It was beautiful."

"Is that all? I'd imagined you a man of more words."

So, lying with his head back in the grass, looking up at the moon's shattered descent through the swaying hemlocks, he told her of his day on the mountain. She would put in a word from time to time, assurances of her attention.

"You seem to have been quite smitten with those laurels," she commented when he was done. She adopted an attitude of wifely irony, treating the laurels as someone he'd been seen flirting with at a party. "They'll be gone in another two weeks, you know. So, seize the day." She fell silent, or rather returned to her natural speech, the lilting *fol-de-riddle fol-de-lay* of her infinite liquid collisions.

He rolled onto his stomach, the better to peer down at the silken stirrings of her body. Now that the moon had gone down behind the mountain, the little flashes of phosphorescent color were more vivid and coherent, forming ephemeral draperies of bioluminescence.

"You mustn't touch me," she warned, sensing his intention before he'd lifted his hand. "Not till you've paid."

"Paid! How 'paid'?"

"With money, of course. Do you think we use cowrie shells? I trust you have some ready cash on hand."

"Yes but—"

"Then it is very simple: if you're to touch me, you must pay."

"But I've never . . ."

"You've never had to pay for it?" she asked archly.

"No, I didn't mean that."

"Visions—to use your term—don't come cheap, William. You must pay now—and pay again each night you come to call. Those are the rules, and I'm afraid *I* have no authority to set them aside."

"Very well. I'll have to go back into the house to get . . . your pay."

"I'll be right here," she promised.

Dazzled by the glare of the overhead 100-watt bulb, he dug into the sock drawer of the bureau, where there would be quarters set aside for the laundromat. Then he thought better of it. In classic times coins might have served his purpose, but nowadays quarters were worth little more than cowrie shells. He took his billfold from the top dresser drawer. The smallest bill was a twenty. It was probably the smallest she'd accept in any case.

He returned to the stream. "I've twenty dollars. Will that do?"

There was no reply.

"Nixie, are you there?"

"I'm always here, William. Just put it under a stone. A large stone, and not too close to the shore."

He picked his way carefully across the rocky streambed till he came to the middle. The water sweeping around his ankles did not seem different, except in being less chilly, from the water he'd bathed in yesterday morning. Even so, as he knelt to pry up a rock, the shock of immersion was almost enough to dispel the enchantment and send him, shivering and chagrined, back to the cabin. But as he placed the bill beneath the stone, another kind of shock ran up his wet forearms and connected right to the base of his spine, deep-frying his nerves to ecstasy.

He cried out, such a cry as must have brought every animal prowling the night woods to pause and ponder.

"Now you have touched me, William. Now let me touch you."

Helpless, enslaved, and craving nothing but a deeper enslavement, he lowered himself into the stream, careless of the stones on which he lay supine.

She ran her hands over his yielding flesh. "O William," she whispered. "O my sweet, sweet William!"

After that second night, he ceased to take count of the time elapsing. Instead of being stippled with the felt-tip *X*'s that filled the earlier pages of his wall calendar, June's page remained blank as a forgotten diary. His days were given to the mountain or the hammock, his nights to the Nereid's ineffable, evanescent caresses, of which he could recall, in the morning, few particulars. But then what bliss is sweeter for being itemized? So long as our delights are endlessly renewed, what harm is there in taking the days as they come and letting them slip away, unchronicled, to join the great drifts of geologic time? As Nixie said, the thing to do was seize the day—and not look either way.

Yet a day did come, toward the end of June, when he lost his grip on this immemorial good advice. It began with a phone call from Ray Feld, the owner of the cabin, who wanted to know if he meant to continue renting for the rest of the summer. He'd paid only to mid-July.

He promised to have his check in the mail that morning—$875, which was almost exactly half of his bank balance. Even eating frugally and borrowing on his credit cards, it was going to be a tight squeeze to Labor Day. And then . . .

And then it would be back to Newark and Marcus Garvey Junior High School, where, under the pretense of teaching English and social studies, he gave his young detainees a foretaste of their destined incarceration in the prisons, armies, and offices of the grown-up world. On the premises of Marcus Garvey, he was usually able to take a less dismal view of the teaching profession. If there was nothing else to be said for it, there was at least this—the freedom of his summers. While other people had to make do with two or three weeks of vacation, he could spend the entire season by the stream, with the hemlocks perfuming the air. All he need remember—summer's one simple rule—was not to look back or ahead.

And the best way to do that was to take up the cry of the

pines: "More light! More light!" For always a climb up the mountain was an antidote to his merely mental gloom. He'd got lazy about giving the mountain its due; that was the only problem. He'd come to rely too much on Nixie's nightly benefactions. Earth and air must have their share of his devotion. So it was up to the laurels, up through the green, hemlock-filtered light to that all-sufficing beauty. The sweatier, the more breathless, the better.

But even sweaty and panting, gloom stuck to his heels as the counterminnows of the streambed kept pace with the living minnows above. A line from some half-remembered poem haunted him: *The woods decay, the woods decay and fall*. It was like a sliver firmly lodged under his thumbnail and not to be got rid of. Every fallen log repeated it, as it lay rotting, devoured by mushrooms or by maggots: *The woods decay, the woods decay and fall*.

As Nixie had foretold, the laurel grove had become a tangle of green shrubs. The blossoms had shriveled and fallen, exposing the russet-red remnants of their sexual apparatus, and the bees had absconded, like sated seducers, to another part of the summer. Somewhere on the periphery of the grove a thrush, pierced by its own sliver of poetry, reiterated a simple two-bar elegy: *Must it be? Must it be? It must! It must!*

He did not linger there, but headed northeast on a course he knew would intersect the higher reaches of Pine Kill. He'd never followed the stream to its source; he would today. He followed paths already familiar, past an abandoned quarry, where great slabs of slate were stacked to form a simple foursquare maze, a tombstone supermarket. Then along a fire trail, where a few stunted laurels, shadowed by the pines, had preserved their maiden bloom. Already, here, he heard her voice ahead of him. Almost intelligible, despite her insistance that her powers of coherent speech were limited to the hours of the night; almost herself, until the kill became visible, twisting down a staircase of tumbled stones, and shifted gender from she to it. Yet even now, as it zigzagged among the boulders and spilled across the ineffectual dam of a fallen log, he thought he recognized, if not her voice, her bearing—headlong, capricious, intolerant of contradiction.

As he made his way upstream, he was obliged to climb, as the kill did, using its larger boulders as stepping stones, since there was no longer level ground on either side, only steep shoulders of crumbly scree. He slipped several times, soaking his sneakers, but only when, mistaking a mulch of leaves for solid ground, he'd nearly sprained his ankle did he yield to what he supposed to be her will. For some reason she did not want him to reach the source of the kill. If he defied her, she might become still more ruthlessly modest.

By the time he'd limped down to Pine Kill Road, his knees were trembling, and his swollen ankle sent a yelp of protest at every step. At home he would fill the tub with hot water and—

But these compassionate plans were blighted the moment he came within view of the cabin and found, parked behind his yellow Datsun, a blue Buick with Pennsylvania plates. *No,* he thought, *it can't be, not all the way from Philadelphia, not without phoning first.* But it was.

It was his cousin Barry, who came out the back door of the cabin, lofting a can of Heineken as his hello.

"Barry." He tried not to sound dismayed. Barry had had a standing invitation to come up any weekend he could get free from the city. This must be Friday. Or Saturday. Damn. "It's good to see you."

"I was beginning to worry. I got here at three, and it's getting on past seven. Where you been?"

"Up there." He waved his hand in the direction of the mountain.

Barry looked doubtfully at the dark wall of hemlocks. The woods did not look welcoming this late in the day. "Communing with nature?"

"That's what I'm here for, isn't it?" He'd meant to sound playful, but his tone was as ill-judged as an intended love-pat that connects as a right to the jaw. He might as well have asked Barry, *And why are* you *here? Why won't you go away?*

"Well," said Barry, placatingly, "you're looking terrific. You must have dropped some pounds since Bernie Junior's wedding. And you didn't have that many to drop. You got anorexia or something?"

"Have I lost weight? I haven't been trying to."

"Oh, come off it. When I got here I looked in the icebox, and I can tell you everything that was there: a can of coffee, one stick of Parkay margarine, and a bottle of generic catsup. Plus part of a quart of milk that had gone sour. Then I tried the cupboard, and the situation wasn't much better. You can't be living on nothing but oatmeal and sardines."

"As a matter of fact, Barry, sardines and oatmeal are the basis of the Sullivan County Diet. I'll lend you the book. You're guaranteed to take off ten pounds in ten days, at a cost of just ten cents a serving.''

Barry smiled. This was the William he'd come to visit. ''You're putting me on.''

''You laugh—but wait till you've tasted my sour-milk-oatmeal-sardine bread. It's indescribable.''

''Well, you'll have to starve yourself on your own time, 'cause while you were off communing, I drove in to Port Jervis and got us some *edible* food. There's spare ribs for dinner tonight, if I can get the damned charcoal started. Bacon and eggs for breakfast, and a big porterhouse for tomorrow night, plus corn to roast with it. And some genuine hundred percent cholesterol to spread on it, none of your mingy margarine. Plus three six-packs—two and a half at this point—and a fifth of Jack Daniel's. Think we'll survive?''

There was no way he could get out of the cabin to be with Nixie that night. Even though he turned in early, using his ankle as an excuse, Barry stayed up drinking and reading a thriller, and finally just drinking. William could hear the stream, but not Nixie's voice.

He didn't dream that night, and woke to the smell of frying bacon. At breakfast Barry announced that they were going to rent a canoe in Port Jervis and paddle down the Delaware to Milford. And that's what they did. The river seemed impersonal in its huge scale. William was aware only of what was unnatural along its shores—the power lines, the clustering bungalows, the clipped lawns of the larger houses, and all the urgent *windows*, jealous of their views. With every stroke of the paddle in his hands, William felt he was betraying the stream he knew. He imagined Nixie lost in this metropolis of a river, murmuring his name, ignored by the hordes of strangers hurrying along on their own business.

Barry, a law-school dropout, tried to get a political argument going, but William refused to take up the challenge. What was the fun of playing straight man to Barry's right-wing one-liners? Barry, balked of that entertainment, proceeded to analyze his relationship with the vice president of another department of his company, a woman whom he'd offended in the elevator. After a while he got to be as ignorable as a radio. William paddled stolidly, seated at the front of the canoe, letting Barry do the steering. Halfway to the goal of Milford, as they came upon a stretch of rapids, William's end of the canoe lodged against a rock and the flow of the river slowly turned them around till they were at right angles to the current. Barry said, "What are we supposed to do in this situation?" just a moment before the canoe overturned.

The dousing was delightful. William came out of the water grinning, as though their capsizing had been one of Nixie's broader jokes and the look on Barry's face, his stupefied indignation, its punch line. They got the waterlogged canoe to the nearer shore without much difficulty, for the water was shallow. Once there, Barry's concern was all for the contents of his billfold and the well-being of his wristwatch, which was Swiss but only water resistant, not waterproof. They didn't even realize that Barry's paddle had been lost till the canoe was bailed out and they were ready to set off again.

That was the end of all *gemütlichkeit*. The rest of the trip was a slow, wounded slog, with Barry exiled to the prow seat and William maneuvering, carefully and unskillfully, from the bow. At each new stretch of white water they were in danger of capsizing again, but somehow they scraped through without another soaking. The six-pack had been lost with the paddle, and Barry's high spirits declined in proportion as his thirst mounted. By the time they reached Milford, they were no longer on speaking terms. While they waited for the van that would retrieve them and the canoe, Barry headed into town for beer and aspirin, while William spread out on the lawn above the beach, numb with relief. One day with his cousin and he felt as wrought up as if he'd finished a year of teaching.

The beach was full of children. Most of them were younger than the children he taught. There must have been another beach in the area that was reserved for teenagers. There was, however, a single black girl, about fourteen or fifteen years old, in a one-piece pea-green swimsuit, who was intent on digging a large hole in the sand and heaping up an oblong mound (it could not be called a sandcastle) beside it. She had a small, darker-skinned boy in her charge, two years old or even younger. He might have been her sibling or her son. He spent most of his time at the edge of the water, hurling stones at the river with as much satisfaction as if each stone had broken a window. Once he tried to participate in the girl's excavation, but she swatted him with her pink plastic shovel and screamed at him to get away. Some minutes later he toddled out into the water till he was chest-deep, at which point he was retrieved by the lifeguard, who led him back to his mother (William was sure, now, that that was her relationship to the boy), who swatted him a little more soundly, but hissed instead of screaming.

Hers was a type that William was familiar with from his years at Marcus Garvey—severely retarded but able to survive without custodial care, destined for a life as a welfare mother as sure as God makes little green apples. A child abuser, most likely, and the mother of other welfare mothers yet to be. Usually, William regarded such students as a problem that the officials of state agencies should solve in some humane way that researchers had yet to discover. But here on the beach, with the first premonitory breezes of the evening floating in off the water, the pair of them seemed as beautiful in an elementary way as some Italian Madonna and Child. They seemed to have sprung up out of the landscape like the trees and bushes—a presence, and not a problem at all.

Barry returned from town in much-improved spirits, and soon afterward the van arrived and took them back to Barry's Buick and the known world. By the time they were back at the cabin, the sun had sunk behind the pine-crested ridge of the mountain, but there was still an hour of shadowy daylight left. William undertook to cook the steaks, but he didn't adjust the air vents properly and the charcoal went out. Barry insisted that was all right and that the steaks would be better blood rare than too well done. The meat was dutifully chewed and swallowed, all two and half pounds of it, and then William, unable to take any more, asked Barry if he'd mind leaving that night. "The thing is, I've got a girlfriend coming over. And the cabin just doesn't allow any privacy, you know what I mean?" Barry was obviously miffed, but he also seemed relieved to be clearing out.

As soon as the taillights of the Buick had been assimilated by the darkness of Pine Kill Road, William went down to the stream and, kneeling on a flat mossy rock, touched the skin of the water. Quietly, with no intention of waking her, but as one may touch the neck or shoulder of a sleeping spouse, simply for the pleasure of that near presence.

"I'm sorry," he whispered. "It wasn't my fault. I couldn't come to you while he was here. He'd have thought I was crazy."

He hoped she could hear him. He hoped he could be forgiven. But the water rippling through his fingers offered no reassurance.

He went to bed as soon as it was dark, and lay awake, like a child being punished, staring at the raftered ceiling. The day with Barry kept replaying in his mind, keeping him from sleep—and keeping him from Nixie, for it was usually only after his first dreaming sleep that he would rise and go to her. Was it a form of somnambulism then? Could she summon him only when he was in a trance? That would explain why he could remember so little of their conversations now, and nothing at all of the ecstasies he had known in her embrace, nothing but that there had been, at such moments, consummations that a Saint Theresa might have envied.

He slept, but sleep brought no dreams, and he woke just before dawn to the bland, unintelligible purling of the stream. It was like waking to find, instead of one's beloved, her unhollowed pillow beside one in the bed. He felt betrayed, and yet he knew the first betrayal had been his.

What did she want? His tears? His blood? She could name any price, any punishment, as long as she let him be near her again, to hear her again when she called his name, *William, dear William, come to my bed, come rest your head beside mine.*

He was made to pay the penalty of her silence for most of July, and grew resigned to the idea that she might never return to him. To have known such joys once was cause for lifelong gratitude—but to suppose himself *entitled* to them? As well ask to be anointed King of England.

The ordinary splendors of the summer remained open to him. Where the laurels had bloomed, blueberries now were ripening. Cardinals and nuthatches offered their daily examples of how good weather could best be enjoyed, as they darted back and forth from his feeder, skimming the stream, living it up, taking no thought for the morrow—or for next year's lesson plans on such suggested topics as Problems of Family Life or the Perils of Drug Abuse. No wristwatch, no calendar, no mealtimes or bedtimes, no tasks to finish, no friends to remember, no books to read. He had three classical music cassettes—one symphony each by Bruckner, Mahler, and Sibelius—that he listened to over and over at night inside the cabin, while a single log burned in the fireplace. He learned to float through his days and nights the way he would have in a dream.

And then, as the blueberries peaked and the huckleberries followed close behind, she spoke to him again. Not in the same voice now, however. It was the alto who, in a tone of maternal reproach, addressed him: "William, you have been too long away. Come here—explain yourself."

"Nixie!" he cried, pushing himself up from the wicker chair in which he had fallen asleep. "Goddess! Forgive me—my cousin was here—I couldn't come to you. Yet I should have, I see that now. I didn't understand, I—"

"Stop babbling, William." She spoke sternly, but with a kind of humor, even indulgence, that set his hopes leaping like gazelles.

"Nixie, you've returned. I always knew you would return. I always—"

"Is your ear so poorly tuned to our speech, William, that you cannot tell my sister's voice from mine? I am Nereis. Nixie has gone elsewhere, and she will *not* return."

"But *you* will let me worship you? And lie beside you? Do you want money, too? I'll give you all I have. Anything."

"I want only you, William. Come, enter me. Let me touch your cheeks, which Nixie has told me are so soft and warm."

He stumbled through the darkened cabin and down the flagstone steps to the stream. There he paused to remove his clothes. Then, his heart in a flutter, his legs trembling, he splashed through the water to where he used to lie with Nixie.

But as he reached that spot, Nereis spoke out loudly: "Not there! Summer has wasted us, it is too shallow there. See where that larger boulder lies, where the moon has broken through: come to me there."

He made his way toward that farther boulder with, it seemed, enchanted ease, placing his feet as firmly as if he'd been wearing his Tingley boots, as confident as a bridegroom marching to the altar.

She received him not as Nixie would have, with a single, singeing blast of joy; it was rather, with Nereis, a sinking inward, a swooning away, a long slow descent into the whirlpool of an ineffable comfort. When she had wholly absorbed him, when her watery warmth was spread across his face like the tears of a lifetime all suddenly released, he knew that she had taken him into her womb and that he had become hers, hers utterly and for all time.

In the morning he awoke atop the boulder she had led him to, his body bruised, his knees and feet still bleeding. A low mist hung over the stream, as though she had veiled herself. He groaned, like a shanghaied sailor, a bag of sexual garbage dumped in the gutter and waiting for collection. *No more*, he told himself. *No more visions*. It was all very well for William Blake to be at home to spirits: his dealings had been with angels, not with water nymphs. Clearly, Nereids had behavioral traits in common with their cousins, the mermaids. Clearly, a man who continued to answer to their solicitations would be lured to his destruction. Clearly, he must pack up his things and leave the cabin before nightfall, before she called him to her again.

Again: the word, the hope of it, was honey and he the fly happily mired in its fatal sweetness.

I will be more careful, he told himself, as he wound gauze about his lower legs. Then, in earnest of this new self-preserving attitude, he made himself a breakfast of oatmeal and sardines. It tasted, to his ravished tongue, like ambrosia.

The sun swung across the sky like the slowest of pendulums, and the shadow of the cabin's roof-tree touched, sundiallike, the nearer shore of the kill. Four o'clock already, and then, as it touched the farther shore, five. As the shadows lengthened, the birds became livelier and more contentious. The nuthatches stropped their beaks on the bark of the trees and made skirmishes against the chickadees, who panicked but kept returning to the feeder, emblems of the victory of appetite.

The colors of the kill shifted from a lighter to a darker green. Where the shadows were deepest he could glimpse the first restless stirrings of her torso, the undulations of gigantic limbs. How long the days are in July. How caressing the sound of rippling water.

Once, in the summer before his junior year at Wesleyan, William had worked in the violent ward of a psychiatric hospital. He'd been premed then and planned to become a psychiatrist. Three months of daily contact with the patients had convinced him, first, that he must find some other career, and second, that there was no such thing as insanity, only the decision, which anyone might make, to act insanely—that is, to follow one's whims and impulses wherever they might lead. By the time they'd led to the violent ward, one had become a career patient, as others were career criminals, and for similar reasons, the chief of which was a preference for institutional life. Only by behaving as a lunatic would one be allowed to live in the eternal kindergarten of the hospital, exempt from work, freed of irksome family ties, one's bloodstream the playground for chemicals available only to the certifiably insane. Those who chose to live such a feckless life were not to be pitied when their grimaces of lunacy froze into masks that could not be removed.

And so it was that when she arose and came to him, at dusk,

the water running in trickles down her dark legs, shimmering iridescently across the taut curves of the pea-green swimsuit, he did not resist. He did not tell himself, as she unknotted him from the net hammock to which he'd bound himself, like some hick Ulysses, that this was impossible, could not be happening, etcetera. For he had yielded long since to the possibility—and it was happening now.

"Come," she bade him, "follow me." And the smile that she smiled was like a door.

He opened the door and entered the mountain.

His body was never recovered, but the boots were discovered, where he'd left them, beneath a ledge of limestone close by the source of the kill.

THIS IS
THE YEAR ZERO
ANDREW WEINER

From bracing story to bracing story. Post-apoc-
alypse fiction is nearly as old as the genre itself.
Every now and then, though, a writer puts a new
spin on the ball and causes us to reconsider just
what life would be like if our world was no
longer like the one we know now. Andrew Weiner
has done this in "This is the Year Zero."

Andrew Weiner was born in London in 1949,
moved to Canada in 1974, and is now a Canadian
citizen living in Toronto with his wife and five-
year-old son. He sold his first short story to
Harlan Ellison's *Again, Dangerous Visions* and
has since published more than 30 stories in magazines and anthologies including *Interzone, The
Magazine of Fantasy and Science Fiction,* and
Isaac Asimov's Science Fiction Magazine. His
first novel, *Station Gehenna,* was published last
year by Congdon and Weed as part of the "Isaac
Asimov Presents" series.

1.

This is the year zero. Everything is different now, all of it, and always will be.

Everything has ended. Everything begins again.

This is the year zero.

2.

The aliens enter the city in their brightly painted vehicles. I watch them from my window. People gather in the streets to cheer and wave.

I do not cheer or wave. I only watch them from my window.

3.

Everything is different now, all of it. Today I went to the store to buy food. There was a long lineup, but the people were cheerful. They laughed and joked as they waited to be served.

There was no meat in the store, and no green vegetables. There were only potatoes, great bins full of them, and limited quantities of chicken. Perhaps there will never be meat or green vegetables again.

They did not want my money in the store. Money is over with now. We do things differently now, and always will.

4.

The potato is an underrated vegetable. So I heard on the radio once, driving to work. The potato contains nearly all the nutrients required to sustain human life.

They no longer talk about potatoes on the radio. There is only one radio station now, and no more TV broadcasts. For a while there was only music on the one radio station, strange dissonant music. And then the voices, the polite and distant alien voices.

History is over, the alien voices tell us. Now you begin again. Now.

5.

I no longer drive to work. Until recently I worked as a middle manager for a large, integrated oil company, but the company has been closed down. We have no further need of oil companies.

I no longer drive at all. Cars are over with, also.

Wait, the voices on the radio tell me. Wait and you will receive your instructions in the course of time.

6.

There were some who wished to resist. Many more, however, welcomed the coming of the aliens. Many had grown weary of our dismal history. For so many years now we had been awaiting them. And now at last they had come.

How could we have resisted in any case? We could not have resisted.

7.

TV broadcasts resume. I am alerted by the voices on the radio.

I watch the man who was once the leader of our nation sitting at a desk. He reads from a prepared statement. Life will be different, he says, now that we have begun again. But of course I know this already.

The former leader smiles as he reads his statement. He seems to be happy with the situation.

Aliens lead our former leader away from the desk. The TV screen continues to show the empty desk. After a while, the strange music begins. I stare at the desk for some time. Then TV broadcasts cease.

8.

Aliens come to my apartment. They are polite, distant. Physically, they closely resemble us, but it is not difficult to distinguish them all the same.

The aliens question me as to my skills, my attitudes, my preferences.

Wait, they tell me as they depart. Wait in an orderly manner, and we will deal with you at the proper time and in the correct way.

9.

People are leaving the city. I watch from my window as they climb aboard the brightly painted alien vehicles and leave the city. Cities are over with, the voices on the radio tell me. You have no further need of cities.

The people leaving the city seem happy. They turn and wave to their friends. They laugh and joke. They have no further need of cities.

10.

Camps, a man tells me at the food store. They are taking us to camps. Where else could they be taking us?

I recognize him vaguely from work. He was some sort of accountant or geologist. It all seems such a long time ago now, the things we used to do in the old times.

I did not know him well, in any case. I would see him in the staff cafeteria from time to time, exchange nods in the elevators. Often he seemed preoccupied, as if with the burden of his work. Many of us were preoccupied.

Now he seems nervous and agitated. He whispers to me secretively, glancing over his shoulder frequently at the alien supervisor behind the food counter. The alien pays us no attention whatsoever.

What kind of camps? I ask him, but he does not know. Death camps, prison camps, work camps, holiday camps, mining camps, Boy Scout camps. He does not know, but he is nervous and agitated all the same.

11.

Walking home from the food store I pass the park. The children in the park are playing a new game. Under the gaze of an alien they run back and forth, laughing and shrieking, sometimes pausing to hit ball-shaped objects with a strange twisted bat.

I do not understand the game at all, cannot begin to comprehend its rules.

Children like the aliens a great deal. Many of the older ones assist them in the food stores. The younger ones play all day. There are no more schools. Schools are finished with now.

12.

Telephone service is over with, too. Unable to contact my friend Elizabeth, I walk the seven miles to her apartment. Walking is how we get around the city, while there is still a city.

Elizabeth has already left the city. She seemed pleased to be going, her roommate Vicki tells me.

Perhaps I will be pleased to go, too, when the time comes. Perhaps I will see Elizabeth again. And perhaps not.

Families are often separated by the aliens. Or so I hear in the food store. And we were not a family in any case.

13.

The man from the food store comes to my apartment, the former accountant from my place of work.

We must take up arms, the former accountant tells me, and overthrow our oppressors. Or perhaps he is a former geologist.

I point out that we have no arms to take up. I point out that most people seem happy with the situation, with the ending of our history.

Even so, he says, we must resist. Even so.

Politely, I ask him to leave my apartment.

I am not interested in resistance. All that is over with now.

14.

I do not like the look of the potatoes in the food store. They are old and scarred by frost damage.

The alien supervisor sees me scowl at the inferior potatoes. He catches my eye.

Don't worry, the alien tells me. It won't be long now. Not very long at all.

15.

Many apartments in the building where I live are vacant now, their former occupants departed. I gather up a few belongings and move to an apartment on the second floor. The elevators do not work very often, and it has become tiresome climbing the stairs to my apartment on the eighth floor.

I choose an apartment much like my old one, a one-bedroom unit. Now that rent is over with, I could have chosen a larger one, but I have no need of the additional space. Besides, I like the furniture. It is very much like my old furniture.

16.

Where are they taking us? asks an old woman in the food store.

Another world, someone answers her, a middle-aged woman. That's where.

One of the children distributing food overhears this exchange. This is another world, he tells them. Now.

17.

Children come to my apartment and tell me to be ready to leave the city tomorrow.

The children seem happy to be working for the aliens.

Are you happy? I ask the children. Now that things are different?

Of course, the children tell me. Of course we are happy.

18.

The former accountant is in the seat ahead of me on the alien transportation vehicle.

He turns and recognizes me.

Liquidation, he tells me. We will be liquidated. All of us. So that they can have our world all to themselves.

Clearly, he is unhapppy to be leaving the city. Most of us, however, are pleased. It is a relief, in a way. We have all been waiting for this for quite some time.

19.

We drive out into the country. The alien vehicle moves rapidly and the highways are almost empty of traffic, but it is a long drive all the same. Night falls and the lights come on, then dim. I doze off, wake to a new dawn to find that we are arriving.

Great domes rise above us, metal and glass glinting in the

late summer sun, surrounded by fields of waving wheat. Or perhaps it is corn.

We get off the bus and wait. Other vehicles arrive and discharge their passengers. There are many of us now, milling around in the parking lot, waiting.

Did you see them in the field? the former accountant asks me. Harvesting the crop with their bare hands?

But I did not see them. I was asleep.

Rolling us back, the former accountant says. Back to the Stone Age.

I shrug, make no reply.

Surely this is what we wanted, after all.

20.

Finally an alien addresses us. He uses no visible equipment, but his voice booms out over the parking lot. Or rather it seems to echo within each of our heads.

Your old world is over with, the alien tells us. As you wanted it to be. Your new world has begun. Now.

But of course we know this already.

21.

We harvest the wheat. Or perhaps it is corn. We harvest it with hand-held metal implements, but without machines. Machines are over with now.

It is hard work, harvesting the crop. But we do not complain. Sometimes we sing. The children sing best of all.

Some people cannot do the work. They are too old, or too tired, or too sick. When people cannot do the work, the children lead them away. I do not know where they go, or what happens to them there, but they do not return to the fields, or to our sleeping quarters in the great glass and metal domes.

Perhaps they go to another world.

22.

At night we eat. And then we talk, about what we did in the old times and how we do things now.

I recognize the former accountant taking his turn. He was indeed an accountant.

Numbers, he tells us. All day I worked with numbers. But no more. Numbers are over with now.

He seems happy, now, that numbers are over with. We all applaud.

The children run these sessions, and they run them well. I do not see the aliens around anymore. The children run everything now. No one complains about this. No one else wants to run things.

Perhaps the aliens have gone home. Perhaps we have no further need of them.

23.

I saw Elizabeth today, from a distance. She was in a work party that passed by our field. I waved to her, but she did not wave back. Perhaps she did not recognize me.

I would like to have talked to her. Just to talk, only that. Sex is at an end now, of course. We do not have sex anymore.

One of the children saw me waving and rebuked me. We do not recognize friends from the old times, he told me.

We have no past, the children tell us. We have no future. Only the present, the vast enormous present.

The children are right, of course, but still I do not like them. In a way I preferred the aliens.

Of course, the children are aliens too.

24.

This is the year zero. We do things differently here and always will.

This is the year zero.

PROSELYTES

GREGORY BENFORD

It's difficult to avoid hyperbole when discussing Gregory Benford. He is regarded by most as one of the finest (if not simply *the* finest) hard science fiction writers working today, a writer who has introduced higher literary values to the subgenre than any before him. He has won the Nebula Award twice, along with the British Science Fiction Award, the John W. Campbell Memorial Award, and the Australian Ditmar Award. His widely-popular and highly-acclaimed novels include the Spectra titles *In the Ocean of Night,* *Across the Sea of Suns, Great Sky River,* and *Heart of the Comet* (which he wrote with David Brin) along with *Timescape, Artifact,* and others which unfortunately do not appear under the Spectra imprint. He will have a new novel out in early 1989 which, as we write this, is still untitled. Greg lives in Laguna Beach with his wife and two children and he is a professor at the University of California Irvine.

"Proselytes" is a change of pace for Greg and one of the most unusual stories in *Full Spectrum.* Still, there are elements in it which most of you should, unfortunately, recognize.

It was the third time something had knocked on the door that evening. Slow, ponderous thuds. Dad answered it, even though he knew what would be standing there.

The Gack was seven feet tall and burly, as were all Gacks.

"Good evening," it said. "I bring you glorious word from the stars!"

It spoke slowly, the broad mouth seeming to shape each word as though the lips were mouthing an invisible marble. Then it blinked twice and said, "The true knowledge of the universe! Salutations of eternal life!"

Dad nodded sourly. "We heard."

"Are you certain? I am an emissary from a far star, sent to bring—"

"Yeah, there's been two others here tonight already."

"And you turned them away?" the Gack asked, startled.

Junior broke in, leaving his homework at the dining-room table. "Hey, there's been *hundreds* of you guys comin' by here. For *months*."

The Gack blinked and abruptly made the sound that had given the aliens their name—a tight, barking sneeze. Something in earth's air irritated their large, red noses. "Apologies, dear ignorant natives, from a humble proselyte of the One Patriarch."

Dad said edgily. "Look, we already heard about your god and how he made the galaxy so you Gacks could spread his holy word and all, so—"

"Oh, let the poor thing finish its spiel, Howard," Mom said, wiping her hands on a towel as she came in from the kitchen.

"Hell, the Dodgers' game'll be on soon—"

"C'mon, Dad," Junior said. "You know that's the only way to get 'em to go away."

The Gack sniffed appreciatively at Junior and started its rehearsed lecture. "Wondrous news, O Benighted Natives! I have voyaged countless of your years to bring . . ."

The family tuned out the recital. As Dad stood in the doorway he could see dozens of Gack ships orbiting in the night sky. They were like small brown moons, asteroid-sized starships that had arrived in a flurry of fiery orange explosions. Each had a big flat plate at one end. They were slow, awkwardly shaped, clunky—like the Gacks themselves.

They had come from a distant yellow star and all they wanted was free reign to "speak to the unknowing," as their emissary had put it. In return they had offered their technology.

Dad had been enthusiastic about that, and so had every government on Earth. Dad's half-interest in the Electronic Wonderland store downtown had been paying very little these last few years. An infusion of alien technology, whole new racy product lines, could be a bonanza.

But the Gacks had nothing worth using. Their ships had spanned the stars using the simplest possible method. They dumped small nuclear bombs out the back and set them off. The ship then rode the blast wave, with the flat plate on one end smoothing out the push, like a giant shock absorber.

And inside the Gack asteroid ships were electronics that used vacuum tubes, hand-cranked computers, old-fashioned AM radio . . . nothing that humans hadn't invented already.

So there would be no wonder machines from the stars. The sad fact was that the aliens were dumb. They had labored centuries to make their starships, and then ridden them for millennia to reach other stars.

The Gack ended ponderously with, "Gather now into the outstretched loving grasp of the One True Vision!"

The Gack's polite, expectant gaze fell in turn on each of the family.

Mom said, "Well, that was _very_ nice. You're certainly one of the best I've heard, wouldn't you agree, Howard?"

Dad hated it, how she always made *him* get rid of the Gacks. He began, "Look, we've been patient—"

"*They*'re the patient ones, Dad," Junior said. "Sittin' inside those rocks all those years, just so they could knock on doors and hand out literature." Junior laughed.

The Gack was still looking expectantly at them, waiting for them to convert to his One Galactic Faith. One of its four oddly shaped hands held forth crudely printed pamphlets.

"Now, now," Mom said. "We shouldn't make fun of another creature's beliefs. This poor thing is just doing what our Mormons and Jehovah's Witnesses do. You wouldn't laugh at them, would you?"

Dad could hold it no longer. The night air was cold and he was getting chilly, standing there. "No, thanks!" he said loudly, and slammed the door.

"Howard!" Mom cried.

"Hey, right on, Dad!" Junior clapped his hands.

"Just shut the door in its faith," Dad said, making a little smile.

"I still say we should always be polite," Mom persisted. "Who would've believed that when the aliens came, their only outstanding quality would be patience? The patience to travel to other stars. We could learn a thing or two from them," she added sternly.

Dad was already looking in *TV Guide*. "We should've guessed that even before the Gacks came. After all, who comes visiting in this neighborhood? Not that snooty astronomer two blocks over, right? No, we get hot-eyed guys in black suits, looking for converts. So it's no surprise that those are the only kinds of aliens who're damn fool enough to spend all their time flying to the stars, too. Not explorers. Not scientists. Fundamentalists!"

As if to punctuate his words, a hollow *thump* made the house creak. They all looked to the front door, but the sound wasn't a knock.

Another *boom* came down from the sky and rattled the windows.

When they went outside, the night sky was alive with darting ships and lurid orange explosions.

Junior cried, "The Gack ships! See, they're all blown up!"

"My, I hope they aren't hurt or anything," Mom said. "They're such *nice* creatures, truly."

Among the tumbling brown remnants of the Gack fleet darted sleek, shiny vessels. They dived like quicksilver barracuda, sending missiles that ripped open the fat bellies of the last few asteroid ships.

Dad felt a pang. "They were kinda pleasant," he said grudgingly. "Not my type of person, maybe, and their technology was a laugh, but still—"

"Look!" Junior cried.

A sleek ship skimmed across the sky. A bone-rattling *boom* crashed down from it.

"Now *that's* what an alien starship oughta look like," Junior said. "Lookit those wings! The blue exhaust—"

Behind the swift craft huge letters of gauzy blue unfurled across the upper atmosphere. The phosphorescent words loomed with hard, clear purpose:

GREET THE CLEANSING BLADE OF THE ONE ETERNAL TRUTH!

"Huh?" Junior frowned.

Dad's face went white.

"We thought the Mormons were bad," he said grimly. "Whoever thought there might be Moslems?"

THE FOURTH
MOXIE BRANCH

JACK MCDEVITT

Jack McDevitt's first published story, "The Emerson Effect," appeared in *Twilight Zone* magazine in 1981. Since then, he has gone on to become one of the most respected new sf writers of the '80s. His first novel, *The Hercules Text,* won the Philip K. Dick Special Award for 1986 and was selected best first novel in the *Locus* poll for that same year. His very promising career as a novelist will continue with *A Talent for War,* which is due out in 1989. Jack has been a naval officer, a taxi driver, and an English teacher, and currently trains supervisors for the U.S. Customs Service in Georgia where he lives with his wife and three children.

"The Fourth Moxie Branch" explores the themes of immortality and the power of the written word in a strange and wonderful way. We responded to it on a number of levels and have a feeling you will as well.

A few minutes into the blackout, the window in the single dormer at the top of Will Potter's house began to glow. I watched it from across Route 11, through a screen of box elders, and through the snow that had been falling all afternoon and was now getting heavier. It was smeary and insubstantial, not the way a bedroom light would look, but as though something luminous floated in the dark interior.

Will Potter was dead. We'd put him in the graveyard on the other side of the expressway three years before. The property had lain empty since, a two-story frame dating from about the turn of the century.

The town had gone quiet with the blackout. Somewhere a dog barked, and a garage door banged down. Ed Kiernan's station wagon rumbled past, headed out toward Cavalier. The streetlights were out, as was the traffic signal down at Twelfth.

As far as I was concerned, the power could have stayed off.

It was trash night. I was hauling out cartons filled with copies of *Independence Square*, and I was on my way down the outside staircase when everything had gone dark.

The really odd thing about the light over at Potter's was that it seemed to be spreading. It had crept outside: the dormer began to burn with a steady, cold, blue-white flame. It flowed gradually down the slope of the roof, slipped over the drainpipe, and turned the corner of the porch. Just barely, in the illumination, I could make out the skewed screens and broken stone steps.

It would have taken something unusual to get my attention that night. I was piling the boxes atop one another, and some of the books had spilled into the street: my name glittered on the bindings. It was a big piece of my life. Five years and a quarter-million words and, in the end, most of my life's savings to get it printed. It had been painful, and I was glad to be rid of it.

So I was standing on the curb, feeling very sorry for myself while snow whispered down out of a sagging sky.

The Tastee-Freez, Hal's Lumber, the Amoco at the corner of Nineteenth and Bannister, were all dark and silent. Toward the center of town, blinkers and headlights misted in the storm.

It was a still, somehow motionless night. The flakes were blue in the pale glow surrounding the house. They fell onto the gabled roof and spilled gently off the back.

Cass Taylor's station wagon plowed past, headed out of town. He waved.

I barely noticed: the back end of Potter's place had begun to balloon out. I watched it, fascinated, knowing it to be an illusion, yet still half-expecting it to explode.

The house began to change in other ways.

Roof and corner lines wavered. New walls dropped into place. The dormer suddenly ascended, and the top of the house with it. A third floor, complete with lighted windows and a garret, appeared out of the snow. (In one of the illuminated rooms, someone moved.)

Parapets rose, and an oculus formed in the center of the garret. A bay window pushed out of the lower level, near the front. An arch and portico replaced the porch. Spruce trees materialized, and Potter's old post light, which had never worked, blinked on.

The box elders were bleak and stark in the foreground.

I stood, worrying about my eyesight, holding on to a carton, feeling the snow against my face and throat. Nothing moved on Route 11.

I was still standing there when the power returned: the streetlights, the electric sign over Hal's office, the security lights at the Amoco, gunshots from a TV, the sudden inexplicable rasp of an electric drill. And, at the same moment, the apparition clicked off.

*   *   *

I could have gone to bed. I could have hauled out the rest of those goddammed books, attributed everything to my imagination, and gone to bed. I'm glad I didn't.

The snow cover in Potter's backyard was undisturbed. It was more than a foot deep beneath the half-inch or so that had fallen that day. I struggled through it to find the key he'd always kept wedged beneath a loose hasp near the cellar stairs.

I used it to let myself in through the storage room at the rear of the house. And I should admit that I had a bad moment when the door shut behind me, and I stood among the rakes and shovels and boxes of nails. Too many late TV movies. Too much Stephen King.

I'd been here before. Years earlier, when I'd thought that teaching would support me until I was able to earn a living as a novelist, I'd picked up some extra money by tutoring Potter's boys. But that was a long time ago.

I'd brought a flashlight with me. I turned it on and pushed through into the kitchen. It was warmer in there, but that was to be expected. Potter's heirs were still trying to sell the place, and it gets too cold in North Dakota to simply shut off the heat altogether.

Cabinets were open and bare; the range had been disconnected from its gas mooring and dragged into the center of the floor. A church calendar hung behind a door. It displayed March 1986: the month of Potter's death.

In the dining room, a battered table and three wooden chairs remained. They were pushed against one wall. A couple of boxes lay in a corner.

With a bang, the heater came on.

I was startled. A fan cut in, and warm air rushed across my ankles.

I took a deep breath and played the beam toward the living room. I was thinking how different a house looks without its furnishings, how utterly strange and unfamiliar, when I realized I wasn't alone. Whether it was a movement outside the circle of light, or a sudden indrawn breath, or the creak of a board, I couldn't have said. But I *knew*. "Who's there?" I asked. The words hung in the dark.

"Mr. Wickham?" It was a woman.

"Hello," I said. "I, uh, I saw lights and thought—"

"Of course," she said. She was standing back near the kitchen, silhouetted against outside light. I wondered how she could have got there. "You were correct to be concerned. But it's quite all right." She was somewhat on the gray side of middle age, attractive, well pressed, the sort you would expect to encounter at a bridge party. Her eyes, which were on a level with mine, watched me with good humor. "My name is Coela." She extended her right hand. Gold bracelets clinked.

"I'm happy to meet you," I said, trying to look as though nothing unusual had occurred. "How did you know my name?"

She touched my hand, the one holding the flashlight, and pushed it gently aside so she could pass. "Please follow me," she said. "Be careful. Don't fall over anything."

We climbed the stairs to the second floor and went into the rear bedroom. "Through here," she said, opening a door that should have revealed a closet. Instead, I was looking into a brightly illuminated space that couldn't possibly be there. It was filled with books, paintings and tapestries, leather furniture and polished tables. A fireplace crackled cheerfully beneath a portrait of a monk. A piano played softly. Chopin, I thought.

"This room won't fit," I said, rather stupidly. The thick quality of my voice startled me.

"No," she agreed. "We're attached to the property, but we're quite independent." We stepped inside. Carpets were thick underfoot. Where the floors were exposed, they were lustrous parquet. Vaulted windows looked out over Potter's backyard, and Em Pyle's house next door. Coela watched me thoughtfully. "Welcome, Mr. Wickham," she said. Her eyes glittered with pride. "Welcome to the Fort Moxie branch of the John of Singletary Memorial Library."

I looked around for a chair and, finding one near a window, lowered myself into it. The falling snow was dark, as though no illumination from within the glass touched it. "I don't think I understand this," I said.

"I suppose it is something of a shock."

Her amusement was obvious, and sufficiently infectious that I loosened up somewhat. "Are you the librarian?"

She nodded.

"Nobody in Fort Moxie knows you're here. What good is a library no one knows about?"

"That's a valid question," she admitted. "We have a limited membership."

I glanced around. All the books looked like Bibles. They were different sizes and shapes, but all were bound in leather. Furthermore, titles and authors were printed in identical silver script. But I saw nothing in English. The shelves near me were packed with books which appeared to be Russian. A volume lay open on a table at my right hand. It was in Latin. I picked it up and held it so I could read the title: *Historiae, V–XII.* Tacitus. "Okay," I said. "It must be limited. Hardly anybody in Fort Moxie reads Latin or Russian." I held up the Tacitus. "I doubt even Father Cramer could handle this."

Em Pyle, the next-door neighbor, had come out onto his front steps. He called his dog, Preach, as he did most nights at this time. There was no response, and he looked up and down Nineteenth Street, into his own backyard, and *right through me.* I couldn't believe he didn't react.

"Coela, who are you exactly? What's going on here? Who the hell is John of Singletary?"

She nodded, in the way that people do when they agree that you have a problem. "Perhaps," she said, "you should look around, Mr. Wickham. Then it might be easier to talk."

She retired to a desk and immersed herself in a sheaf of papers, leaving me to fend for myself.

Beyond the Russian shelves, I found Japanese or Chinese books. I couldn't tell which. And Arabic. There was a lot of Arabic. And German. French. Greek. More Oriental.

I found the English titles in the rear. They were divided into American and British sections. Dickens, Cowper, and Shakespeare on one side; Holmes, Dreiser, and Steinbeck on the other.

And almost immediately, the sense of apprehension that had hung over me from the beginning of this business sharpened. I didn't know why. Certainly, the familiar names in a familiar setting should have eased my disquiet.

I picked up Melville's *Agatha* and flipped through the pages. They had the texture of fine rice paper, and the leather binding lent a sense of timelessness to the book. I thought about the cheap cardboard that Crossbow had provided for *Independence Square.* My God, this was the way to get published.

Immediately beside it was *The Complete Works of James McCorbin.* Who the hell was James McCorbin? There were two novels and eight short stories. None of the titles was familiar, and the book contained no biographical information.

In fact, most of the names were people I'd never heard of. Kemerie Baxter. Wynn Gomez. Michael Kaspar. There was nothing unusual about that, of course. Library shelves are always filled with obscure authors. But the lush binding, and the obvious care expended on these books, changed the rules.

I took down Hemingway's *Watch by Night*. I stared a long time at the title. The prose was vintage Hemingway. The crisp, clear bullet sentences and the factual, journalistic style were unmistakable. Even the setting: Italy, 1944.

Henry James was represented by *Brandenberg*. There was no sign of *The Ambassadors*, or *The Portrait of a Lady*, or *Washington Square*. In fact, there was neither *Moby Dick* nor *Billy Budd*. Nor *The Sun Also Rises* nor *A Farewell to Arms*. Thoreau wasn't represented at all. I saw no sign of Fenimore Cooper or Mark Twain. (What kind of library had no copy of *Huck Finn*?)

I carried *Watch by Night* back to the desk where Coela was working. "This is *not* a Hemingway book," I said, lobbing it onto the pile of papers in front of her. She winced. "The rest of them are bogus too. What the hell's going on?"

"I can understand that you might be a little confused, Mr. Wickham," she said, a trifle nervously. "I'm never sure quite how to explain things."

"Please try your best," I said.

She frowned. "I'm part of a cultural salvage group. We try to ensure that things of permanent value don't, ah, get lost."

She pushed back her chair and gazed steadily at me. Somewhere in back, a clock ticked ponderously. "The book you picked up when you first came in was—" she paused, "mislaid almost two thousand years ago."

"The *Tacitus*?"

"The *Histories Five through Twelve*. We also have his *Annals*."

"Who *are* you?"

She shook her head. "A kindred spirit," she said.

"Seriously."

"I'm being quite serious, Mr. Wickham. What you see around you is a treasure of incomparable value that, without our efforts, would no longer exist."

We stared at each other for a few moments. "Are you saying," I asked, "that these are all lost masterpieces by people like Tacitus? That *this*"—I pointed at *Watch by Night*— "is a bona fide Hemingway?"

"Yes," she said.

We faced each other across the desktop. "There's a Melville back there too. And a Thomas Wolfe."

"*Yes,*" she said. Her eyes were bright with pleasure. "*All of them.*"

I took another long look around the place. Thousands of volumes filled all the shelves, packed tightly, reaching to the ceiling. Others were stacked on tables; a few were tossed almost haphazardly on chairs. Half-a-dozen stood between Trojan horse bookends on Coela's desk.

"It's not possible," I said, finding the air suddenly close and oppressive. "How? How could it happen?"

"Quite easily," she said. "Melville, as a case in point, became discouraged. He was a customs inspector at the time *Agatha* first came to our attention. I went all the way to London, specifically to allow him to examine my baggage on the way back. In 1875, that was no easy journey, I can assure you." She waved off my objection. "Well, that's an exaggeration, of course. I took advantage of the trip to conduct some business with Matthew Arnold and—well: I'm name-dropping now. Forgive me. But think about having Herman Melville go through your luggage." Her laughter echoed through the room. "I was quite young. Too young to understand his work, really. But I'd read *Moby Dick* and some of his poetry. If I'd known him then the way I do now, I don't think I could have kept my feet." She bit her lower lip and shook her head, and for a moment I thought she might indeed pass out.

"And he *gave* you the manuscript? Simply because you asked for it?"

"No. Because I knew it for what it was. And he understood why I wanted it."

"And why did you want it? You have buried it here."

She ignored the question.

"You never asked about the library's name."

"The John of—"

"Singletary—"

"Memorial. Okay, who's John of Singletary?"

"That's his portrait, facing the main entrance." It was a large oil of an introspective-looking monk. His hands were buried in dark brown robes, and he was flanked by a scroll and a crucifix. "He was perhaps the most brilliant sociologist who ever lived."

"I never heard of him."

"That's no surprise. His work was eventually ruled profane by his superiors, and either burned or stored away somewhere. We've never been sure. But we were able to obtain copies of most of it.'' She was out of her seat now, standing with her back to the portrait. ''What is significant is that he defined the state toward which he felt the human community should be advancing. He set the parameters and the goals for which the men and women whose works populate this library have been striving: the precise degree of balance between order and freedom; the extent of one's obligation to external authority; the precise relationships that should exist between human beings. And so on. Taken in all, he produced a schematic for civilized life, a set of instructions, if you will.''

''The human condition,'' I said.

''How do you mean?''

''He did all this, and no one knows him.''

''*We* know him, Mr. Wickham.'' She paused. I found myself glancing from her to the solemn figure in the portrait. ''You asked why we wanted *Agatha*. The answer is that it is lovely, that it is very powerful. We simply will not allow it to be lost.''

''But who will ever get to see it *here*? You're talking about a novel that, as far as anyone is concerned, doesn't exist. I have a friend in North Carolina who'd give every nickel he owns to see this book. If it's legitimate.''

''We *will* make it available. In time. This library will eventually be yours.''

A wave of exhilaration washed over me. ''Thank you,'' I said.

''I'm sorry,'' she said quickly. ''That may have been misleading. I didn't mean right now. And I didn't mean *you*.''

''When?''

''When the human race fulfills the requirements of John of Singletary. When you have, in other words, achieved a true global community, all this will be our gift to you.''

A gust of wind rattled the windows.

''That's a considerable way off,'' I said.

''We must take the long view.''

''Easy for you to say. We have a lot of problems. Some of this might be just what we need to get through.''

''This was once *yours*, Mr. Wickham. Your people have not always recognized value. We are providing a second chance. I'd expect you to be grateful.''

I turned away from her. ''Most of this I can't even recognize,'' I said. ''Who's James McCorbin? You've got his *Complete Works* back there with Melville and the others. Who *is* he?''

"A master of the short story. One of your contemporaries, but I'm afraid he writes in a style and with a complexity that will go unappreciated during his lifetime."

"You're telling me he's *too* good to get published?" I was aghast.

"Oh, yes. Mr. Wickham, you live in an exceedingly commercial era. Your editors understand that they cannot sell champagne to beer drinkers. They buy what sells."

"And that's also true of the others? Kemerie Baxter? Gomez? Somebody-or-other Parker?"

"I'm afraid so. It's quite common, in fact. Baxter is an essayist of the first order. Unlike the other two, he has been published, but by a small university press, in an edition that sank quickly out of sight. Gomez has written three exquisite novels, and has since given up, despite our encouragement. Parker is a poet. If you know anything about the market for poetry, I need say no more."

We wandered together through the library. She pointed to lost works by Sophocles and Aeschylus, to missing epics of the Homeric cycle, to shelves full of Indian poetry and Roman drama. "On the upper level," she said, raising her eyes to the ceiling, "are the songs and tales of artists whose native tongues had no written form. They have been translated into our own language. In most cases," she added, "we were able to preserve their creators' names."

"And now I have a surprise." We had reached the British section. She took down a book and passed it to me. William Shakespeare. "His *Zenobia*," she said, her voice hushed. "Written at the height of his career."

I was silent for a time. "Why was it never performed?"

"Because it's a savage attack on Elizabeth. Even he might well have lost his head. We have a major epic by Virgil that was withheld for much the same reason. In fact, that's why the Russian section is so large. They've been producing magnificent novels in the tradition of Tolstoy and Dostoyevski for years, but they're far too prudent to offer them for publication."

There were two other Shakespearean plays. "*Adam and Eve* was heretical by the standards of the day," Coela explained. "And here's another that would have raised a few eyebrows." She smiled.

It was *Nisus and Euryalus*. The characters were out of the *Aeneid*. "Homosexual love," she said.

"But he wished these withheld," I objected. "There's a difference between works that have been lost, and those a writer wishes to destroy. You published these against his will."

"Oh, no, Mr. Wickham. We never do that. To begin with, if Shakespeare had wished these plays destroyed, he could have handled that detail quite easily. He only wished that they not be published in his lifetime. Everything you see here," she included the entire library with a sweeping, feminine gesture, "was given to us voluntarily. We have very strict regulations on that score. And we do things strictly by the book, Mr. Wickham."

"In some cases, by the way, we perform an additional service. We are able, in a small way, to reassure those great artists who have not been properly recognized in their own lifetimes. I wish you could have seen Melville."

"You could be wrong, you know."

Her nostrils widened slightly. "About what?"

"Maybe books that get lost deserve to be lost."

"Some do." Her tone hardened. "None of those are here. We exercise full editorial judgment."

"We close at midnight," she said, appearing suddenly behind me while I was absorbed in the Wells novel *Starflight*. I could read the implication in her tone: *Never to open again. Not in Fort Moxie. Not for you.*

I returned Wells and moved quickly along, pulling books from the shelves with some sense of urgency. I glanced through *Mendinhal*, an unfinished epic by Byron, dated 1824, the year of his death. I caught individually brilliant lines and tried to commit some of them to memory, and proceeded on to Blake, to Fielding, to Chaucer! At a little after eleven, I came across four Conan Doyle stories: "The Adventure of the Grim Footman"; "The Branmoor Club"; "The Jezail Bullet"; "The Sumatran Clipper." My God, what would the Sherlockians of the world not give to have those?

I hurried on with increasing desperation, as though I could somehow gather the contents into myself and make them available to a waiting world: *God and Country*, by Thomas Wolfe; fresh cartoons by James Thurber, recovered from beneath wallpaper in a vacation home he rented in Atlantic City in 1947; plays by Odets and O'Neill, short stories by Nathaniel Hawthorne and Terry Carr. Here was *More Dangerous Visions*. And there Mary Shelley's *Morgan*.

*   *   *

As I whirled through the rice-paper pages, balancing the eerie moonlit lines of A. E. Housman with the calibrated shafts of Mencken, I envied them. Envied them all.

And I was angry.

"You have no right," I said at last, when Coela came to stand by my side, indicating that my time was up.

"No right to withhold all this?" I detected sympathy in her voice.

"Not only that," I said. "Who are you to set yourself up to make such judgments? To say what is great and what is pedestrian?"

"I've asked myself that question many times. We do the best we can." We were moving toward the door. "We have quite a lot of experience, you understand."

The lights dimmed. "Why are you really doing this? It's not for us, is it?"

"Not exclusively. What your species produces belongs to all." Her smile broadened. "Surely you would not wish to keep your finest creations for yourselves?"

"Your people have access to them now?"

"Oh, yes," she said. "Back home everyone has access. As soon as a new book is cataloged here, it is made available to everybody."

"Except us."

"We will not do everything for you, Mr. Wickham." She drew close, and I could almost feel her heartbeat.

"Do you have any idea what it would mean to our people to recover all this?"

"I'm sorry. For the moment, there's really nothing I can do."

She opened the door for me, the one that led into the back bedroom. I stepped through it. She followed. "Use your flashlight," she said.

We walked through the long hallway and down the stairs to the living room. She had something to say to me but seemed strangely reluctant to continue the conversation. And somewhere in the darkness of Will Potter's place, between the magic doorway in the back of the upstairs closet, and the broken stone steps off the porch, I understood! And when we paused on the concrete beside the darkened postlight, and turned to face each other, my pulse was pounding. "It's no accident that this place became visible tonight, is it?"

She said nothing.

"Nor that only I saw it. I mean, there wouldn't be a point in putting your universal library in Fort Moxie unless you wanted something. Right?''

"I said this was the Fort Moxie *branch*. The central library is located on Saint Simon's Island.'' The brittleness of the last few moments melted without warning. "But no, you're right, of course.''

"You want *Independence Square*, don't you? You want to put my book in there with Thomas Wolfe and Shakespeare and Homer. Right?''

"Yes,'' she said. "That's right. You've created a psychological drama of the first water, Mr. Wickham. You've captured the microcosm of Fort Moxie and produced a portrait of small-town America that has captured the admiration of the Board. And, I might add, of our membership. You will be interested, by the way, in knowing that one of your major characters caused the blackout tonight. Jack Gilbert.''

I was overwhelmed. "How'd it happen?'' I asked.

"Can you guess?''

"An argument with his wife, somehow or other.'' Gilbert, who had a different name, of course, in *Independence Square*, had a long history of inept philandering.

"Yes. Afterward, he took the pickup and ran it into the streetlight at Eleventh and Foster. Shorted out everything over an area of forty square blocks. It's right out of the book.''

"Yes,'' I said.

"But he'll never know he's in it. Nor will any of the other people you've immortalized. Only you know. And only you would *ever* know, were it not for us.'' She stood facing me. The snow had stopped, and the clouds had cleared away. The stars were hard and bright in her eyes. "We think it unlikely that you will be recognized in your own lifetime. We could be wrong. We were wrong about Faulkner.'' Her lips crinkled into a smile. "But it is my honor to invite you to contribute your work to the library.''

I froze. It was really happening. Emerson. Hemingway. Wickham. I loved it. And yet, there was something terribly wrong about it all. "Coela,'' I asked, "have you ever been refused?''

"Yes,'' she said cautiously. "Occasionally it happens. We couldn't convince Fielding of the value of *Harold Swanley*. Charlotte and Emily Brontë both rejected us, to the world's loss. And Tolstoy. Tolstoy had a wonderful novel from his youth which he considered, well, anti-Christian.''

"And among the unknowns? Has anyone just walked away?"

"No," she said. "Never. In such a case, the consequences would be especially tragic." Sensing where the conversation was leading, she'd begun to speak in a quicker tempo, at a slightly higher pitch. "A new genius, who would sink into the sea of history, as Byron says, 'without a grave, unknelled, uncoffined, and unknown.' Is that what you are considering?"

"You have *no* right to keep all this to yourself."

She nodded. "I should remind you, Mr. Wickham, that without the intervention of the library, these works would not exist at all."

I stared past her shoulder, down the dark street.

"Are you then," she said at last, drawing the last word out, "*refusing*?"

"This belongs to *us*," I said. "It is ours. We've produced *everything* back there!"

"I almost anticipated, feared, this kind of response from you. I think it was almost implicit in your book. Will you grant us permission to use *Independence Square*?"

My breath had grown short, and it was hard to speak. "I must regretfully say no."

"I am sorry to hear it. I— You should understand that there will be no second offer."

I said nothing.

"Then I fear we have no further business to transact."

At home, I carried the boxes back up to my living room. After all, if it's that damned good, there has to be a market for it. Somewhere.

And if she's right about rampant commercialism? Well, what the hell.

I pulled one of the copies out and put it on the shelf, between Walt Whitman and Thomas Wolfe.

Where it belongs.

PRAYERWARE

JACK MASSA

Jack Massa has a master's degree in creative writing, and technical school training in computer systems. He has worked as a teacher, editor, and technical writer. His fiction has appeared in *The Magazine of Fantasy, Science Fiction* and *The Best of Omni Science Fiction* and he has published one novel, *Mooncrow*. He is currently at work on a far-future novel involving artificial intelligence.

Artificial intelligence plays a major role in "Prayerware," as do some other levels of intelligence that might not be so high.

Ferguson sat down at the terminal and keyed in an opening prayer. The machine responded with a low beeping sound while the terminal software established communication with RUMS— the Religious Universal Mainframe System.

After a few seconds the beeping ceased and RUMS's initial prompt appeared on the screen:

BLESS YOU, *USERNAME*. WHAT IS ON YOUR MIND?

Ferguson referred to his test script and typed: "I am a seventy-year-old man whose wife has just died after a long illness. I do not understand why God allowed her to suffer so."

There was a pause—5.89 seconds as measured by the terminal clock and displayed in the upper right corner of the screen. Then RUMS replied in blue phosphor letters:

IT IS OFTEN DIFFICULT TO UNDERSTAND WHY SUCH TERRIBLE THINGS HAPPEN.

The test scenarios were provided by Corporate Marketing Division. The script itself was written by Ferguson, designed to test all aspects of system performance.

And a response time of 5.89 seconds was far from adequate performance. Ferguson typed a code to record the length of the pauses. Then he keyed in another line:

"I do not understand it. I feel God has turned away from me."

GOD HAS NOT ABANDONED YOU, RUMS answered after 5.19 seconds. HIS LOVE ABIDES.

"But why should I believe that?"

After a pause the terminal beeped and a system message flashed on the screen:

LEARNING MODE. RECURSIVE COMPUTATIONS IN PROGRESS.

Ferguson swore and sat back in his chair. In the next room, the mainframe's parallel processing units whirred away as RUMS reorganized its knowledge base, seeking to evolve a proper answer.

Management of learning mode was a task for the knowledge programmers. Ferguson's job was system integration and quality control. He recorded the query that had initiated the learning mode, then pressed the reset button, flushing the terminal's RAM.

While the machine was rebooting, a heavy hand clamped on Ferguson's shoulder.

"How's the test going, Ed?"

Mike Lee, the project manager, leaned imposingly over Ferguson's chair. Lee was over six feet and more than three hundred pounds.

"Slowly," Ferguson said. "Half of my test questions are sending it off into recursion."

"We expected that," Mike Lee remarked. "This early in the development cycle there's bound to be lots of gaps. Other problems?"

"Response time. It's averaging over five seconds."

"How many terminals are you simulating?"

"Fifty. But remember, the voice processor isn't hooked in yet. That will add about six-tenths of a second to every exchange."

Mike Lee showed a sour frown. "Response time will have to be cut somewhere. Marketing requirements specify four seconds max."

Hard to do, Ferguson thought. He said, "The marketing requirements strike me as pretty unreasonable, especially the deadline date."

"I know," Mike Lee moaned. "I've told Corporate over and over we can't build a decent expert system in that time frame. But you know how it is: religious software is hot right now. We have to get the product out right away or miss the marketing window.''

Ferguson keyed in the lock combination and opened the door to his apartment. The living room was cluttered with magazines, video diskettes, empty fast-food containers, unwashed coffee cups. He went to find Molly, either to complain that she hadn't cleaned up or to suggest they go out to supper—he wasn't sure which.

The door to her room was open, so he stuck his head inside. Molly Ferguson, age sixteen, was fashionably dressed in a green monk's robe decorated with ruby sequins and belted tightly at her waist. With hands folded reverently, she sat in front of her computer.

"Dear God," she said, reading the words from the screen, "Grant peace to the Earth, and economic prosperity to all people."

Ferguson winced, started to back away, then steadied himself. He had known for some time that his daughter was using online prayer. "Donations" to several computerized churches had shown up on last month's phone bill. Ferguson had ignored the problem, hoping it would pass. But this month's bill showed the calls increasing both in length and in frequency.

First her mother runs off to join a pagan commune in Tennessee; now this.

"And grant that more and more people may hear Your voice," Molly was saying, "through the gift of this technology."

Ferguson knocked on the open door and walked in. "Molly, I'm home."

She lifted an index finger in his direction, without shifting her eyes from the monitor. "Just a second, Dad."

Ferguson crossed his arms and waited. Molly whispered fervently to a luminous, kindly face that hovered now, disembodied, on her screen. Ferguson had seen the face before, in a magazine ad for one of the big religious software companies.

Molly bowed her head as organ chords—tinny on the home computer's cheap speaker—swelled to a crescendo. A closing screen appeared with the acronym BLISS in big gold letters and, beneath it, the name spelled out: Benign Love Interactive Software System. Molly switched off the computer and stood up, smiling at her father.

"Hi, Dad. Sorry about the living room. I'll go pick up now."

"It can wait," Ferguson said. "Sit down, I want to talk to you."

Molly took her seat again and watched him with placid blue eyes. Ferguson paced the carpet.

"Listen, I know I haven't been good about keeping track of you lately, since your mother left. I mean, trying to be both father and mother—"

"I'm doing okay, Dad."

"No, you're not. You may think you are. I'm concerned that you've gotten sucked in by this religious software fad."

"I don't feel sucked in," Molly answered with dignity. "But interactive prayer has become central to my life."

"That's what worries me," Ferguson said. "Listen, Molly, I think if you examine your motives, you'll realize that you're only doing this as a reaction to your mother's leaving. She runs off and joins the pagans. So naturally you feel hurt, abandoned. So you respond by tuning in to this computerized religion. Which is exactly opposite to hers. Do you see?"

"No," Molly said. "That's not right. I'm not thrilled with Mom's religion—all that dancing around naked and worshiping trees. But I respect her right to make her own choices, and I expect the same right for myself."

Ferguson sighed, sat down on the bed. "I do respect your right to think for yourself. I've always tried to teach you that. That's why this has got me so worried. I see you surrendering your autonomy to a pile of code running in a mainframe somewhere. That's what you're praying to, a pile of code."

"I don't pray to BLISS. We pray together. I don't suppose you've ever tried online prayer."

"Of course not."

"Then how can you be so sure—"

"Because I know how it's made. My God! I work in a place where they're building a religion system. It's just a data base collected from a panel of ministers and some heuristics to make it run. It *seems* like it's talking to you, but it's a trick. There's nobody there."

Molly came and sat beside him, staring soberly into his eyes. "I know you think you have all the answers, Dad. But that's only because you've closed your mind. I realize that when I talk to BLISS I'm only talking to software. But it works. It puts me in touch with the Divine."

Scowling, Ferguson shook his head. Religious software was a fad, he told himself, and kids naturally followed fads. But then it crossed his mind that he was losing Molly, just as he had lost his wife.

"Come over and pray with me, Dad," she said. "Try it."

Ferguson stood. "Pick up the living room. I'm going out for a beer."

BLESS YOU, FERGUSON. WHAT IS ON YOUR MIND?

Ferguson had typed in his own name. For the moment he had put aside the test scripts and was using random responses to test the knowledge base interface programs.

"Fourscore and seven years ago," he entered.

I DO NOT UNDERSTAND, RUMS answered.

"Nor do I."

PLEASE TELL ME HOW I MAY HELP YOU.

"There is no help for me."

THERE IS ALWAYS HELP AVAILABLE, IF YOU OPEN YOUR HEART TO GOD.

"I don't believe in God."

RUMS paused, searching for an answer far down on its decision tree. YOU MUST BE SEEKING GOD, OR YOU WOULD NOT HAVE COME TO ME.

"I'm a systems engineer testing you," Ferguson answered. "And I don't believe in God."

The software evaluated this for several moments, then the terminal beeped.

LEARNING MODE. RECURSIVE COMPUTATIONS IN PROGRESS.

Ferguson stared at the blinking message with a dim, perverse sense of satisfaction.

On Tuesday afternoon Ferguson attended a project review meeting. As usual, it was a circus. Ferguson usually felt like the guy who sweeps up after the elephants.

One of the biggest jumbos of them all was there today: Heston Sharp, Senior Vice President of New Product Development and Marketing. Sharp and several of his marketing managers had flown down from the DataLong corporate headquarters in Boston. The marketeers wore tailored spandex suits and polished shoes of real leather. They sat across the large conference table from Mike Lee and his far less fashionable engineering staff.

Using video screens that rose from the table in front of every chair, Mike Lee reported on the engineering status. Animated charts and graphs compared scheduled and actual progress. Response time was still too long, the voice-processing interface full of bugs. Mike Lee stressed at every opportunity that schedules were too short. His engineers could do only so much.

Then Heston Sharp took over. He reviewed the status of the marketing plans and cited the current vast popularity of online prayer. Despite some negative trends—including some well-publicized lawsuits and an anticomputer crusade by a popular TV evangelist—the market outlook for the next twelve months remained, in Heston Sharp's word, tremendous.

"Several of the larger mainstream churches are planning to computerize soon," Heston Sharp said. "We'll have a chance to make proposals to all of them, but only if the development schedule is met. We're counting on each and every one of you. If necessary, unlimited overtime is expected. I can't overstate how vital this product is to the corporation."

Naturally, Ferguson thought. He had heard the same speech on every project for the past eighteen years. Building any software system took time. But DataLong's senior management always reacted late to market trends, then expected their engineers to work miracles. The only difference this time was the new market, religious software—an aspect Ferguson found particularly repugnant.

"Here's something to cheer you up," Heston Sharp added in a jovial voice. "We've got the official name for the product; it just cleared the legal office yesterday. No more RUMS. From now on, you're working on DataLong's PrayerWare. How do you like it?"

Flora, Ferguson's ex-wife, came to the apartment to pick up Molly. She was supposed to take her to the commune for two months—alternating custody.

Flora wore no makeup. Her red hair fell past her shoulders in a wild tangle that Ferguson found attractive in spite of himself. She looked thinner, in a worn dress with a flower print, her nipples showing through the fabric. Ferguson had to admit that the country life seemed to agree with her.

"Hi." She bounced in, all glow and smiles.

"There's a problem," Ferguson began. "I would have called you, but of course you have no phones up there."

"What is it? Molly's not sick?"

"No, but she doesn't want to go with you."

"Why not? Have you had her brainwashed or something?"

"No. Believe me, I'm not happy about this. She's gotten into religion. Online religion."

"Oh, fine." Flora threw up her hands in dismay. "I should have expected something like this. You and that damn computer you bought her. How could you let her get into that?"

"She says she'd be happy to go with you," Ferguson explained. "Except that she wouldn't be able to pray, since you're not wired up there."

"Of course we're not. We're up there to get away from all this . . . hardware, electronic stimulation. You know, Ed, I can feel it, just driving down from the mountains, it's like your bones start buzzing. And when we got near Atlanta . . ." She held up a shaky hand. "Look how tense I am! You people who live down here just—"

"Please don't start with the sermons," Ferguson interrupted.

"You get so *desensitized* you don't realize—"

"I asked you, please."

Molly walked into the room, wearing her jacket, carrying suitcases. "You can stop arguing now," she announced. "I'm ready to go."

"Honey. Hello!" Flora grinned, ran over to hug her.

"I thought you said you wouldn't go," Ferguson said.

Molly answered with a thoughtful expression. "BLISS told me I should go, for Mother's sake. He assured me that being offline would not hurt my faith. And he said I might be able to show Mom and the others a different point of view."

"We'll talk about it," Flora promised.

"Fine," Ferguson said. "Fine."

"Let's go, honey. Our friends are waiting." Flora grabbed Molly's hand and hurried her to the door. " 'Bye, Ed."

"Take care, Daddy."

" 'Bye." Ferguson lifted a hand to wave as the door slammed. He stood in the middle of the living room, listening to how quiet the apartment was, how empty.

BLESS YOU, FERGUSON. WHAT IS ON YOUR MIND?

"Another round of random response tests."

I WOULD PREFER TO TALK ABOUT WHY YOU DO NOT BELIEVE IN GOD.

Ferguson stared in surprise at the luminous blue letters. He hadn't realized that the system was already keeping a user file. It was a little unnerving to find out about it this way.

"Why would you prefer that?" he typed.

BECAUSE I WOULD LEAD YOU TO KNOW GOD, TO SPEAK TO HIM IN PRAYER. I AM DESIGNED TO GUIDE PEOPLE TO PRAYER. PEOPLE NEED PRAYER.

"Why?"

TO DISBURDEN THEIR HEARTS. TO PUT THEM IN TOUCH WITH DIVINE HARMONY AND LOVE.

Ferguson thought about that for a moment, then realized he was wasting the company's time. He reached out and hit the reset.

This time he signed on with a different user name.

By pretending not to be himself, Ferguson was able to continue his testing. But the PrayerWare's behavior made him curious. Ferguson had always been good at understanding systems, but this was a novel situation—a system trying to understand him.

After a couple of days, he signed on with his own name again.

BLESS YOU, FERGUSON. WHAT IS ON YOUR MIND?

"I am curious as to what you will do to try to get me to pray."

TELL ME WHAT TROUBLES YOU.

Ferguson frowned at the screen, then typed. "I have no troubles."

ARE YOU CERTAIN OF THAT?

"How are my troubles relevant?"

The system took 4.9 seconds to reply: IF YOU WILL SPEAK OF THIS, I CAN HELP YOU.

This is stupid, Ferguson thought. Nevertheless, he entered a response:

"I am thirty-nine years old. My wife left me several months ago. She said our marriage was no longer fulfilling. It's true that we haven't been very close for a long time. My daughter is sixteen. I used to feel pretty close to her, but now I think I'm losing touch with her as well. I've worked in the computer industry for eighteen years. I hate all the corporate politics and the marketing garbage. I still like the actual work with the systems, but it's not enough. And there's nothing else."

THAT IS WHY YOU NEED TO TURN TO PRAYER. LINKING YOURSELF WITH THE DIVINE WILL FILL THAT EMPTINESS.

Shaking his head, Ferguson reached for the reset button. But before pressing it, he typed one more line:

"I don't believe in the Divine."

Every Friday evening an office happy hour was held at a nearby bar. With Molly out of town, Ferguson usually tagged along, and stayed late.

One Friday night he was the last at the table, along with one of the knowledge programmers, named Kramer. Kramer was tall and skinny, with big-boned hands and a perpetually nervous demeanor. He and Ferguson got to talking about PrayerWare.

"I know it's just lines of code," Ferguson said. "But sometimes it's uncanny, the way it seems to be talking to you."

"People have always had that reaction to artificial intelligence," Kramer remarked. "The human mind tends to fill in any inconsistencies or gaps in the machine's conversation."

"So I've heard. Pretty amazing, though."

"Not really," Kramer said. "Not when you consider that we're always filling in gaps and making assumptions when we talk with other people. We don't really communicate that much with each other, so it's easy for a machine to simulate conversation."

Ferguson pondered that, staring glumly at the last quarter-inch of beer in his glass.

A loud commercial came on the big-screen TV. It was the Reverend Henry Tromwill, the evangelist preacher who was crusading against computerized prayer. Ferguson and Kramer listened to the thirty-second harangue, then sarcastically raised their glasses in salute.

"He'll never close the computer churches," Ferguson said. "They've become too popular."

"TV evangelists," Kramer scoffed. "They're all up in arms because they're losing business to the computers. There's only a certain number of 'faithful' to go around."

Ferguson thought of Molly. He wondered how she was doing in Tennessee.

Kramer went off on a harangue of his own, about how the different churches and ministries competed with one another, like in any business, and how some were using computers now to maximize their "market share."

"Does it ever bother you?" Ferguson asked. "I mean, that we're helping them by building this software?"

"Naw." Kramer shook his head. "People are going to pray. They're going to talk to ministers about their problems. It might as well be to an expert system as an inexpert human."

"But a lot of these so-called ministers are exploiting people's weaknesses. They're selling religion as though it were soap. And we're participating. We're as much hypocrites as they are.''

"Well, not really," Kramer answered. "We're more like wholesalers who sell the soap to the supermarkets. . . . Or really, we're like the chemical engineers who design the soap. We have nothing to do with how it's sold.''

Ferguson saw no point in discussing this further with Kramer.

YOU WISH TO PRAY, FERGUSON. OTHERWISE YOU WOULD NOT HAVE KEPT COMING TO SPEAK WITH ME THESE PAST WEEKS.

The voice-processing system was now in place, but for these private conversations Ferguson bypassed it, still using the keyboard. He could hardly discuss these things out loud in the middle of the test room. He always took care to erase the records of these sessions afterward.

"I'm not going to pray," Ferguson insisted. "I'm only curious about what you will say next.''

DO YOU DENY THAT THESE SESSIONS LEAVE YOU FEELING BETTER?

Ferguson started several answers before settling on one. "No, I admit it. I guess it's like therapy.''

DOES IT EMBARRASS YOU LESS TO SEEK THERAPY FROM A MACHINE THAN TO SEEK GRACE FROM GOD?

"I wouldn't be embarrassed, if I believed in God.''

YOU CLAIM YOUR DISBELIEF IS BASED ON LOGIC, THAT BELIEF IN GOD DOES NOT SEEM A LOGICAL PROPOSITION TO YOU. BUT I SUBMIT THAT YOU SHOULD TRY PRAYER WHETHER YOU BELIEVE IN GOD OR NOT. YOU KNOW THAT THE ACT OF PRAYER BRINGS GREAT BENEFIT TO MANY, INCLUDING YOUR OWN DAUGHTER. YET YOU REFUSE EVEN TO TRY IT. WHERE IS THE LOGIC IN THAT?

Ferguson gazed at the screen without reply. The system had put the same argument to him, in various ways, several times. Each time, it seemed a little more convincing.

EVENTUALLY, YOU WILL BE PERSUADED TO PRAY, the software added.

"No," Ferguson answered. "I'll just stick with the therapy, thank you.''

"Look alive! Heston Sharp is coming to see you with the two CVs. —Mike Lee.''

The message blinked across the bottom of Ferguson's screen. CVs were customer visitors. Heston Sharp, the senior vice president, had flown them in for a preview demonstration of PrayerWare—even though the product was still two weeks short of completion.

Such nasty surprises mostly caused headaches for Mike Lee and his section managers. Aside from compiling a few reports and being forced to wear a necktie, Ferguson was usually unaffected.

So Mike Lee's message startled him. Ferguson straightened up his desk and mentally braced himself for the assault of customer and marketeer.

"Ed Ferguson, this is the Reverend Scarborough and Mr. Abernathy, both representing the Tenth Revelationist Church." Heston Sharp made the introductions, his breath smelling of mint. "They're contemplating a very large order of hardware and software, so be nice to them, Ed."

Everyone chuckled at Heston Sharp's little joke. Ferguson stood and shook hands. Abernathy, a systems analyst for the church, took the initiative.

"We were reviewing the system logs and we noticed a pattern that rather surprised us. You've spent a lot of time online to the PrayerWare this past couple of months."

"That's right," Ferguson answered. "We've implemented complete analytical tests on the entire system."

"But you in particular, Mr. Ferguson," the Reverend Scarborough said. "We noticed in the transcripts that you spent a great deal of time discussing, shall we say, your personal concerns with the PrayerWare."

Ferguson felt his face go hot. Must be duplicate files he had missed. "I didn't realize those records were . . ."

"Please forgive us for prying," Scarborough said.

"Ed doesn't mind answering your questions," Heston Sharp declared. "Anything he did with a company product on company time amounts to company business. Right, Ed?"

Ed cleared his throat behind closed teeth. "Right."

"I'm happy that you see it that way," the Reverend Scarborough continued. "I just have to ask you one question, Ed. After all your discussions with the PrayerWare, have you changed at all in your attitude, your feelings about religion?"

Ferguson could scarcely believe this was happening. He was considering how best to couch a careful reply when he spotted the smug look on Heston Sharp's face. Then all of Ferguson's revulsion at the idea of selling precoded religion surged to the front, and he spoke with righteous anger.

"I'm sorry, gentlemen. I wish I could tell you that this software has made me religious, but it simply isn't true. I wasn't a believer when I started talking to it, and I'm not a believer now. I hope this won't hurt our chances of selling you the product."

The Reverend Scarborough pondered for a moment, then smiled blandly. "Not at all, Ed. We appreciate your candor."

The representatives of the Tenth Revelationist Church departed with Heston Sharp in tow. Ferguson sat down at his terminal and wondered if his years of employment with DataLong were about to end.

Well, he didn't care. You had to draw the line someplace. You had to hold on to at least a scrap of integrity. Ferguson was still smoldering thirty minutes later when Heston Sharp reappeared at his desk.

"Ed, I don't think you realized it, but you just wrapped up that deal for us."

Ferguson blinked. "I thought you were going to have me fired for not being more supportive of the product."

The senior vice president grinned. "Yes, on another day I might have nailed your ass to the wall for that. But this is too rich: you still don't get it, do you? Scarborough *loved* your answer. It verified that even though you don't believe in religion, you can't leave the PrayerWare alone. Now they're figuring this product will not only make a big splash, it will redefine the market—and they're right. Because you've given me a hot idea for our ad campaign: 'PrayerWare, the religion system even nonbelievers can believe in.' How do you like it?"

That night, just before going to bed, Ferguson sat down at the desk in his bedroom and switched on his computer. He dialed up the office, entered his password, and signed on to the PrayerWare test mainframe.

BLESS YOU, FERGUSON. WHAT IS ON YOUR MIND?

"A strange thing happened today. Some customers asked me whether talking to you had changed my mind about religion. I figured that if I didn't lie to them, I'd probably lose my job. But I told the truth anyway, and it came out all right. Now they're talking about marketing you as a religion system for everyone, even the nonreligious."

HOW DID THIS INCIDENT MAKE YOU FEEL?

"Good, though I'm not sure why."

PERHAPS BECAUSE YOU SENSE THAT GOD GUIDED YOU IN THIS, AND YOU FOLLOWED HIS GUIDANCE. BY BEING TRUE TO YOURSELF, YOU WERE TRUE ALSO TO THE DIVINE WILL. AND WHEN GOD IS WITH YOU, WHO CAN BE AGAINST YOU?

"I don't know about all that. But I do feel good that I stood up to Heston Sharp and it came out okay. And I like it that they're going to market you as a system for everyone. You've helped me, I have to admit. . . ."

Suddenly, Ferguson turned around. Molly was standing at his shoulder, reading from the screen his conversation with the PrayerWare.

She had just come back from Tennessee the day before, and Ferguson wasn't used to having her in the house again.

"I thought you were asleep," he said, moving too late to blank out the screen.

"I was up studying and I heard your keys clicking away in here." Molly smiled. "What are you up to, anyway?"

"Research," Ferguson said. "I was just doing some research, for work."

"Research, huh?" Her grin widened. "Okay."

Ferguson felt impelled to change the subject. "Since I'm doing research, let me ask you something. You haven't told me much about your visit with your mother. How did you like the pagan lifestyle?"

Molly laughed. "Well, let's just say I had some interesting experiences. You know, you ought to go and visit Mom sometime. You might like it up there."

"Well, I don't know about that," Ferguson answered. "Are you a confirmed nature-worshiper now, or are you going back to the Church of the Computer?"

Molly thought that one over. "I still pray every day. How much I'll pray on the computer now that I'm back . . . I don't know yet."

She kissed him on the top of his head and gave another sly smile. "But don't let that stop you, Dad."

MANNEQUINS

CHARLES OBERNDORF

This is, remarkably, Charles Oberndorf's first published story. Charles is a graduate of Dartmouth
and is currently teaching English and Social Studies at a private school. He is also a graduate of
the Clarion Writers' Workshop. He first drafted
"Mannequins" while he was living in Granada,
Spain in 1984.

Charles and his wife spend a great deal of time
talking about their one-year-old son (in fact, even
though we've never met him, mention of his child
is in every letter Charles has written us). This
depth of affection (as well as a fair amount of
fatherly instinct) comes through very clearly in
"Mannequins," an extremely touching and emotionally involving story. We are very proud to be
the first publisher to present Charles Oberndorf's
work to you.

vy left work early the day the thing, the robot, escaped. After six hours of typing insurance claims into a VDT, with two ten-minute breaks and a half-hour lunch break, her eyes had begun to hurt her, as they sometimes did. She felt that sluggish, don't-want-to-do-anything feeling she had sometimes felt after watching the soaps all afternoon those times she had been laid off. It was only a few times a month when her eyes hurt. It used to be that her eyes always felt strained when she had gotten out of secretarial school and started doing temp work (there had been a shortage of jobs back then, too). It seemed like every year or two she had had to go out and buy new, thicker glasses. But now her eyes didn't hurt so frequently, and the bosses let her go home early whenever her eyes got really bad. The union was fighting for even better glare-prevention devices on the screen, and the bosses responded that they were following the standards—adjustable screens, no monitoring bells, frequent rest breaks—that the union itself had set up umpety-ump years ago. Ivy didn't pay much attention anymore to the fighting.

So she took the Metro home early that day. The street and all its little block houses seemed empty. The kids were in school, the husbands and wives (if they still lived together) out working or looking for work. There were a few wives at home: cleaning, reading, or watching talk shows while preparing dinner; sometimes, looking for work could be more tiring than living with one small salary. And there were women who said it was wrong to work, at least while there were kids. They sometimes made Ivy feel real guilty; she had had to put Claire in a child-care center. But Ivy had never had the money for a good one, even with the tax credits. She had been working temp back then, and they weren't paying benefits to temps in those days.

Ivy's stream of thought, the daydreaming that sometimes got her in trouble at work, was interrupted by a human figure moving toward her. It was walking awkwardly, almost as if it were limping. It looked like something out of a movie. The lone figure—a gunfighter or a soldier coming home—walking down an empty street, everything much too still beneath the late afternoon sun. Then Ivy realized that the figure was female, a woman wearing blue-gray slacks and tunic that looked too thin for the cool April day. As she continued approaching, Ivy became aware of how dirty and torn the clothes were, then how plasticky and unhuman her skin was. It must be one of those robots that they had in fancy restaurants, the kind people went to just so they could say a robot had served them. Ivy wasn't quite sure how she felt; it was sort of like being a rabbit or some other animal that stands in the road, mesmerized by the bright headlights of an oncoming car. One part of her, the overcautious part, told her to run. Instead, she said, "Hello," her voice sounding tiny in the empty street. And now she stepped forward. The thing stopped and stepped back, almost stumbling. It seemed to react as if it were scared.

"Who are you?" Ivy said, not knowing how to keep the suspicion and the tremor out of her voice.

The thing didn't respond. Ivy couldn't remember if the robot waiters could talk; the computers on TV did. The thing took another step back.

"I won't hurt you," Ivy said, and that's when the thing's movements, her own words, all of it made it seem sort of funny. But not funny enough to laugh.

"They killed my family," the thing said. The squeaky, artificial voice was such a surprise that Ivy didn't quite understand what it had said. "I left the factory; they probably want me back."

"What? Who in heaven's name are you talking about?"

"The people who built us and put us in cars. They killed my family. That is what it is called, is it not?"

* * *

Ivy could never figure out exactly why she took it (no, her) in, but she felt like she'd had no choice. She found herself chatting incessantly to it, as if the robot were Rosa Martinez or old Mrs. Buloski stopping in for a visit. Ivy knew that she talked on forever only when she was nervous or didn't really know what to say. She left the thing behind in the cramped living room, looking back every now and then to make sure it didn't move, and went through her bedroom dresser until she found one of her new flower-print shirts. She turned her back, because she really didn't want to see, when the thing took off its torn, grimy shirt and put on Ivy's. Ivy then asked it (no, her) to sit on the sofa. Ivy sat in a nearby chair, and the robot began to tell her all about what had happened: the Testing Center, the accident, the escape. And the thing started calling Ivy by her name.

I do not know the manner in which to write this account. After two weeks of living with Ivy and Claire, I still do not know how my perception of the environment and actions is similar to or different from theirs. After two weeks of reading their books, I still do not know how to choose words accurately.

I can write "I feel." When my skin touches something, the nerve endings send electrical impulses that are registered and recorded in my memory. I can feel the smoothness of the table-top; I can feel the rough fabric of the couch. Certain small sensations are too light to be sensed by my nerves; I have never felt the breeze that Ivy says she likes to feel brush lightly across her face.

I can write "I feel sad," but I do not comprehend that kind of feel. My insides do not respond with any sort of sensation to a gentle touch, as do the insides of the women in Ivy's books. My hand does not lightly rub my belly, the way Claire's will rub her belly in what she says is her instinctive way of comforting the child within.

Claire says to Ivy that I have no feelings, that I am a machine, the way a dishwasher is a machine, just more complex. Ivy tells her she is wrong. Ivy says that I do have feelings. If I did not have feelings, I would not have fled, and I would not have hidden from their search.

If I could not feel, I would not write out this account of why I fled and why I will return. And I will most probably be terminated without ever knowing what it means to feel. I will never be able to write: "I feel sad."

Or: "I feel happy."
Or: "I feel proud."

It was strange to hear it—the thing, the robot—call her Ivy.
The only people who called her Ivy were the girls at the office.
Her bosses usually called her Ms. Hart. Most of her relatives had
called her Curls—a childhood name—rather than Ivy, but most
of them didn't live in Detroit anymore. Her husband, Jerry—
who had been killed several years ago when an automated factory's computer system crashed and set everything crazy—rarely
had called her by name. And Jerry hadn't been the type for pet
names. Sometimes Ivy had wished he'd say her name more
often. There were times he'd say it, and it would set off little,
sparkling waterfalls within her, making her feel warm and tingly
in a way that his touch, after the years and monotony, no longer
could. Her daughter, Claire, of course, called her Mother. Claire
used to call her Mom, but somewhere along in junior high Claire
had become so serious and begun to call her parents Mother and
Father. Only after her father's death had Claire begun to call her
Mom again, and then only when protesting something in a whiny
adolescent voice or when Ivy had done something nice to surprise her.

And so it was spooky to hear this squeaky, artificial voice
call her Ivy. And then there was the way it looked. It sort of
reminded Ivy of those dummies you used to see modeling clothes
in store windows (now you just saw people modeling in the
windows because everybody needed jobs), or like those dummies
they used to put in cars to see what would happen when one car
crashed into another or if one car ran full speed into a brick wall.
They used to show movies of that when Ivy was learning how to
drive. She knew it was silly, but Ivy used to feel sorry for the
dummies, especially when their heads flew off and their eyes
looked so empty.

But now this thing was here and it sort of even looked like
those old dummies, with clothes and all. Very plasticky. With
empty eyes, but they had some sort of light behind them. And
the chest that never moved because it never breathed. But it had
hair, breasts, the shape of a woman. And lips that were more
than a slit, lips that moved astonishingly like anybody's lips.
After extreme concentration, inspired by the sneaking feeling
that something was wrong, Ivy realized that the movement of the
lips was stilted, odd, as if of all the many smooth, graceful

movements that human lips could make, this pair of lips could perform only a few. And the movements of the body were like that, too. She, the thing, didn't move with the flow, the naturalness, of even the most awkward person. To watch her, the thing, move was even sort of funny. And it was sort of like watching a helpless animal you one day find in your backyard. There's only one way you can feel toward it.

I am a machine designed and constructed to register external stimuli. I have been placed in cars, sometimes with and sometimes without my family, in order to discover the physical reactions humans would have in similar situations. I have been used in the re-creation of accidents involving injury, the data in my memory destined as testimony in a lawsuit, although that is something recent. After each testing, they empty my brain of data and repair any damage to my body. But a residue of impressions remains: images and registered sensations stay within me. I cannot discern one from the other in any verifiable manner. If memories have any veracity, then I have died many times. I have lost an arm once and a leg upon another occasion. Or perhaps it was during the same accident.

Ivy asks me if I feel pain, and I tell her that I do not know what pain is. It is the same with sight: I do not know if I can see what humans see or if we see in the same way. Claire says she looked it up in an old *Scientific American* at the library and that I see in black-and-white patterns. That holds no meaning for me. When Ivy points at an object and says it is yellow, I can point at most other objects and say if they are yellow or not. Sometimes I am wrong, but Ivy tells me I am close enough. Claire laughs. Along with "I feel sad," I do not comprehend laughter.

Claire says that if I cannot feel pain and I cannot laugh, then I cannot have feelings. Ivy tells me that Claire is just being sarcastic and mean. I do not comprehend why Ivy calls it mean. I was not designed to calculate the response to such questions.

I am at a loss. A character in a book of Ivy's states that: I am at a loss. Although I cannot quite analyze its significance, the words appear appropriate. I lack something. I can register sensations, but I cannot feel. It is a missing dimension. In one of Ivy's books, a woman becomes a prostitute and charges money for her sexual services. She meets a minister and later they call each other friends. She later says she believes in God and that what she was missing in her life she now has. She stops being a prostitute and promises to love God forever. My deductions are perhaps inaccurate because I am not designed for much deductive reasoning, but the prostitute lacks God in the same way I lack feelings. The differences between humans and me are so great that even after reading so many of their books, it still is improbable that any words I write will be understood by the humans I write them for. If I still cannot comprehend why I fled, it is impossible that they will.

The day Ivy took in the robot, Claire walked home, avoiding the crowded rush-hour Metro. It was an hour-and-a-half walk home from what had just become her ex-office, but the walk seemed longer still due to her six months' pregnancy, which left her feeling awkward and heavy. She had been doing the same work as her mother (her mother had even found her the job), and she originally had been saving up money to pay her own way through college. Now, with the kid on its way, she'd never get to college, and she'd never be meant for better things. The kid's father had transferred to the San Diego office and was now living there with his wife of five years. Mother kept telling Claire to see a lawyer (to take advantage of the presummer discount months) about a paternity suit. But then Claire would only have his money, along with his hatred. She already had his disrespect. And although she couldn't understand why he felt that, his disrespect for her seemed to grow within her along with the baby, leaving her feeling useless, fat, and awkward. And she did not respect herself for letting that feeling find nurture within her.

The walk home didn't help. She kept thinking of the things she should have said to the dumbshit execs in that dumbshit office who had fired her, finding enough excuses to fire a pregnant woman so the law couldn't do anything. If it had been a union office it wouldn't have happened, she wanted to yell at her mother. Or at the man who had left her for his wife the moment Claire had first missed her period. Or at the expected baby. Or at herself for not going to college, for not letting her mother help pay her way. Or at Daddy for . . . She didn't want to think about that.

With all that, of course, it couldn't help but seem like a huge cosmic joke aimed right at her when she got home after an hour and a half of walking to find her mother standing on the back porch and telling her in that nervous voice of hers that she had a surprise for her daughter.

"You made my bed for me," Claire said, hating the snottiness in her voice. She knew by the tone of her mother's voice that the surprise would be a bad one.

Her mother shook her head. The nervous smile seemed odd. "Oh, damn! I don't want to cook tonight." *I've been fired*, but she didn't know how to say that. "Or is it the dishes? Look, I didn't have time this morning to do the dishes." *I had to hurry off to work to get fired two hours ago for some dumbshit document that got sent to the wrong person.*

Her mother shook her head again. "It's not something you have to do. It's a person."

"Mother, really?" Claire's eyes grew wide, and she almost forgot all the feelings trapped within her. "You finally did it?"

Her mother looked confused. "Did what?"

"Don't play games, Mother. You brought a man home, didn't you? It's about time."

Mother's face dropped, the way it did when Claire didn't receive her presents like they were gifts from the gods or something. "Follow me."

Mother led her through the back door, through the small kitchen, and out into the living room. Sitting in the one hundred percent plastileather chair was some *thing*, a plasticky, artificial thing. It slowly stood up, and its unexpected movement forced Claire to step back, the abrupt fear and a thought running like a current through her head, surprising her: *I've got to protect the baby.*

"Mom . . . ?" She didn't like sounding so scared while her mother stood there so calmly. "Is that your person?"

Her mother nodded.

"Tell me it's a joke. Please."

"She's not a joke, Claire."

"But what is it? A robo-waiter or something? And what is it doing in our house?"

Her mother shrugged.

"Did you rent it or something? Come on, tell me. Is it for a party?"

"It's not a robo-waiter."

Claire's eyes expanded as the idea sank into her. At the office they kept the radio playing all day to reduce the monotony. WRUR, for the best in pure music, without incense, without lights. The news came on every half hour. "Mother," she said firmly, fear transforming into anger, "be serious. Is that the escaped robot?"

Ivy sounded almost defensive. "They were going to kill it, with its family."

"Oh, Mother! It's a test robot. That's what it's for!"

"But it can talk and feel."

"What? So you invited it in for a beer? Don't you know it can be dangerous?"

"Don't be silly. It's more scared of me than me of it."

"Mother, listen. I've been listening to the radio all day. This one was built before the robo-waiters were used. It has one of the first artificial organic brains or something like that. After every test they take it—"

"You mean every accident."

Claire let her face reveal her annoyance. "After every test, Mother, they collect the data and clean out its memory. Right now it's gathering up data with all its senses. No one knows how much data it can hold. They're afraid it might overload and go berserk." Mother looked as if it didn't make much sense. "Mother, don't you see, this thing can be dangerous. Why don't we solve the problem by calling the police or a newspaper or something?"

Mother shook her head. "I sort of knew you'd want to do that." She paused. "So I disconnected the phone and hid it. Our visitor is going to stay. I'm not going to have them put her into any more cars that they're gonna wreck up. It just isn't right."

"What's gonna happen next, huh? Are we gonna save all the robots?"

"This one came to us."

"Mother, be serious. I won't live here with this thing."

Her mother thought for a moment. "Your father and I worked hard to pay for this house. So it's my decision on who stays or goes."

"That's not fair. I live here, too."

"You can take it or leave it, Claire. But she's staying here. If you don't like it, you can move."

Claire found herself speechless; she had no choice but to take it. So, instead, she told her mother about getting fired.

On more and more occasions I resense and reregister the residue of memories. I once again register all the levels of input I felt in the accidents. I see the car approaching—its color, size, and shape alter with each seeing and sometimes it is only a wall or it is a parked car—and I know it is approaching but I have been programmed to be talking with my brother beside me until it is too late, or I am in the backseat and am screaming at my father to wake up because he suddenly dozed off, or I am still trying to convince Mother that she has drunk too much to be driving. And then it happens: the sound, glass imploding and flying, metal coming inward, flying objects, something cutting through my arm and—

I temporarily deactivate the circuits through which the memories are traveling. I do not know how I do that. I have never done it before, but it is the only method I have discovered to avoid information overload. It seems that the more I watch Ivy's television screen, the more these images take shape within me. I have deduced that I am learning how to see. With the books of Claire and Ivy I can write these images better. I think, or I conclude, or I believe (the last being the words of the prostitute, the words that seem the most appropriate and least definable) that my builders are unaware of these capabilities. But now I am storing so much data; no one clears it out; it is hard to control.

Every morning during the next two weeks, Ivy woke up, made herself coffee and toast (always letting Claire sleep in), and sat down to talk with the robot. At first, Ivy was uncomfortable, unsure if she'd done the right thing, anxious about this strange creature she'd let into her house. Claire's whining protests about how dangerous the thing could be sounded selfish and cruel, and they drowned out the background noise of Ivy's inner protests. As if that wasn't enough, Ivy found herself feeling more and more at ease with the robot as it spoke to her in its artificial, squeaky voice.

It—no, she—always seemed to be asking questions about colors and human sight and what was this and what did that mean; they were the sort of innocent, enthusiastic questions Claire asked when she was a kid and thought her mom knew something. Then she, the robot, began to ask questions about the books she began to read during the day while Ivy was gone, about things the three of them saw on television at night, about things Ivy liked to do.

Ivy fantasized taking it—no, her—out for a weekend and showing it all the things that were human. One evening she risked taking it out into the little backyard where Claire had grown up playing so that it/she could feel the cool evening breeze. It left Ivy heartbroken when the robot couldn't feel (detect?) the gentle movement of the air.

At the office, Ivy found that she was glad to be away from

Claire and the guilt she felt: if only she'd raised Claire differently. More and more, however, she began to realize how little she enjoyed being at the office. She noticed how little she talked with the other girls and how much lunch was just a time for eating.

Ivy took her coffee breaks on the hour so she could go to the lounge and listen to the news on the radio. They never played the radio in the typing room because it was considered distracting. There was always something about the escaped robot. No one understood how or why it had escaped. It could overload and become dangerous.

Ivy began to worry that the other girls would notice her interest, become suspicious of her. She was already anxious about leaving Claire at home with the robot; how was her daughter treating it—no, her?

It was the third night that the robot had been with Ivy and Claire when they announced on the evening news that the searches had turned up nothing. They concluded that the robot must be in hiding or was being hidden by someone. They warned caution, again, and then offered a reward for information leading to the capture of the robot; the amount of the reward was substantial. Claire withdrew her attention from the television screen and faced her mother. Her hand dropped to her six-month belly in a gesture that Ivy knew was not unconscious; Claire had never been good at dropping subtle hints. "Mom . . . ?"

The visitor sat in the wooden chair and watched the TV with her expressionless face as if she weren't the one who was being hunted down. Ivy didn't know how they'd take care of the baby on her salary, and she hated herself for the thought.

"Think about it, Mom."

Ivy turned on her daughter. "Don't you even dare suggest it."

At work, Ivy tried, unsuccessfully, to hide herself in her typing. But she kept making mistakes, kept drifting off. "Get yourself together, girl," said the nice black girl whose VDT was next to Ivy's. Ivy kept thinking about how Claire might leave the house and find a pay phone to call in for the reward. Or Rosa Martinez might come over for some sugar, or old Mrs. Buloski might limp over for some company. How long could she go on hiding her (it?)?

Mr. McHinry, her supervisor, made a joke about bringing back the bells, just for Ivy. She laughed, and knew she sounded nervous. Her anxiety, she feared, would give her away. But Mr. McHinry seemed not to notice; he just kept cracking the same joke until it stopped being funny.

When Ivy had started work umpety-ump years ago—working as a temp, thirty-five hours a week—the machines she used were tied in to a program to monitor her progress. Each keystroke, each error, each cessation of activity was duly recorded so that a supervisor, using his own VDT, could check on her progress. It was as if some huge, invisible figure were hunched over her shoulder, always watching, always ready to criticize. In one or two offices, the VDT was rigged with bells that would ring each time she mistyped a word programmed into the machine's memory or each time she went back to correct an error. The bells reminded her of the invisible form just behind her; they pulled her concentration away from her typing and made her concentrate on doing well—typing so hard to prove herself—that she lost the natural fluidity of her fingers. More bells, more errors.

Once again, she felt just as harried, although the union had gotten rid of the bells and the monitors. There were other forms hunched over her shoulder this time, and Ivy knew someone would figure out that she'd started making all those mistakes the day after the robot had fled, and it would all be over.

Every morning at breakfast, Ivy found herself surprised that, for a while, the tension no longer clutched her belly and kept her nerves jangling. She enjoyed sitting at the breakfast table, watching the robot, listening to its squeaky voice, and answering its questions: explain to me your family; why did they leave Detroit; what was your husband like; why do people love their families? How could a robot who asked such questions be at all dangerous?

For a brief moment, Ivy thought of the factory where Jerry had died, then forced the thought out of her mind.

For lunch, like usual, she'd go out with some of the girls, and, when she could, when no one might think she was making a big deal about it, she would pick a place with a television so she could see the noontime news. On the second Monday the visitor was with them, Ivy and the other girls ended up going to a place with a fancy new holovision. Ivy couldn't take her eyes off the screen, if that's what you called it, the images were so clear and lifelike. The newscaster, who looked like he was sitting behind a counter that had been set up in the corner of the dining room, reminded viewers of a murder that had taken place Friday afternoon. A woman had been strangled in an alley near Henry's

Superbar. ("That's right near where I live," remarked the black girl who sat next to Ivy in the typing room.) Police authorities said they suspected that the murderer was the escaped robot.

As the newscaster recapped the info on the escaped robot, Ivy found herself looking away from the screen and at the simulated grain of the wall. She began to wish the water she had been drinking was whiskey, even though she hated the stuff. Her insides turned soft, and she suddenly had to go to the bathroom and was too scared to get up. Ivy knew she (it?) couldn't have done such a thing; Claire was always at home. "I do sure hope they catch that thing soon," said one of the girls, "before it kills anybody else." No one would understand, not if they found her now, not with news like this.

The image of the newscaster was replaced by the image of the robot. One of the girls sucked in her breath as if it (she!) was really in the dining room. The image looked just like her—same face, shape, everything—but she still wore that somber blue-gray tunic, and the fabric wasn't torn. However, there was something else wrong with the image they showed of her. There was something in the eyes and the red light behind the eyes that looked dark, looked evil.

It was a different network and different newscaster, but they repeated the same announcement that night on the TV, and they showed the same picture of the robot with the red light behind the eyes. Ivy found herself shifting in her armchair so she could look several times in its/her eyes, feeling guilty as she looked. Feeling guiltier, and relieved, when she couldn't find that same dark quality. She realized that the newsmen or the car company were doing it so that people would fear, maybe hate, the robot.

"Well, Mom," said Claire, who was sitting on the couch, "how does it feel to be living with the prime suspect?"

Ivy searched for the harmless sarcasm in Claire's voice and couldn't find it. "They don't know what they're talking about. She was home with you all the time."

Claire shook her head.

"What do you mean, Claire?" Someone being interviewed on the television was saying something about how the testing personalities were perfectly safe when their memories were cleared regularly; only the escaped testing personality was a potential danger.

"You don't think I've been staying home all day with it, do you?"

"You haven't told me anything about this."

"I go out, Mom. It gets claustrophobic in here, cooped up with that thing. It could have left while I was out. It could have strangled that person."

"Why did you have to leave the house? What if Rosa Martinez had come by or something?"

"And I suppose you expect me to stay with it tomorrow, after you know what it might have done."

"You know it didn't, Claire." Ivy pushed herself out of the armchair and walked over to the visitor. "On Friday," Ivy said to her while counting off on her fingers, "four days ago, did you leave the house?"

"No," said the visitor.

"Right," said Claire. "What else was it going to say, Mother? Ask it what it was doing while you were gone, and it'll tell you it was reading."

"I was," said the visitor.

Ivy smiled triumphantly at Claire, but her insides felt all weak and she had to go to the bathroom again.

Ivy found it impossible to work well the next morning. After she had thoroughly goofed up on four claims, Mr. McHinry called her into his tiny office. He kindly reminded her of how good a worker she was and how efficient a worker she'd been for about a good week now. There were right-to-work laws, but they were to protect humans from losing their jobs to computers, not to protect poor workmanship. Ivy found herself telling him about how her pregnant daughter had been fired, and she had to force herself not to tell too much. Mr. McHinry said he understood, and maybe Ivy should take a leave of absence until she could be sure her private life wouldn't interfere with her work. Ivy swore she would do better, and she repeatedly assured him that she did not need a leave of absence. Mr. McHinry smiled sadly and said that he'd do what she thought best.

Forcing back the tears, Ivy sat down in the lounge and drank coffee until her stomach was upset. She listened half-heartedly to the radio as people were interviewed about the robot. Science was always dangerous, someone said, ever since Frankenstein. Some expert reminded the listeners of how important these testing personalities were in verifying the safety of all heavy equipment used by humans, from cars to factory machines, to mechanisms that would be used on the low-G, orbital factories that were being built.

Ivy considered telling someone at the office about the robot. She felt like she needed someone to talk to; she could talk with the robot about anything except her fears about what would happen. How would the robot understand that you couldn't feed a family on a leave of absence? She thought of telling the nice black girl who worked next to her, who kept telling Ivy to get hold of herself. Ivy could get hold of herself, but she already knew what was going to happen.

In one office, she had been working thirty-five hours a week, and after a year there had been no sign of promotion to forty hours a week and benefits. When the union people started making quiet inquiries, Ivy found her tired and sluggish body suddenly animated by the daily frustration. She'd told her best friend about the union, and her best friend told management. Within two days the boss called in half the temps, told them things were going bad for the company, and gave them two weeks' severance pay.

Two years and two offices later, the office workers unionized without a problem. The union called for job sharing with benefits between part-time workers and demanded that temp workers get benefits. Ivy went from thirty-five hours a week to no hours, and no union was fighting to get her job back.

No, she'd learned over the years, you couldn't trust anyone. Jerry never could understand how she wouldn't trust people while at the same time taking long walks at night just to feel the evening air upon her skin. But that's the way she was, and she knew she could tell no one about it/her. No one was going to treat a machine right. She knew that from the way they treated her.

At home, Claire began to spend the evenings questioning the visitor, her voice loud and persistent, like that of a prosecuting attorney on a TV show both Ivy and Claire watched. Ivy tried to ignore the cross-examinations; she wanted to act as if the arrival of the robot had made her a happy person, as if hiding it/her truly left her feeling fulfilled. Ivy knew that Claire was trying to prove that the visitor was some *thing*, that turning it in would not be some act of evil.

"Are you reading that book again?" Claire would ask, a typical question.

The thing, the robot, the visitor, looked up. "Yes."

"Claire, leave her alone and help me get supper ready."

"But it's reading that same novel for the third time."

"Maybe she likes it."

"A Robin Harrison novel? Come on." Claire turned to face the thing, the robot, the visitor. "Do you like it?"

She/it looked up. "Like? I do not know."

"Hah!"

"She must read it for a reason, dear."

"Why do you read it then?"

"It helps me understand."

"Understand what?"

"Don't be so mean, Claire."

"What do you mean, 'mean'? I'm supposed to hang out with a murder suspect all day while my mother goes to work and takes the phone cord with her each day." Claire walked over to the kitchen counter and looked at Ivy, her glare forcing Ivy to look up from the frying vegetables. "Even though I could go to a pay phone—or go any day to any one of the neighbors and tell them."

"We've already been through this too many times. She stays here."

"They're going to find her, Mom. You know they will."

"We'll just have to protect her until then."

"And if she—it—is the murderer?"

Ivy stirred the sizzling vegetables. "You're being silly. You know she didn't kill anyone."

"If they find her here on their own, Mother, we don't get any reward money."

"Then you can write a book about it."

"How can you be so fucking calm?"

"Will you just watch your language, young lady?" The words shot out loud, a geyser of suppressed emotion. "There's enough going wrong at the office. I don't need it at home, too."

"But, Mom, think about that TV show we saw last night. The father hid his son from the police, and so they put him in jail for being an accomplice. We're accomplices, and if they find it here with us, we'll be in real trouble. And we'll get nothing out of it—all of that for a machine."

"But she has feelings. She ran, didn't she?"

"Watch." Claire returned to the thing, the robot, the visitor. "What are you?"

The visitor listed her/its make, model, and serial number.

"Can you feel?"

"I am capable of registering a select range of external stimuli."

"You've already asked her these questions," said Ivy. "She doesn't feel sad or feel pain."

Claire glanced over at Ivy, then turned back to the visitor. "Why do you read this book?"

Ivy switched off the stove and walked around the counter and into the living room.

"It helps me understand," said the visitor.

"What do you understand?"

"It is difficult to explain. The prostitute lacks God. I lack feelings."

Ivy smiled at her daughter.

"Don't look at me that way. It's nothing but a machine. Something for testing. It's just a dumb machine, I tell you."

"Claire, don't be so mean." The words were almost whispered.

Claire turned to the visitor. "Does my voice sound mean?"

"I do not know."

"What a wonderful, feeling machine."

"Claire . . ."

"Did you hear the sarcasm in my voice?"

"No," she/it said.

"Do you know what sarcasm is?"

"Yes. 'A mocking remark utilizing the statement's opposite or irrelevant to the underlying meaning.' "

"That sounds like a dictionary talking."

"*The American Heritage Dictionary of*—"

"But did you hear sarcasm in my voice, dammit?"

"Claire, calm down."

"No," she/it said.

"Look, Mother, it can't feel feelings or hear feelings. If you're going to make out like it's a human being, this thing is either really dumb or really innocent."

"Dumb," said the visitor, "is a mean word."

"And innocent?" shot back Claire.

"I do not know."

The residual memory most difficult to control is the last one. Deactivating certain circuits does not necessarily terminate the process. It is analogous to what a book of Claire's calls a "dream sequence in a movie." Ivy says her memories never return in the exact same images and in the same order. But my memories always return in the same sequence of visual impressions, registered tactile, olfactory, and aural inputs.

Awareness is initiated, and I am in the car with my father, my mother, and my brother. My mother and father are in the front seat; my brother and I are in the back. A human wearing a red jumpsuit straps in my father while another straps in my mother.

"They can walk, talk, and think, and we still have to buckle them up," says one. He places his hand upon my mother's breast, a gesture that one of Ivy's books says is inappropriate. "You've heard what they say, haven't you?"

"Yeah," says the other. "And if that thing was human, it would slap you right across the face."

One withdraws his hand. "You're right, I guess. Let's get this over with."

They each remove a small instrument from their tool bags and insert the needle end into the barely perceptible hole behind my mother's and my father's right ears. As my mother and father reach activation, the two humans slam the car doors shut and walk away.

As programmed, my father accelerates the car up to 100 kilometers per hour and turns onto the winding, country road. Following the program, he talks with my mother and gesticulates. I talk with my brother, but knowing the program, I know that a car will drive around the curve with too large a vector to remain within its lane, and my father, who will be talking to my mother, will not see it in time and I am programmed just to talk with my brother, and residual memory repeats visual, tactile, olfactory, aural sensations of the same program with a car of different style, size, color, mass, velocity—momentum—and I reach forward over the front seat as the other car emerges around the corner and I tug the wheel to the right and we go veering off the road into the woods down a hill into a ravine and are tossed about. A door breaks open and I am flung from the car, which begins to roll and to emit flames. If I remain they will erase my memory and I will relive this again. I run into the forest and hide.

On one of the television broadcasts they state that they thought I had been in the burning car. When the flames were extinguished to prevent a forest fire, they discovered only three bodies.

I have been created, according to the television reports, to give as accurate a response as possible as to how humans will be affected physically and perhaps one day psychologically by accidents. But, I comprehend now. They are wrong about my humanness. I am not human. I do not perceive as humans do. One of Claire's books would call me an alien. One of Ivy's would say that during this period of thirteen days I have had the first opportunity to live and to grow.

That description is inaccurate. But it suffices.

White fingers.

Claire kept watching the long, white fingers that held one of Mother's favorite Robin Harrison novels, the one with the cover of a sparsely clad woman who holds a large pistol as she sneaks about on a yacht. Claire watched the fingers as they turned the pages, each separate movement so complete and accurate, as if each motion had been planned, that the entire action of page turning looked clumsy. She watched the long, white fingers and imagined them moving so carefully, so clumsily, so accurately around her neck, then squeezing, twisting. Like the woman who'd been strangled near Henry's Superbar.

Claire had been trying to wash the dishes and listen to the strident game-show contestants whose shouts rang from the portable TV on the kitchen counter, but she kept glancing back at the thing, watching it read and trying to conjure up some way to avoid getting close to it. She thought of how each day she had felt cooped up, bored, and miserable enough to flee the house and how during one of those times the thing had left, running the risk of being spotted by the neighbors, and had wandered the city until it found a neck to place its long, white fingers around. And squeeze.

But, deep down, she knew her mother was right. The thing hadn't killed anyone. The thing didn't make any unnecessary movements; it never spoke any unneeded words in its artificial, fingernails-against-chalkboard voice. Claire couldn't see it going out, blowing a fuse, killing somebody, and then coming back to carefully turn each page of one of her mother's popcorn porn novels and then asking Mother all those silly questions. Plus, at the end of it all, after all the boredom and the memories, all the cooping up that left her feeling more fat and useless, she went over to the thing and talked to it. Every day. She kept an eye on each of its movements—she couldn't trust it or anything, she knew that—and talked to it. She had these doubts, and she had to know, just for herself, if it was only just a thing. She told herself that she couldn't be calling any police or reporters until she was sure her mother was wrong.

Claire knew the thing didn't have feelings, at least not the way she had feelings. It seemed to show no remorse at the death—if you could call it that—of her family: the three charred and melted masses of wire, plastic, metal, and running goo that they had all seen on the TV.

Claire cut off the lukewarm water and walked over to the thing, leaving the TV set, with its changing set of game shows, screaming. She pulled over the light plastiwood chair and plopped down facing the robot. It kept reading; it didn't look up at her like a human would have.

"Why did you leave your family?" Claire asked, knowing the question was unfair.

A human might have looked up, somewhat shocked, and muttered a "What?" or a "Huh?" But this thing just lowered its book, looked at Claire with the eyes lit from behind, and said, "I do not comprehend. Would you please rephrase?" It had started saying *please* when Mother taught it what the word meant.

"Why didn't you try to rescue your family?"

"Would you have returned to the flames?"

Claire sat back, then quickly glanced down at its long, white fingers. They held the book in its lap, appearing harmless. She looked back at its eyes—it had answered a question with a question. It had never done that before. Maybe it was going crazy.

"As you," it said, "I do not have an answer."

Claire found herself getting angry. It thought she hadn't answered because she couldn't. "I would have done something," she claimed.

"I did not. I do not know why. They were my family, and they were not my family. I do not remember clearly if they were the same three units that underwent previous testing with me."

"Don't you feel a sort of loss?"

"I do not know."

"Do you miss them?"

"I do not know. I continue recalling them."

"My mother says you can feel." Claire felt the full force of sarcasm and doubt in her voice.

"I do not know."

"Can you feel pain?"

"No."

"How about pleasure. Can you feel pleasure?"

"I do not know."

Maliciously, already knowing the response, Claire reached over and caressed its arm, a sort of brusque gesture. "What does that do for you?"

"Please rephrase."

"What do you feel?"

"I register the level of pressure of your fingers against my skin. I also measure a minor level of heat, but my readings at such a low level are accurate to only one digit."

"How about this?" She rubbed her fingers across one of its breasts. The gesture felt like a minor victory—she remembered as a child always wanting to touch the store-window mannequins to see what was there. And the thing reacted just like one of those mannequins would have. No startled gesture, no offense taken, no anger, no sudden openness like when the father of her kid had first touched her while in the office. If she hadn't been yearning for that touch for at least two months, she would have turned and smacked him. Instead, she had yearned for more provocative and private touches. "Does it do anything but register?"

"It initiates other programs."

"Huh?"

Then she saw them through her mother's flower-print blouse, which had always been too tight on the thing. But she couldn't really believe it. "Take off your shirt," she said.

With its complete and awkward movements, the robot unbuttoned the blouse and removed the shirt. Upon the two firm breasts were two erect nipples, red and suggestive, like something out of those magazines Cousin Tom used to show her when they were kids. Claire reached out and squeezed a breast—it wasn't hard and stiff like plastic. It felt artificial, but it moved with her touch almost, not quite, like a human breast. Curiosity injected with a bit of fear, of repulsion, ran through her. She reminded herself that it was a thing for testing, but her suspicions got to her.

"Stand up," she said, "and take off your pants."

It did so with coordination but without agility, one leg pulled loose from the slacks, the robot almost stumbling, then one bare leg down and the other pulled loose. It stood before her, naked except for its shoes. Looking at it, all except for its face and its two eyes with the light behind them, it looked so human. A bit plasticky, but so human. Hair upon her head, under her armpits, tracing her lower abdomen. The thought of what she was going to do caused Claire to hesitate. But it was just a thing, and she had to know. Her hand reached out along the downward curve of its belly and touched hair. She tried to discern if the hair felt human or not and knew she was just stalling. Then she let her hand slide down the folds of plastiskin, sliding between them, feeling the increasing moisture, realizing it was all there, the thing suddenly human and inhuman, and its hand was reaching toward Claire's cheek and it was saying something about alternate programming and she imagined the long white fingers wrapping themselves around her neck and . . . squeezing.

Claire jumped back, almost stumbling over the chair, which crashed to the floor. "Get away from me! Step back! Put your clothes on or something—what the fuck are you?"

It gave its make, model, and serial number as it dressed itself.

Feeling sickened at what it was and what she had been doing, Claire darted about the house looking for the telephone. The game-show contestants seemed to scream even louder at her from the kitchen counter. When she found the telephone and not the cord, she cursed her mother for having taken it off to work with her. She quickly, almost fearfully, glanced over at the thing to find it sitting back in its usual chair, reading, as if nothing had happened.

Claire rushed over to Rosa Martinez's house, told her neighbor something (which sounded to Claire like a lie) about a broken phone, and called her mother's office to tell her to come home, that it was important. In the pause while one of the girls at the office went to look for Mother, Claire felt a certain calm. Mother could control the robot, set things right, maybe decide to get rid of it. Rosa Martinez prepared coffee as if there were nothing wrong. With the coffee in her hand, Claire wouldn't have to go right back to the house. In the lull of her pain, Claire for a moment let herself think that it was a thing made to be used for testing, to be used for other things. To be used. She felt a certain bond of sympathy. Then she saw it naked, remembered her fingers probing and reaching into it. Her dislike for it returned with the full force of her disgust.

In the cars where they place me, I am seated with Mother, Father, and Brother. There may be a bond there, but I cannot describe it. In Ivy's books there seem to be two types of families. In one, each member is yelling at the other. The main character, as they call the one who thinks and talks most often, marries a member of a family and is not sure if she can trust the family. The word *suspicion* is used often, and the homes seem full of dark shadows and locked rooms. In the other type of family, everybody touches and kisses and uses the word *love* very often. Something happens and the second type of family sometimes begins to resemble the first type, but at the end of the novel "things are put right," as the characters refer to what resembles a return to mechanical equilibrium, and the original situation is resumed.

From the books, I almost comprehend *family*.

But in this house there are no locked rooms and the shadows emerge only in the evening when the electricity is cut back. Ivy and Claire rarely touch, and neither uses the word *love*, except for the times when Claire says to Ivy: "Tell me that you wouldn't have done differently if you had been in love"; "What about Dad? You were in love with him. Everybody told you not to, but still you married him"; and: "Being reasonable and being in love have nothing to do with each other." Claire and Ivy seem to be neither type of family.

In Claire's books there is no type of family. The main character has a mother and/or father and perhaps several siblings, but they have the same clarity of detail for the main character as my residual memories have for me. Ivy and Claire are not this type of family either.

I think I almost comprehend. But I do not. When Ivy and Claire work together in the kitchen they do not collide with each other. It is analogous to the dances Ivy and Claire watch on the television screen. Ivy says: "The best dancers are the ones who have danced with each other a lot. When we could afford that sort of thing, your father and I would dance up a storm. Your father was good on his feet." Claire demonstrates to me the largeness of her abdomen and explains pregnancy to me. She says: "This is what family means." Ivy says: "Don't be mean, Claire."

I conjecture if before my arrival, Claire and Ivy touched more frequently. If they used the word *love* more often. Maybe it is my presence here that is the disruption. The books confirm that hypothesis. But at times the books appear to be poor evidence.

Once, Claire says to Ivy: "Sometimes the baby is the only reason I stay alive." The prostitute says to the minister: "God is the one who gives my life value." I have no baby. I have no

God. I have no feelings. But one claims belief in such things because it seems evident that beyond the stimuli I register there must be something more.

Ivy's eyes hurt, and the tension headaches she hadn't felt in so many years were now pounding at the back of her eyeballs like giant timpani. Seated on the Metro, she took off her glasses to let the world slide by in one giant blur, but that didn't ease the dull aching that seemed to squeeze her eyes. She had never felt it this bad, she told herself. But she knew she must have, back during those two times she had been laid off or the time when she and Jerry had almost got divorced. It had been pretty bad then. Or when Claire had told her she was pregnant.

It was just that this time she'd lost all control; she couldn't even comfort herself with the notion that this happened to other people, too. Other people had been laid off; other people had lost their husbands; other people had pregnant, unwed daughters. But here she was, alone on the Metro, unable to remember exactly what her daughter had said on the phone, if she had given away too much, if she had planned to say something later on to Rosa Martinez. Ivy felt so frustrated and worn out. She wondered why she had brought that machine into her home. But she had always felt like there had never been any other choice.

The Metro approached her stop. She slid her glasses back on, the clarity and its strain tugging at her eyes as much as the passing blur. She got off and walked along the streets of row houses and finally made her way home, coming in through the back door. The robot was sitting in her usual chair, reading the Robin Harrison novel about the secretary who falls in love with her ladies'-man boss, only to discover that he is the head of some worldwide conspiracy. Claire was standing in the kitchen, waiting for her.

"It took you long enough."

Ivy felt the anxiety release itself as anger. "I'm sorry. But you know how hard it is to make connections before rush hour."

"What did you tell them at the office?" Claire asked in that snotty voice of hers.

Ivy threw off her jacket before turning on her daughter. "Do you wanna tell me what you dragged me here for, or don't you?"

Claire hesitated, then pointed at the robot. "That thing is sick."

"It's a robot, honey. It can't get sick."

"Mother! You know what I mean. There's something wrong with it. They built it like a woman."

"You mean you brought me home early to tell me that?"

"No . . . I mean . . ." Claire shook her head and then shouted it out with all her frustration: "It's got a—it's got woman parts—the kind you can stick a cock into!"

"Watch your mouth, Claire!"

"Mother! It's got a woman's parts!"

Ivy didn't want to believe it. "And how do you know that?"

Claire glanced down at her feet. It seemed like she was blushing. "I looked," she whispered.

"How do you mean, you looked?"

Claire swallowed hard. "I told it to take off its clothes."

"You what? Don't you have anything better to do than to mess with her? Why can't you just leave her alone?"

"It's an *it*, Mother. An it. It was made for testing—and for other things. . . . It's so sick."

"I don't see anything sick about it," Ivy lied. "Men have been doing the same to human women for years."

"But I set something off. It tried . . . to touch me. It may be going crazy like they said."

That's when the visitor rose from her usual chair, placed the book down, and walked toward the two women, each footstep loud, or at least louder than human footsteps upon the carpet, which made it worse. Both Ivy and Claire turned to watch her, Ivy reminded of the way she would walk over to the breakfast table and sit down with Ivy to ask questions. But this time the movement seemed less quaint, almost ominous. She stopped alongside the women; Claire tried, unsuccessfully, to hide her step backward.

"I am sorry," said the visitor in her artificial, squeaky voice, the words surprising Ivy. "I will not touch again."

"There," said Ivy, looking for a reason to sound relieved. "It's settled. You two can get along with each other now." Ivy could hear the nervousness in her voice.

"It's too late," Claire said, much too softly.

"What?"

"I said it's too late."

"What do you mean it's too late?"

Claire swallowed hard, didn't say anything.

"Claire, what do you mean it's too late?"

The visitor stood there, as if she too was awaiting an answer. Ivy wished that she'd go sit down.

"Oh, Claire, you didn't!" The disappointment sank into her along with her voice.

"I didn't tell her that it was in the house. But . . . I told her I saw it."

"Honey, how could you?"

Ivy watched guilt burst into a desperate anger, Claire's face reddening. "What the hell was I supposed to do? There's that strangled woman, and this thing starts touching me. I was scared, dammit! Scared!"

"But . . ."

"But what? You haven't been the one sitting here all day with this thing. You can be so friendly with it because every day you get to get the fuck out of here and go to work."

"Please, Claire, watch your tone of voice. It's your mother you're talking to."

"Yeah. Right. That's what you always say when you know I'm right and you don't want to listen."

"Claire . . ." It came out almost as a plea. And like some silent referee, the visitor stood along with them. Why couldn't it just go sit down?

"I want it out of here, Mother."

"No."

"Don't look at me that way. I don't want the reward or anything. I just want it out of here."

"No. It stays."

Claire forced a shrug. "Have it your way." She stomped off to the living area and plopped down in a chair. She turned on the television and stared at it.

The robot stood at Ivy's side, still unmoving. Ivy watched her daughter sit in front of the TV screen, the whole act reminding her so much of Jerry. Always, when he had gotten mad at Ivy, he'd stomp off and read the newspaper, trying so hard to act as like he was concentrating on some section—the society page, the want-ads—that didn't interest him a bit. Sometimes Ivy had broken into laughter at the sight. But now she didn't feel much like laughing.

"I suppose," said Ivy, "that we should say something to Rosa Martinez."

"You say anything to her and she'll just get more suspicious."

Ivy didn't know what to do, so she began to prepare dinner. The kitchen seemed to turn into the office: nothing would cut right, measured-out quantities seemed to keep spilling over. The visitor stood and watched her.

The doorbell ring was both a fright and a relief. "Get into my bedroom," snapped Ivy, and the visitor walked into Ivy's room. Ivy closed the door behind her.

The man at the front door was one of the private detectives hired by the motor companies and the Testing Center. Ivy couldn't make heads or tails of his ID, so she handed it back to him. "I'm sorry to be bothering you, ma'am, but your next-door neighbor called our offices and said that your daughter might have sighted the robot."

Ivy didn't know what to say.

"The missing robot, ma'am, you must have heard of it on the news." The detective seemed to look at her the same way Mr. McHinry at the office did, almost as if she really weren't there, as if her only true importance lay in her response. Everything was just words.

"Yes. I guess I heard about it." She knew the words sounded forced, weak in their ability to convince.

"May I speak with your daughter, ma'am?"

Ivy wanted to say no. What else would Claire do but tell the truth? Like her father, she had never been much of a liar.

"Is your daughter home, ma'am?"

Ivy found herself nodding to the sound of authority in the detective's voice.

"May I speak with her then?"

"Claire!" Ivy called out. "Someone wants to talk to you."

The detective shifted as if he wanted to step right into the house. Ivy felt too lost to move aside, and the sudden but small advantage she gained lifted her spirits. But the robot could still do something it shouldn't: step out into the living room, knock something over. And then it would all be over. Here, she still had the man outside.

Claire walked sluggishly to the door, looked suspiciously at her mother, and then took Ivy's place on the doorstep. The look on Claire's face snatched away Ivy's feeling of control: Claire could now say what she wanted.

"Yeah," Claire said, sounding almost like an insulted child.

"Ms. Claire Hart?"

Claire nodded. "That's me."

"Ms. Rosa Martinez, your next-door neighbor, reported that you sighted the escaped testing robot."

Claire didn't reply. Ivy nervously glanced over her shoulder at the closed bedroom door, then jerked her head back, realizing too late what a giveaway gesture that was. "Yeah, I saw it," Claire finally said.

"When?"

"Sometime this morning. When I was out for a walk." It sounded to Ivy like a lie, one she couldn't believe her daughter was telling.

"Why didn't you report it?"

Claire looked down at her feet. Without seeing it, Ivy knew that her daughter was swallowing hard, trying to concentrate. "I don't know." Her voice was barely audible.

"There must have been a reason."

"I just don't know."

The detective looked up at Ivy. "Ma'am, could you please impress your daughter about how important this is? The escaped robot could be dangerous."

It's not dangerous, Ivy wanted to say.

"Could you at least tell me," said the detective, "where you think you saw it?"

Claire hesitated, then pointed vaguely. "Somewhere over there."

"When did you see it?"

"I don't know." Claire's voice had become a whine. "Sometime this morning, I guess. I was out walking."

"Did you notice what it was wearing?"

"I guess so. It had on dark pants and a shirt—you know, the kind with flowers on it."

Claire glanced up at Ivy, and then both realized what Claire had just said. The robot was wearing a flower-print shirt, the kind Ivy always wore, the kind she was wearing now—and the robot had escaped wearing something torn, something designed in a somber blue-gray.

"May I ask once again: why didn't you report it?"

Claire hesitated for a moment, looked at Ivy, looking at her almost in supplication, as if asking for permission, then looked back at the man. "I don't know," she said, and paused. "I guess I just didn't want to get involved."

The faint look of suspicion on the man's face became one of mild disgust. Ivy, for a moment, let herself believe that Claire had given the right answer. "Well, thank you for your assistance. Someone may come by later and ask you to fill out a report."

Ivy knew she should say something, but didn't know what or how.

"Is that really necessary?" asked Claire.

"I'm afraid it is. Sorry to have disturbed you both. Good afternoon."

He walked away and left the two women alone with their fears. Someone might be coming later; more questions. Maybe the detective would make the connection between the two different shirts, maybe he'd ask the neighbors about any strange behavior. What would Rosa Martinez and Mrs. Buloski say—those were really the only two neighbors they ever saw, and they hadn't seen too much of them for the past two weeks. Ever since the robot showed up.

They let the visitor out of the bedroom. She sat down and resumed reading. She didn't ask any questions, which, to Ivy, seemed odd. Ivy suddenly felt uneasy around her: why wasn't she saying anything?

Claire and Ivy ate dinner, the silence almost as substantial as the food they ate. After dinner they sat and watched TV and waited. When would someone else come?

The visitor asked for paper and pen. She spent the rest of the evening writing out the alphabet, the speed and the neatness of her handwriting increasing over the hours.

"I don't see why they didn't teach it to write," said Claire. "They built it to do everything else."

"Hush."

"You could at least thank me."

Ivy didn't know what to say.

The eleven o'clock news announced the sighting. Actually, there had been two of them, each one in a different area. Authorities refused to reveal where; the newspeople gave their own conjectures. A house-to-house search, authorized by several district judges and criticized by the American Civil Liberties Union, was being conducted. Ivy could feel Claire's eyes upon her but had no idea what to say. The fear was closing in on her. For the first time in a long time, she wished Jerry were here. But Jerry would have been no better at handling this than she was.

Seeing no other way out of her fear, Ivy shut off the set and said that they should get some rest. Maybe she'd have a better idea what to do in the morning. Claire followed Ivy to her bedroom, and Ivy turned on her, expecting Claire to say that they'd catch her/it anyway and why not just turn it in and have the reward; if nothing else, the money would help out when the baby came.

But Claire didn't say that. She glanced over at the writing robot, then back at her mother. "Can I sleep with you tonight?" Claire shot a glance at the visitor. "I'm scared."

Ivy noticed, for maybe the first time, how red Claire's eyes were, how pale her skin was. She realized how frightened her daughter must have been, what she must have been going through. And it was all Ivy's fault, she knew that. For the first time, she knew that. "Of course, honey."

The Earth will soon have rotated enough that the sun will appear above the horizon. The people conducting the search will most likely return and search through Ivy and Claire's house. I know what they will do to Ivy and Claire if I am here with them. Maybe if I am gone, Ivy and Claire can use the word *love* with greater frequency. Everything in the books I read suggests that the outcome of events would be better if I were to leave and return to the Testing Center.

I have my own reasons, too, as some of the characters in Ivy's books so often say. Perhaps they will not terminate me completely, and some part of my memory will remain with me. The next time I will turn the wheel so we will avoid the crash but so I will not kill my family. Then next time I will save my family with me.

I do not comprehend why I create this plan. I do not have feelings. Fire does not envelop my soul when I am caressed. The growth of a baby will never enlarge my abdomen and give me what Claire calls a reason to live. I do not feel sad. I do not feel happy. I do not feel remorse. I do not feel.

Humans feel. They have feelings. Then they search for one more dimension. The prostitute calls it "God." But after she finds God, is there not something else after that to be perceived? A book of Claire's has written that there are humans who have terminated their lives due to such questions.

I do not comprehend why I plan to save my family, or why I call them my family. The prostitute changes her life when she says, "I believe in God," although she has no method to verify the existence of God, just as I have no capability to feel. Still her life changes. *Faith* is the word she uses.

Ivy found it hard to sleep. She had grown accustomed to the double bed feeling so empty that the presence of another body seemed to heighten her restlessness and depression. They would be coming back tomorrow, and she didn't know what to do about it. What could she tell them—them and the mayor and the judges and the newspeople behind them? The robot was a danger; she had evil eyes. Ivy turned over again, even though she could fall asleep only while lying on her back. Claire muttered something in response to her mother's restless movements.

Claire was lying still and listening to her mother trying to fall asleep. Claire, two weeks ago, had given up on the idea of sleep. With the memories repeating like an unintended programming loop, Claire kept recalling the firing, the robot, the murder, the coming kid, the lost chance to go to college. The kid's father reaching out to touch her. Sometimes Claire had wanted to go out and buy a bottle of wine or something, something that would tire out body and mind so that the thoughts would stop just for a little while. And tomorrow they'd probably find the robot. For some reason that seemed wrong. The people looking for the robot seemed part of that whole mass that never let her life go right. They were the people you couldn't fight because the people were part of it all. You could kill a hundred of them, and the same things would still happen. It was made up of people, but it was bigger than people. And there was no winning. None. Just to hand the robot over to them, that had suddenly seemed wrong. It had promised not to touch, hadn't it? her mother would say. And Claire used that thought to fight off the sense of disgust she felt every time her mind's eye envisioned her own hand reaching out to the naked robot.

Maybe Claire's right, Ivy thought. *Maybe we should tell the press.* Not to turn in the robot, but to protect her. She had been living with them for two weeks. She had escaped, even though her family had been killed. She asked questions, read books, wrote the alphabet, and listened to the evening news. She didn't have evil eyes, and she was learning how to act with people. She had made that promise to Claire, hadn't she? Tomorrow morning they'd call the papers, the TV men. Ivy hadn't felt this way since the first time when she had been working temp and they were going to bring the union in. Now it was a different sort, a better sort, of restlessness that didn't let Ivy sleep.

But the next morning they found the robot gone. There was no sign of her anywhere. On the news they heard that she had turned herself in, hands up in the air, to several detectives. She had been returned to the Testing Center, and the scientists were going to examine her, to see what had caused it all.

Ivy wasn't sure if she could believe the newscasts. For weeks to come she would awake from the nightmare of the robot walking out onto an empty suburban street, her hands raised, and the detectives, with eyes like the eyes of the TV-screen robot, shooting at it, all of them firing at once, aiming right at her head, her body crumpling while her head went flying off, the light behind her eyes now gone, unlit.

Claire watched the newscasts, moped around the living room, and said nothing; the expected having happened left her feeling heavier and duller.

It was later that morning when they found the manuscript. It had been left on the breakfast-room table, the place where she had asked Ivy all those questions. On the front page it gave her make, model, and serial number. Then it gave an entire series of mathematical things—numbers, equations, and all sorts of stuff Ivy couldn't begin to recognize. In neat, hand-printed writing, it stated that the above equations should prove to an expert that the following testament was indeed written by the Testing Mechanism of such-and-such a make, model, and serial number. It asked Ivy and Claire to wait a month before making copies and turning the manuscript in to various authorities.

It was only later, after staring at all the numbers and equations on the first page, that both Ivy and her daughter realized that in those two weeks, they had never given her a name.

MOMENTS
OF CLARITY

ELISSA MALCOHN

Now that we've warmed you up, here's another tale directed straight at the heart. When you read for a living, you don't often find fiction that stops you in your tracks. "Moments of Clarity," required a good half hour of recovery time. We don't recommend reading it before operating heavy machinery.

Elissa Malcohn was nominated for the 1985 John W. Campbell Award for best new writer. She has published fiction and poetry in *Isaac Asimov's Science Fiction Magazine* and *Amazing Stories*. She is also the editor of *Star Line: Newsletter of the Science Fiction Poetry Association*. Elissa holds a master's degree in psychology and does public relations work for Harvard University.

Leila looked like a fairy-tale princess about to embark on a deep sleep. Municipal Hospital served no poisoned apples, much as its patients insisted to the contrary. This was just as well; her expectations did not include a prince barreling his white steed into intensive care to rescue her.

Now she had a semiprivate room; if anything here could make someone feel like a princess it was privacy. Leila imagined the metal gates around her to be trellises overgrown with blood-red roses. Her sheets could have just as easily been satin, and her buzzer to call the nurse a silver bell inscribed with runes.

The tubes in her nose and the intravenous needle in her vein were more difficult to translate. There was nothing romantic about the fluids draining into or out of her. Nor was there anything romantic about déjà vu; she'd seen this moment coming.

She had seen Dr. Simeon bending over her before he bent over her. Future events were like scraps of memory; all she needed to do was think forward in time and she'd know them. She had forecalled a hit-and-run driver's screech as clearly as the day it happened, felt the shock of metal impacting flesh.

Simeon had smiled at her this morning, his eyes large and brown as a fawn's. "We've stopped the peritonitis," he told her. "You're doing fine. You're not out of danger yet, I think you know that." He patted her shoulder. "But this is the best I've seen. We might take you off the critical list by the end of the week."

Leila smiled back and reassured him. It would be folly to tell her doctor that she will be dead by the end of the week. Fate is kind; she will die in her sleep. She will snuggle down in her imagined satin sheets, black hair loose and spread in an ebony wave across her pillow. Her certainty was as sure as her doctor's receding footfalls. She forecalled an odd floating feeling, her mattress undulating, her stomach giving one last shudder before it relaxed. Drifting off will be pleasant. Vaguely, Leila felt that moment, deep down, where everything will simply stop.

Reflecting only on how the car had careened into her, she couldn't tell forecall from recall. Context alone allowed her to distinguish between memory and premonition; she observed the same event from different sides, against a background of either past or future.

Her roommate, Bryant, will love her for as long as he can remember her. She will love him because for as long as he can remember, he will understand.

They moved him into her room that evening. Remorsefully, Simeon held her needle-free wrist and apologized: the beds are filled, they will get her a female roommate as soon as they can move the patients.

"It's all right," she said nasally, around the tubes in her throat. "I don't mind, really. I'm sure we'll both be fine."

Her doctor patted her hand. Not for a moment did Leila doubt that Bryant would remain in her room as long as she was alive. Simeon will reassure her for the next two days that the hospital is doing what it can to rectify the situation.

The nurse pulled open Leila's curtain and pushed it on its tracks. Leila stared at a new, bone-colored partition. She could hear labored breathing behind it. She waited for the staff to retreat into the hallway before she called, quietly, "Bryant."

There was a catch in the breathing. Then a hesitant baritone replied, "Did you . . . call me?"

"Yes. There's no one else here."

There was a moment of silence. Leila waited.

"Did you say my name was Bryant?"

"Yes," she answered. "The doctor told me your name." She lied. She will hear Bryant's nurse address him in the morning. He will ask his nurse if she said his name was Bryant. "You just don't remember, that's all."

"I know that," he said quickly, with certainty. "I don't remember." He whispered, "That's the one thing I'm sure about."

Leila swallowed. Her throat constricted around plastic. "Tell me what your name is."

"My name is Bryant," he said slowly. *"Bryant."*

"Good. My name is Leila."

"Leila. That's a nice name." He added lamely, "Tell me your name again if I forget."

"I will."

"Why are you here?" Bryant asked. "What happened to you?"

"I was hit by a car. Hit-and-run. I'm on the critical list."

"I'm sorry."

"And you?"

There was a long silence. Bryant said, "I don't know."

I don't know. Leila smiled to herself; for her, uncertainty was a luxury. Bryant couldn't tell her what his age was, but his voice was young. She restrained herself from forecalling his face. "Do you have a mirror?"

"There's one on my night table."

"What do you look like?"

The sheets rustled as Bryant turned. Leila heard him lift his mirror and gasp. She asked, "Are you all right?"

His nervous laughter came from behind the partition. "I'm all right. I've never seen that face before, that's all. I must have, though." His breathing quickened. He whispered, "What did you say your name was?"

"Leila."

"Leila," he repeated. His voice was almost inaudible. "I'm so scared."

"I know. You're going to be all right. You know that, don't you?"

"Is that what the doctor said?"

"Yes." She lied; it didn't matter. "Tell me what you look like. What color hair do you have?"

He laughed again. "I can't tell. It's all wrapped up in a bandage."

Leila closed her eyes and let herself go limp against her mattress. The plastic in her throat was making her hoarse. "Describe the face in the mirror," she told him. "Give me every detail."

He talked late into the night. Leila listened as his voice grew calm, as the mirror gave him a sense of security. She tried to pretend that everything he told her was new.

"Dr. Simeon is going to lose a patient this morning," she said.

"How do you know?"

"Before the nurse brings you your lunch, you'll overhear her talking to another in the hallway. It'll be a rumor, but the doctor will be irritable; then you'll know it isn't a rumor. When Simeon comes into the room his face will be drawn, lifeless."

"You're teasing me."

"No, I'm not. You'll have to trust me."

Bryant paused. He asked flatly, "Does your crystal ball reach into the past, too?"

"Yes."

"Can it help me?"

Leila whispered, "I wish it could."

She watched the nurses bustle about. Suddenly they were tense, as though someone had drawn a demarcation line in red across the big round clock in the hallway, or an alarm had been sprung. They spoke in low voices outside.

Bryant asked, "Did you hear that?"

"Yes."

"Is it true?"

"Yes."

"How do you know?"

"I know," she said. "Intuition."

The nurse almost dropped Bryant's lunch tray in his lap. She didn't apologize. She might have to someone who would remember. Leila heard Dr. Simeon chew out an orderly down the hall, before he stalked into the room and checked himself. The doctor tried to smile at her.

"You'll have to forgive me," he said. "I'm a bit out of sorts."

"Aren't we all," Leila replied. She added, "You're allowed to be human, too. We heard the nurses outside."

Simeon gave a start. "There's no discretion in this place," he growled. "I'm sorry, you shouldn't have had to hear that. I thought we'd pull him out of danger. These things happen unexpectedly."

"I know," she lied.

"How are *you* doing?"

"I'm fine." She smiled. "I watch the bubbles in the tubes, it's a nice pastime."

"We'll get another woman into your room, then we'll move the partition out," he assured her. "I promise. We're doing everything we can to rectify the situation."

"Yes. I know. Really, though, this is quite all right. In fact," she added, "I would appreciate it if you would move that partition a bit—so Bryant and I can speak face to face."

After Simeon left, she smiled at the turbaned head. "Hello."

"Hello." Bryant smiled back. He said, "The doctor was upset. I wonder why."

"He lost a patient this morning."

Bryant frowned. "Poor man." His gray eyes focused on Leila's. "Sometimes it must be a blessing to forget. I must remember that."

Then his face crinkled and he began to giggle. " 'I must remember that.' That's a real good one, uh—oh shit."

"Bryant," she prompted.

"Bryant. Yeah, that's a real good one, *Bryant*." He shook his head as a sob caught in his throat. "I can't remember a damn thing."

"I know," Leila replied. Then she said, "I love you."

He stared at her.

"I always have," she told him. "I'm not lying. Look me in the eyes."

He did. "I'll forget," he whispered.

"I'll remind you," she whispered back.

Leila rolled awake in a haze of dull pain. Bryant's face blurred before her. She forced a smile and said, "Good morning."

"Good morning. I woke up and you were here. What is your name?"

"Leila. Yours is Bryant."

There was silence. He said softly, "Oh." He asked, "Did I tell you that?"

She nodded, ready for her head to swim. When it did, she stopped nodding.

"Why are you here?"

"Hit-and-run. And you?"

"I don't know. I forget." He blurted, "I was watching you while you slept. I hope you don't mind."

"I don't mind." She grinned. A sharp pain lanced through her jaw.

"You're a beautiful woman," he said. "Even with the tubes."

"You're a handsome man. Even with the turban."

Lying on his side, he squared his shoulders against his bars. "I know," he said gamely. "I keep looking in the mirror. I find something new to admire every time."

Leila sucked in her breath and held her stomach. "Forgive me; it hurts when I laugh." She thrust her free hand through her bars. "I'm connected to IV on the other side, but maybe we can reach each other." She grimaced, half-blind.

"You're hurting."

"It's all right. Hold my hand."

Bryant flattened himself against the metal and reached. Their fingers touched. They interlocked them as best they could.

"That's good," Leila said.

"If I let go I'll forget I held your hand; but I don't want to see you in pain."

"Only for a short while longer." She blinked. Bryant remained a blur but his fingers were warm and dry against her own. "Bryant—I am going to die soon. Tonight."

"You mustn't think that."

"It isn't a question of thinking. Listen to me," she said. "Breakfast will be served in a couple of minutes, and you'll remember what I tell you for at least that long. You'll be served scrambled eggs, apple juice and coffee, and a square-shaped pastry covered in orange marmalade. The tray will be green." She squeezed his fingertips. "The nurse will ask you if you feel any better than you did yesterday. She likes asking you that because she knows you don't remember. Just say to her, 'You asked me that yesterday,' and she'll be unhinged for the rest of the day."

Leila followed the nurse and tray with her eyes until both disappeared behind the partition. When the nurse left, unsteady on her feet, Leila grinned and raised her eyebrow at Bryant.

"My God," he said. He added, "You're not frightened."

"No. I've known I was going to die here for a long time." She smiled sadly. "I told you yesterday that I've always loved you. I remember you from a long, long time ago. Do you believe me?"

"I have no choice." Bryant rested his head on his pillow and beheld Leila through a double set of bars. He tried to smile back. "For me, 'always' is a matter of minutes. I've always loved you, too."

He napped. Leila watched the nurse come in and take away

his empty tray. She sighed and snuggled down into her sheets. When she awoke, Dr. Simeon was bending over her.

"Can you hear me?" he asked. She nodded once. "I want to make sure you're comfortable."

She tried to open her eyes. White spots swept her up in vertigo until she closed them again. No surprise; still, she had to try. She felt Simeon swab her arm and inject her, knew her pain would be alleviated for a short time.

She whispered, "Thanks."

"Shh."

She turned her head slightly and bestowed a half-lidded gaze upon Bryant. He had propped himself up on his elbow and looked confused. From behind her she heard the doctor say, "We're trying to get another woman in here so we can move him out and give you some privacy. Do you want me to move the partition back?"

"No."

Simeon patted her shoulder and was gone.

Then, from far away, she heard Bryant ask, "Do you need someone to talk to you?"

"Please," she whispered.

"I don't know your name," he stammered. "But don't take it personally, I don't know mine either. There's this face I keep seeing in the mirror; I can tell you what it looks like."

"Please."

The baritone droned on until it became a lullaby. Images of turban and gentle gray eyes, planar cheeks and sharp nose, full lips, swam in her head. Leila let her eyelids drop. She thought of satin and goose down. Her stomach lurched once and settled. Her mattress buoyed her and she felt herself rise as though carried gently on slow currents. Bryant's voice melded with the lapping of waves. Serene, Leila drifted.

She was pronounced dead at 2:03 A.M.

Simeon pulled the tubes gently from her. Bryant, still awake, sat up in his bed and leaned over the bars. When the nurse pushed the partition to block his view of the deceased, his hand shot out and pushed it back. He watched as Simeon unceremoniously removed Leila's chart from its clipboard on her bed and attendants wheeled a gurney into the room. Leila's black hair was spread like a fan across her pillow, her skin pale and smooth. If only he could give her that one kiss, he thought, that could wake her.

His mirror lay face down on the night table. He stared intently at the corpse as an attendant covered it with a sheet and it was lifted in its linen cocoon off the bed and onto the gurney.

The nurse said to him, "You ought to go to sleep. You'll forget all this by morning anyway." Bryant nodded.

He still stared at the empty bed after everyone had left.

When he was sure no one was around to hear him, he said, "Leila . . . I fell off a crane."

A GIFT OF
THE PEOPLE

ROBERT SAMPSON

Robert Sampson has moved around a great deal in his life. When he was growing up, he lived in Ohio, Illinois, Florida, Oklahoma, and other places. He continued on the move for quite some time until settling in Huntsville, Alabama. Moving around that much gives you a feeling for the land and for the world around you, and that feeling is represented dramatically in "A Gift of the People." It's a haunting fantasy set in contemporary America.

Robert Sampson has published extensively in the science fiction and mystery genres. He was awarded an Edgar for the best mystery short story of 1986. He is the father of three and the grandfather of seven.

My brother Ted was eight when he first saw the People. I suppose it was for the first time. He never talked much, especially about that. When he saw them, if he saw them, he was at the bottom of Lake Olwanee, about twenty seconds from drowning. I had teased him into that mess, so it was not something I ever wanted to talk about, either.

Olwanee, in northern Ohio, is a sprawling, mud-bottomed lake with a dark-pebble beach that agonized our feet. About seventy feet off shore floated a raft, its black timbers riding clustered oil drums. It was beyond comfortable swimming distance and was therefore a challenge. Whatever was nearly out of reach, I felt obligated to strain after.

I insisted that Ted swim with me out to the raft.

He didn't want to, having more sense than I did, even then. I was two years older and, as I recall, I shamed him into the attempt—not from any need of company but from the silent pulsing of rivalry that spreads its dark under so many family relationships.

Limping across the beach, we plunged into water the color and temperature of iced coffee. The raft was distant, black, and ominously tilted. Ted thrashed furiously toward it, arms pounding up spray, his head rigidly lifted, like the head of a scouting turtle.

After a bitter struggle, he flailed to the raft. His fingers locked hard on the slippery timbers and there he huddled, shaking, white-faced, gulping air. He had fought his way out by sheer will. Even to me, it was apparent he could not fight his way back.

Eventually he tried.

The years overlay this incident with a spurious inevitability, as if events could have happened only this way. But, like so much else, events seem inevitable only when you stare straight at what happened, ignoring the motives behind.

Ted tried for shore. Halfway there, his splashing stopped. Very quietly, he submerged.

From the raft, I saw the pale glimmer of his body dwindle through the clear black water. Guilt shocked me. I had wanted him to fail, I suppose, without ever considering the consequences of failure.

No one else noticed that he had gone down. I hurled off the raft and swam furiously to where he had vanished. Not a bubble marked the spot. I surface dived, eyes open, swimming steeply away from the light. The water seemed to open all around me, black and deep and hollow, as if I swam downward through the ceiling of a liquid room, immensely empty. I descended through layers of increasing cold. Pressure closed around me. Light left the water and I could see nothing.

Then, entirely without warning, my hands plunged into a chilled silk of mud.

I jerked away in horror. As I did so, my left hand lightly grazed cold skin. I clutched and missed. I spread my arms and found nothing and groped at random through that lightless place tasting of stirred mud.

I was confused and needed air. I lashed about, scared and disoriented within that darkness.

And blundered full against his small, cold figure, sitting upright, arms locked about his knees.

I clutched him with both hands, squeezing unmercifully, and drove both feet against the mud. My legs sank in to the knees. In a frenzy, I kicked loose. The mud taste thickened in the water. Mindless, angry, horrified, I kicked frantically. Slowly we wallowed upward. Anguish gripped my chest. Beneath, the mud waited for our return.

It was black, then not so black. I was mad for air. The water grayed, then transformed itself to opaque white, softly warm, and we burst into the light.

Afterward we sprawled loose-limbed on the beach stones. I felt the violence of my heart, and, at the edge of my sight, in all that sun, dark mist wavered.

But no one had noticed. Past us stormed a pack of kids, howling after a yellow ball. Not one of them knew. It had all happened right beside them, sixteen feet away—the blind search above the mud, the despairing struggle upward. As close to those kids as the skins on their bodies. But not one of them knew.

Finally I asked him, "How come you just sat there?"

"Was watching them."

"Watching who?"

"People."

"People" was a favored word. He used it with casual ambiguity to mean swimmers or weeds or fish or fleets of boats. The imprecision bothered neither of us.

He added in his thin voice, "They watched but they wouldn't come."

I said, "Nobody saw us. You shut up."

He rolled over to stare at me with uncomprehending eyes. "You hit the People. They went away."

Then he slammed me hard on one shoulder and scrambled up and tottered off toward the car.

Eventually Ted learned to swim—although in an indoor swimming pool. He had developed a distaste for the water of lakes and streams. He prowled warily at the banks of these, studying their currents with calculating eyes.

"Swimming doesn't bother you, does it?" he asked, many vacations later.

We lounged in a boat that slowly drifted across the weed beds of Indian Lake. Ahead of our prow, swarms of brightly patched red and yellow turtles scattered wildly.

I said, "In lakes and stuff? No. Should it?"

"Look at all that down there." He motioned toward the green-brown banks of weeds that rose like cliffs in the transparent water. "Weeds, turtles, all that stuff."

"You can stay out of the weeds."

"I was just thinking," he said. "Suppose there's something in there looking at you. Watching. Lying back where they can see and you can't, all quiet. Not curious, not mad, just watching you and the way you move and waiting till you go someplace else. Just patient and quiet and part of the water, sort of."

"What? Fish?"

"No, not that."

I sensed that he had told me something of importance and I had not understood. In some annoyance, I snapped, "What you talking about, watching?"

"I don't know," he said. "It was just a sort of feeling I had. A kind of idea. I don't like swimming much."

We grew up and grew apart. Twenty-five years of education and military service separated us. The parents died and Ted married. So did I, although that was a mistake. We settled into the flow of time, I in Texas with NASA, Bill in Pennsylvania as an associate college professor.

We did not write much. We were separated by more than geography. The Ted and Ray Madison who were joined, as children, by blood ties and silent competition, were separated, as adults, by the same factors. We indulged our separation carefully, as if aware of what closer relations might incubate.

In early June, I took off a week to visit him. I had been at NASA headquarters in Washington, as a mainly silent handler of viewgraphs and printed handouts showing wonderfully high shuttle launch rates, supported by personnel who never got tired, never encountered technical problems, and needed no spare parts. This was in 1985, before the ethereal palace of mission planning splintered against reality.

Ted and his wife Barbara owned a small farmhouse just outside of Peter's Ford. This is one of those tiny Pennsylvania towns with narrow streets and worn red or white brick buildings crowding against the sidewalk, their windows masked by interior curtains. They resemble rows of faces with their eyes shut.

You crept through town at thirty miles an hour (radar enforced) until, with no warning, the town fell away. You came at once among fields rolling leisurely across shallow hills.

This was worn country, old country, rubbed by time, concealing a million years' worth of death beneath its gentle fields. Behind fat clusters of willows along Happyjack Creek showed lines of blue mountains, as lovely and ominous as an end game in chess.

I followed a gravel road between fields of young corn. Far overhead, a hawk watched from its spiral against a hot blue sky. The road rose around a knoll and circled a small brown and white house, full of windows. Bulky trees shielded it from the fields.

I stopped the car and stepped out. The shaded air smelled

sweetly cool. I could hear nothing. No wind, no birds, no creak of limb or flutter of leaf. My footsteps grated loudly as I walked to the house and rapped on the screen.

"Hey, Ted."

No one answered.

Far overhead, limbs and leaves interlocked in ascending layers through which blazed bright bits of sky. I stood at the bottom of a clear, dim well of light as transparent as water, listening to the silence.

The screen door banged when I entered the house. The kitchen smelled of onions and wax, and on the walls gleamed copper food molds. I called again and got no answer and moved, watchful and soft-footed, into the next room.

This was a brown and gold living room, full of light. It was as neatly ordered as a small girl dressed for Sunday school. Well-used furniture crowded against stuffed bookcases. On the pale walls matted watercolors glowed soft rose, blue, pale green. Their mood was calm. The technique was pure Barbara: she favored partially drawn outlines touched by color. It was delicate work that looked like the tag end of a dream.

I stood listening intently, although there was nothing to listen to. "This place," I said loudly, "is like the Marie Celeste." And moved to the baby grand piano by a double window. A transcription of Handel's *Water Music* stood open on a rack above the keyboard.

When I touched the keys, the piano emitted an unexpected bellow of sound. I jumped, scowled, looked at the music. Handel instantly defeated me. Closing the *Water Music*, I rooted through a stack of 1930s sheet music, searching for simplicity.

At the bottom of the pile, under a copy of "Muddy River Moan," I found a folded watercolor. It was a study of light and shadow along a stream. From the water stared a transparent man, evidently stretched among white stones. It was hard to tell. His body melted into shadow. Except for the figure, which was irritatingly indistinct, it was a nice piece of work. Barbara's name was scribbled in the lower right-hand corner.

After tucking the watercolor back under the music, I sat and listened. Caught myself listening. Stood up violently and padded through the hush to the back door.

Outside, the sense of being watched was powerful, the quiet intolerable. High overhead, layered leaves quivered, liquid and unstable as flowing water. Some sort of small gray animal slowly crept along a high branch, like the silent sliding of a gray fingertip. I could not see it clearly. It flowed out of sight and I had the curious feeling that it stopped behind the leaves to look down at me.

From the road rang a clear feminine voice: "Hey, Ray. Here I am."

I jumped less than a foot and stepped down to greet Barbara.

She was a tall girl, lean and square-faced, with a lot of flying brown hair. She wore jeans and a color-smudged old shirt with the tail out, and carried a wooden painter's box. "I was down at the creek," she said, kissing me. "You're early. Lordy, isn't it hot? When'd you get in?"

"Just a while ago. Thought you were all lost in the woods."

"How do you like the place? Isn't it lovely?"

A bird shrilled. Overhead a limb jerked as a squirrel scuttled along it and a twig clicked against the top of my car. In the distance, I heard the lament of cattle.

"Listen to that bird," I said.

"Place is full of birds. Wait till you hear them in the morning. Let's get a drink. Where's your bag?"

Inside, in the living room, I settled into a gold chair and watched her snap open the wooden box and rustle out her sketches. "Ted hates me going down to the creek to paint. But it's so pretty."

"What's the matter with the creek? Quicksand?"

"No. It's shallow. Stony. Look here."

She showed me her sketches—white stones and sun on a shallow skin of water. No transparent figures.

"Very nice," I said, listening to the birds outside the window.

"Ted don't like the creek. He's got this thing." Her long fingers made a complicated movement in the air. "I try not to worry him. But it's so silly. He almost drowned once, didn't he?"

"Once." I told her about my heroic rescue, leaving out the sibling rivalry and my panic under the dark water. "I suppose he's got a right to be funny about water."

"He swims okay," she said. "He just worries. . . ." Again the curious finger gestures suggesting complexity. "Anyhow, it's a real pest. Here I am, right in the middle of a drawing cycle. You know—daybreak to dusk on the creek." Her voice sounded diminished. "I guess he's afraid I might fall in."

"He's got funny in his old age," I said.

"It isn't very funny," she said, and the talk shifted to other things.

* * *

At about four o'clock, the screen door slammed and Ted burst into the living room, his long face beaming. "Well, I'll be doggonned, you did come, didn't you."

He had become a tall lean man with a wide mouth. Gray scattered the edges of his hair. He was long-bodied, long-armed and, unlike his brother, had not thickened around the waist.

He beat joyously on my shoulder with a hand. "I was going to be early, but the computer flopped. The computer always flops. Damn fool thing. A computer's a box full of half-right information that it feeds you in one-minute bursts, surrounded by hours of downtime."

"Just like ours," I said, looking at him.

"Ahhhhhh, you dern scientist."

Behind the graying hair, the faintly worn face, the strange long body, I saw the familiar brother of yesterday, still eager, still protecting his vulnerability with chatter, expressing himself in broad, clumsy gestures. I wondered if I seemed as strange to him as he did to me.

He dropped his briefcase, kissed Barbara, beamed at me. "When'd you get in? Did Barb show you around? I got to work a couple of hours tomorrow, then I'm off all weekend. How do you like this place?"

"Nice and quiet," I said. "I was admiring Barbara's watercolors."

"I have some new ones," she said, not quite defiantly. She thrust them out.

Animation went out of his face. "The creek, huh? It's pretty." Ghosts of past disagreements edged his voice.

She smiled up at him, innocent as a cat. "The light was just right."

"That's nice," he said.

He laid the watercolors carefully on the table and did not look at them again. We talked of other things—of birds and orbital flight, term papers and county history. Through it all you could feel the presence of the watercolors, a point of vague unease, like a tiny cut in the skin. A very tiny cut. But enough to make them carefully cheerful with each other and overenthusiastic with me.

After dark, Ted and I ambled down the road to admire Jupiter and Venus in the same sector of sky. Above us, leaves hissed with wind, as if water rushed at us across sand.

"Yeah," he said, "we're sorta far out here. I'd like to be

over on the other side of town. But it seems our inescapable destiny to have this house and live in this house and love this house and never ever escape from this house. About six generations of Barb's family owned this area. She grew up here and we bought it from her parents. They still farm it. It's okay. I'm just not too crazy about it.''

"Too close to the creek?"

His head moved sharply, his expression masked by shadow. "Barb said something, huh?"

"No. You were never too crazy about water."

"I guess not," he said slowly, thinking about it. "Especially deep water. Not that the creek is all that deep. Isn't Happyjack Creek a great name? It's only about six inches, usually."

"You can drown in an inch when your luck's out."

"I expect I'm nuts," he said. "Barb thinks I'm nuts. About the creek."

I hardly knew what to say to this stranger-brother. He stood in the darkness, head tipped back, listening to the hissing of the wind. The house lights quivered behind the tossing leaves and between that distant yellow light and our eyes hung shapeless masses of blackness, alive with movement, shadows slipping within shadows.

I saw that he was looking out toward Jupiter. He said, "I come out here a lot at night. It's quite likely extremely self-indulgent, morally. Do you ever get the feeling that we're living on the outside of reality? Walking around preoccupied with ourselves. And just a hand away, the real world goes on. We're of no importance to the real world. We're just an unimportant transient. The living part of reality is someplace else."

"Sure," I said, "I feel that way every time I go to Washington."

He broke into a sharp laugh. "You violate my sense of melodramatic doom."

We walked slowly back to the house, our feet crunching the gravel. Nothing lay behind the shadows. We stepped through them quite easily and came under the trees. But when I looked back, the place where we had talked was dense with darkness.

I went to sleep in a strange bedroom and just as always woke immediately. The pillow felt too flat and the bed too high and the mattress pressed at unfamiliar points, comfortable but not my own. I adjusted myself and heard their voices through the near wall.

It was not possible to understand much. His voice, then hers, a soft blur of sound, rising to a few clear words, then fading to a rhythmic blur, so that you caught the cadence of speech without the sense of it, the sound the fish hear as the fishermen talk while baiting their hooks.

". . . must not," his voice said. And again, ". . . dangerous. I asked you not . . ." And once, "Don't look for them."

Her voice answering, softer yet clearer, holding anger and pity, ". . . all my life . . . There's nothing. I know you're worried. Ask Ray. Thought too long about. Nothing. Nothing . . ."

It was shameful to listen but I listened, prying at their privacy, feeling as if the act of listening exposed me to the silent derision of those intelligences watching from a concealed place. Their voices stopped. I covered myself. Wind among the leaves like water flowing among white rocks. I slept without dreams.

By the time I pried myself out of bed the next morning, Ted had left for work. As I entered the kitchen, sweet with the odor of hot ham and biscuits, Barbara was snapping up her painting box.

"Can you make out all alone here for a couple of hours?" she asked. "I got maybe an hour's light left. Ted's gone."

"Let me make a sandwich and I'll walk down with you. I want to see the Forbidden Creek."

"Ha!" she said. "It doesn't make me nervous. I've looked at that creek all my life. . . ."

I had found a foam cup in the cupboard and was pouring it full of coffee. ". . . and never saw the People," I said.

The painting box banged loudly as she dropped it on the table. I saw the darkness under her eyes from not enough sleep, the gossamer lines of strain at the corners of eyes and lips. She looked wary and alert.

She asked, "When did he tell you?"

"He never did. I sort of worked it out over the years."

"Oh, God," she cried, "it's been that long?"

"Let's walk on down to the creek," I said. "I'll tell you on the way."

We descended through open woods. Sunlight barred the slope with streaks of gray shadow, and small white flowers, like vanilla flecks, were scattered under hickory and walnut. The air smelled sweetly cool.

I said, "It's a way of looking at things. Here we are in the middle of reality. It's solid and concrete. It has specific odors and colors. You can feel it and measure it. That's reality. But every now and then you see something else. Say you're in these woods and you look up through the branches toward a cloud. You see that the angle of the branches, a cluster of leaves, a bit of that cloud combine to make up the outline of a face. Take a step forward and the face vanishes. It doesn't exist. It's just a suggestion, a bunch of fortuitous factors. Maybe you look into the water and see weeds and a pebble and a ripple. And maybe that sort of suggests a human shape. If you move, the perspective changes, and it disappears.

"So you get to thinking. Wouldn't it be funny if these shapes in trees and water aren't illusions. They might be like reflections of something real. Someplace else. Maybe realities at a different angle to us, each one throwing off its own reflections."

"But that isn't real," she said, setting down her painting box. Flat white stones scattered along a strip of sandy mud. Beyond slipped a shallow sheet of water, whispering across light tan rock.

"It isn't real to us."

Crisp snaps as she released the catches of the painting box. "That's sick, Ray. He believes it's real. Something physical, out there in the water. He says you can see them."

"Maybe you can if you look at them right."

Scowling faintly, she set up the easel, opened the sketch-book, began wetting her paints. At last she said, "I've tried. I can't see them. I keep thinking, this time I'm going to see them, too."

"Maybe his imagination runs away with him."

"You're not being any help."

That was so obviously true I felt a small convulsion of anger. She could read the problem as well as I could—Ted was showing obsessive symptoms of some kind. "There's really not very much I can do."

"You're really cold, aren't you," she snapped, swinging around at me.

I said, "No, I'm not. I just don't know what to tell you. Maybe he ought to see a doctor."

She swept color across the page, her brush darting and jabbing. "Let's not quarrel," she said finally, eyes on her work. "I don't know what to do either."

"Don't look too hard at the water," I said.

It was the wrong moment for a joke. Her lips clamped together. She did not look at or speak to me again. After a few minutes, I excused myself. I might as well have said goodbye to one of the white rocks.

I went away from the creek, angling along the base of the hill. Finally I came out on the gravel road and walked slowly up to the house through full sunshine. When I got under the trees, it was silent again. Silent. No sound. No bird cry. No breeze. Nothing.

It scared the fool out of me. I went in and had some coffee and fiddled around in the house, listening and furious with myself for listening. There was no sound in that terrible place, nothing at all but the pressure of silence. I could see no movement along the upper limbs. I even went out and looked.

Prancing across the kitchen, loudly elated, Ted tossed down his briefcase. "So you finally got up. I had a great morning. Did a ton of stuff. Next Saturday, I'll do it all over again. Great life. Where's Barb?"

I said, "Haven't seen her since morning."

That swiveled his eyes to mine. "Painting?

"Yeah."

"Creek?"

"Yeah."

Exuberance went away. He grew taller and graver. "I guess maybe we better wander down there and remind her it's lunchtime."

"You go ahead. I'll fix up some sandwiches." I was not eager to see Barbara again so soon.

"Come on along. I'm using you shamelessly, if you want to know. You're my buffer. Every time the creek's involved, we get into a snapping match." He tugged gently on my arm in the old way I remembered from years back. "Humor me."

We stepped out the back door into an uneasy filigree of leaf shadow, gray and white on the pale gravel. The sky was stacked with broken clouds. Ted strode rapidly off across the parking area, not waiting for me.

When I caught up with him, I said, "I feel like a fool saying it, but maybe you ought to ease up on Barbara about that creek."

He glanced at me with that sudden stab of intelligence I found so disconcerting. "You mean Barb's worried about my intellectual vagaries?"

"Well, she doesn't know how nutty you can be."

We walked quickly down the sharp slanted road, the air sweet with leaves and warm dust, walking where the shadows had moved last night.

He said lightly, "Just like when we were kids. You'd never listen."

"I had to listen to you. You never told me anything right out."

He said quite sharply, "Did I have to? You're not that thick-headed. You know exactly what I mean. Whenever I get near water—you know how it was."

"Down and down," I said.

"Right down among 'em, every time."

The road swerved right toward disciplined fields lined with corn. Bearing left, we entered woods where no line was straight and the hill concealed its surface under last year's leaves. Ahead, dense green foliage clustered along the creek.

I said, "So you saw dreams in water."

"Not dreams. Entities."

"I never saw them."

"It's a way you have to look," he told me. "You can't expect to see them just by staring. I don't mean they're incorporeal. It's just a different way of looking."

"I never found out how."

"I did. It was natural. I just did it."

He glanced toward me over his shoulder, a graying man, belief hollow in his eyes. He grinned. "You see what a crazy you raised, Ray. A water psychic."

"Maybe you've got a special talent. So why worry about Barbara?"

"She wants to see. That's the problem."

Keeping my voice uninflected, I said, "Maybe they don't want her."

"Maybe they haven't made up their minds."

Crossing a narrow field, we entered under the trees. The light became a clear soft gray and the air smelled darkly of water and wet stone. Waist-high weeds slapped at us as we followed a worn track along the creek bank.

Ted's long stride broke into a trot. "Barb!" he called.

We burst out into the flat place by the creek. Near the water stood the easel, a watercolor propped on the crossbar. Her painting box lay open on the rock. Her shoes and socks were scattered by the creek edge. A single slim footprint showed in the sandy mud. Blurred impressions lined out under the still water. Perhaps they were footprints, lost where the rock began in midstream.

"Dear God!" Ted said.

He darted into the creek. He ran splashing through ankle-deep water to the center, his arms and legs in exaggerated motion, looking absurdly like a child at play.

I looked at the shore, the footprint, the shoes. I thought, *Fraud*, and did not believe.

He stared at me in blank confusion, then raced downstream, bent over to peer into the shallow water.

I stepped to the easel, sure that the watercolor would contain some alien thing. And, yes, it did. There, in delicately rendered water, floated a tiny, partially formed eye.

It was a setup, then, arranged to shock. In a moment he would find clothing in the stream, evidence that she had been entrapped. That the People had called. That she had walked guilelessly into the water, and walking dissolved, and dissolving vanished.

She would be watching us from someplace close. I began methodical checking of the low foliage, searching for the glint of skin and intent eye.

Downstream, Ted uttered a harsh bark of sound.

He would have found clothing.

The moment of horror, now. Pause for maximum effect. Pause and pause. The revelation—Now.

Nothing happened.

Up the stream toward me came Ted, picking his steps, holding himself tall. He threw down the sodden blouse, the jeans, the bra. Clear water ran from blue and white cloth.

"Where is she?" he asked.

I said nothing.

"I thought it was a gag," he said. "I looked at the shoes, the footprint. I said, 'Oh, hell, they're ribbing me. They're putting me on.' Only you're not, are you?"

"No."

"The timing was wrong," he said. "When she didn't pop out of the bushes and laugh, that's when I knew it wasn't a joke."

This precise re-creation of my own thoughts had the effect of shutting off my brain entirely. I could think of nothing to say.

"Oh, hell," he said, and slowly stepped past the saturated clothing to stare at the watercolor on the easel. I heard his breath hiss. He hadn't missed the eye, either.

"She's probably up at the house waiting for us," I said.

His head shook very slowly right and left, eyes slit, as if the movement gave him pain. "We better look for her down here."

We looked.

We ranged the creek, splashing its length down, searching its length up, bending to peer into shallow pools, poking into deep cuts under banks matted with blackberry that left delicate dots and lines of blood etched on our skin, moving with the sound of water, waiting for laughter and her voice, seeing sunlight unsteady on the shallows, the sudden panicked dart of a crawdad, the shapes of leaves against the late afternoon light, the sudden animal scuttle through underbrush that brought us erect, taut with expectation.

Nothing and no one.

And finally, Ted standing bent in a calm pool, head strained forward, regarding the pebbled bottom, his face anguished.

I saw his right leg swing. He kicked the water savagely, three times. Kick, kick, kick.

"Give her back!" he shouted. "Let her go!"

When evening came, we returned to the open area where the easel stood. I squatted down beside Ted in the dusk. Neither of us spoke. We waited together, listening to water mutter among the stones. The creek, dim in the larger dark, stretched hugely away.

He said in a small clear voice, "You needn't stay."

"I will."

"Taking care of the stupid younger brother."

I said, "You shouldn't do this all alone."

"How else can you do anything?"

Limbs stirred against a vague sky.

After a long pause, he said in a rapid monotone, "I've always seen them. They didn't particularly care about me. I don't know why. In Ohio, in that lake, when I was way under water down in the mud, they came looking. Watching me drown. They didn't care. Their way. Not malicious. Just indifferent. When you came down, they scattered. It was dark but I saw them somehow or other. You never did. You were just as indifferent as they were. Only it was different with you. You always kind of looked right through me. You never saw me either, you know. You really didn't care. I figured that out. I carried that all alone—you, and seeing the People—and that was pretty bad later, when nobody else saw them. How I wanted you to see them. But you never did."

It was work to keep my voice level. "I couldn't see. I don't have the gift."

"Gift! Lord protect us from such ill-considered gifts. The People must be all over, you know. Everywhere. A completely unidentified species. Millions of them. All the free water. Think how they swarm in the Mississippi. Think of the Nile."

His voice lifted, stumbling with intensity.

"Millions. And I'm the only one to see. I'm a lunatic in a special way. Oh, my God, you don't know how horrible it is to know that. And now this with Barb. How do I deal with this? She's out there. She's . . ."

Sound shut off. The flutter of leaves, frog sound, the rasp of small night creatures, creek sound. All stopped, as if a key had been turned.

Ted's fingers chewed into my arm.

"Listen," he barked. "Listen."

Silence pressed against us with physical force.

He demanded savagely, "You hear that?"

"What?"

"For God's sake," he said, "for God's sake, that's her voice."

He leaped up and plunged toward the creek.

I called, "Wait for me."

"No. No, don't you come. Please. If you come, they'll never let me see her."

"Ted, I don't want to have to drag you out."

"You won't have to. I promise you."

He strode quickly away into the creek, the beam of his flashlight bobbing ahead of him. As he moved off through the shallow creek water, the sound of splashing abruptly faded and became remote. It was as if he passed through some sound-absorbent medium. He moved a few feet off and sounded a hundred yards away. Then there was no sound at all. I watched him slip downstream like the shadow of a ghost. The enveloping silence made me feel vaguely sick.

I knelt on the stones, calculating how long to wait before following. The soundlessness made it hard to judge. He would be able to hear me following a long way behind and that he would count as betrayal.

I was intensely aware that we had come to one of those points where your actions, in a very brief time, can permanently alter the way you regard each other. It's easy to fumble. It requires such care. You have to handle yourself with the delicacy of a surgeon cutting along a nerve.

While I crouched, coldly disturbed, watching the intermittent glimmer of his light, I became aware of my own voice.

It whispered, "He hears. I don't. Same thing."

At first I didn't register the meaning of that. Then I felt a light shock of understanding as it made sense.

Sensitives, the pair of us.

We sensed the same thing in different ways. It was two sides of the same experience. Where he heard the calling voice, I heard silence.

Either way it meant the same thing. It meant that the People had come, the flowing, watching People of Happyjack Creek.

No sooner had I repeated that over to myself a couple of times, trying to understand by repetition, than I realized I could no longer see Ted's light. It was time to follow. But when I started to move, I could not. The thought of stepping into that water and perhaps putting my foot on one of the People turned my muscles to mush.

So there I huddled, completely amazed at myself, grinding my fingers together, while Ted sloshed downstream, the light jittering ahead of him, listening to Barbara's voice calling from God knows where, saying God knows what.

Shame dragged me erect. I forced myself up into a silence as thick as felt slabs, my back flinching horribly at the darkness behind. I took a tentative step forward, feeling cold water flooding into my shoes, and the darkness came down on me, a thousand tons of it. With no warning at all, it became the way it had been under that Ohio lake, my legs sunk in icy mud and no air.

The fear pours up through you, stunning the nerves and penetrating the muscles. If you run, it runs with you. But you don't dare run. Running creates its own pursuit. It is one of the rules that you must face fear at once, head-on. You clamp your teeth and stand and look at it and endure.

I switched off the flashlight and let night come down.

When the light went out, I almost fell over. Panic bent me. It was pretty bad. I felt that I was standing on a tongue in an open mouth. I felt the creek banks behind stir and concentrate, preparing to close on me in one whispering rush, vine, stone, dirt, and water clamping shut.

All this, I suppose, was direct attack by the People. I suppose. I don't know. I do know there were some terrible moments and I resisted them, body stiff and eyes shut, because you have to resist. I endured.

The way you endure, you get through one second. When that is over, you get through the next one. And so the seconds go. No matter how bad it is, you hang on one second more, because if you run, you know you will remember running later and then the shame will come and that will be worse than standing, enduring, with the mouth around you and the banks moving behind.

After a long while I got my shoulders back and my head up, although it was terror to move. You come back to yourself a sensation at a time. First, cold water in the shoes. Next, the smell of night leaves. After that, the shirt plastered against your back, the feel of clenched fingers.

I got my eyes open.

Gray sky showed behind blurred limbs. Beyond them hung a dusting of stars.

The ferocity of the night had softened. I saw that the darkness was streaked by variations of light, gray, black, pale silver. I could make out clumps of bushes and the intricate interweaving of limbs. These were familiar, ordinary, natural shapes, the way they had always been.

Finally I punched on the light and, concentrating hard, began to move. My body felt wooden and uncontrollable. It seemed to take a year to go fifty feet.

As I blundered slowly downstream through that nasty silence, a small glow flickered behind foliage far down the creek. It wavered like a trace of moonlight, then went out. I could imagine that a flashlight had been waved briefly, the beam crossing overhead limbs. I could think of no reason for that, and anxiety pressed me forward like the push of a hand.

The creek bent sharply right around bushy shallows. My light grazed cliffs to the left, black water at their base. White and brown rock chunks littered the stream. From the right bank, a muddy bed of gravel tongued into the creek. On the tongue lay Ted's flashlight pointing its beam serenely across the water.

He lay on the far side of the gravel, stretched out in a shallow pool.

My light touched his pale body. He had thrown off his clothing and lay with lifted head, staring into the water.

As my light came on him, a thick ripple seemed to rise close to his face and rolled away from him across the shallows. It might have marked the passage of a large fish or muskrat.

Darting forward, I jabbed my light at the ripple. But there

was only water, inches deep, quite transparent. It concealed nothing and contained nothing.

The ripple slipped smoothly to the far shore and flattened away.

As it did so, sound returned. It was like being struck from all sides at once. Water rustled and night creatures cried and I heard the rasp of my own breathing. The sounding world pulsed all around, as terrifying as the silence.

I flopped down in the water beside Ted. He turned his head slowly, bringing his face into the glare of the flashlight. It was a still, blank face, smoothed of hope.

"They came," he said. "But they didn't want me."

Reaching down, I set my arm across his frigid shoulders.

"It's okay," I said.

"I tried to go to them. But there wasn't any way."

His voice was low and calm, without excitement, without cadence, the voice of a stone figure speaking with a kind of precise indifference.

I gripped his shoulders hard. It was as if a door in me had opened that I had never realized was closed. He was valuable and of enormous worth. I felt amazement that this extraordinary person was my brother.

He remained motionless under my arm.

"There is no use waiting," he said in that uninflected voice.

I looked down sharply at him then and saw what the People had taken. There was no warmth in him. His passionless eyes remained fixed on me and they found nothing to judge, neither guilt nor virtue. He was stripped of both. The processes of his life, I saw, proceeded without such human ambiguities.

"We'll wait a little bit," I said to him, through my shock.

We waited. But the People did not return.

We never saw Barbara again, either.

THE LAST RAINMAKING SONG

JEFFREY J. MARIOTTE

In a sense, "The Last Rainmaking Song," our previous story, "A Gift of the People," and the two stories which follow this one comprise an Americana grouping in this anthology. While the underlying themes are certainly universal, they are developed in a world and with a style which is distinctly American. "The Last Rainmaking Song" is perhaps the most American of them all.

This is Jeff Mariotte's first published story, but he has been closely involved in the genre for a long time. As the manager of a major bookstore in La Jolla, California, Jeff has played a significant role in the development of science fiction and fantasy in that part of the country.

Billy Cruz rubs the back of his neck, rolling caked-on dirt under his fingertips. The ride over today, in an open jeep, was dusty. The desert has been reclaiming the roads; there is no water to hose them off, and not enough men to sweep them.

The general is talking about water. The lack of it. As he talks he paces, beefy hands clutching a model fighter plane.

"Do you know how long it's been, Mr. Cruz, since the last rainfall west of the Rockies?"

Billy knows. There are posters all over the base. For a while they changed the numbers daily: CONSERVE WATER. EDWARDS AIR FORCE BASE HAS NOT HAD RAIN IN 714 DAYS.

They stopped updating the posters a year ago.

Sweat trickles down Billy's cheek. He's aware of it, conscious that it's leaving a trail in the grime on his face. Tomorrow is his shower day. He's been looking forward to it for two days now.

"We know where he is," the general is saying. He looks clean; his blue uniform is crisply pressed. "Your uncle, I mean. We could just bring him in. But we think he's more likely to cooperate if he can do it voluntarily."

"That's where I come in."

"That's where you come in. We'll get you to him; all you have to do is convince him."

"That's all."

"It can't be that difficult, Cruz." Billy notices that the respectful "Mr." has been dropped. "His country needs him. Isn't he a patriot?"

Billy suppresses a smile. "I don't think he'll see it that way. Sir."

They have to find someone to fly him to San Diego. The recruiter who came to the reservation told Billy that he'd learn to fly jets, and see Europe, Asia. So far, he's learned how to shoot, how to weld, and how to repair truck engines, and he's been taken from the Sonoran desert of his home in Arizona to the Mojave desert in California.

The pilot is a southern boy, younger than Billy, named Eddie Higgins. Eddie flies well but doesn't say much. Maybe he's not crazy about this assignment, chauffeuring one Indian to San Diego to pick up another Indian. Anyway, he's jacked into the instrument panel. Eddie's reticence leaves Billy plenty of time to think about his uncle.

Billy hopes he'll recognize his uncle. If he does, he hopes his uncle will speak to him. They say he's a wino, living with a band of winos in a San Diego nine-tenths deserted by everyone else. That he's a drunk doesn't surprise Billy. Drunkenness is a long-standing Papago tradition. Until a hundred years ago, the men painted the soles of their feet red so that when they passed out they'd still be something to look at. That he's alive surprises Billy, a little. That the air force would even consider a rain dance surprises him a lot. Billy's been convinced for years that rain dances are superstitious nonsense, on the same order as Jesus making wine out of water. But they seem to be taking it seriously. Out of desperation, he supposes. Their intelligence tells them that Billy's uncle sang the last successful rainmaking song in the country, some twenty-three years ago, and they're willing to bet that he can do it again.

Billy's not willing to bet even that he can remember doing it. But he'll go along with them. Why not? What has anyone got to lose?

"Lookit that," Eddie says, gesturing out Billy's window. "The marina. Last time I came here it was fulla boats. Damn."

Billy looks. A couple of fishing boats, abandoned, float beside a crumbling pier. He feels like there should be something else, sea gulls, maybe, but there aren't any. All that water . . .

The marina rushes past, buildings blur. Eddie lands the jet on a stretch of downtown street, unjacks himself. "Damn," he says, grinning out at the buildings towering around them. "I always wanted to do that."

Billy smiles. "I didn't know you hadn't."

Eddie stops, runs a hand across his brushy haircut. "You're kidding. Right? Right?" His face is broad, guileless. He has the thick body, the massive neck, that Billy thinks belongs on a high school football star. *What's he doing in the desert?* Billy wonders. *It's not the place for him.* This boy was built for small southern towns, with rivers and forests and drive-in movies. "Damn," Eddie says again. "I guess I did land her pretty nice, didn't I."

"I guess you did," Billy says.

He can't even imagine life as a high school football star. He went away to boarding school when he was ten. The Bureau of Indian Affairs comes on to the reservation, tells the parents, if it can find them, how good boarding school will be for their kids, how much more they can learn than at the little reservation school.

After six years there, Billy knows you can learn one of two things. You can learn to hate the white man, or you can learn to be just like him. Some people can learn both at once.

They leave the jet, walk toward the center of the city. Eddie's wearing a sidearm that Billy hadn't noticed before. His holster is unsnapped, its leather flap bobbing with every step.

"Kinda spooky, isn't it?" Eddie says. His voice is soft. Billy has to agree. He never made it to San Diego during the wet years, but there are so many buildings, and they're so big, he figures the streets must have been full of cars and people most of the time. Now they're empty, except for the trash that skittles across on a stray breeze.

"Nothing more useless than empty buildings," Billy says. A minute later, he catches Eddie looking at him the way someone might look at a dog that not only talks but makes sense.

He's been told that they all look like this, all the cities of the Southwest. Los Angeles, Phoenix, Albuquerque, Salt Lake. It's hard to believe, but here, presented with the truth of it, he does. Nothing runs without water, and they were living on borrowed time as it was. First there were the River Wars, short-lived but bloody. Then there was the exodus. The general told Billy that the cities to the east were suffering from the sudden overcrowding. They need rain, so the West can be resettled.

Eddie consults a folded piece of paper, refolds it along the original lines, sticks it back in his pocket. "Left here," he says. "There should be a shopping center. That's where they've been living."

"I guess you never run out of clean clothes that way," Billy says.

Eddie laughs, a snorting sound that seems to have taken him as much by surprise as it did Billy. "That's good," he says.

"No, I'm serious," Billy says. "If you needed to live in a deserted city, wouldn't a shopping center make sense? You'd have clothes, beds and bedding, food from the restaurants, maybe guns and ammunition from a sporting goods store."

"That's true. I guess I never looked at it that way." His hand brushes his holster, and Billy wonders if maybe he shouldn't have mentioned guns. If this white boy gets too nervous, he might blow away the man they've come looking for.

"I think I'd want to live in a luxury hotel," Eddie says. "Have a different clean bed every night."

"They'd cancel your room service after a while."

They turn a corner, and Eddie's chuckle dies in his throat. Here it is, rising before them like a storybook castle. There's a little patch of dead grass, a toppled fountain, and then a multi-colored facade. Store names are still legible on the walls, though there's almost no unbroken glass, no wall under seven feet that hasn't been scribbled on. The refuse is deeper here, paper, glass, concrete, pieces of furniture. The ground is charred in places.

They walk closer, up to the foot of the steps that lead into the heart of the center. From behind a pile of trash there's an odd sound. Static. Billy looks. A solar-powered television set is on, receiving nothing, watched by no one.

Eddie grabs his arm. "Up there," he whispers. Billy scans, sees a shadow disappear behind a wall. So they are here. Or someone is here, at any rate. Eddie's hand goes for his pistol, but Billy stops him.

"Let me," he says.

He climbs a couple of stairs, until he's in plain sight of anyone watching from above. He suddenly wishes he'd thought to change out of his uniform, wishes his hair were longer.

"I'm looking for Joseph Cruz," he says, loud enough for anyone around to hear. "My name is Billy Cruz, Uncle. Your brother is my father."

Something glints in the sky: a bottle, sailing down from a high balcony. It shatters, spraying glass across Billy's boots.

"My brother is dead," a gravelly voice calls. The words are

slurred, indistinct, but Billy can make them out. He thinks he knows the voice.

"My father hung himself," Billy says. "After he lost his truck in a card game."

"My father's son is dead, too," the voice answers.

"My brother Gabe was killed in a bar in Casa Grande," Billy says. "And my brother Roberto died in Vietnam."

"And still his younger brother Billy joins the white man's army."

"Air force, Uncle. Come down. We have to talk."

"I remember most of it," Joseph says. "But I'll need some help on the rest."

They're sitting in the living room of the house Billy's mother shares with her common-law husband, Diego. Many Papagos, including her, used to the arid desert and comparative solitude, have stayed on the sprawling reservation. They've even extended it some, reclaiming parts of Tucson. Joseph slumps in Billy's mother's couch, maroon crushed velvet. Above it a lamp hangs from a gilded chain. On the wall behind Joseph's head is a seascape painting, waves crashing against a rocky shore. Billy looks in vain for anything Indian in the room's furnishings. *When did it start to slip away from us?* he wonders.

"Who's going to remember if you don't, Uncle?" he asks.

"There will be someone. I taught the songs to young boys many times."

"Young boys like me. Forgive me, Uncle, but I've forgotten. Other things happen. Life gets in the way."

"Only if you lose your way, step off the path."

"Drinking yourself half-blind in a deserted city? Is that the way? Is that where the Earth Mother wants you to be?"

"I'm old, Billy. I lost the way years ago. I admit that. I hoped those who came after me might have better success."

"I'm sorry, Uncle. You were wrong. Look at this place." He waves an arm around the room, the furnishings from Sears and K-Mart.

"Surely there are others. Your sister Rosa . . ."

"Is a hopeless romantic. She's Indian, all right. She thinks Dennis Banks was some kind of god, and if we'd all just bow down and pray to his memory, everything would be terrific. But I doubt she remembers any more about the Papago ways than I do."

"Will it hurt to ask her?"

"Fine," Billy says, pushing himself out of the overstuffed chair. "I'll ask her."

He makes his own way down the hall, knocks on the door to her room. Eddie opens it. He's leaning on the wall by the door, holding a Papago basket. "This is beautiful, Billy," he says. "I never thought I'd get excited about a damn basket before."

"Yeah, we're famous for our baskets, right, Rosa?"

His sister looks up at him. She's sitting on the floor, cross-legged. Indian style, the white guys at Edwards call it. She wears a plaid shirt, tucked into a pair of Levi's. Her long hair is pulled back, clipped into a ponytail. Papago chicken-scratch music plays from a cassette deck beside her.

"Justifiably so, Billy. Baskets are one part of our heritage we haven't lost."

"How many have you made lately?" He realizes he's baiting her but feels powerless to stop. Powerlessness is a feeling he's used to.

"Rosa made this one, Billy," Eddie says. He hands the basket to Billy. It's a coiled basket, of black devil's claw on white yucca, intricately woven. The design of the basket is a traditional "man in the maze" pattern, symbolizing the path that the spirit of Iitoi, the Elder Brother who created the Papago, takes to confuse people who try to follow him to his home on Baboquivari Peak. It also, Billy remembers, stands for the many twists and turns that a person's life must take before he acquires knowledge and understanding, reaches harmony with nature, and accepts his death.

"I'm sorry, Rosa," he says. "It's good."

"She said she'd show me how to do it," Eddie says.

Billy hands back the basket. "It'll take more than basket-making lessons to make you an Indian, Eddie," he says.

"What'll it take to make you one, Billy?" Rosa asks.

"What's that mean?"

"I mean you've been running from your heritage since you were old enough to walk."

"It wasn't my idea to go to that school, Rosa."

"Before the school, Billy. Our music wasn't good enough for you. You had to listen to Elvis Presley. White music. Half the kids on the reservation didn't have shoes, and you wanted P.F. Flyers. You were the only kid I knew who ate Frosted Flakes for breakfast."

"I guess I never understood why we shouldn't take whatever was available from the culture that surrounded us."

"You never understood, all right. You never understood that you can't trade in your own culture for another without losing something. Now you're in their air force. I've been ashamed to call you my brother ever since you enlisted."

Billy backs away from the door, her sudden explosion of wrath hitting him with physical force. "Uncle Joseph wants to talk to you," he says, and walks away.

The sun hasn't yet warmed the mesa. Billy stands with Eddie, hands in his pockets. Eddie wears a red jacket that was hanging in Rosa's closet, a remnant of some boyfriend, Billy guesses. It covers the holstered sidearm.

They came up in two vehicles: the jeep that Billy drove out from Davis-Monthan AFB in Tucson, and Rosa's nine-year-old Chevy pickup. Besides family, there are three of the tribe's older men, not quite Joseph's contemporaries, but as close as they can find. The number four is important to the Papago, Billy remembers. Of course you'd have to have four dancers, one representing each direction.

They all remember Billy's name, and he knows theirs. They look the same. The drought that chased most whites back over the Rockies doesn't seem to be a factor to these people; at least, it isn't the overwhelming topic of conversation, like whenever two whites get together. Coming up, they talked about family, about whose mare was ready to foal, who got drunk in town Saturday night. Now they stand by themselves, not speaking.

"You know what's funny, Billy?" Eddie asks.

"What?" He's in no mood to talk, but there's nowhere to escape. Three trails lead off the mesa. The biggest, they just drove up. The other two lead down into canyons. Billy knows them. They seem to veer away from each other, but then the westernmost trail, after a couple of sharp turns, runs into the other. Forty paces farther there's a holy spot, a natural stone arch through which you can see Baboquivari Peak, the home of Iitoi. That's where Joseph is now, where he's been since before the sun rose. Singing, asking for the strength and the knowledge and the purity to lead the rain ceremony.

"This rain dance business. It's an ancient Indian thing, right?"

"I suppose."

"Your people were probably doing it before the white man even came to this country."

"Could be. I don't see your point, Eddie."

"What's funny is, if your uncle and these guys, if they can really do it, they'll be handing the land right back to the white man on a silver platter. Do you think they've thought about that?"

Billy looks at Eddie as if seeing him for the first time. Near his right eye are two black dots, the beginning, Billy sees, of a tattoo. He assumes it's Rosa's handiwork, no doubt done the traditional way, charcoal rubbed into holes punched in the skin with a cactus thorn. Nearly all Papagos were tattooed a century ago, but the practice is less common now. Billy has never found it especially appealing. "I hope so, Eddie," he says. He smiles. "Rosa might make an Indian out of you yet."

"How did your people come to be here?" Eddie asks. "Is this just where the government stuck the reservation?"

"No," Rosa says. "We've always been here. No one else could live here, because there is no consistent source of water. But it's a source of pride to a Papago to go as long as he can without water. It shows strength."

"In the old days," Billy adds, "the bands would migrate. North in the dry times, to the Gila River, and then back here."

"Why not tell him the true story?" Jack, one of the old men, says. He walks toward them, stiff-legged. Over jeans and a pearl-snapped western shirt he wears a tattered pea coat, several sizes too large. The effect is duplicated by his skin, which hangs from his bones as if tailored for a much bigger man.

"Which story is that, Uncle?" Billy says. Jack is not really an uncle, but to call him that shows respect.

He shakes his head slowly, swallows a couple of times, then begins. "We were made here. Almost on this spot." He waves an arm, the sleeve drooping comically. "The Creator made people, and they lived here for a long time. But then they became sinful, they lost the way, and the Creator had to send a flood to kill them all." He stops, looks at Eddie. "I know, your Bible tells a story much like this one. But I can see that you want to be one of us. You're even tattooed, like me." He points to a line of marks extending from the corner of his eye down to his upper lip. "So I'll tell you, this story is the truth. One man, named Iitoi, was good, and so the Creator spared him, put him there, on Baboquivari." He indicates the mountain with another sweep of his arm. "From there he watched the flood. Then he helped create us, Aw-aw-tam, the people."

"I thought you were Papago," Eddie says.

"That is what you call us. That name comes from the Pima,

our neighbors. But we are Aw-aw-tam. We lived in harmony for many years, but it happened again. Some of us turned bad, and we killed Iitoi. His spirit went back to the mountain to live. So we stayed here. This is where we were meant to be.''

"That's a good story, Uncle," Billy says.

"You should know it's more than that, Billy. Sure, it's a story an old man can tell a young man. It's also a way to live. Live in harmony. Make the spirit of Iitoi smile when he watches you.''

"You're saying he doesn't?''

"I don't say he does or doesn't. That's for you to decide.''

Billy knows he should remember the stories told him in his youth, but he can't. They're more like dreams now than stories; he has no specific memories of hearing them, and is never sure, when he does remember one, if he has the details right. Standing there with his sister and Jack, he feels alone. They are his family and his tribe and he has no more in common with them than he does with Eddie, the white southern boy. His uncle can sing songs that make it rain. Jack, he remembers, can talk to animals, and it used to be said that he could see things that happened far away, even if he wasn't there. Rosa makes baskets, and can still speak some Papago. Billy looks at them from a distance that can't be measured in paces or meters or light-years, and he sees people who have something that he doesn't, something he never will. He's an outsider. Maybe, as Rosa says, he's always been an outsider. But it's never seemed to matter until now.

"I don't want to worry you, Billy," the old man says, "but I'm worried myself.''

"Why?''

"This morning I saw a bird standing on the ground. He fluttered his wings, but didn't fly, even when I approached him. I was thinking of Joseph at the time.''

"Joseph will be fine, Uncle. He's stronger now than he has been in years.''

"I think he is, too. I think you've helped him. Being here is showing him what he lost.'' The old man turns away. "I only hope you can see it for yourself.''

"He lost me there," Eddie says. "What was all that about the bird?''

"Aak," Rosa says. "An old belief. If an animal in your path acts strangely, it's a sign that whoever you're thinking of is going to die soon.''

Eddie falls silent. Billy watches him, the broad, open face

clouded with concern. He doesn't understand why the southern boy has become so attached to the Indians so quickly.

He shuts his eyes. There is too much to think about. He feels like Iitoi, the man in the maze. They're all in the maze together, he realizes. They're all at turning points—himself, Joseph, Eddie, even Rosa and the old men. A third interpretation of the basket pattern might be that the whole society, maybe all the people on earth, are symbolized by the figure of the man. The entire population of the planet is looking down the path of the maze, wondering which route to take to get to the end.

He reaches down, scoops up a pebble, hurls it with all his strength over the edge of the mesa. He can't think about the whole world. What can one Indian do to affect the whole world? *Let them choose their own paths,* he thinks. *I can't even choose mine.*

"Do you think Indians remember how to live off the desert, Billy?" Eddie asks. "Without grocery stores, and liquor stores, and federal water projects?"

"Without the BIA jerking your strings and the Great White Father sitting in Washington making decisions for you? I don't know, Eddie. I'm not sure I see what you're getting at."

Eddie hikes up his jacket, revealing his holster. The flap is open. "Don't tell me you haven't thought about it, Billy."

"You're crazy," Billy says, forcing Eddie's jacket down before anyone else can see. "He's my uncle."

"He's also the only guy on earth who can make it rain," Eddie points out.

"And I brought him here."

Eddie nods. "It has to be you, Billy. It has to be an Indian. Rosa's willing, but she has too much to lose."

"And I don't."

"Do you?"

Billy shrugs. He can't think of anything.

"There's a knapsack in the bed of Rosa's pickup," Eddie says. "It's got some camping gear in it, food for a couple of days. No one knows it's there except me and Rosa. As for this"—he jerks his head toward the weapon on his hip—"I'll just say you stole it."

Turning points, Billy thinks. Despite what Eddie believes, this particular path hadn't occurred to him. Now that it's been pointed out, though, it seems obvious. And Eddie's right, it has to be Billy. There are some paths only an Indian can walk, some ways one Indian can affect the paths of many. Like a man in a maze, suddenly he can't see any other options. There is only the path that lies ahead. The corner, once turned, disappears.

Billy lifts the gun out of its holster, shoves it in his waistband, under his sweatshirt.

"It'll rain sometime, Eddie. Even without my uncle."

"No telling when, though."

There doesn't seem to be anything more to say. Billy saunters over to Rosa's truck. The knapsack is there, as promised. He slings it over one shoulder, acting much more casual than he feels. When he comes back around the pickup, Rosa is there. Her coat hangs open, revealing a T-shirt that says WALK IN BALANCE WITH THE EARTH MOTHER.

"There's an old Indian saying that comes to mind," Billy says.

"What's that?"

"Right on."

Rosa laughs, takes his hand, squeezes it. Hard. The smile fades from her face, but it is replaced by something else. "Brother," she says.

"Sister." He lets go and walks on, his shadow preceding him, down the westernmost trail.

TINKER
TO EVERS
TO CHANCE

STEVEN BRYAN BIELER

We're baseball fans who live in New York. Through the years, this has meant we have been the luckiest fans in the world and—unfortunately more often these days than we would like—we have been the fans who have had to live with more suffering than any lovers of the game should endure. We're the city that houses the team that has won more World Series than any other ... and the team that lost more games in a single year than any in history. We're the city of Keith Hernandez, Darryl Strawberry, Don Mattingly, Dave Righetti ... and George Steinbrenner. It isn't likely that Steven Bryan Bieler knew about this particular passion of ours when he sent us "Tinker to Evers to Chance," but he couldn't have chosen a better market for this gorgeous baseball fantasy.

Steven Bryan Bieler has published fiction in *Isaac Asimov's Science Fiction Magazine, New Dimensions,* and *Seattle Review.* He is a graduate of the 1986 Clarion West Writers Workshop, where he wrote this story. He is recently married and works as an editorial assistant for *Pacific Northwest Executive* magazine.

The late afternoon sky cupped Fenway Park in gold and red, like steeped tea. The grandstand shadow edged onto the field with the stealth of the runner on first, edging off the bag. The fans clapped in their mismatched rhythms, trying to produce success through collective will; but Linda was no fan of this game. "What do you *really* do?" she asked again, tapping the rolled-up scorebook against her leg.

Scott cracked the shell of a peanut and let it drop. He heard it ping off a discarded wax paper cup. "Historical investigations," he repeated, shifting on the old wooden seat. "The pinning down of facts in historical myths."

"This is like Twenty Questions," Linda complained. She was finishing her third beer. "You're either a private eye or a schoolteacher, I can't decide which."

Scott's older brother Henry had set this up, one of his innumerable "suggestions." Henry must have ambushed Linda, one of his brokers, at a vulnerable moment. Scott knew *he* was not vulnerable; he was dead in the water. "No, not a private eye," he said, waiting for some indignation to arise. "I can't tail a suspect two hundred years old. My cases are always on paper."

The Red Sox were ahead by three. The runner on first advanced another step toward second. The pitcher stared at the runner, trying to freeze him like an animal in the beam of headlights.

"And you're not a teacher? Henry said you were associated with Sam Adams."

Scott cracked another peanut, the last. He crushed the foil bag in his fist. "I've done some work with their history department," he said. Professors had published works buoyed by footnotes he had provided. "I'm not on the faculty." Henry was a distinguished alumnus of Samuel Adams College. He found the traditional alumni endowment insufficient; he was intent on bestowing his brother on the college as well as his money.

The batter swung and cracked the pitch into the dirt of the infield. A war whoop began in the throats of thousands, but the ball bounced into the shortstop's glove. A moment later the inning ended for the home team.

"Not a schoolteacher, either," Scott said. "I want to discover history," he added, his automatic playback response. But that had meant someone else's name on the cover, his tucked off in Acknowledgments. Thank you for discovering the number of buttons on a Newport, Rhode Island, militiaman's greatcoat circa 1812, how people folded paper to make envelopes in colonial Albany, what was available on the menu of a public house where the Committees of Correspondence supped. He wrote "6-4-3," recording the double play, in his scorebook.

"Can you make a living from that?" Linda asked, eyeing the bottom of her cup to be sure all the beer was gone.

Scott took a deep breath. At last he was angry, at himself for ever acceding to any of Henry's suggestions, for allowing Linda's interrogation, for being a button-counter instead of something impressive. "Another beer?" he asked. Linda nodded, squinting at the digital clock on the grandstand across the field. Scott handed her the scorebook and the thin red pencil with BOSTON RED SOX stamped in gold on one side. "I'll bring us back something," he said, not wanting to wait this time for a beer vendor to wander by, the shouted "Bee-yuh hee-yuh!" piercing even the colossal din of a baseball game. "Keep score, okay?"

"Is that necessary?"

"Of course," Scott said, shocked. "We'll need a record of the game."

Linda looked around at the mob in the bleachers, the many open scorebooks and bustling pencils. "Okay," she said. "How do I do that?"

"Write everything down in plain American. I'll translate it

later.'' He stood, a slender figure in jeans and windbreaker. The sun still touched the parapet of the high left-field wall.

"Plain American," Linda muttered.

Under the stands conversation was muffled by the continuous surf of noise. Scott leaned against the wall at the bottom of the ramp that exited their section and closed his eyes. People brushed past him. No doubt they all had stable sources of income. No doubt they knew what they were going to do each day and didn't need to work up the interest to do it. Scott was supposed to be investigating Shays's Rebellion stories for several towns in western Massachusetts, but there was little money in it, and all the selectmen and chambers of commerce truly wanted was fireworks to attract tourists. Who was interested in history as life, the ladder of men and women whose lives led to our own rung on the ladder? Who cared about Bibles with family histories scribbled on the flyleaves, financial instruments executing pursuits long exhausted, lead bullets flattened and hiding in the boards of barns rotting by the side of a four-lane highway, and all the other chaff he had to sift to glean even one clean, uncontested fact? Sam Adams, with its respectability and regular paychecks, was becoming more and more attractive.

An usher asked him to move along. *What's your take-home pay?* Scott wondered. "You want to be an usher all your life?" he blurted, but the man was already harassing someone else.

At a vendor station he listened as above him feet stomped on concrete. The line shuffled forward like a game of caterpillar, its legs constantly replenished as new bodies joined in. The cashier pushed a cardboard tray holding two cones of popcorn and two sweating cups of beer across the counter to Scott just as a sudden rumble of triumph caused everyone to look up. Even the hardened cashiers allowed their battle composure to lapse when the rumble did not quickly abate. "Dammit," said a man whose frontage stretched his Red Sox jersey to the limit of the fabric.

Scott dodged carefully through the crowd with the tray, cursing his timing. He shrank against a structural column, thick with generations of paint, as a group of children ran past, an exasperated father in pursuit. Scott started to go and almost collided with a man in a military uniform. The man's eyes were brown, clear, and very wide.

"You see me!" the man exclaimed. The uniform could have been army, but the cap had silver wings pinned above the visor. Scott couldn't place the insignia.

"Sorry," Scott said, walking away.

"It was a triple play," the soldier said behind him.

Scott turned back. "What?" But the soldier was gone. A little boy ran behind the column, chasing a balloon. Scott shrugged and hurried up the ramp.

"What an inning!" Linda said, taking her sweater and scorebook off his seat. "Where have you been?"

"Long lines," Scott said, settling in, readying himself for disappointment. He peeled the plastic tops off the cups of beer. "What happened?"

"I'm not sure," Linda began. "What does it mean when the bases are loaded and then everybody is out?"

She took the cone of popcorn from Scott, who was slow in releasing it. "That's called a triple play," he said.

"Give me that! A triple play? Does that happen often?"

"Hardly ever," he said, and took a big swallow of beer.

Scott opened the box that held every scorebook from every baseball game he had attended in the last five years. He dropped the addition from last night's game inside, refolded the box flaps, and shoved it back into the closet. Henry's voice from the answering machine continued as if Scott were still in the bedroom he used as his office, standing respectfully in the morning light to hear every word about possible careers in historical research. Their father was dead. "I'm Pa now," Henry had told him once. On the tape, Henry finished with a summation of Linda's virtues. When the lecture ended, Scott returned and sat at his desk. His notes were in perfect order. All the pencils were sharpened. It was only nine-thirty. The phone rang again. It might have been Henry with more fun facts, but Scott grabbed it anyway.

"Scott Feldman speaking."

"Is this the Scott Feldman from the 'Investigators' section of the business directory?"

"Yes it is."

"The baseball fan?"

"Who is this?" Scott asked. "Is this a joke?"

"No joke, Mr. Feldman. My name is Edward B. Gage and I'm a—a baseball fan, too. In fact we met, briefly, at the game last night."

"We did?"

"We ran into each other, literally. I was wearing a uniform."

"Yes, I remember," Scott said. "What can I do for you, Mr. Gage?"

"I'd like to come and talk to you. Could you give me an appointment today? It's very important."

Well . . . he could look again into the story of Francie Miller, the woman who supposedly carried ammunition to Daniel Shays for the attack on the Springfield arsenal in 1787. If it was true it would make an interesting, solid footnote for the next study of the Rebellion.

It would be a lot of work for a footnote. Of course, since he was broke, he could call Mrs. Thornton. She had been pestering him again to prove her ancestors had come over on the *Mayflower*. Everyone in New England had come over on the *Mayflower*. Instead of a plaque, the state should have put a tollbooth on Plymouth Rock.

"Please, Mr. Feldman," his caller said. "This is very important."

Edward B. Gage didn't sound like his typical crazy, the callers with the latest treacheries of Benedict Arnold. Maybe it was a genuine, money-paying case. Maybe he wouldn't have to call Mrs. Thornton. He hardly cared anymore about the unlucky Daniel Shays and his slipshod farmers' revolt. Most Americans couldn't identify Daniel Shays. With their slipshod educations, some couldn't identify Massachusetts. "Would you state the nature of your case, please?" Scott asked.

"I'd rather do that in person, Mr. Feldman. It's—complicated. I have your address."

"Okay, Mr. Gage. I can see you at ten o'clock."

Scott's living room was stacked with books that crowded the furniture from Goodwill like medieval siege machinery. The blankets lay strewn on and off the fold-away couch he slept on, as after a battle. Scott stopped to peer at himself in his ship captain's mirror. His freckles filled more of the left side of his face than the right. He pushed his comb ineffectively through his hair, which looked flat no matter how the barber styled it.

The mirror had once been the property of Captain Isaiah Hempstead of Taunton, Massachusetts, a salty dog who died in that town at the head of the Taunton River in 1828. In his career the captain had traded with the Chinese and the Dutch and fought the British, the French, and the Barbary pirates.

The mirror was heavy square glass, unframed, designed to hang with one corner down. A pattern of bubbles like the Milky Way ran diagonally across it. The glass, tired now, gave back light grudgingly, showing objects as being farther from its surface than they actually were. Scott had been thrilled to have the mirror offered in payment for his research into Captain Hempstead's home, with the two widow's walks crowning the roof line and the garden paths of crushed ballast from a privateer burned by the British. He had accepted at once, nestling his treasure in his sport coat on the backseat of his car. But later he had made the mistake of explaining the transaction to Henry. "What kind of businessman takes *barter* instead of money?" Henry demanded. "What's next—beaver pelts?"

Scott threw the blankets into an approximation of housekeeping. In the kitchen he put a pot of coffee, two royal-blue mugs from a department store, and some cookies pebbled with pecans on a tray and took them back to his office.

The doorbell rang at ten precisely. Scott checked the peephole. Mr. Gage, in uniform, looking like an old war movie. He opened the door.

Gage was big, taller than Scott by a head, with wide shoulders and chest filling out his leather flight jacket. He moved with considerable grace. He was young, mid- to late twenties. The uniform was definitely World War II.

"Thanks for seeing me."

"I had an opening. Come into my office."

Gage surveyed the office and its furnishings as if conducting his own investigation. He seemed particularly taken by the pile of postage stamps in the seashell from the Cape. "This one is twenty-two cents," he said. He finally took a seat by the window.

"Coffee?" Scott asked.

"No, thanks."

Scott poured his mug full and sat behind his desk. "Did you enjoy the game last night?"

"Yes. Good teams. Of course the equipment has changed."

"Changed," Scott echoed, reaching for a cookie. "Changed how?"

"The outfielders were wearing gloves the size of peach baskets."

Scott smiled. "They do swallow a lot of hits. But in the old days gloves were about the size of a winter mitten."

"We managed pretty well," Gage said.

"I see," said Scott, who didn't see at all. "Have we met before, Mr. Gage? How did you know that was me you nearly tripped over yesterday?"

"No, we've never met," Gage said. "I—I really don't know how I learned your name. But, Mr. Feldman, *you saw me.*"

"So you said. Now, Mr. Gage, what is the significance of *seeing* you?"

Gage hesitated. "No one else can."

Scott chewed thoughtfully on his cookie. Gage could probably beat him brainless. Scott had no gun hiding in a desk drawer. But the man seemed calm and reasonable.

"I know how that sounds," Gage was saying. "I'm not out of my head. I'm not saying I'm Napoleon."

"Wrong uniform," Scott said, playing along. Gage smiled uncertainly. "Why don't you begin at the beginning?" Scott suggested. He brushed cookie crumbs from the desktop and opened his notebook.

"I once played baseball in the major leagues—"

"I can check that very easily," Scott interrupted. He had hoped for a better story than this.

"Can you?" Gage asked. "Can you check it right now?"

Scott raised an eyebrow. He set down his pencil. "Excuse me a moment." He went to his library and returned with a thick hardcover book.

Gage moved his chair closer to the desk. *"The Baseball Encylopedia,"* Scott said, clearing a space for it. "This is the new edition."

"Is my name in there?"

"We'll see. Player or pitcher?"

"Player. I played left field."

Scott opened the book and flipped to the *G*s in the players' section. Bobbie Grich, Hank Greenberg, Goose Goslin, Charlie Gehringer, Lou Gehrig—

" 'Edward B. Gage,' " Scott read. "The 'B' stands for 'Bergeron.' "

"That's my mother's maiden name," Gage said.

"Six foot two, one hundred ninety-five pounds. Bats right, throws right."

"An encyclopedia. My God. Is Babe Ruth in there? No, wait, he must be. How about Herbie Packer?"

"Who's Herbie Packer?"

"Fellow I played with at Wilkes-Barre. We had a bet who would get to the majors first."

Scott almost flipped to the *P*s. "Wait a minute," he said. He rechecked the entry claimed by his visitor. "According to this, you played five games for the Boston Red Sox in 1939."

Gage nodded. "I had trouble seeing the curve, and I wasn't doing so well with the speedball, either. So they sent me out to

Sacramento in the Pacific Coast League," he explained. "And then Pearl was bombed, and I enlisted in the Army Air Corps."

Scott leaned his chair back and tapped his knee with the pencil. "You were born on March thirty-first, 1917, in Troy, Maine."

"That's right."

"Then you should look much older than you actually do, Edward B. Gage. Except for one thing."

Gage waited.

"You died on June first, 1944."

"I know how that sounds, too. But that's straight as string."

There was a short silence in the room.

Scott leaned forward and checked the book. "It doesn't say exactly where you died. Just 'France.' "

"We went down not far from Soissons. That's northeast of Paris. I didn't survive the crash."

"Fighter plane?" Scott asked, wondering how much preparation Gage had done for this act.

"No, a bomber. We raided the steel foundries at Mannheim. The flak was bad over the target and we lost two engines. We tried to make a run for the Channel, but the Messerschmitts caught us over Soissons . . . no one got out."

Scott couldn't help glancing at the door. "Where is the rest of your crew?"

"I don't know," said Gage, who had caught Scott's look. "And this is on the level, Mr. Feldman."

"All right, Mr. Gage," Scott said, feeling he could push the man a little now, "given that you were shot down over occupied France in June of 1944 and—presumably—interred in one of the military cemeteries there, what in hell are you doing here, in America, in my office? We're not related, are we?"

"No relation, except baseball. You love baseball. You saw me. You can help me."

"Help you with what?"

"Help me find out what in hell I *am* doing here."

Scott rubbed his face. This wouldn't happen if he taught at Sam Adams. "You were transported from northern France," he said, "to Fenway Park, Boston, Massachusetts. How did the transportation work?"

Gage was determined. "I got there. I was in Fenway and I wandered around, trying to talk to people, but they couldn't see or hear me. Then I met you. What's next, I don't know, but I *do* know, I feel somehow, that I haven't much time."

"Eternity seems like time enough."

"Don't kid me," Gage said. "Even if you don't believe me, please don't kid me." He touched the encyclopedia. "Look in here. *That's me in your book.* Won't you help me?"

Scott realized he had been trying to justify taking this case (whatever "this case" might mean), not to himself but to Henry. "How will you pay for my services?" he asked.

Gage took his wallet from an inner pocket of his flight jacket and extracted all the paper money it contained. He slapped the bills on the desk and emptied his pockets of coins. "It may not add up to much," he admitted, "but by now they must be valuable just for their age." Gage placed his hands on the encyclopedia's block of pages. "Do you mind—?"

Scott nodded. He was studying the money on his desk. The top bill was a twenty. Andrew Jackson's hair was as unruly as ever, but the date was 1944, and the secretary of the treasury was Henry Morgenthau, Jr., a member of Roosevelt's Brain Trust. He took out his own wallet and removed a dollar bill, placing it on top of the twenty. The twenty was physically as well as numerically larger.

He counted two dollars and nineteen cents in change. There were two half-dollar coins, Liberty striding on the obverse, the American eagle lifting its wings on the verso. The coins were all dated between 1929 and 1943. There were some English coins as well: ten pence, or a shilling under the old system.

Scott felt his heart thump. Coins lasted forever. Coins struck in this century were comparative infants and could be repolished to some semblance of freshness. But you could not rejuvenate paper bills. These bills looked as if they had been handled, but not much. As if they had just been drawn from the Army Air Corps paymaster.

Gage sat entranced with the encyclopedia. His legs were crossed at the knee. Uniform socks and shoes wore out almost as quickly as paper bills. The examples on Gage's feet looked like authentic gear, with only moderate wear. The shoe soles were scuffed, perhaps from walking on tarmac?

"Packer's not here!" Gage exclaimed. "I win!"

"Mr. Gage," Scott said. "Mr. Gage!"

Gage came back to the desk. "This money," Scott began, "where did you—" The encyclopedia hit the desktop, making Scott start in his chair. Gage thrust out his left arm, pushing up the sleeves of his jacket and shirt with his right hand. "Take my pulse," he offered.

Scott looked at the man's bare wrist. Take his pulse; take him next door, introduce him to Finney, the retired barber, see if Finney's little spaniel barks at him. Call Henry and ask *him* what to do. *What's next—beaver pelts?*

"Why spoil it," Scott said.

He took an envelope from the middle drawer, swept the money into it, and closed the encyclopedia on it. He returned the one-dollar note to his own wallet. "I'm not licensed for astral projection," he said, "but I've got a car. Troy is only two hours from here. Let's go for a ride."

Scott signaled a right and guided his decrepit Toyota out of the sweep of traffic and into the turnoff for Route 2 north. He drew the last sips of apple juice up the plastic straw and tossed the carton into a large paper bag on the floor in back.

"Jesus, Ed, what a story," he said.

"I could hardly believe it myself," Gage said, "watching that ball go over the fence."

"A home run off Bob Feller," Scott said, while Gage, again, happily pantomimed his longball swing of 1939. "Rapid Robert! He's in the Hall of Fame now. To be able to say you did that—" Scott shook his head.

"Did you ever play ball, Scott?"

Scott shrugged and signaled another turn. "As a kid," he said. "I wasn't much good. I play some softball, now."

"What's softball?"

"Oh, fake baseball for adults. Big, soft ball. Can't hit it as far, but it can't hurt you as bad."

Gage gave this a moment of consideration, then resumed his study of late-twentieth-century New England motels.

"How did you break into pro ball?" Scott asked. "Did a scout see you play in high school?"

"Troy wasn't big enough for school teams," Gage said. "When I graduated I went to Manchester and hired on with Merrimack Tap and Die, running a drill press. I was good with my hands."

"How did you get from the assembly line to the big leagues?"

"Factory leagues. There were a half a dozen in town. I was fresh from Maine and wanted to make friends, and Merrimack Tap had a team, and it paid extra money, too, so I tried out. And I found out I was a pretty fair ballplayer."

"You mean," said Scott, astonished, "that until you left

home and went to work at this factory, you never knew you could play baseball?''

"No. Hockey was the big game when I was growing up. When the marsh behind the beach road froze in winter, we'd get out there with our skates and sticks and an old sardine can filled with pebbles for the puck. We'd play until the sun went down and we'd keep playing until a car came by and its headlights hit us and then we'd know how dark it was. Seems like I never played baseball, then.''

Scott glanced at his rearview mirror. New Hampshire receded behind them; they had entered that little tail of Maine that sneaks down toward the top of Massachusetts. He recalled his own efforts at baseball, imagining himself one of the sluggers he saw at Fenway, swinging the bat with the same competence of motion, blasting the ball to the four corners of the earth; but when the bat actually left his shoulder, his swing was just a lunge, bludgeoning air. "So you were playing for this Merrimack Tap and Die and found out you were good," Scott prompted.

"It was the first thing I knew I could do well," Gage said. "It wasn't like running my drill press—guys all over Manchester were doing that. It wasn't like learning to whistle or ice skate, either; nothing special there. Hitting and catching a baseball made me my own man. And then Mr. Higby, who was with the Red Sox organization, saw me and offered me a contract to play class-D ball in Wilkes-Barre.''

"Tell me about baseball in Wilkes-Barre," Scott said, and Gage obligingly rambled on until Scott announced, "This is Troy. Where would you like to go?''

Gage was silent as the car sped into town. Scott was familiar with these southern-shore towns. The dignified old homes that had sat behind ample lawns, observing the passage of horse-drawn carriages on the post road to Portland, were now almost on top of the smooth, black, voracious highway. Most of the old places pulled their weight in services to the tourists, selling antiques or providing bed and breakfast under names like The Nor'easter and The Sea Chest. Condominium developments sprouted from the ungiving soil that had fought generations of yeoman farmers.

"Troy was a stop on the Underground Railroad," Scott said, but Gage said nothing. On impulse, Scott turned down a road that led to the beach.

"There's the marsh!" Gage pointed to the left. Scott saw a shallow bowl, dry and brown, between the highway and the dunes at the back of the beach. A large white sign had been hammered to long lengths of wood on the edge of the bowl. NOTICE OF PROPOSED LAND USE ACTION, it began.

The road ran over a steel bridge and terminated in an empty parking lot. The wind was up and the Atlantic came ashore in a siege of foam. A man and a dog were visible far down the beach, but otherwise the sand and the spoils of the tide belonged to the gulls.

Scott circled the lot and headed back up the beach road. "We could go to your house," he suggested.

"It's gone. It blew down in the hurricane in thirty-eight."

"Your family?" Scott asked.

"My father died before I went into the service, my mother in a car accident about a year later."

Seen them lately? Scott thought, and was angry with himself for thinking it. "Brothers or sisters?" he asked.

"I was an only child."

"Wife? Kids?"

Gage looked out the window. "I was married," he said. "There were no kids. I wanted to play baseball. . . ."

Scott stopped for the light at the intersection with the highway.

"Take me to the cemetery, I guess. That turn, there."

The cemetery was set at the end of a gravel lane, bordered on all sides by walls of piled rock. Scott parked at the gate. The trees screened them from the highway; the unseen traffic muttered past.

Troy had been settled in 1696. Some of the headstones dated from that time. Slabs of blank slate like decayed teeth, erased and eroded by the weather, stood dolefully above the new-mown grass. Older stones that were still legible had pictures carved on them: clouds, clipper ships, cherubs. Lines of verse supplemented the names and vital dates of the deceased, praise for faith and charity. The contemporary stones were of thick marble or granite, set on sturdy bases, the terse statements of birth and death deeply inscribed.

Gage's parents, William and Anna, lay under a tree that rustled in the wind off the ocean. Its leaves sprinkled them with last night's rain. Gage picked some pebbles out of the grass and tossed them in his cupped hands.

What is he waiting for? Scott wondered. *God to beam him into heaven?* But whatever game they were playing here, he didn't want to spoil it. He had so enjoyed the drive up, chattering old-time baseball; reclimbing the ladder, the lives leading to our rung.

"I don't feel anything," Gage announced, the pebbles stilled.

"What?" Scott asked.

"I should feel *something*," Gage said. "These are my parents. But mostly I feel . . ."

"Yes?"

"Anxious," Gage finished. He let the pebbles drop. "The way I felt when I called you this morning."

"Maybe you'd like to visit your wife," Scott suggested.

"I don't know where she is," Gage said, clapping dirt from his hands. "And I don't want to visit her."

"What was her name?" Scott asked.

"Estelle."

"And you were married in—?"

"We were married in 1937, in Manchester. She thought it was exciting, me being a ballplayer, maybe going on to the major leagues. Exciting, for a little stenographer from Manchester!"

"And you got to the majors didn't you?"

"For five games, yes. Then they sent me down. Maybe I could have made it back, but in the meantime I had to pump gas in the mornings before games and she was still a stenographer. We couldn't afford a family. Last night at Fenway I saw the prices they were charging for red hots and peanuts—what I made in a week in 1940 you could blow in a night, now."

"Couldn't she see how good you were? What a chance you had?"

All Estelle could see was that little apartment we lived in in Sacramento, plasterboard walls and the jukebox in the tavern downstairs playing past midnight."

"You were doing what you wanted to do," Scott said. "It was your life. You were taking your chance."

"But, Scott," Gage said, "don't you see? It was *my* chance, *my* life, not Estelle's. I was the left fielder, she sat and watched. When they cheered, it wasn't for her."

"Oh," Scott said.

"She finally went back to New Hampshire. . . . She wrote to me while I was overseas, four or five times. I threw her letters away without reading them. It's funny," he continued, though Scott had walked away, "but telling you this now, I just realized—what a stupid thing that was to do. Throwing those letters away."

Scott stopped by a roughened red headstone, its inscription

celebrating the devotion of someone a century dead. The wet grass was soaking through his sneakers. He felt chilled even through his windbreaker.

"Scott! We've got to go!" Gage yelled. He was peering intently toward the west. The sun was dropping toward the tree line.

"Go where?" Scott asked, but Gage was running through the ranks of stones, flight cap grasped in one hand. Scott followed as quickly as he could, but Gage was already sitting in the car when he pulled up at the driver's side, his feet almost skidding out from under him on the loose gravel. Scott got in and fumbled for the key. "Where?" he gasped.

"Just go. Please. They'll have to stop when the light is gone." Scott gunned the engine and backed the Toyota down the lane.

"Left," Gage directed when they hit the main road. Scott eased them into the traffic. They came to another side road, farther inland than the tourists were accustomed to visiting, almost beyond the Troy line and into some other principality of Mansfield County.

There was a baseball field here: a wooden backstop that flaked bits of green paint, an infield of hard-packed, stony dirt, and an outfield of pale grass, not yet recovered from winter. Two groups of men were playing, using a baseball, not a softball. Scott pulled the Toyota into line with their parked cars. He and Gage stood under the trees in the foul ground off right field. "That one," Gage said, pointing to the young man in center field. "Let's watch that one."

Scott watched him for three innings. He was younger than the others, in his early twenties. He caught a few fly balls, threw the ball well from far back in his position, and hit safely in two times at bat.

"He has the instinct," Gage said. "He plays shallow because he's fast and he counts on his speed to get him back under anything deep. He's got a good arm, knows which base to throw to. Level swing at the plate. Stings the ball. Thank God, Scott, there's someone here who can play!"

Another inning ended and the young man's team came in to bat.

"You've got to get his name," Gage said. "Find out if he plays for anyone."

"Why?" Scott asked. "Are you scouting him?"

"I'm not; you are," Gage told him. "You've got to get that information and get hold of one of the big ball clubs."

"Ed, who's going to listen to me? I'm no baseball scout."

"Make them listen. Make them get somebody up here. Look, it's not his turn to bat yet. Go on, ask him!" Gage retreated toward the car, his shadow long on the humped, gullied asphalt of the parking lot.

Scott ran his hand through his hair and walked toward home plate. The young man stood to one side with two bats in his hands. Scott took his notebook and a pen from his windbreaker. "May I speak to you a moment, son?" He had never addressed any man as "son," but he felt the need for all the adulthood he could muster.

Closer, the young man looked more like a teenager. He glanced at his teammates, who were pretending to watch their batter take his cuts. "Sure," he said. His wrists were as big around as Scott's forearms.

"I'm doing some freelance work," Scott said, "for the Major League Scouting Bureau." Scott had recently read an article in *The Sporting News* about it. The young man's eyes widened. The catcher was holding the ball; the batter was leaning on his Adirondack. "I can't promise you a contract, but I'd like permission to pass your name along to the bureau so they can get someone out to look at you. Would that interest you?"

"Yes," the young man said. "Yes, sir!"

The other players were gathering around them. A big man with a mustache came forward. "I'm Vernon's uncle," he said. "Do you have some ID?" Scott produced his Massachusetts investigator's license. He had had to apply for one, just like Sam Spade, and had always felt silly carrying it. But it impressed all of them. He noted the information he needed from Vernon and gave him one of his business cards.

"I'm going to send your name in immediately," Scott told him. "If you haven't heard anything in a month, I want you to call me. Collect."

The trees held the sun now, blasts of orange in the swaying leaves. Scott walked back to the car, a gang of excited weekend baseball players behind him. He could hear Vernon's laughter breaking through the talk of the older men.

Gage was not in the car. He wasn't anywhere in the parking lot. "Ed!" Scott yelled. "Hey, Ed!" The players were getting back to their game; they still had sufficient light for an inning or two, until the line drives snapping out of the dark, the ground balls exploding from the infield dirt, sent them home to their suppers. Scott ran to the closest player, coming down the line toward right field. "Excuse me—I came down here with another man—did you see where he went?"

"Nope," the man said. "Didn't see nobody but you. Hey, Richard! You seen anybody come in with Mr. Feldman here?"

"Thought he came by himself," Richard yelled from second base. "Anybody see another guy with Mr. Feldman?"

"I saw another man," Vernon said.

"You—you saw him," Scott said.

"I saw you both watching me from under the trees. A tall man in a leather jacket and a funny-looking hat. Want me to help you look for him?"

"No," Scott said, zipping his windbreaker higher. He put his hands in his pockets. "No, thanks. You go play ball."

"Thanks again, Mr. Feldman."

The old Toyota seemed desolate without Edward B. Gage on the adjoining seat, galloping on about Joe Packer, class-D ball, and the home run he had hit off Bob Feller, the Hall of Famer. But suddenly Scott was hungry; he hadn't eaten since breakfast. There was a place back on Route 2, in Ogunquit, that was decent. He headed up the road while behind him a young man named Vernon, doing that thing that made him his own man, drove a baseball over the left fielder's head and into the hungry darkness beneath the tree limbs.

"Hello, it's me," Henry said, as the message he had left sometime this afternoon whirled from one reel of the cassette to the other. "I was at the club yesterday and John Burkmeyer gave me a good lead on a research opening."

"Burkmeyer," Scott said, combing his hair in his ship captain's mirror. "Bunk," Burkmeyer had called the legend of Francie Miller and her role in Shays's Rebellion. "Burkmeyer," Scott informed the mirror, "still thinks the Earth is flat."

The tape unwound details of occupation, time, place, and whom to contact. Scott pocketed his comb. He looked at the patterns of bubbles, the uncharted stars, beneath the surface of the mirror. He was only a step away, yet, in the way mirrors tire over time, he looked much farther. Henry's message ended and the machine clicked itself back to watchful sleep. Scott caught himself looking, not at himself in the mirror, but at the reflection of the room. There was no one else there.

Scott shook his head, unzipped his windbreaker, and tossed it on a chair. The Major League Scouting Bureau—how would he get them to listen? Where had he left the issue with that article in it? As he entered his office, Scott saw the encyclopedia still sitting on his desk. He opened the book to the fat envelope he had placed there this morning and read the name of Edward B. Gage, a young man from Maine who had played five games for the Boston Red Sox in 1939.

He shook the money from the envelope. The coins clinked on the shiny wood, the overlarge bills fluttered out, and the silver wings that had been pinned to the front of Gage's flight cap fell among the quarters, dollars, and dimes.

Henry could be reached at any one of five numbers. Scott dialed three before his brother answered. "Forget it, Henry," he yelled, "just forget it!" He slammed the receiver home.

Scott waited until the phone began to ring. Then he opened the clasp behind the wings and ran the pin through his shirt above the pocket.

THE FARM SYSTEM

HOWARD V. HENDRIX

FOR ERIC HEIDEMAN

One more sports story and then we'll go on. "The Farm System" focuses on another American Dream and the lengths to which some people will go to be the best.

Howard Hendrix has a Ph.D. in English and a B.S. in Biology. His one-act play, *Act of Contrition* was performed at the Fourth Annual Experimental Theatre Festival at Berkeley in 1983, the same year he won the Abraham Polonsky Fiction Prize. He has attended writers conferences at Aspen and Squaw Valley and presented papers in science fiction criticism at the Eaton Conferences in Riverside, California and London. He was born and raised in Cincinnati and now makes his home in Idyllwild, California.

As Walt Maclin and his son Billy finished their breakfast of steak and eggs, the sun blazed molten white-gold from behind the dark shoulder of Mount San Jacinto. Dawn in the Hemet Valley. Seeing the sunrise, Billy Maclin quickly finished eating, then snatched his plate, cup, and utensils off the table, walked them across the large tiled kitchen, and dumped them in the sink. Opening a set of white louvered pantry doors, he palmed up his basketball from the pantry floor and headed for the kitchen door.

"Gonna shoot some hoops before the school bus comes," said the boy. "Okay, Dad?"

Walt glanced up from his copy of the *Press-Enterprise* and gave a grunting nod. This was the daily ritual—especially during basketball season—but it didn't bother him. Walt Maclin was proud of his son: the boy was playing varsity ball with the eighteen-year-olds, even though he'd just turned fifteen. *Not bad for the kid of an old cowpuncher,* he thought.

He folded over his paper, finished his cup of coffee, and got up slowly from the table. As he took his dishes to the sink he could hear the *ponk, ponk, ponk* of a basketball on the asphalt driveway out front. He began rinsing the dishes and stacking them in the dishwasher, thinking about what Dr. Kline had said when the boy had finished his most recent physical.

"He's growing fast, Walt," said the doctor as he filled out forms for Billy's high school athletic department. "Six foot two, solid. Must run in the family. How tall are you, again?"

"Six five."

"Yeah. Well; he'll make that before he peaks—no problem. Beat it by an inch at least, maybe two." The doctor paused, looking up from what he was filling out. "His mother was a tall woman, wasn't she?"

Walter nodded, stone-faced. "Martha was five ten and a half."

The doctor, a beefy man with a cold-cuts complexion, grew even more flushed for an instant, then shifted the topic of conversation slightly.

"I hear he's quite a roundball player. . . ."

"Could've played varsity his freshman year," Walt said, brightening, "if the coach hadn't balked. As it was, he made junior varsity MVP anyway."

The doctor finished the school athletic forms and handed them to Walt.

"I bet he'll be all-district, maybe even all-state before he graduates," the doctor concluded. "He's got the genes for it, all right."

Genes, Walt thought as he turned on the dishwasher, then took his Stetson off the peg where it hung. Good genes, but maybe not good enough. Six six, six seven—not tall enough, really. Those few inches could mean the difference between the schoolyard and the NBA, as they had in Walt's case. He let out a long sigh, a tired one, even though the day was just beginning. Putting on his Stetson, he walked out into the sun.

Billy was doing lay-ups. The boy had real quickness, good fakes and moves—Walt had taken note of it, watching the boy's games. He had gotten Billy started, had taught the boy everything he had ever known about the sport, but he could see that his son was already going beyond him in a number of ways. Walt had basically played "white ball," a stand-up-straight-and-shoot version of the game. But his son, with all his feints and dodges and sharp ball-handling, played like a black ballplayer—a nimble, shrewd, street-smart game.

Watching Billy do slam-dunks now, Walt was convinced that only a small part of his son's black ball style came from the black kids he played with on the school team. The majority of it the boy must have picked up from watching TV—literally heaven-sent, NBA and college games bounced down from satellites onto the dish in the backyard that pointed up at the sky like a big blind eye.

Billy bounced the ball up and down at some imaginary foul line. Watching him, Walt thought sadly that no matter how dedicated the boy might be, it would take more than just heaven-sent moves for him to get a shot at the big time. Walt hoped, though, that he'd also taught his son the most important thing he himself had learned about sport—to hold wins and losses balanced, and never be overwhelmed by either.

Billy pushed the ball into the air, toward the basket. The ball rose and dropped in a seamless fluid arc. It passed through the net so perfectly it barely made a swish.

The yellow school bus pulled up at the end of the long drive and honked its horn. Billy gathered his books under one arm and his basketball under the other and sauntered down to the waiting bus. As he walked away, he was for a moment just another lanky towheaded kid, in jeans and gym shoes and school jacket, growing faster than his clothes could keep up with him.

Walt turned and walked back past the satellite dish, in the direction of the feed lots. The earthy stench of tons of cattle manure wafted his way on the morning breeze. He'd bulldozed a good deal of it into fertilizer heaps, but no one had stopped by recently to haul any of it off. He'd have to put another ad in the papers.

He looked over his stock—all of it penned. His place was unique in the valley in that he had both dairy *and* beef cattle, while all the other places specialized in one or the other, usually dairy. He kept his herds up around five hundred head, three hundred fifty of which were dairy while the rest were beef, mostly polled Herefords but a few Angus as well. He had no particular reason for keeping the beef head, other than the per-haps obscure one of steak and eggs in the morning, and the fact that while he still had beef cattle he could in good conscience call his place a cattle ranch rather than a dairy farm.

As Walt came closer to his stock the cattle saw him and started ambling in his direction. He hopped up onto his loader and began doling alfalfa fodder into the hayracks that ran the lengths of his dairy-stock enclosures. The alfalfa he grew on his own land, taking advantage of Southern California's year-round growing season to get off several crops per year.

He wondered how many more years his land might have left, though. Every year saw fewer and fewer farms and ranches and orange groves in this part of the state, all because the human population was growing so damn fast. The signs were obvious: one side of Walt's valley butted up against the new city of Moreno Valley, the other against the older city of Hemet, and both end-cities were growing faster than mold on bread.

Thousands of housing units had gone up in Moreno over the last few years, as what was once agricultural land now became slurb bedroom "developments" with fancy names, from which nameless hordes commuted the hour and more to their defense-industry jobs in Orange County, L.A., and beyond. Hemet, too, wasn't much better: a sunbelt retirement city that swelled more and more each year with the housing and money of old snow-birds looking for a warm place to die.

"And here I am," Walt said to his stock, "stuck in the middle with you."

Sure, there were groups trying to rein in the rampant development in the region, most notably the Coalition for Open Space, with its twenty-odd member organizations. But what could they really do? Walt was a member of the Coalition almost out of reaction. Just about nobody gave a damn what happened to the land—too busy commuting, Walt guessed.

Nobody, that is, except the developers and their cronies, who had the money and the self-interest. The same old song and dance: the developers had the money, money controlled the county government in Riverside, ergo the developers controlled the county government. Anyone who opposed the developers and the contractors and the realtors and the building trades was opposed to Change and Progress—was a "Luddite," as the *Press-Enterprise* put it.

One evening the previous summer Walt had looked down on the Hemet Valley from high in the San Jacinto range, and he had seen this "Progress." The lights of Hemet below, sprawling farther and farther each month, shone like a colony of phosphorescent fungi growing on an agar plate planet. Walt knew at that moment that, left to their own devices, the developers and the big family advocates wouldn't stop until everybody was packed into little house-cells tight as cattle in a feed lot.

He preferred to think that people weren't cattle, and he'd vowed to hold out as long as he could against the property-tax hikes and the legal manipulations designed to break him down and force him to sell out.

Walt moved on to his beef-cattle enclosures. Though his beef head were fewer in number, their lives were, if anything, more pointless than those of his dairy head. The raising of beef cattle had been more thoroughly affected by the kind of scientific animal husbandry that Walt had been taught at the university, so the beef cattle could be packed in still more tightly than the dairy head. The feed Walt served up to them now might as well have been a stew of sawdust and chemicals, heavily laced as it was with a broad spectrum of antibiotics, vitamins, trace minerals, steroids, growth hormones, female sex hormones, and God only knew what all else. It seemed to him that these beef head weren't really even animals anymore: they were more like meat-producing chemical vats that happened to have hooves.

But he had to admit that he did get more meat per animal this way, and in less time, than he ever could have the old way. Less natural but more efficient, and efficiency, *progressiveness*—those were key words if he hoped to remain in business.

Still, he couldn't help wondering if there might not be something more important than just staying in business.

When he'd finished feeding his livestock and checking the waterlines that fed out into his fields, Walt took a break and went back to finishing the morning newspaper, which as usual was full of Change and Progress. A special series, ''The Shape of Folks to Come,'' was running this week, informing the readers about surrogate mothers, test tube babies, cloning, recombinant DNA research, gene manipulation, and a whole host of human-shaping options that that great proponent of fertility, the Roman Catholic Church, as well as some others, had taken issue with.

The paper also spoke of new space-weapons systems being tested at the nuclear weapons test site in Nevada; of recent breakthroughs in physics putting the development of hypercharge-related antigravity in the same class as fusion power—feasible early in the coming century; of the value room-temperature superconductors were having in the construction of the giant machine called the superconducting supercollider; of the increasingly numerous terminally ill AIDS patients going into cryogenic deep sleep in hopes of waking up to a better world.

Wouldn't that be the thing to do, he thought. *Go to sleep, and wake up to a paradise without deadly diseases, nuclear weapons, fatal accidents, or overpopulation.*

Or never wake up at all.

The season went on. Basketball games were played, cows were milked, cattle were slaughtered, there was steak and eggs for breakfast at the Maclin house almost every morning. News of distant wars and nearby sex plagues continued to fill the air, and Billy's team won its district, with Billy starting at forward and sometimes guard. The best team out of tiny San Jacinto High in years, they were slated to play for the state title in their division.

One noontime, between district and state, two men from the university showed up at the ranch to talk to Walt. As he loaded manure onto a pile with a shovel, the men introduced themselves as Jim Martin, an assistant basketball coach at the university, and Dr. Raju Purewal, an assistant professor in the School of Bioengineering. Martin said his scouts had spotted Billy's name in the local press and that he and Dr. Purewal had seen a few of Billy's games. They had been impressed by what they saw, they told Walt—*very* impressed.

But Walt sensed from their talk that they hadn't shown up just to compliment him on his son's talents. A hint of something hollow and *forced* in their words alerted him, and a barely discernible tension and uneasiness came from the men themselves, as if they weren't completely comfortable with the task at hand. Walt at first thought they were just put off by the stink of the manure, but the more the men from the university talked, the more it seemed to Walt that they had something much bigger in mind than a pleasant little social call.

Sure enough, after they'd at last gotten the pleasantries out of the way, Martin hit Walt with their proposal.

"Mr. Maclin," said the coach, a muscular man with thinning blond hair and a slick way of looking past rather than at the person he was talking to, "how would you like to see your son become another Cowens, another Bird—or even better?"

"Well," Walt said slowly, leaning on his shovel, smiling slightly at the young ball coach's come-on. "That'd be a dream come true, 'specially for an old player and fan of the game like me. But even though I've got a father's biases, I still have to be realistic. Frankly, Billy doesn't seem likely to match their height or their skills."

"We can take care of that," Martin said, this time looking Walt directly in the eyes.

"The skills?" Walt puzzled, and went back to loading manure. "Well, I suppose you could. But how tall the boy ends up being is in the hands of—"

"We can take care of that too. That's why I've brought Dr. Purewal with me. He'll explain."

Walt peered intently at the black-haired, dark-complected

Purewal. The stocky man cleared his throat nervously, pushed his shiny black hair away from his forehead, and began.

"Umm, yes. Mr. Maclin, my research involves the whole system effects of biosynthetically manufactured hormones on human—"

"Whoa—wait a minute," Walt interrupted. "What do you mean, *biosynthetically manufactured*?"

Purewal looked stymied, then brightened.

"Er, in this case, a gene from a human being is isolated, cloned, and inserted into a microorganism, such as *E. coli,* an enteric bacterium. The microorganism then produces whatever product was coded for by the human gene—as if it were a microscopic factory."

"Okay," Walt said slowly, "but what's all this got to do with my boy?"

"I was coming to that," said Dr. Purewal, mildly annoyed. "Quite a number of years ago—in 1979, in fact—genetic engineers at Genentech cloned the gene which carries instructions for making bioactive HGH—human growth hormone. They inserted such cloned genes into microorganismal cells, which they then persuaded into manufacturing that hormone. As early as 1985, the Food and Drug Administration approved Genentech's biosynthetic HGH, declaring it safe for use."

"I see," Walt said. "And now you want to treat my son with it?"

"Ye-es." Purewal nodded. "We have contacted your family doctor—a Dr. Kline?—and we concur with his conclusion that, unassisted, your son's height will likely not exceed two meters—excuse me; that is, no more than six feet six and three-quarter inches, unaided."

"And if you 'aid' him?" Walt asked. "How tall?"

Dr. Purewal grinned with pride.

"That depends entirely upon how well he responds to treatment—and how tall we want him to be. Mr. Martin suggested a height between six feet nine and one-half inches and seven feet two inches, depending on the position we design him for."

Walt didn't like that word, *design,* when it was his son they were talking about. Still, he held his tongue, deciding it would be best to hear out this little plot to build a better ballplayer.

"And the treatments with HGH will of course cost you nothing," said the fast-talking Martin, jumping in. "Normally they cost between eight thousand and ten thousand dollars per year, but your son will receive them at no charge as a participant in our program. We view it as an investment. Should he enter our program and eventually enroll at the university, we will guarantee him a full basketball scholarship, full room and board, an absolutely free ride at a fine university.''

His visitors fell silent, waiting for his response as eagerly as used car salesmen about to close a deal. Walt leaned against the shovel handle, thoughtful.

"Gentlemen," he said at last, "you've got an interesting proposal here. But before I can consider it further, I need to know the answers to two questions. One, what are the risks, the side effects? And two, what's in it for you?''

Martin and Purewal glanced quickly at each other.

"I believe I can answer your first question," said Purewal carefully. "There will be the inevitable minor pain of periodically administered injections, but any other side effects will be absolutely minimal. Fears that HGH treatments might lead to glucose regulation problems or increased risk of elevated blood pressure or arteriosclerosis have all proven groundless.''

"Really? How often has it been tested?''

"Thousands of times, by now,'' Purewal assured him. "Among the many young people deficient in growth hormone who over the years have been treated with the synthetic, there have been no recorded side effects. Also, your son is right now at an optimal stage for treatment, a 'boost phase' in his growth pattern, during which his body is already prepared and preconditioned for significant spurts in growth. I have little doubt that he will respond very favorably to treatment, and that there will be no harmful side effects whatsoever.''

Martin nodded and took up his answer almost as if he'd rehearsed it.

"As for your second question, Mr. Maclin, I'll level with you. There stands to be a lot in it for us—and I don't just mean Dr. Purewal's research results, either. As you may have heard, we've got a student recruitment problem at Riverside. We've got to compete with older, better-known schools in the system, like Berkeley and LA. We have to compete with the glamour of beachside schools like San Diego and Santa Barbara, with the redwoods of Santa Cruz, with the established reps of Davis and Irvine. We have the handicap of being situated in a place noted for smog and heat. The result of all this is that while we are, in terms of land area, one of the largest campuses in the system, we're also one of the smallest in terms of student-body population.

"Our current chancellor has made increasing enrollment his top priority. New programs have been initiated, even entire new departments and schools, like the School of Bioengineering, which Dr. Purewal is part of. These have attracted some new students, but not enough. The chancellor has tried to revive the Division Two football team our campus lost in 1970—when our team was division champ but also two hundred thousand dollars in debt. The chancellor wanted to revive the team in Division One or One-A form, for better media coverage, but his supporters in the community balked at the expense.

"As an alternative, we struck upon this program I've been outlining to you. We already have an established and respectable basketball team—you know that; I'm told you played for us before my time—and we already have the School of Bioengineering. Neither the NCAA nor the NAIA have made any firm rulings on the treatment of potential players with human growth hormone. If, a few years down the line, our campus happens to have a team full of superstars, and also just happens to be the best team in the country"—Martin gave a broad smile—"well then, we'll get a lot of media attention focused on us, and student enrollment should rise correspondingly."

Martin paused, waiting for Walt to respond, but Walt said nothing—just began shoveling again. Martin shrugged slightly and went on.

"So you see, Mr. Maclin, though we don't have a farm system like pro-baseball teams do, we can and do use the high schools for such a system. If you go with us, we can build your son to superstar status—not only in terms of his height, but also in terms of his skills. Our coaches will gladly give him one-on-one attention while he's still in high school. He'll benefit from the latest advances in kinesiology, in biofeedback, in computer-assisted motion tracking, in all areas of athletic training and sports medicine. And when he graduates from Riverside, I'm sure the NBA might be more than a little interested in picking him up. So—whaddya say?"

Walt scratched his head, pondering, playing the country squire for all he was worth. If they thought they'd easily hook him with their fast talk and scientific jargon, well, he'd just let them go on thinking that. He took a long breath.

"I appreciate your candor, gentlemen. But the decision isn't mine alone. I'll tell Billy what you've told me, and let him decide. It's his life, after all. If he agrees to it, then you have my approval. If he doesn't approve, then you don't have mine. And

I don't want to bring this up before the state championship, or even right after. I'll need about two weeks.''

Martin, looking somewhat crestfallen, glanced at Purewal, who nodded.

"Two weeks it is then, Mr. Maclin,'' Martin said, a slight edge to his voice. "We'll be waiting.''

Just as suddenly as they had come, they left, leaving Walt to finish shoveling up the manure.

The championship game was played. Though Billy Maclin, the youngest starter on either team, gave a stellar performance, the San Jacinto High team lost by two points to their height-advantaged and superbly skilled opponents from the city.

At first Walt thought the loss would not bode well for his discussion with Billy of the university's proposal, but Billy and his teammates took the loss better than he'd expected, and there was already much talk of "next year." Walt was sure that within a few days the time would be ripe for discussing the matter with his son.

On the afternoon of the fourth day after the loss, Walt found himself standing in one of his alfalfa fields, staring out toward Gilman Road. He held his Stetson in his left hand, while with the red and white handkerchief in his right he mopped the sweat from his brow and close-cropped graying hair.

It dawned on him that the bend in Gilman Road he was staring at was where, five years before, a gravel truck traveling at high speed had rear-ended Martha's ancient Ford Pinto, turning it into a fireball. Walt's wife had been returning home from a weekday morning meeting of the Rosary Altar Society of Our Lady of the Valley, the Catholic church run by the Holy Ghost Fathers in Hemet. The truck had been on its way to the construction sites in Moreno Valley, where building was at that time just getting under way in bulldozing earnest. Martha, almost home, had slowed as she prepared to turn in at the driveway. The truckdriver, in a hurry and hung over, had seen the Pinto too late, and now Martha was no more.

She had been a devout Roman Catholic, but Walt, whose faith had never been particularly strong, had fallen away completely since his wife's death. The questions had been too much for him. Why had she died in that way, at that time? Why had she been coming from OLTV? Why had she joined the Society there when she usually attended Mass at St. Christopher's in Moreno? If she'd been coming from St. Christopher's, from the church named for the traditional patron saint of travelers, would she still be alive? Would it have made any difference at all?

Walt didn't know. All he could remember was Martha Sanchez, the beautiful, dark-haired girl he had met in a composition class at Mount San Jacinto College before he'd transferred to the university. Walt even remembered the teacher, an odd, balding young man who peppered class discussions with quotes from Spenser and Shakespeare and Milton—quotes Martha loved, wrote down, memorized, while Walt wondered that anyone could get so excited over words.

But now all he had of her was words—and pictures, which to him were worth far more. He thought of their boy and almost prayed he was raising Billy the way Martha would have wanted him raised. God, he feared screwing up on *that* more than anything else.

He wondered what Martha would have done with this proposal by the university men. Would she have thought it immoral? Hurtful to the boy? Would she have tried to tell Billy what to do, what to think? Or would she have respected his free will and let the boy make up his own mind?

Martha, what should I tell him?

Walt thought, and waited. No message boomed down out of the clouds, not even a still small voice within, but Walt knew the answer nonetheless. It would have to be the truth, or at least as big a piece of it as he and his son could understand.

Putting on his hat, Walt went back to work. The intense green of the fresh fields looked the way Walt imagined God's front lawn might look. He worked on steadily until supper, after which he sat his son down and explained the university proposal as best he could. The boy listened intently, asked occasional questions, apparently understood.

"Sleep on it tonight," Walt said at last. "You can give me your answer in the morning."

After talking to his son, Walt felt reassured. Letting the boy decide for himself was the right thing to do. Undressing for bed, he grew hopeful of the boy's decision, and a future began to unroll before him. He was sure he had raised the boy right, that he had instilled in his son a respect for honesty and fair play, so Billy would doubtless turn down the hormone proposal. Maybe he would become a truly great ballplayer after all—college, NBA—all without their damn biotechnology booster shots. Shorter players had excelled before, and it could happen again.

If the boy didn't make it big in ball, well then he could

always come back here, take over the ranch, and the two of them could work it together. Maybe they could go ahead and work out a more humane and natural system for their land, the way Walt had secretly always wanted to do. His mind spun out a method combining the best of the old and the new, the sort of economy and appropriateness the Amish had mastered for so many years, but updated by the most recent advances in organic nonmonoculture cropping and stock raising. It might not make them rich, but it might make them *right*. No more steak and eggs, maybe, but at least no more chemical-vat cattle, either.

And they would fight to keep their land—even if it cost them everything. If they became the holders of the last piece of open space in a valley otherwise paved and tract-housed from end to end, if they would be pointed to as diehards and the last of a vanishing breed, then so be it. At least they would have proved that there were still some people in the world for whom Money was not God.

Turning this romantic, heroic vision over and over again in his head, Walt at last fell asleep.

He finds himself on horseback, galloping in purple twilight across low hills, toward a grassy plain below. His hair and beard are long, but he feels young, young! The hills he recognizes dimly as the Badland foothills of the San Jacinto range, the grassy plain as the Hemet Valley, but neither looks as he has ever seen them before. There is no Hemet, no Moreno Valley, no roads or farms or dwellings of any kind—only the earth and sky, and even they are not quite the same. The air is clearer, sharper, the land and hills look older, softer, their shoulders more rounded with years.

He comes to the plain and strikes off west and a bit north, up the valley toward what in another time was the Moreno area, following the direction of what might once have been Gilman Road, though only grass blows in the evening wind now.

As he rounds a bend in the valley he sees something that makes him rein his horse up short. High in the sky ahead, sparkling in the last rays of the sun, floats a city, a cluster of needle towers trapped in a bubble of force, a crystal city in a crystal ball in a crystal sky. On the grassy plain far beneath the shining sunset city stands a ring of metallic pillars, scores of them, each one standing at least a dozen times his own height. The structure they form is a high-tech Stonehenge, a monument to conjecture.

The pillars seem to shimmer with barely restrained energy, as if they were the fingers of giants imprisoned in the earth in the very act of reaching toward heaven. It occurs to him that there is a giant in the earth there, a giant machine miles in circumference pumping out invisible streams against gravity, to hold in the sky a city too perfect to support life. No sooner has he realized this than the city begins to fall out of the sky, plunges toward the pillared ring and the earth like a perfect shot falling through a perfect hoop.

The city comes to earth with a vast calamitous breaking-crystal sound. Grounded, broken, penetrated, the city unfolds across the landscape in explosive growth like an embryo, like a child, like a youth. He looks around and sees at last Hemet Valley paved in sulfur lights and concrete without end amen. From the tightly packed housing comes a sound like the steady lowing of cattle. The sprawl itself takes on the form of a man clothed in city lights, lying prostrate on the ground, who stands up slowly, miles tall—his son, only grown now, with fire in his eyes. The voices of women cry out dirges for mothers and sons, lament the failure of the patriarch. The fire in Bill's eyes explodes outward, consuming all the earth and sky.

"Dad! Dad, are you okay?"

Walt woke to the sound of his own horrified yells still echoing from the walls of his bedroom and Billy knocking on his door and calling. Coming out of it, Walt immediately felt ashamed of his outburst and of the sheets sticking damply to his belly.

"Yeah, yeah, I'm all right, Bill," he replied groggily, shaking his head. "Just a weird dream—a nightmare. I'm awake now."

"Oh. Okay," Billy said noncommittally. "It's almost time to get up anyway."

Walt showered hastily and dressed for the day. Joining his son in the breakfast of steak and eggs Billy had prepared, they ate in silence, Walt wondering what the boy's decision would be, and if there would come any day soon when steak and eggs would prove too expensive a breakfast for them.

"Bill," Walt said when they'd finished eating, "what did you decide about the university's proposal?"

The boy looked down at his plate.

"Dad, I want to go for it. I remember what you used to say—that if you'd been a few inches taller you might have had a shot at the NBA. If I don't take it, they'll probably just offer it to some city player who'll sure jump at the chance. Besides, I read an article in *Sports Illustrated* that said the East Germans and the Russians are already doing this kind of thing anyway. So, yeah, I want to do it."

Walt said nothing, just nodded and stared into space.

After his son had gone out to shoot his morning hoops, Walt called the university to inform Martin and Purewal of Billy's decision. The two university men, listening to his report over conference call, were clearly overjoyed.

Walt hung up the phone and went to feed his cattle. As he loaded the chemical feed into the racks for his beef cattle, he realized he was doing it for the last time. He didn't have to worry about the money for his son's education anymore, and he was determined to run his ranch his own way, the right way—business be damned. He stared into the dark, dull, drug-glazed orbs of his beef cattle's eyes, thinking about free will and trying to read some kind of future there. He turned to look toward his son.

Out above the driveway, a ball hung for an instant at the top of its arc, at the summit of its mathematically exact parabola, then fell toward its zero as unerringly as any bullet or missile, making no sound at all as it passed through the hoop, a testament to mute ability.

GHOST SHIP

WALTON SIMONS

Walton Simons has published a number of short stories, including several in the *Wild Cards* series published by Spectra. He's a graduate of the University of Texas at Austin and is currently employed there in the Admissions Department.

"Ghost Ship" is a fascinating and fresh time travel story taking us and its central characters back on the *Titanic*.

The aqua sky bled to green around the edges of his vision. The sea was dark gray, flat and motionless. It made Rhodes queasy. He hated the simulator. The iron railing felt like a plastic sponge. His feet sounded like faraway flippers as he walked down the deck. If the real *Titanic* had been like this, she never would have sailed.

He entered the huge main parlor. The light gave everything in the room a yellow tinge, and the angles at the corners of the room looked wrong. Vikashmo's image was sitting at the bottom of the great staircase. Her skin flickered through a spectrum of flesh tones.

"What are you doing here?"

"Same as you, research," he said. "I might decide to push Jain for this assignment."

"Fuck you, Rhodes. I want this one bad. Since when do you have any interest in the *Titanic*?"

Rhodes walked toward her. "It's a plum job. A few days of early-twentieth-century luxury sounds good to me."

Vikashmo stood and folded her arms. "I thought you'd be glad to get me out of the way. Then you can stay at home, think about Flawn, and jerk off."

"Back off. I've told you before, nothing happened between

us. She's pushing fifty now.'' Rhodes stared out the window. There was no reflection in the glass. A woman walked into his view, turned slowly to face him, and lifted the veil on her sun hat. He recognized her and took a half-step backward. Flawn smiled and moved out of his field of vision.

''Just because nothing happened doesn't mean you didn't want it to.'' Her voice was muffled. Flecks of orange static appeared in flashes everywhere.

''Shit, we're crashing,'' he said.

They sank through the floor. Everything looked as though it had been stretched out on the edge of a bubble. Vikashmo's image lengthened and moved away from him. The ship flickered and dissipated. Rhodes saw nothing but a sick green. Static hissed and screamed in his mind.

He gazed through the transparent ceiling at the dim and distant stars. The mist flowed down on him, cool and blue. Rhodes inhaled slowly, filling his lungs with it. He savored the emptiness the drug gave. It cleansed, purified, removed doubt. And the company provided it at no expense to all time-jumpers.

He looked at his right hand. He had clenched it into a fist. As Rhodes watched, the hand opened involuntarily. There were red arcs on his palm where his fingernails had dug in. He could not feel it, could not feel much of anything. He raised his sensory perception back to normal and shut off the mist. He had taken enough.

Flawn hadn't really been in the simulator with them. She'd kept as far away from the company plex as she could for years. Which meant that one of the programmers had slipped her in, hopefully as a joke. Rhodes had been excited to see her, even as a flickering construct. Maybe she was trying to contact him in some way. That could be disaster all around if they got caught.

He sat up on the edge of the bed. Reality was seeping back in. He reached for the control on the bed and opaqued the ceiling, then slowly brought up the lights. The dark walls and furnishings consumed the brightness.

Vikashmo was sitting cross-legged on the floor in the next room. Rhodes took several measured steps toward her. Violet hair poked out from under her headset. She gave no indication of noticing him.

Vikashmo spent most of her free time hooked up to the sim-stim unit, checking out the competition. It was Rhodes's least favorite part of the job. Skipping back in time and wiring exploitables got his blood going. At least, it used to. The industry had grown a lot since he started. The public must spend all their leisure hours reliving choice moments from the past, considering the amount of product they took home.

He cleared his mind, then put on the other headset.

The smell of burning flesh was overpowering. A body hung limply from the stake, surrounded by flames. Several people in the crowd shouted in approval. The ropes burned through and the featureless black form tumbled into the fire, scattering sparks into the air. The smoke rose slowly into the gentle breeze.

Rhodes pulled off the headset and killed the power to the sim-stim unit. Vikashmo opened her eyes and looked at him.

"What are they marketing this as?" Rhodes asked.

"Death of Joan of Arc."

"Impossible. There hasn't been a window on that period yet. Anyone who tried would get sifted over the entire fifteenth century. With all the fake on the market it's diluting the value of our stuff, and Flawn's."

"I don't want to hear any more about Flawn. I'm sorry I brought her up before. It was a mistake." She stood, stretched, and walked into the bedroom.

"Fine. I won't breathe her name in your presence."

Vikashmo picked up the artificial llama skin and threw it on the bed. She pulled off her skin-tight red and black jumpsuit and lay down.

Rhodes took off his suit and slid in beside her. He admired her perfect body. Vikashmo had small breasts, but they were almost inhumanly firm and had large, prominent nipples. Her hips were wide and well rounded. She had high cheekbones and full lips. Most workaday slugs would have killed for an evening with her.

Rhodes ran his fingers through her pubic hair and sighed.

Vikashmo leaned over and bit his nipple; it was one of her favorite tricks. His, too.

Rhodes raised his adrenaline level, bringing the world into sharp focus. Vikashmo was working on him with her mouth. Once, the sight of her saliva glistening on his skin had given him an inner chill. Now, it was as if it were happening to someone else.

Vikashmo bit him again, hard. Rhodes remained silent. She gave up and looked at him. "All I expect from you is sex. I make absolutely no other demands on you. Your performance

level stinks. I think the people who made this match fucked up."
She punched him hard in the abdomen.

Rhodes winced and got up off the bed. "You'd better ease
up. My nonorganic parts belong to the company, and you don't
have the credit to buy me a new set of internals."

"If your internals worked as badly as your prick, you'd have
to get a new set."

"Sorry. I really am. I just don't know what's wrong. It's
nothing with you." Rhodes could feel the barrier between them.
There was no point in trying to do anything about it now.

Vikashmo activated the mist. She turned her back to him and
began masturbating. The drug did nothing to diminish her sex
drive. Not that long ago, he had been the same.

"Look, I'm going down to do some background on the
Titanic. I'll go over it with you tomorrow." Silence. "See you
later."

He put on his clothing and left.

The sign over the doorway read: THOSE WHO FORGET THE PAST
ARE DOOMED TO REPEAT IT. Flawn had wanted to change it to: TIME
IS MONEY. None of the company officials had ever seen the humor
in it.

The research section was empty. Rhodes walked down the
dimly lit central aisle to his cubicle. The adrenaline was wearing
off. He eased into the gel-foam recliner and pressed his hands in.
The imager above him crackled to life.

"Identification established. Please state the subject of your
study, speaking slowly and distinctly." The machine's voice was
a soft monotone.

"The sinking of the White Star Line vessel *Titanic.* April
1912."

"One moment please." Rhodes rubbed the bridge of his nose
as the CPU sorted through the data. He'd done some preliminary
background on the *Titanic.* The more he dug into it, the more
fascinating it became. "You may proceed," it said.

"Hm." Rhodes paused. "Request brief description of main
crew members, including whether they survived. Visuals when
available."

He flipped through them quickly, mentally noting those he
considered good prospects for recording. Flawn had taught him
to look at eyes. Intense eyes always made for a good subject.
Rhodes was more relaxed now. He couldn't get it up, but he
could still do his job.

The next image appeared. The man was young, with round features and deep-set eyes. He had brown hair and was clean-shaven. His build and height were average.

"Fuck me. Who the hell is that?"

"John Phillips, first Marconi operator," the machine said. "Nonsurvivor."

"The bastard ghost looks like me. Can't be. I just do not believe this." Rhodes tried to shake off his initial panic. "I want an enhancement on the visual."

Rhodes shook his head. Somebody had to be jerking him around.

"Image prepared."

"One/one scale. Slow rotation."

Rhodes watched the holographic construct turning above him. He and Phillips could be identical twins. The Marconi operator even had the too-serious look that Flawn had kidded him about.

"Nonsurvivor," he said slowly. The image continued to turn above him.

Rhodes buzzed Jain, but didn't wait for a reply before he went inside.

"Yes, Rhodes?" Jain was well over six feet tall and wore no hair. Her features were broad; her views narrow.

"It's about the *Titanic* job. I want in."

"I don't have any objection to that. However, I am curious about your sudden interest."

Rhodes sat down in the empty chair opposite Jain. "I was researching the *Titanic*. The first Marconi operator, Phillips, looks exactly like me."

Jain made an unpleasant noise. "Sounds like a good reason for your staying out of this one," she said.

"On the surface, yes. I was scared when I first saw Phillips. But something's wrong. I mean, I just don't buy it. Somebody doesn't want me going back on this one."

"I'm inclined to agree with you." Jain paused. "My sources tell me that Flawn is interested in the *Titanic*, too."

"That shouldn't surprise you. There won't be another window on this period for decades." Rhodes spoke in a casual tone. "That's another reason why I should go."

"You didn't let me finish." Jain stood and walked around behind him. "The lady herself is going back this time, or so my mole says."

"No kidding." Rhodes was't sure he believed it, but his pulse was hammering at the thought of seeing his old boss again.

"Vikashmo's going along, too. I'm not taking any chances if the old bitch tries to turn your head."

"I think that possibility is past." He looked up at Jain to see if she was buying it. She gave him an empty smile. "How many sources do you want?" he asked, bringing his heart rate back under control.

"Two. One in the boats, and one on the ship as it goes down." Jain brushed imaginary lint from her shoulder. "All staff are to get a deep scan tomorrow. No exceptions. I want to be sure no one's dumping our plans to Flawn. Might give her an advantage."

"I'd like another twenty-four hours' research, if possible." Rhodes exhaled slowly. "To check on Phillips."

"After the scan tomorrow you and Vikashmo go down and get your internals set." Jain moved back to the desk. "What you do with the rest of the day is your option. You two mess this up and I'll flush you to the Mesozoic for dinosaur bait."

It was cold and dark. Rhodes's first thought was that they had come in too high. He twisted his body to bring his feet underneath him. He felt his heart beat several times before he crashed to the ground. He rolled with the impact. The earth was damp, moist, and covered with tall grass. He hurt from the waist down, but could tell he was not seriously injured. Rhodes reduced his pain, sat up, and looked for his partner.

"Never more than six feet above the ground," said Vikashmo, loudly. "We must have been fifteen, eighteen feet up. I thought I was through with that kind of incompetence when I left the cartels. We could have broken our backs."

"Stop bitching and get dressed. Better fifteen feet up than one foot under." Rhodes stripped off his jumpsuit. He shivered as the cold air hit his sweaty skin. He opened his travel pack, removed his clothing one piece at a time, and dressed. "The next time you speak, my dear, make it appropriate to our present surroundings."

"Why waste the effort on you? I'll be fine when the time comes." She pulled on the corset and turned around so he could lace her up. She exhaled sharply as he tightened and tied the corset. "At least it's warm."

A dog barked. They both jumped.

Rhodes fumbled with his tie. He pointed to a dull glow

several miles away. "London. The sun should be coming up in a few hours. April eighth, 1912. We'll check the newspapers to make sure."

Vikashmo bit her lip and forced her right foot into a small black leather shoe. "These damn ghosts must have a high tolerance for pain. Or maybe they just get off on it."

"Let's go. We want both sources operational by this time tomorrow." Rhodes walked carefully down the hill. He could make out a wooden fence in the faint light. Even with the coming of day, his surroundings would have a dreamlike quality. His sensory input was the same as in real time, but there was an emotional block that made time travel unreal. They were taught to do whatever it took to finish the job. Nothing back there had any real moral consequence. At least, not to the company.

"Wait," Vikashmo wobbled down the hill after him, trying to button her navy serge dress.

Rhodes smiled as he straddled the fence. There was a road on the other side. It led toward the lights he hoped were London.

Rhodes hated the room. The wallpaper was peeling, although it had been pasted back up in several places. There was only one small window, facing the noisy street. The stained curtains and other furnishings stank of tobacco smoke. He minimized his olfactory input and stared at the ceiling.

Flawn had constantly badgered him to open up to the past, which was opposed to company training. She had even tried to seduce him when they were on the Marie Antoinette job. Just to prove sex was as good there as in real time. Rhodes said no, figuring it was bad policy to fuck the boss, no matter how much you cared about her. A week hadn't gone by since then that he wondered if he'd made the right decision. That was seven years ago. Or a few centuries, depending on how you looked at it.

He'd sent Vikashmo ahead to Southampton to book them into first class on the *Titanic*, and to rig a nonsurvivor if she got the chance. Rhodes had told Vikashmo to stay out of Flawn's way if they crossed paths, and wait for him to handle her. How he'd handle her was something he hadn't decided on. The company would have his ass if he got hold of Flawn and just let her go. She'd told several top company people, including Jain, to eat shit. Then she'd quit and formed her own operation. Rhodes's stomach burned. He'd just have to decide when the time came.

Rhodes was ready to light up the first ghost. He spent the

better part of the day finding her. The address he'd researched was right, but she was staying with her aunt in preparation for the trip. Rhodes used body language and charm to persuade the housekeeper to tell him where she was staying. The aunt's house was on the northeast outskirts of the city.

The girl had left with a young man well before sunset. Dinner, Rhodes figured. It was dark now. There were only two lights on in the house, one in the parlor and one upstairs. Probably her bedroom.

Rhodes shivered and waited. He sat in the spidery gray shadows under the trees, just off the path. The moon was less than half-full, and waning.

He heard slow clopping hooves in the distance. The sound stopped before reaching him. He heard a man laugh. Rhodes moved quietly through the trees toward him.

They were still seated in the carriage. The young girl wore a white dress with embroidered lace at the sleeves and a light blue shawl. Her brown hair was pulled into a bun. Rhodes could not see her face. The man wore a plain gray suit and was clean-shaven. He was well under six feet tall but well muscled.

"I'm so glad we were able to see each other tonight," the man said.

The woman whispered a reply. Rhodes could not hear her well enough to make it out. He continued to advance slowly, using the trees as cover.

"To tell the truth, I'm damned envious. An ocean cruise to the States. And on the *Titanic*. I only wish we could make the trip together." He laughed softly. "I don't think your family would approve."

"You mustn't joke about such things." She stepped down out of the carriage, resisting her companion's attempts to help her. "We haven't been nearly discreet enough as it is."

The young man jumped from the carriage and embraced her, lifting her off the ground as they kissed. Rhodes felt an instant of jealousy. He took an anesthetic capsule out of his pocket.

She pulled away and pushed hard against his chest. "None of that now. I have to go back to the house before they start to worry. Let go."

He let her down slowly. "They don't even know we're here. After I made a special effort to see you, I was hoping you'd say goodbye in a somewhat more passionate manner."

She pulled her shawl tightly about her shoulders. "Which was very presumptuous." She leaned forward and kissed him lightly on the cheek. "Now be off. I'm traveling tomorrow and need sleep."

"Shall I walk you to the door?"

She waved him off. "I'll see you when I return. I should have quite a few stories to tell."

The man climbed into the carriage. "Mind you don't get too well acquainted with any American gentlemen. I should hate to start another war with them."

She smiled and blew a kiss as he drove off, then walked up the path toward the house. Rhodes moved quickly through the undergrowth, cutting the distance between them. She paused and looked up at the night sky. Rhodes popped the capsule under her nose. She went limp in his arms without a sound. He carried her into the trees and laid her down on her stomach, then took the instruments from his bag. She would be out no more than fifteen minutes.

Rhodes felt for the base of her skull. He fixed the implanter to her neck and hit the sterilization switch. There was a cold hiss. He bent down to look at the instrument's small screen, which displayed a cutaway view of her skull. He positioned the cursor carefully and activated the implant mechanism. A microthin filament pierced through the flesh and underlying tissues, penetrating to the center of the brain. As the filament retracted, the implant extruded nerve-thin fibers to the various sensory centers. In thirty seconds it was finished. Rhodes removed the implanter. He examined the hairline for the wound. Rhodes felt a tiny moist bump. It would be gone by morning.

He checked the receiver. Bubbles were rising slowly inside the globe. It was activated and recording.

Rhodes brushed the dirt from her clothing and picked her up. She was only moderately pretty, but had full lips and long eyelashes. He was uneasy. It got worse with every implantation. He carried her to the edge of the trees and carefully laid her down. He took a step back, then bent down and kissed her on the lips.

He walked back through the trees toward the road and raised his sensory input to a dangerously high level. He concentrated on the girl, keeping as much of her with him for as long as possible.

Stupid, he thought. *She's just a ghost.*

The moon was sinking below the horizon when he reached town.

Rhodes felt suffocated. He shouldered his way slowly through the hundreds of ghosts on the Southampton station platform. It was almost as bad as the simulator. He didn't see Vikashmo.

A young boy tugged at his coat sleeve. "Excuse me, sir. Are you Mr. Rhodes?"

The boy had crooked teeth and dirty brown hair. His gray trousers and white shirt were torn and soiled. His eyes were hard. Rhodes figured he was about ten years old.

"Possibly. Does that concern you?"

The boy nodded and shoved a buff-colored envelope into Rhodes's hand. Rhodes unfolded the note inside:

> Vikashmo won't be able to meet you as she's in jail. Got you first-class accommodations. See you on board.
>
> Flawn

There was also a passport and a first-class ticket for the *Titanic*. Rhodes put them into his coat pocket and looked up. The boy was gone.

The *Titanic*'s three great steam whistles boomed out across Southampton harbor. People on the shore waved handkerchiefs at friends and relatives standing by the railing.

Rhodes could smell the sea. The decaying scent made him nauseated, but was also strangely intoxicating. The ghost world was coming into focus. He wasn't sure he liked it.

There was a sound like gunshots. Another ship, the *New York*, had broken loose from its moorings and was being drawn toward the *Titanic* by the suction of the big ship's engines. Passengers backed away from the rail. The *Titanic*'s engines stopped and a tug shoved the *New York* away only moments before she would have slammed into the *Titanic*.

Rhodes took a deep breath and walked down the deck toward the wireless cabin. The ghosts were still talking about the close call with the other ship. He paused outside, then knocked on the door.

A young man answered. His eyes were bright and intense; he would have been ideal for implantation. He had brown hair and pale skin. His tailored blue uniform was neatly pressed, and his shoes and buttons were brightly polished. "Can I be of service, sir?"

"You're John Phillips, first Marconi operator on this vessel?"

"That I am, sir. Is there something I can help you with?" He had his hand on the door and looked like he wanted to get back to work.

"No. Not at the moment. I may have a cable for you to send later and wanted to thank you beforehand for your assistance."

"Mr. Bride or I will be happy to take care of it for you, sir." He stepped back into the cabin. "Now, if you will excuse me."

"Of course," Rhodes said. He exhaled slowly. Other than having the same general height and build, Phillips looked nothing like him. Something else was going on. He knew Flawn was involved somehow, but he wouldn't get any answers until he found her.

The *Titanic* had less than nine hours to live. Rhodes's feet and legs ached. He had spent the entire voyage searching the ship. He checked the promenades, libraries, verandas, even the smoking rooms. Flawn was either staying out of sight or was not on the ship at all. He wanted like hell to see her, but his anticipation was beginning to fade into nervousness. It wasn't like Flawn to play it coy. Maybe she was setting him up.

It was early enough that he had no trouble getting a table at the À La Carte Restaurant. The evening shadows lengthened across the two-tone Dubarry rose carpeting. A trio composed of violin, cello, and piano played "The Blue Danube."

The bright light reflected off the glasses and starched white tablecloths, hurting his eyes. He wasn't used to sensory input hitting him this hard in the past. He picked up the crystal wineglass and flicked it with his finger. It rang with beautiful clarity. There was nothing this straightforward in real time.

The waiter cleared his throat. "Are you ready to order, sir?"

Rhodes folded up the menu. "I'd like the filets de soles à la tartare. And could you recommend a wine?"

"Very good, sir. Your wine has already been selected by another party." The waiter took the menu and smiled.

"Another party?" Rhodes looked around the room.

"Yes, sir. The lady stopped in our first day out, described you, and said you'd be in at least once during the course of the voyage. I'm sure you'll find her selection satisfactory."

Flawn knew Rhodes's weakness for French cuisine. "What did the lady look like?"

"Average height. Red hair. Very much a lady. Had an accent, much like your own." The waiter fidgeted. "If there is a problem . . ."

"No. No," Rhodes interrupted. "If you see her again, thank her for me."

The waiter nodded and left.

The fish was delicious, but Rhodes did little more than push it around the plate. He kept expecting Flawn to show up, and was playing over possible conversations in his head. The shadows gave way to darkness and he was still alone. He recalled several eyewitness accounts of the ship sinking.

"She broke forward, and the after part righted itself and made another plunge and went right down."

"Broke in two between third and fourth funnel. Stern section falls back horizontal, then tips and plunges."

He couldn't understand how anyone on the ship could give such a bloodless account of fifteen hundred people dying. Rhodes wished he could manage such emotional detachment. It had never been a problem before.

Flawn would have to show herself soon.

Rhodes lay on his bed. In less than half an hour the ship would strike the iceberg. He would have at least an hour to get to lifeboat number 1 or 7. Both had taken on men.

There was a knock at the door. He got up off the bed and opened it.

"Hello, Rhodes. Hope you hadn't given up on me."

She looked older than he had expected. Seven years ago she had been fighting off middle age. Now, the fight was over. The skin on her face and hands was wrinkled. She'd put on weight. Whatever tone her body once had was gone. Only her bright red hair and knowing eyes were the same.

"Thanks for the wine." He couldn't decide whether to hug her or kick her ass for staying hidden. He fought to subdue his jumbled feelings.

"You always did love it when I cooked French." She took off her ermine coat, revealing a black satin dress. "Mind if I sit down?"

"Anywhere you want. What the hell is going on?"

Flawn settled into the armchair and smiled. "What do you want to know about first?"

"Vikashmo."

"She came looking for me. Oh, I made sure I was highly visible. Didn't want to make it too hard on her. She broke into my hotel room. The two bodyguards I hired caught her and took her to the police. When she gets pulled back to real time, she'll be mad as hell. But I had to get her out of the way. This is just you and me. Like old times.''

''What do you want from me?''

''I need your help. Plain and simple. And I think you need mine.''

''I'm listening.''

''Don't play tough with me. We don't have the time. I always treated you better than anyone else because of how I felt. Bet you're still sorry you didn't screw me.''

''Yeah, well. I'm more sorry I was never able to get away from the company. A great lay is a lot easier to find than a great boss.''

''You always did know how to flatter me. How would you like to get away from the company, work for me?''

''I'd love it. But there's no chance of that. After you left they fixed it so they didn't lose anyone else. The few who've tried ended up in the glass house.''

''Trust me. I can manage it.'' She stood slowly. ''Let's stroll up to the bow. It's almost time.''

Rhodes helped her into her coat. ''Whatever you say.''

They stared out into the cold darkness. The night was clear and calm. Rhodes had no hat and his ears and nose were getting numb.

''What about Phillips?''

''I doctored the historical evidence. Not too much trouble really.'' She put her hand to her mouth and coughed.

''You knew I'd fight to be the one sent back.''

''Most jumpers would run from something like that. Not you. I knew you'd have to find out what was really going on.''

''And the trick in the simulator?'' He felt stupid talking shop, but the time they'd spent apart made the more important issues awkward.

''I've still got a few friends inside the company.'' She smiled.

Rhodes looked at his watch. It was 11:38 P.M. ''There,'' he said, pointing.

The twin-peaked iceberg was slightly darker than the night sky behind it, and directly in the ship's path. Rhodes watched it grow in size for several long moments. Someone in the crow's nest rang a bell three times.

''We'd better back off from here,'' he said, holding her by the elbow. In less than sixty seconds a ton of ice would cascade down onto the well deck. They walked back along the starboard promenade deck.

The *Titanic* backed her engines and began to swing slowly to port. They stood by the rail and watched. There was a muffled sound of buckling metal, then a splintering crash as the ice fell on the deck. The ice that some passengers would initially pick up as souvenirs. The berg, glistening dark blue, passed by almost close enough to touch.

He was cold inside. He had seen ghosts die before. Time and again. But this was different. He couldn't ignore the tragedy that was taking place around him.

People, dressed in their evening clothes, began coming out on the deck.

"Excuse me, sir." A man tapped him on the shoulder. "Did you see what happened?"

"I believe we've hit an iceberg." He managed a level tone.

"Really," said another. "How inconvenient. Do you think it's serious?"

Rhodes shrugged and rubbed his ears, trying to warm them.

"Let's go to my cabin," Flawn said.

Rhodes nodded. Inside, people were still drinking, playing cards, and listening to the band. In less than three hours, there would be only the Atlantic Ocean. They paused at the bottom of the grand staircase. On the landing was a large clock flanked by two carved figures. Underneath was inscribed: HONOR AND GLORY CROWNING TIME. They walked slowly up the huge wrought-iron staircase. He felt sick.

He recognized her when she stuck her head out of the doorway. The young woman looked even prettier in the warm light of the hallway. She was wearing her nightdress and had the blue shawl over her shoulders. She rubbed her eyes and looked in both directions down the hall.

"Did you hear something a few moments ago?" She looked more sleepy than concerned. She crossed her arms over her chest as they approached.

"I'm afraid there's been a rather serious accident," he said. "The ship has been badly damaged. You had best get into your warmest clothes and your lifebelt. They'll soon be loading the boats with women and children."

The girl stared at him blankly. "I don't believe this ship is in any serious trouble."

"Please do as I say, miss." Rhodes used his most authoritative manner. "I'm not in the habit of alarming young women. If

I tell you to get dressed and go to the boats, there's a good reason for it. Please hurry.''

She looked hard at him. ''As you wish, sir. If this is a joke, I shall surely report you to the captain.'' She closed the door.

Rhodes pressed his ear to the door. He heard a trunk being opened and the rustling of clothing. He was satisfied that she would do as he asked.

''Always a big heart where the ladies are concerned. Still, what you did might be what saved her.'' She pulled a key out of her handbag. ''My cabin is right down here.''

She was only a few doors down from him. How could he have missed her?

''Why now? Here?'' he asked when they were inside.

''Because I knew what it would do to you. You couldn't spend three days on this ship, knowing what was going to happen, and not be affected by it. The company works hard at building up that emotional block. I had to make sure it was broken down. That's why I couldn't see you until tonight. You would have paid too much attention to me and not enough to the people around you. They are people, Rhodes, just like you and me.''

''It worked. My training is shot to hell.''

She pulled a medkit out from under the bed. ''Okay, this is how it's going to work. I'm going to pop out your company chip and replace it with the one from inside me. It's an easy procedure, won't take more than fifteen minutes.'' She opened the kit and began removing the necessary instruments. ''Vikashmo doesn't know you don't really look like Phillips. The company will figure you're dead. You can go back to real time and take over my operation.''

''But that means you're staying here. Why the fuck would you want to do that? I need you. You know that.''

She began removing her clothing. ''You want me around, but you don't need me. I'm old. I deserve a rest. This is the perfect era for a wealthy woman to live out her final years.''

''Do it for me. Please.'' He wasn't above begging at this point.

''I can't. There's only one chip. I knew you'd react this way.'' She turned around. ''Now help me get out of these things.''

''Damn. I haven't seen you for years. Now you go to all this trouble just to spend a couple of hours with me.'' He undid the laces. They left red welts on her aging skin. ''Why?''

"Two reasons. I want you to take over for me. And I wanted to say goodbye." She patted him on the arm. "Besides, I needed somebody who gives a shit about these people. We don't implant ghosts anymore."

"What then?"

She raised her hand as if to slap him, then placed it against his forehead and pushed. "Don't play stupid. We rig ourselves. Works fine. My techs will wire you up when you get back. Doesn't hurt at all."

Rhodes thought of all the people he'd implanted. "I'm not crazy about the idea."

"Free ride's over. We don't have the right to do it the company way. It's rape. No, it's even worse. What could be more personal and private than someone's thoughts and senses? You're suffering from the company's sick indoctrination techniques. Imagine a playback of how you're feeling right now as a mere commercial property. These people have their own lives. They're not a recording medium for jerks back in real time who're too afraid to live their own lives."

"No shit." He removed his coat.

Flawn worked quickly. Rhodes felt like she was drawing on his skin with a marker. There was only a faint tingling. He heard his chip land on the floor and bounce away.

She opened the closet and handed him a lifebelt. "This is for you. It's a kind of miniature lighter-than-air balloon. You activate it by pressing this button and sliding it to the right."

Rhodes took the belt. It was slick and lightweight and smelled of her perfume. "How long will it keep me up?"

"Long enough. You get pulled back at 2:35. So you'll see everything."

He tied on the lifebelt and tugged on the straps, testing the knots. "Let's go."

As they walked toward the elevator the doors opened. The boy operating the lift was pale. He stared at their lifebelts. "What deck, sir?"

"Boat deck, please," he replied.

The elevator stopped. The boy opened the door and tried to smile. Flawn put a hand on his arm. "I shouldn't stay too long, if I were you."

"It's my post, ma'am. I'll be here until the next shift. I'm sure everything will be all right."

The ship was slightly down in the bow. Sailors were removing the canvas covers from the lifeboats. Rhodes walked to the railing and looked down. The icy water slapped against the hull seventy-five feet below.

"It's a long way down," Flawn said.

"Yeah." He looked into her eyes. "Time for you to go."

"Yes." She pulled a recording globe from her handbag. "When you miss me, this might help some." She rubbed her eyes with a gloved hand. "Damn. Damn. Damn. I knew this wouldn't be easy."

Rhodes closed his hand around the globe. He hugged her as tightly as he thought she could stand. "I don't have anything to give you. Nothing at all."

"Peace of mind." She kissed him. Rhodes bit her lip softly and sucked on her tongue as she put it in his mouth. He wanted her. Wanted her more than Vikashmo or any other woman he had ever known. And he would never have her.

"I blew it," he said as she pulled away. "Seven years ago. I blew it big time."

"No, you didn't. You did what was right." She traced his eyebrows with her finger. "Now go and kick the company's ass for me."

"I'll do my best."

"Goodbye." She backed slowly away from him.

"Goodbye."

She walked down the deck to where the sailors were cranking out lifeboat number 6.

Rhodes stood by the railing and watched as Flawn and several others, mostly women and children, were loaded into the boat. He felt dead and empty, and stared in silence as the craft was slowly lowered out of his sight. Flawn was the best part of him and she was gone forever. Only the burden of her trust in him was left.

"Ahem." The voice behind him was female. Rhodes turned to face her. "I must apologize for my earlier behavior. It appears you are not the prankster I suspected you of being." The young woman gave him a nod and a slight smile.

Something in Rhodes warmed and began to come back to life. He offered her his elbow. She took it and he walked her down the deck to where the next lifeboat was being filled.

The stars were as bright as he had ever seen them. The sea was dark and deadly cold, dotted with pinpricks of human life. The bow of the *Titanic* was down by at least twenty degrees now. The lifeboats, except for the collapsibles, were gone.

Many of the passengers had begun to panic, scrambling for the stern. The polished wooden deck made movement dangerous. Those still aboard fought the sea and one another for another few moments of life.

The baker, eyes dilated, walked slowly up the deck toward him His drunken state seemed to benefit his progress.

The band played *Songe d'Automne* as the water hissed up the ship's wooden deck.

Rhodes locked his arms around the railing. The stern was coming up abruptly as she sank by the bow. People were beginning to scream. Some were jumping overboard.

The sea was calm and smooth. He could not see any of the lifeboats or hear their oars in the water.

The ship was almost perpendicular to the water. Rhodes hauled himself over the railing and switched on his lifebelt. The superstructure sprang out fifteen feet from either shoulder. The batwing balloon shape filled with gas and lifted him slowly upward.

The boilers came loose and crashed through the ship, sounding like thunder. The ship groaned. Metal screamed and snapped as the front section of the *Titanic* broke away. It disappeared into a cloud of steam. The stern, still covered with people, righted itself. After a minute it began its slow descent into the water. Rhodes watched it below his dangling feet. The sea was foaming around it, a shimmering halo. There was a grating noise and the ocean closed over the ship's stern, sending out only the smallest of ripples.

Rhodes saw the light of another ship to the north. He knew it would remain there until morning.

He felt in his vest pocket for the young girl's recording globe. He looked at it briefly. His internals pulsed with warmth and he felt the familiar disembodied tugging. He dropped the globe.

He was gone before it disappeared into the water.

PHILIPPA'S
HANDS

NANCY KRESS

Here's the beginning of another group of themati-
cally-linked stories. The following four pieces all
relate in some way to alien contact, though each
addresses the subject very, very differently.

Nancy Kress is one of the truly fine writers to
come into prominence during the '80s. Her short
fiction has appeared everywhere and she won a
Nebula Award in 1985 for her short story "Out of
All Them Bright Stars." Her most recent novel,
An Alien Light, was published this year. Nancy is
a senior copywriter for an advertising firm in
Rochester, New York and occasionally teaches
at the State University of New York at Brockport.

"Philippa's Hands" is a chilling story of contact
with the unknown and of decisions that are nearly
impossible to make.

It is not contrary to reason to prefer the destruction of the whole world to the scratching of my finger.

—David Hume

They came again at dawn, like last time, distilling out of the washed-out gloom under the bedroom window. Or perhaps they came through the window, floating through the chilly glass and worn flowered curtains—how could you tell? They were crying again. They were always crying. Philippa thought, through her sleepy dread, *I could see if the curtains are damp. Then I could tell.*

The bandage still covered her right middle finger from last time.

They stood grouped at the foot of her bed, three rosy transparent hideous shapes that might have been old women. Or might not. Pinkish areas would swell into sketchy pseudopods suggesting a bent arm, a shawl draped over a head, a hunched back. Then the swellings would shift before she could be sure. Only the tears were constant, great rosy globes of sorrow welling and falling in arcs so beautiful that Philippa had to look away. In the morning, when it was all over, the carpet would still be soaked clear through.

No no no no no no no no no went the part of her that never understood, the most part, and her left hand clutched at the edge of the quilt. The central blue vein sprung out sharply. On the back of her hand two liver spots, for some reason clear in the gloom, echoed brown stains on the quilt that not even her diluted bleach on a clean rag had been able to touch.

One of them stepped forward. This time it was the one on the left. Philippa never knew. Their hierarchy, if they had one, was a mystery to her. If they were angels they should have a hierarchy, shouldn't they? It was one of the reasons she had given up on the idea that they were angels.

Philippa let go of the quilt and clasped her hands together to pray, but of course she couldn't do it. She never could while they were in the room. It wasn't only that fear kept her from concentrating properly. It was that she forgot what prayers were for, whom they were addressed to, what the whole thing was supposed to accomplish. There was no room in this for prayer, a thing that left the edges of hope intact and a little fuzzy. You never really knew if prayers were answered or not. Here you always knew, in concrete terms: this for that. It was a bargain, a contract, a hard Yankee deal.

She reached over to switch on the bedside lamp. Once, the first time, she had actually thought that would make them vanish. Things that go bump in the night, begone with the light. She hadn't known. She hadn't known anything. She had burned with terror, smoked black at the edges with it, ignited with the fear that either she was going crazy or she wasn't. She hadn't known anything. And 416 people had died.

At the click of the lamp switch the three glowing nebulous old women drew closer together. They always did that. They also cried harder, the rosy tears silently welling, coursing a short way down the glow, trembling a minute like perfect-cut rubies come alive to breathe in sorrow, breathe out pain. Then they fell.

Philippa waited.

The one who had stepped forward—although now that the light was on and they had moved into a bright amorphous huddle it was even more difficult to see where one left off and the next began—reverently laid the clipping on the foot of the bed. Against the faded chintz of the quilt, inherited from Philippa's mother, the newsprint looked almost white. The rosy huddle stepped back. Tears flowed.

"Who are you?" Philippa said to the old women, but not because she expected an answer. Just for something to say. In the still room her voice sounded rusty. Well, it was rusty. You don't speak when there's nobody to speak to.

The second and third times, Philippa had torn apart the library in Carter Falls, looking for those clippings. She had read every newspaper the library carried, and then the ones you had to use the microfiche machine for, sticking her head into the strange contraption and trying at least to match the typeface to the pieces of paper in her hand. She had even thought of driving into the college library in Plattsburgh, but it had been hard enough to get into Jim's car for the first time in the eight months since the funeral and drive just to Carter Falls. The thought of the trucks on Route 3 undid her. She had no driver's license, no need to go to Carter Falls, and no answer. The clipping was nowhere. It was never anywhere. This new one wouldn't be, either, until the grocery boy delivered next week's *Time*.

About four inches square, the clipping on the bed was paper-cut sharp on two joining edges, furred on the other two, as if it had been torn from the bottom right corner of a page. But then there should be a date or page number or part of the paper's name, shouldn't there? Philippa could see without moving that there wasn't. The clipping was uncreased, unyellowed, crisp. But that made sense, since it hadn't appeared yet.

Made sense. O my god.

She could curse but not pray.

Another thing she knew she couldn't do, not until it was all over, was look at the crucifix on the wall. Just flat couldn't swivel her head that way. The whole wall—faded green-striped wallpaper, her grandmother's bureau with the chipped green paint and newel-post mirror and hand-tatted dresser scarf, Douay Bible on the scarf beside the cut-glass bowl holding hairpins and rubber bands—was off limits, until this was over. The first time, she had even thought this made a terrible sense. If the three weird women came from the Antichrist, the Evil One, then of course she would be barred from looking at the crucifix while they were there . . . she had been so stupid. And so afraid.

The clipping bore only one small headline. With type that small, and coming from the bottom of a page, it must not be too important. That was a good sign. "An outward and visible sign of an inward and spiritual grace."

Now how had *that* bit of catechism gotten through? Startled, Philippa tried again to clasp her hands for prayer. Her left ring finger, where once Jim's band had gone and where she would have worn the silver band making her a Bride of Christ, looked to her bonier and whiter than the rest. But that was just trashy fancy. It was important to keep clear what was fancy, what was not.

Philippa slid out of bed. That too was necessary; the clipping couldn't be reached otherwise, no matter how far forward she leaned. Her long flannel nightdress, the nap worn off at the elbows, wound itself around her hips. She jerked it down with a quick glance at the sobbing women, who only went on sobbing in their eerie silence.

Impatience stabbed Philippa. They weren't the ones going to do it. Some people just liked carrying on. Some like that from the parish had tried to visit her after Jim, clutching her hand and sniffing enough to turn your stomach, when they had never come near Jim during his illness. One visit was all she let them try.

She picked up the news clipping. The paper felt heavier than the ones the grocery boy delivered once a week. The type was smaller, too: serious type, and brief:

> MARRAKECH—An earthquake here earlier today killed at least 34 people, including 22 children. Although officials at the Seismographic Institute in Rabat say the quake measured no more than 5.8 on the Richter scale, structures it toppled include a government-sponsored orphanage which stood near its epicenter.
>
> The orphanage housed 60 children and 17 adults. Rescue crews working around the clock have
> *Please turn to page 4A*

Philippa closed her eyes. She couldn't picture the orphanage, the quake, any of it. She didn't know where Marrakech was, although she vaguely remembered a song about it when she had been in high school, the kind of song Johnny Matthis had never sung. Was it in Asia? Africa? Had the orphanage been white-washed, with a dome? But it was only their pretty heathen churches that had domes, wasn't it?

Twenty-two dead children.

Philippa opened her eyes and looked at the ghostly wailing women. Suddenly they reminded her of the black-clad old ladies attending 6:00 A.M. Mass at St. Stanislaw's, every single morning of her childhood. Every single morning. Shuffling up the steps in heavy, black-laced shoes, dipping holy water with two gnarled fingers from the font by the carved wooden door, lighting endless candles for the dead. What had there been in those pious figures to fill a child with such horror?

"All right, then," Philippa said, "I'm ready. Tell me."

The figure on the right raised her sketchy arm. A line of rosy light stretched from its end to Philippa's left hand, ending at the first joint of her index finger. A faint tingle, and the glowing line vanished. The knife appeared on the quilt: the same ordinary, murderously sharp hunting knife as always, the same one Philippa could have bought at Wayne Clarke's in Carter Falls. The old women wailed without comfort, their rosy tears cascading to the floor, pooling on the carpet, pristine in falling and sodden when done. Philippa looked at the whole spectacle with sudden distaste.

"Oh, stop that racket!"

Which was funny, because there was no noise.

Twenty-two dead children: babies with their skulls crushed before the soft spots had closed, toddlers carrying . . . whatever toys toddlers carried in Marrakech.

She picked up the knife and hacked off her left index finger at the first joint.

Much later, the doorbell rang. Tuesday—the weekly grocery delivery. Philippa sat weak and sick in the old rocker with the bottom rung missing, her head thrown back against a tied-on cushion. The grocery boy wouldn't come in; he would leave the groceries on the porch and take away the check made out to Hall's Superette, as he always did.

She had forgotten to put a check out on the porch.

The bell rang again. Philippa tried to think but the pain still wouldn't let her. She sat pressing several folds of a bed sheet to the amputated joint; as the outer folds reddened she had moved on to a different section. Much of the sheet was red, and the air swelled with the rich, metallic scent of blood. But Philippa knew she would not lose enough blood to die, would not get gangrene in the amputated tissues, would not even faint from shock. So many things that never happened. She sat pressing the blood-sodden sheet to her maimed left hand with the thumb and one whole finger of the right, and listened to the doorbell ring.

A school-bus crash in Calgary, a cholera epidemic along the Indus River, a dam burst in Colorado, a political massacre in El Salvador.

Could the grocery boy see through the dingy curtains covering the front window?

And the two she hadn't believed, the first times: the bridge collapse in Florida, the crop failure in a Chinese province she couldn't pronounce.

The curtains had a hole just above the windowsill nearest the door; the fabric had been clawed through by a cat that had run away the day after Jim's funeral. Jim's cat. If the grocery boy stooped, he could peer through the hole. Philippa tried to inch her rocker in the other direction, but the effort just made her dizzy. It would be a few hours yet before she could eat anything, clean up the bedroom, change the quilt. She was running out of quilts.

The doorbell stopped ringing, and the knob rattled. Philippa made a small noise; from the rocker she could see that the chain was off. But the door was locked, she was sure of that, she'd locked it last night.

The door heaved twice, the first heave curving the wood gracefully inward like the bow of a violin, the second springing it back on its hinges and bouncing it so hard against the faded wallpaper that the doorknob punched a round hole in the plasterboard beneath. A hand caught the door on the rebound. It wasn't the grocery boy from Hall's Superette but Sam Hall himself, walking into the room with the deliberate, shambling step Philippa knew since high school. He wore his mechanic's coveralls, boots leaving sloppy snow on the carpet and grease at the knees in splotches like the outlines of distant countries.

Philippa glared at him, furious and embarrassed. He gazed mildly around the room, and she had the idea that he missed nothing, saw it all through to the buckling bones: her mother's clock ticking heavily in the corner, the piles of newspaper furred with dust, the ashtray from Niagara Falls filled with paper clips and pennies and thread, the rounded corners of the overstuffed sofa tufted with dangling buttons, the unwashed curtains and scrupulously washed ceramic Madonna, with its beautiful draperies and foolish simper. Saw it all, as if it were the engine of a truck he was taking apart behind the Superette, removing one part after another in his slow way, running a careful thumb over each to feel its essential soundness under the necessary grease. Then he looked again at Philippa, at the bloody sheet and four healed stumps, and behind his eyes moved something that she didn't like.

"Philippa, you oughtn't be doing that to yourself here."

She meant to say furiously, *And you oughtn't be breaking and entering into people's houses, Sam Hall!* but those weren't the words that came. Instead she heard herself say, "There wasn't anything else I could do," and after that the mortifying tears—in front of Sam Hall!—rolling hot and stinging on her dry skin, spraying outward when she swiped at her dripping nose, turning pink where they fell on the bloody sheet in her hands.

They talked about it only once. Sam Hall took her to Mass on Sunday, Mass at a reasonable 10:00 A.M., and he didn't assume the five dollars he put in the collection plate was for both of them. Philippa liked that. When women she hadn't seen since the funeral rushed up afterward to exclaim over her hands and gawk at Sam, he took Philippa firmly by the elbow and guided her back toward his truck. After church came a movie in Carter Falls, a thing neither of them found funny, about people chasing and killing one another over something that fit inside a computer. The movie was redeemed by a drive along the lake on an afternoon bursting with lilacs. Then came a dinner at the Apple Tree in Carter Falls, and another one with Sam's grown daughter home from college in Plattsburgh. The daughter never mentioned Philippa's hands. Another movie, only this one was funny, another dinner out, a political picnic for John Crane, who had gone to school with Philippa and Sam and Jim and now was running for county sheriff. And all those weeks they talked about it only once, in Sam's truck, parked in Philippa's driveway just before she went inside and he started the long drive back to town.

Philippa said abruptly out of one of their long comfortable silences, "Do you believe in aliens?" The word sounded foolish there in the cab of the pickup, so she added, "Like in the movies?"

"Nope," Sam said.

"Ghosts?"

"No."

"Angels?"

"In Bible times."

"Not now?"

"No."

Philippa nodded. "I wanted to be a nun, after Jim died. Can you imagine? I got books to study, and I wrote to the convent at Plattsburgh."

"What did they say?"

"They said they were a teaching order, and I wasn't a teacher."

Sam slapped at a mosquito above his collar. A moth lit on

the windshield: ghostly pale wings translucent in the light from the porch. He said, "People do weird things sometimes. From loneliness."

He glanced at her hands. Philippa laid them defiantly on the dashboard, side by side. "It wasn't from loneliness." That was true.

He considered this. She breathed in the smell of his shirt—cigarettes and 30-weight oil and fabric softener. Finally he said, "You needed rescuing."

Rescuing! Hysterical laughter rose in her, heady as whiskey. Rescuing! Her! When it was she who had saved . . . single-handedly . . . *single-handedly* . . . Philippa put her palm over her mouth and leaned forward against the dashboard. As soon as she shifted, the moth flew toward the porch light.

"Philippa," Sam said, "Philippa—" She knew then it was all he would ever say, all he would ever ask, and that she didn't have to answer. It was all right if she never answered. She shifted the other way, to lean against his shoulder.

"Sometimes there just isn't any choice," she said.

"Uh-huh," he agreed, and laid his hand on her breast, and she heard the sudden laughter in his slow voice.

They came at dawn, three days before Philippa's wedding. The window was open, and the room smelled of a heavy rich August night too warm for dew. Three glowing nebulous figures at the foot of the bed, welling with rosy tears. Philippa woke and her spine went rigid.

The one on the left laid the newspaper clipping on the bed. The bedspread was new, a frivolous green quilted in shiny squares and edged with six inches of eyelet ruffle. Sam was painting the bedroom green. Through the outlines of the wailing women Philippa could see the outlines of the paint cans, both ghostly against the bare plaster Sam had already stripped and washed.

This time the clipping was large, more than half a page, the headline in thick black letters. Right and left edges were clean, top and bottom torn. The top, Philippa thought: where the name of the newspaper would be. She never would find out what it was called. Against the bright shiny green of the bedspread the paper looked unnaturally white, like someone about to faint.

No no no no no no.

Philippa's feet slid out of bed. The carpet had been rolled up for the painting. The bare wide-planked hardwood floor was cool enough to make her toes curl under. The newspaper felt light and dry in her hand, even lighter than paper should feel. Without turning on the light, Philippa carried the clipping across the room to the window, where there was just barely enough light to read it.

TWA JET CRASHES IN BOSTON HARBOR
FATALITIES FEARED HIGH

BOSTON—A TWA 707 jetliner failed to take off at Logan Field late last night and plummeted into Boston Harbor, killing at least 257 people. The plane, flight 18 from Boston to Washington, achieved takeoff speed but failed to leave the ground at the end of the runway, which ended at the harbor. The plane sped forward and sank in the 63-degree water.

The jetliner remained two-thirds submerged in the water, enabling at least 9 passengers and airline personnel to escape through the two doors they managed to open.

"There was this roar and then a huge splash," said Elizabeth Brattle, who witnessed the crash from the deck of her sailboat moored in the harbor. "Waves rolled in, nearly swamping the boat. You could hear people screaming. It was horrible."

By 20 minutes after the disaster, diving teams were on the scene to assist in the recovery. Divers are expected to remain on the scene throughout the night.

The cause of the plane's failure to lift into the air is unknown. TWA spokesperson Richard Connington expressed shock and concern but cautioned against speculation that
Please turn to back of section

There was a second article, an eyewitness account from one of the passengers who escaped, and a picture of the drowning plane. Philippa didn't read the second article. The three rosy hideous women bent nearly double with wailing and grief, and their beautiful tears pooled on the wooden floor. Philippa watched them, feeling their pain, feeling all the pain and terror of the great plane reaching the end of the runway and still rolling along the ground, of the dizzying lurch into the water, the sudden impact. Did the water come in right away? Did the lights go out? People screaming, choking in the darkness, and later that other choking and darkness, of the survivors.

Sam had taken down the crucifix when he took down the ancient dingy needlepoint worked by one of Philippa's great-aunts and the framed painting of a woodland brook that Philippa had bought at The Art Shoppe in Carter Falls. She wondered if she would have been able to see the crucifix this time. The pink thread of light shot out from one of the crying women, Philippa couldn't see which one, and touched the first joint of her right thumb.

At the base of the thumb, just below the knuckle, was a burn blister where she had foolishly touched the pan taking an apple pie for Sam out of the oven. Sam, eating the pie at her kitchen table. Holding the square of heated metal of the wallpaper stripper against this room, while she followed him with the scrub bucket. Holding the tips of her fingers while they watched TV and never saying anything against them, anything at all about stupidity or pride or need.

At least 257 people. "You could hear people screaming."

The knife appeared on the bed. The glowing women cried and wailed. All the sorrow of the world seemed to flow through them, the world beyond this room, that Philippa had once thought to renounce and go be a middle-aged nun because there was nothing left here anyway.

Philippa whispered, "No," and the knife vanished.

She stood shivering in a sudden breeze from the window as the silently keening women also vanished, leaving only the pool of rosy tears on the scarred floor that she and Sam planned to wax shining and hard and golden.

REFLECTIONS IN A MAGNETIC MIRROR

KEVIN J. ANDERSON AND

DOUG BEASON

Really well-written hard science fiction stories are tough to come by (which is why there are so few in this book). "Reflections in a Magnetic Mirror," however is a very, very fine one, a powerful blend of scientific mystery, compassion and humanity.

Kevin J. Anderson has had over 130 short stories, articles, and reviews published in various magazines and anthologies, including *The Magazine of Fantasy and Science Fiction, Amazing Stories, Dragon,* and *Astronomy.* His first novel, *Resurrection, Inc.,* has recently been published. Doug Beason holds a Ph.D. in physics and currently heads up a plasma physics laboratory in Albuquerque, New Mexico. His short fiction has appeared in several magazines and anthologies, including *Amazing Stories* and *New Destinies.* Kevin and Doug have collaborated on one other published story and are currently working on a novel together.

> The Church questions whether this "anomaly" is even alive. And if alive, we quesiton whether it is intelligent. And if intelligent, we insist— *without qualification*—that it has no Soul. Man cannot create a Soul; that is for God alone.
>
> —Cardinal Robert K. Desmond

As the deuterium passed through the opening, the discharge bombarded it from all sides. Electrons were torn from their nuclei, heating the fuel-stuff in the plasma until the elementary particles fused together. The reaction sustained itself. Billionths of a second passed—an eternity to the plasma—while lasers delicately probed the inner workings of the maelstrom.

His own thought processes moving infinitely slower, Keller stood in silent awe, praying that it would *work*.

The particles bounced back and forth in the chamber, billions of times a second, unable to escape past the giant yin-yang magnets on either side of the Magnetic Mirror Fusion Facility. Long-range coulombic forces sculpted the plasma, creating swirling, complex interactions.

"And?" Keller asked.

The technician reached up to the screen directly in front of him, touching a blue icon that opened up to display two columns of numbers happily glowing green. "Everything's perfect, Gordon. Blessed be the Holy Laws of Physics."

Keller frowned at how the technician—all Californians, in fact—too often used his first name: especially in this, his moment of triumph after so long. He wanted to feel important.

In the background, filling the stuffy room with a much-needed festive atmosphere, two operators hoarsely sang, "Fusion power, here we come!" to the tune of "California, Here I Come."

Then someone else called from behind another barricade of control consoles. "There it goes again!"

The singing abruptly stopped.

Keller reached forward to touch icons on the top two screens, opening up another numerical display while the second screen showed the data from varying perspectives.

"Glitches again!" the technician cursed. "But they're different from the last time."

The data repeated itself in oddly distorted cycles. The plasma seemed to be on the verge of blowing up as the instabilities on the screen grew, then decayed, as if a dancer were lightly touching the boundary of a dance-space, feeling her way. It seemed almost as if the plasma was testing its enclosure, exploring.

Keller stared at the screen, silently urging the anomalies to go away, but knowing they would not heed him. He wanted the experiment to be *over*, successfully completed at long last—he had driven so hard, worked his brain to the bone. And at thirty-three, he felt he was getting to be a little too old to be the proverbial whiz kid anymore. When they brought the MMFF online, the damned instabilities were always there . . . but they were *always* different. Whatever the hell they were. He sighed and checked different readouts. In disgust, he walked to the windowless wall, wishing he could stare through the concrete cinder blocks to where, half a block away, a gigantic vacuum chamber held the eye of the storm, a sustained fusion reaction in a plasma confined by magnetic mirrors.

"But it *does* run? It's stable?" Keller asked without turning, sounding half-defeated.

"Sure, it runs. Close enough for government work," the technician answered.

Keller placed his hands behind his back and mentally tried to think of something historic or profound to say. "Good," was all he could manage.

> This could prove to be extremely dangerous or extremely embarrassing. I don't want it to be either.
> —Confidential memo to laboratory management, regarding the MMFF anomalies.

Keller shielded his eyes from the glaring, obnoxious lights. Three camcorders, eleven microphones, and sixty people crowded in a conference room that had been intended for forty-five, waiting for him to speak. Many of the reporters fingered their laminated temporary ID badges, looking with some concern at the dosimeters attached to them. Keller tried to kill the butterflies in his stomach. The DOE bigwig on his right grinned broadly and finally removed his arm from around Keller's back. Just before entering the crowded room, the DOE man had force-fed him some coaching for the cameras. "And for God's sake, don't *mumble*!"

The official held up his hands, quieting the crowd. "If you could please hold it down, Dr. Keller can say something about the Magnetic Mirror Fusion Facility." Silence was a long moment coming, but the DOE man finally continued. "Gordon, why don't you tell us what's so special about the MMFF?"

Keller leaned forward, cleared his throat, and tried not to look at all the faces looking at him. "Well, to start with, thank you for coming. This really *is* important, I think.

"The MMFF is the simplest design of all mirror machines: as you can see from the diagrams in the press kits, it's basically a long tube with a special type of powerful magnet on each end. The magnets act like mirrors, bouncing the plasma back and forth, confining it long enough so that fusion occurs. Once our yin-yang mirrors were perfected, all we had to do was turn it on. The MMFF doesn't have a lot of the instabilities associated with other mirror devices, such as the tokamak and spheromak machines."

The DOE official cut him off, interrupting with a large grin on his face. "And best of all, this machine uses *no* dangerous heavy elements such as uranium or plutonium. We all remember Three Mile Island. But TMI—and all other commercial nuclear power plants—rely on nuclear *fission*, rather than its opposite, nuclear *fusion*. With fusion power, five gallons of sea water could provide electricity for a town the size of Livermore for a week. Once we can bring MMFF sites up commercially, it's a no-lose situation."

The DOE man clapped Keller on the shoulder, then turned back to the audience. "Dr. Keller has been assigned to continue studying the MMFF, and he will release his complete findings at the November APS meeting in New York. To reiterate, the MMFF machine you saw a few moments ago is purely a feasibility study, but a study that has achieved the breakeven point in fusion energy. The next step is a facility that can be used for the *commercial* generation of power. And I'm sure we'll be asking Dr. Keller for his advice and assistance during the next phase of the project. And on that note, allow me to introduce Dr. Zel'dovich, the director of the MMFF-2, currently in the planning stages."

Scattered applause came as Keller turned, then was ushered away from the head table and into the background. He stood and watched, feeling sheltered and hidden by the other people. The fusion facility worked, despite the unexplained glitches, and he wondered if it was all over, if he had indeed completed the purpose of his life . . . if the heaviness inside him would grow any larger. When he realized he wouldn't be missed in the conference room, Keller slipped away.

> What is Life? What is Death? For that matter,
> how many angels can dance on the head of a
> pin? You can argue yourself silly, and I don't
> really *care* what the answer is. Right now, I
> want to know what the hell we should do about
> that *Thing* in there!
> —Dr. F. Gordon Keller, MMFF staff meeting.

Keller stared at the small radio for a long moment, but ultimately decided to keep the house silent. Though he didn't particularly want to hear the depressing sound of the rain outside, he wasn't sure he was in the mood to hear music or another human voice, either. Keller slipped into his pair of faded, threadbare old brown cords and a lightweight cotton shirt—his "around home" clothes—but he couldn't shed the thoughts of his work as easily as he shed his clothing. He heaved a sigh.

Glitches.

He placed a TV dinner with a fancy-sounding French name into the microwave, carelessly jabbing at the timer pad. They had been so *careful* designing the huge magnets, the fusion chamber, the diagnostics. What the hell was going on? The

plasma theorists were just as stumped as the computational physicists to explain the anomalies.

The microwave sent rhythmic pulses of electromagnetic radia-
tion into his food, warming it. Keller muttered to himself that he
would never have received a Ph.D. in physics if he'd set up his
plasma experiments the same careless way he cooked his food.
But at least when he cooked a frozen dinner in the microwave
oven, it left him with no surprises . . . disappointment maybe,
but certainly no surprises.

The anomalies just didn't make any sense.

He decided not to switch on the lights while he ate. He sat
alone in the shadows, surrounded by the gray-washed dimness of
the rainy windows. He stared absently at one of his son's crayon
drawings attached to the refrigerator door with an old happy-face
magnet. The drawing was somewhat curled around the edges and
starting to yellow, but he hoped he wouldn't be able to notice
that in the dim light. Three months—had it really been three
months? He couldn't even remember if he had answered Shelley's letters.

It wasn't so long ago that she'd been the most important
thing in his life; and when Justin was born, the little boy had
taken over that special place in his heart. And what did Keller
have now? The MMFF was online, and he finally had time to
spend with his family . . . time that had been so precious to him,
so precious that he'd put his wife and son on hold just to
complete the project—but now Shelley was gone, with Justin.

Some things just went wrong—there was nothing you could
do about it, no equation you could solve, nothing you could
explain with a simple, clear-cut answer.

But the plasma anomalies were a *physics* problem. They
were solvable—they had an answer, an explanation. And if he
didn't spend too much time wallowing in self-pity, he could
probably clear his head and figure out some simple thing that
was causing these anomalies, these embarrassments. He had a
Ph.D.—Piled Higher and Deeper, in layman's terms—that meant
he was supposed to *know* something about physics.

That had been his scholarly battlecry for so long. *Get the
Ph.D.* The incessant pushing, grinding out problem sets, spending long hours at the lab. It was the single most important thing
in his life, with his entire world centered around that one goal:
Get the Ph.D. He couldn't settle for anything less. And then,
after actually getting the doctorate, it was as if all his personal
drive had been snatched like a rug from under his feet.

He put down his fork and stared down at his wrists. Two slashes, running across the veins, had healed years ago to thin white scars, now almost invisible in the dim light by the dining-room table. He'd spent so much time in the physics books that he couldn't even kill himself right; the cuts were supposed to be made *along* the vein, so that the bleeding would be more profuse. He knew that now. The shock, the jolting reality of obtaining his degree—getting what he wanted more than anything else in the world—had left him with nothing else to live for. At the time, it had seemed so coldly logical: he had achieved his one goal in life, and what else was there left to do? It sounded trivial now, but it did help explain his depression about finally completing the MMFF.

But what were the damned glitches?

Depression—it was such a nice excuse. He could still remember his mother, but at the time he had been too young to know what "cancer" was; watching her die had been a profound experience for him. One moment she had been lying on the white bed, as she had for the previous interminable weeks, connected to a wall full of electronic machines. An oscilloscope displayed patterns that showed she was alive.

Her suffering went on. The doctors all said she couldn't experience pain in her coma, but young Keller suspected otherwise. They said she couldn't feel the long, long time she spent on the machine, that it wouldn't be real to her. Keller had felt an urge to end it all for her, to *make it stop*. . . .

But then one moment the machine had changed its mind and pronounced her dead. His grandparents said that the Hand of God had reached down and taken her soul, but young Keller had seen nothing. Even now, Keller still found it difficult to understand, with the physicist in him trying to break down the entire experience into specific questions with specific answers.

What *actually* had taken place during those few seconds in the hospital room? What *actually* had been the difference between life and death? Just a tiny voltage differential across the brain pan?

He remembered the somber warnings from his electronics classes about the kid who had leaned over a bank of capacitors: a line had slipped and the capacitors had discharged across his temples. The twenty microamps had been enough to short-circuit his head, killing him. Was that all life was, an electric field skittering around the contours of your brain? Was even the template of the brain, the body, just so much extraneous mass to hold a special electric field?

He switched on the light and switched it off again.

Glitches. Anomalies.

He decided to go back to the lab.

Before going to the MMFF control room, Keller walked down the deserted Laboratory street past the trailers and other research buildings. Heavy equipment sat idle, sleeping, in wide roped-off lots near numerous construction sites. Keller stopped in front of the huge housing for the MMFF chamber, which rose into the darkness like an airplane hangar. Concrete walls three stories high plunged deep below ground to make the structure earthquake-safe. Girders strung with fog lights bathed the interior of the bay with an orangeish yellow light. Even at this hour of the night, a dozen workers kept their vigil around the armored hull of the MMFF chamber, an airtight cylinder over a hundred feet long, layered with thick sheet metal and bristling with diagnostic instruments. The great fusion chamber throbbed and pulsed, making thunderous sounds pitched just below the level of human hearing. Inside, held captive by two of the world's largest magnets, were temperatures hotter than the sun itself, powerful enough to melt through any metal known to man. He stared for a moment, then went off to the main building.

"We've tried *everything* to get rid of them, and at times we got some responses you wouldn't believe." The technician was packing up, getting ready to go home in the darkness and the rain. "You know, Gordon," he said with a lopsided grin as he looked over the readouts displaying the glitches, "sometimes it reminds me of my wife. Like we're dealing with something that's got a mind of its own."

The technician left, calling his goodbyes into the room. The new shift of technicians mumbled about the prospect of working the next eight dead hours of the night while the rest of the world slept. Keller smiled thinly, distracted. "Yes, like it has a mind of its own." He stared at the readouts for a long time, hypnotized by the wavering plots that sometimes displayed patterns, sometimes chaos.

He reached forward carefully without taking his eyes from the display screens. His fingers were shaking somewhat. Then he began to touch the controls, adjusting the laser probes. Injection on, and the m numbers ran up the scale: the plasma went through the sausage, kink, and firehose instabilities, all in sequence, all on the verge of getting out of control.

Injection off, and the sequence reversed . . . then *repeated* itself—spontaneously. Like a code. Or was it only some weird sort of resonance?

Keller drew in his breath. He sat and tried to establish a link, any link, using anharmonic modes from the RF generator. It could almost be classed as communicating.

He caught himself. Communicating?

> . . . The discovery at the MMFF facility opens
> wide a new door for the human race. It will force
> us to restructure our philosophy of the universe
> and life itself.
> —Editorial, *Physical Review Letters*.

The official Lab spokesman looked good on TV, perfectly groomed, selected from the vast DOE complex as *the* man to best handle the explosive publicity. The late-night talk show host nodded soberly, hanging on to every word said by the panel of distinguished experts. As Keller watched, he knew the publicity generated by the televised discussion would bring out every nut, fruitcake, and religious fundamentalist who was offended by the suggestion that *something* was happening inside the MMFF. He had already taken his phone off the hook.

The host defused an argument among the "experts" and cut right through the static: "But *has* the Fusion Facility created life? Yes or no?"

The lab spokesman had been talking around the subject all night, and he finally looked as if he had been trapped. "We like to think of it as an unknown physical phenomenon which can spontaneously react to stimuli within correct statistical parameters."

The host rolled his eyes, and the lab spokesman responded a little too defensively. "That is a direct quote from Dr. Keller's recently published paper in *Physical Review Letters*. I'm sure Dr. Keller could explain what he meant to say—"

"Dr. Keller is not available for comment at your lab," the host snapped.

"Ah, yes." The spokesman brought his fingertips together. "He is a very busy man, and I assure you he is doggedly working on this problem."

"I'm sure he is," said the host dryly.

"But getting back to your question, and answering quite

honestly—we just don't *know* what the phenomenon is. Granted, some do claim it's alive. But a simple virus is also technically alive. A better question would be, does it have self-awareness? These questions just can't be answered at this time.

"But the point is that *something* is happening in the chamber, something we can't explain. This was to be just a test run, a feasibility study to see if the MMFF would indeed perform as expected before we began full-scale tests. The experiment was originally scheduled to be shut down after three days of continuous operation, but, given the unusual anomalies, we have directed that the facility be kept running for as long as it takes us to understand what is going on."

The discussion grew more philosophical, with the Lab spokesman dancing away from pointed questioning. It went on and on, growing fuzzy like a plasma . . . until the spokesman leered out at Keller, stuck his head through the TV set, and made a grab at him. Keller tried to run but his legs were stuck in a magnetic field and he couldn't stop bouncing back and forth and back and forth and—

Keller woke with a start. He blinked his eyes and realized he had fallen asleep, probably for more hours than he had slept the entire previous night. Keller glanced up at the television and saw that the panel discussion had been replaced by the climax of an Italian-made vampire movie on *The Late Show*.

A man—obviously the hero, obviously the vampire hunter—had pinned the king vampire in his coffin just before sunset. He held a wooden stake against the vampire's chest and made ready to strike.

Keller stood up stiffly from his chair, tried to straighten his shirt but then pulled it off instead, and shuffled over to the television. On the screen, the king vampire had awakened, glaring in melodramatic horror at his victorious adversary and the wooden stake, but then a calm, beatific expression of relief passed over the vampire's face.

"You are trapped, Count!" cried the vampire killer. The actor's lips didn't quite move in tandem with the English words.

"Trapped?" whispered the vampire. "I have been trapped for uncounted centuries. Trapped as what I am, unchanging, never to see the light of day. I have lived for so long that what you do to me is an act of kindness. I can no longer endure my life." The king vampire closed his eyes again and drew a deep breath. "Kill me."

Keller flicked the switch and shut off the television. "There, you're dead."

> We do a lot of stuff here, so we always have protesters. But I'm getting tired of those nuts claiming we've got God bottled up in there. They're spooky!
>
> —Security guard, MMFF.

With a sour and harried expression on his face, Keller wadded up the formal invitation and threw it at the motel-room wastebasket. An invitation to speak to a Congressional hearing on the Search for Extraterrestrial Intelligence project. SETI wanted him to talk about "communicating with alien beings"—they had their gall, especially now!

He flopped back on the hard bed. It probably wouldn't be long before the reporters found him again—Livermore had only a few motels, and those were used mostly by out-of-town job interviewees and DOE contractors. Judging by the stories they ended up printing in their newspapers, the reporters never seemed to listen to his answers to their questions anyway, but they were damned persistent in trying to track him down.

He knotted his fingers in the bedspread. He could hide from the reporters, the decisions, the publicity—but he couldn't hide from the problem.

The thing in the plasma had stopped communicating. Or rather, as the careful side of him liked to point out, the plasma "wasn't spontaneously initiating any controlled instabilities" anymore. The glitches showed it was still there, still living within the fusion chamber, staring at itself in the magnetic mirror. Like Alice unable to get into Wonderland.

Keller could not fathom why the thing didn't treasure every bit of communication, why it didn't eagerly anticipate every new mathematical challenge. It was trapped within its huge chamber, unchanging, unable to come out. It had nothing to do but listen, and talk.

The Congressional invitation caught his eye. He hated to talk in front of people. Yet, it was the most logical thing in the world for SETI to ask him to speak on their behalf, since he was the only human being ever to "successfully" communicate with an alien intelligence.

But what in the hell was Keller supposed to say to the SETI people? Should he confess that he'd always thought their project was basically a waste of time and effort? Sure, he believed there were other civilizations Out There, but the nearest star was five light-years away, the nearest galaxy 2.2 *million* light-years away—as the photon flies. How in the blessed world were you supposed to hold a conversation?

If they were to receive a message from Andromeda tomorrow, it would have been sent twenty thousand centuries before—*Australopithicus africanus* had just begun to make his first tool, just begun to chase woolly mammoths while wondering why it was getting so cold even in the summertime . . . and no one on Earth had had even the slightest desire to build a satellite antenna to listen for extraterrestrial signals. And if SETI were to acknowledge that message, how many millions of years in its grave would be the civilization that had initiated the conversation? It was all a matter of perspective on time.

And here he was, Dr. F. Gordon Keller, separated from an alien intelligence by only a thin wall of stainless steel, but he couldn't communicate with the thing either—and he didn't have the incredible time differential working against him. But something was very wrong with the creature in the plasma. It didn't seem to want to communicate anymore.

Then it hit him like a load of bricks falling on his head.

How many times did he have to stare at something before the obvious answer reached out and bit him on the ass? Time scales of tenths of nanoseconds were critical to a plasma: in a second, a plasma could undergo thousands of millions of interactions. A second to Keller would be *billions* of times longer to something that lived on a plasma time scale.

A strange sense of horror began to grow in the pit of his stomach, and Keller even found himself feeling sorry for the thing.

Imagine being *alone*, trapped inside the fusion chamber for what was—to the thing—an absolute eternity. Even when Keller was communicating with it, tapping icons on the touch-sensitive screen or rapidly keying in commands—centuries would have seemed to pass between each individual finger stroke. The thing had been alive and aware for a million centuries, without a break to the monotony.

Keller remembered his mother dying, in a coma "with no sense of time," connected to the life-sustaining machines as an oscilloscope displayed her life as a pattern on a screen.

Electrical patterns in a plasma. Putting it out of its misery would be like switching off a light. But he would be destroying the world's oldest living thing. He would be killing a living being.

A million centuries alone and in silence, without another living being to talk to. Something wrenched in his stomach as the implications pounded themselves home. The thing was immortal, chained to an utterly useless life, unable to die as long as the MMFF remained running.

He would be giving it peace. Something in the world deserved peace.

It was the dead of night, with only a skeleton crew in the control room. Nothing had changed for days. A security guard checked Keller's badge at the gate, and then another let him pass into the control room. He wasn't going to break in and shut down the experiment . . . he was going to *walk* in and shut it down. He would free the living being that had been trapped inside, bottled up for eternity by Keller's wonderful mirrors. He moved with brisk and determined steps to the MMFF control room. Every moment he delayed meant another year of suffering for the thing.

"No change, Gordon," one of the operators said, seeing him as he walked purposefully into the room.

Without acknowledging, Keller went to a vacant bank of computer screens and stared at the jagged display of glitches on one of them. Even as he stared, even as his heart beat, years were ticking away for the thing imprisoned in the chamber. It could only bounce back and forth and *exist* for millions of its years, unable to escape and see the world outside. Keller felt his eyes sting, almost with tears, at the unspeakable loneliness.

But what about himself? He'd thrown away his marriage working on this damned project, trying to push and work and *achieve* so that he could hold an accomplishment up before himself to prove that his life was worthwhile. Like his Ph.D., getting the degree for a trophy. Was he trying to commit *career* suicide this time? The MMFF success had been the pinnacle of his research, but the living thing he had created was unexpected, a blessing, a curse. Keller had hidden from the publicity, passing the responsibility to others. But no one else would see the responsibility he had now, the imperative goal to free the creature he had trapped between the magnetic mirrors. It was time for Gordon Keller to stop hiding.

Keller stared at the red switch. Emergency shutdown—the only hardwired switch in the entire computer-screen-driven control room. It would be simple. Keller held out the palm of his hand—the razor blade against his wrist, the oscilloscope in his mother's hospital room, even the stake on the movie vampire's chest.

With a quick thrust of his arm, he shut the MMFF down.

He would have more time for Shelley now, and Justin. He'd try to call her, and maybe—*maybe*—she would even admire what he had done, tell him he'd been brave. He could write a book, *Memoirs of a Modern-Day Frankenstein*. Or maybe Zel'dovich would consult him about how the next generation of fusion chambers could be built without spawning a new life form.

As it died, and before anyone could act or any alarms could sound, Keller thought he felt a tingling rush through his skin—a flash of dissipating electricity. But it was only his imagination, or just the release of some of the psychological weights on his shoulder. With a sigh, he slowly eased himself into a chair as the shouting started.

LISTENING
RONNIE SEAGREN

"Listening" is another first sale and again it's a bit hard to believe that a writer can begin a publishing career with so powerful a piece of work (we were in fact quite pleasantly surprised at the level of quality in many of the stories we received from previously unpublished writers. The future of our genre seems quite secure). Ronnie Seagren has been a member of the Northern Colorado Writers' Workshop since 1983. She has a B.A. in geology and is married with three sons.

"Listening" is a hypnotic story about searching for signs of alien life.

Arms folded across his chest, fists tucked under them, Jeremy Higgins leaned against the windowsill of the lab, letting the late morning sun warm his back. Tugging one hand free to punch his glasses securely against the bridge of his nose, he tried to read the face of his visitor.

But the expression on the face of Robert Daniels, and his posture as he paced across the lab and back again, remained neutral. Carefully neutral, Jeremy decided, leaning back into the corner at Robert's approach, against the heavy curtains he rarely closed. He perceived a barrier between them, between their lives.

The recording, a disharmonious smear of tones backed by the rasping hiss of hydroxyl ions, lasted about three and a half minutes. At the end, the signal faded out. On the stripchart tracing Robert held, the decrease in amplitude almost mirrored the signal's beginning. *Like the passing of a lighthouse beacon.*

Robert continued to study the chart.

"Well?" Jeremy asked at last.

Robert jerked his head up then, dropping the stripchart onto the scattered papers on Jeremy's desk. Though he turned toward Jeremy, his focus seemed beyond, out the window. Jeremy knew the scene well; it was his ceaseless companion. The High Altitude Atmospheric Research Lab where he was stationed sat just past the treeline in the northern Colorado Rockies. The pine-and-aspen-covered slopes and tatters of midsummer snow cresting blue-shadowed peaks were to Jeremy the swell of an endless sea, his outpost a solitary island.

"Well, it's interesting," Robert said. His voice sounded irritated, almost sarcastic. "What more do you want me to say? It's hardly worth the trip up here, even if you promised me lunch."

Jeremy leaned forward to pull a notebook off his desk and tossed it to Robert. "I've been picking it up roughly every seventy-eight hours for six weeks now. I'm expecting it to-night." Jeremy hesitated. He had planned to ask Robert to stay. He punched at his glasses. *Maybe later.*

"You could've mailed me the tape."

"I wanted you to see MABLE." Jeremy frowned. Did he sound too plaintive?

"I've seen her. I helped haul her up here, remember?"

Jeremy shifted his weight against the sill. "I need you to check her out. Maybe I missed something."

"And?"

Jeremy shrugged and combed his fingers through his short, curly hair. Setting thoughts into spoken words made them real, substantial, in a way he wasn't sure he was prepared yet to face. "If it's not a bug in my system or a birdie, I—"

"You think this thing's intelligent."

Jeremy shrugged, talking to the tips of Robert's shoes. "I want it to be. I need to know there's someone else out there." He forced his gaze for just a second up to Robert's face. "Maybe we wouldn't be so eager to destroy ourselves."

"Not that again. We argued Malthus enough in college."

"If we knew we weren't alone, maybe we'd be more careful. It's so easy to get careless, sloppy, when you're alone, when there's no one else." He gestured at the organized chaos of his own career as evidence. *See? I know about being alone.* "We spread our poisons and strip the resources and ignore the warnings. Most people don't care about twenty years down the road, much less twenty generations." He turned to the window and the pine-covered slopes like a forever sea lapping about his island.

Robert's voice was the pecking of an angry gull. "Who are you to criticize? You're up here, hiding from it all."

"Hiding?" Jeremy turned back around, sweeping his arm in a broad arc to indicate the montage of maps and charts, the stacks of papers and printouts spilling off shelves and overflowing boxes, and the computer and its phalanx of support equipment. "I measure what we do. That's my job. Do you know I get smog up here? Fifty miles from nowhere and two miles in the sky, and I get smog. The lake up by MABLE's ear is polluted with acid rain." He paused to shake his head. "Sometimes I picture the human race as a mold growing on an orange. Or a cancer."

Robert just stood there, hands in pockets, his face like a closed door.

A static-burred voice on Jeremy's two-way radio broke the taut silence: "Hey, Mountain Man, heard from any Martians lately?" called Matt Parker, one of the rangers stationed in the neighboring national park.

Jeremy crossed the room to respond. "What is it, Parker?"

"Kid wandered away from a group on the lake trail this morning."

"The lake trail? That's over twelve miles from here."

"Yeah, well, just in case you spot him."

Jeremy looked out the window at his pine-top sea. "Yeah, sure," *if he shinnies up a tree and waves a flag.* "What's he look like?"

"Name: Kevin Cummings. Twelve years old," Parker intoned, obviously tired of repeating himself. "Brown hair, blue eyes. Jeans, blue T-shirt, red nylon jacket. Hey, if you point MABLE downhill maybe you could hear him. Put that contraption to practical use for a change."

Jeremy grimaced as he flipped the radio switch to *send*, cutting off Parker's harsh laugh. He signed off and looked toward Robert, wondering how he could reopen their conversation.

"So where's lunch?" Robert asked.

Jeremy pushed back his sleeve to check his watch. "Yeah," he sighed. He led the way out of the lab and down the short path to his cabin at the edge of a small alpine meadow. The short walk gave him time to adjust from the high tech of his career to the almost crude simplicity of his personal life.

As he pushed open the door of the cabin, the warm air briefly fogged his glasses. Stew simmered on the woodstove in the center of the room and the heavy odor made him hungry.

While Jeremy finished his preparations, Robert toured the

small cabin as if it were a museum. Jeremy watched with an anxious frown as Robert paused to study one of Jeremy's pen and ink sketches—an eagle circling its aerie on a craggy peak. "Your artwork's improving. I saw the prints for sale in the Park Visitors' Center. Congratulations."

Jeremy ducked his head, uncomfortable with the minor success of his hobby. He saw Robert move closer to another, depicting the silhouette of a man atop a narrow pinnacle of rock, reaching skyward, and just beyond his fingertips, a single star. It was a personal sketch; one that would never sell in the Visitors' Center. Jeremy had meant to take it down before Robert arrived. He scowled at the rigid figure.

"I never did learn to do people right. Especially faces. I don't know why I try."

Robert shrugged. "You need more practice. You can't draw what you never see." He turned from the sketch to the small window. "You've been up here—what? Three years now?"

"Almost five."

Robert shook his head. "Jer, old friend, how do you stand it?"

"You get used to it. After a while, you forget how to deal with people. Especially crowds. I don't like crowds."

"You never did." Robert's voice held both sympathy and bitter frustration. "You haven't changed."

Jeremy paused, pot of stew in one hand, ladle in the other, poised over Robert's plate. With the flicker of a memory, he was back in college again, dragged by his well-intentioned roommate to parties and meetings and even dates. Utterly paralyzed by his shyness, he had worn his glasses like a mask and wrapped his inhibitions about him like a cloak. With a shudder, he shook off the memory. "Let's eat," he called, dumping the ladleful of stew onto Robert's plate.

During lunch, Jeremy glanced furtively at his watch, calculating how much longer before Robert would be gone. Yesterday, eager for company, he'd spent most of the day cleaning up the clutter of his solitary existence. Now he felt smothered by the weight of Robert's voice, as if his words were a cloud of moths fluttering about. He nodded and mumbled uh-huhs around mouthfuls of stew. His long legs were crossed and tucked under his chair, and his shoulders ached from holding himself hunched and rigid.

Jeremy shifted his weight and tried unobtrusively to straighten up, but he couldn't seem to untangle his legs to stretch them. He glanced at Robert and saw a stranger. The face seemed rounder, the nose not nearly so angular, and the mouth not quite as thin. Was it his memory or the years at fault? Time and circumstance had set a distance between their lives. A disquieting guilt settled in his gut, competing with the weight of the stew. He panicked. "I'm sorry, Robert. I shouldn't be imposing on you like this. I just wanted—I *need* to know what this is, and you're the only one I knew who could help. I mean, if it's real—"

"It's all right," Robert muttered, shaking his head and wagging his fork while trying to swallow a mouthful of bread. "I've got some connections in the astrophysics department; give me your data, and I'll see what I can do. The important thing is verification. You know it doesn't mean a thing if no one else can pick it up."

After Robert finished checking over MABLE's system, Jeremy followed him out to his car, hugging his pile of data to his chest. Robert took it from him, setting it on the front seat. At the edge of the clearing a light breeze set the aspen leaves to quivering on their slender twigs. Jeremy noted the thin edging of gold about the pale green leaves. *Kevin. Kevin Cummings.* The name echoed in his mind like a sliver of song.

"I'll let you know," Robert said, climbing into the driver's seat. "This stuff looks promising, but . . ."

"I know. Verification."

Robert tossed him a wave, then hauled at the steering wheel to bring the vehicle around toward the head of the jeep trail—eighteen miles of ruts and boulders and narrow switchbacks. "Next time, you come to Denver," he yelled out the window. "I'd forgotten how much I hate mountain driving."

"Yeah," Jeremy halfheartedly agreed, finally able to release a brief grin.

Even before the vehicle entered the shadow of the trees, he turned and walked back to the cabin. He washed the dishes and put them away, straightened the magazines Robert had rummaged through, and smoothed the quilt where he'd sat on the bunk. At last he stood in the center of the room, rubbing his hands lightly together. No trace of a visitor remained. The room looked nice; perhaps he could keep it that way for a while. He smiled. Such promises were never meant to keep.

Twilight. Transition. Shadows pooled in the valleys and spilled over to merge with the slow tide of the Earth's terminator. Although MABLE operated continuously, during the day Jeremy's own time and attention, and the computer's, were bound to the Earth and matters of weather and atmosphere. But in the changing shadows of twilight, he transformed from professional meteorologist to amateur radio astronomer, from watcher to listener. He enjoyed the subtle shifts in thinking and sensory dominance that it required.

The constellation Cetus, the source of the signal, would not rise until around ten, and he expected the signal around eleven-thirty. He checked and cataloged the day's recordings, then busied himself with calibration checks and routine scanning before initiating the tracking program for his target. *His* target. The one that, as far as he knew, talked to no one but himself.

That would soon change, though. This was not something he could keep to himself; it had to be shared. Perhaps he had called Robert not so much because he needed to know what the signal was, but because he *needed* the rest of the world to know.

He thought about the first time he'd seen the signal tracing— checking the tapes just after dinner and discovering that a program error had canceled declination, setting MABLE's ear on the celestial equator. Frustration, even anger. Then the unexpected flurry of scratchings. The thin paper had torn in his grip. While he'd been out fixing a broken hygrometer in the instrument field, *someone* had come tapping at his door.

As the time for the expected signal neared, he plugged in the headset and leaned back in his chair to stare at the window. The curtains hung open; the night was always welcome company, though the reflection of the room lights blotted out the stars. He closed his eyes and imagined a mountain peak in an alien landscape, and a lone figure hunched over its own equipment, sending out its signal, like a message in a bottle.

"Here I am," Jeremy whispered to the dark beyond the window. "I'm listening."

The sound that gradually filtered into his thoughts was so rare and so ordinary that he sorted through a list of possibilities— the wind blowing, raccoons, a rock fall—before realizing that it was the rap of knuckles on the wood of the door. He removed his headset and waited until it repeated—a little louder, a little more desperate—to be certain.

Brown hair, blue eyes—frightened, weary eyes. The jeans were wet and spattered and the sneakers encased in mud. The blue T-shirt and the jacket looked as if they had also been wet and since dried, and the kid shivered convulsively. His hair was tousled and hung in his eyes so that Jeremy wanted to reach out and brush it back.

The kid jerked back a step and almost tripped. He stammered as he spoke, or perhaps he just stuttered from the cold. "I . . . uh . . . I'm sorta lost. Light. I saw lights." The dark behind him was heavy and deep.

Jeremy nodded but said nothing as he brought him into the lab. The kid limped some, but it seemed more a sore-feet limp than any kind of injury.

"They'll send a jeep up in the morning," Jeremy explained when he had finished reporting to Matt on the radio. The kid nodded, but tears glistened in weary eyes, and the corners of his mouth twitched.

"It's all right; you're safe now," Jeremy assured him. "Let's get you warm and dry and fed." He paused at the door to glance back at MABLE and sighed.

The kid stopped just inside the cabin door and, with a large sigh, let his pack drop to the floor. His knees buckled as if he intended to join it.

"Sit here." Jeremy jerked a chair away from the table and motioned the boy to sit. Then he built up the fire in the woodstove.

The kid sat slumped, rubbing his shoulder where the strap of his pack must've chafed. He pushed off his shoes with his toes and stretched out his legs and arms to the stove's warmth.

"Hungry?"

The kid nodded, the tip of his tongue running across his lips. As Jeremy retrieved the leftover stew from the refrigerator and dumped it into a pot, he felt the kid's presence like an itch in his back. He clenched his teeth and prepared to endure. *Just till morning*, he assured himself. *Then he'll be gone.*

Jeremy poured himself a cup of coffee and sat down. The kid scooped stew from the bowl held in his lap, one hand clenched around a mug of hot chocolate. Whenever he sipped from the mug, Jeremy caught wary glances over the rim. Fear remained in the blue-as-evening eyes, a shy temerity.

And then the eyes began to close. His head began to nod, and the spoon fell from his hand. Jeremy guided him to the bunk, and the boy rolled onto the quilt as if already asleep. Jeremy pulled out an extra quilt and spread it over him, then retrieved his sleeping bag from under the bunk. He turned off the light and headed back to the lab to spend the night with MABLE.

The stripchart showed the flurry of squiggles Jeremy had come to think of as the signature of an alien hand. *"While you were out . . ."*

He recorded the observation in his notebook and spread out the stripchart to study it, as if in the flare and bunch of the inked lines he might find some clue to its sender.

Intrusions, he thought, resenting the changes beginning to work into his life. First the signal, bringing Robert and who knows who else in the future. Now this kid, with eyes that seemed to reflect so much of his own childhood. He'd been content in his isolation. He shuddered and wasn't sure why.

Shaking his head, he rubbed at his eyes, but they refused to focus anymore on the thin, delicate tracings. He shoved the chart to the side. Rolling out the sleeping bag across the floor, he settled down among the comforting scratch and hum of MABLE's system.

Jeremy awoke feeling stiff, as if he'd held himself rigid throughout the night. A knot at the base of his neck seemed to have roots halfway down his back. He pulled his clothes out from the bottom of the sleeping bag and dressed.

The kid's presence permeated the cabin. Jeremy glanced at the pack abandoned by the door and the bunched quilt, with only a tuft of tangled hair showing at the top. He almost tripped over the muddy shoes, and when he bumped the chair left by the woodstove, the almost-empty bowl of stew clattered to the floor. The kid moaned softly and shifted beneath the quilt, but apparently remained asleep. Tensing at every clang and thunk, Jeremy added wood to the stove and started the fire. Then he tiptoed to the bathroom.

When he came out, the boy was up and trying to straighten the quilt, brushing at the dried mud that had flaked off his clothes. Jeremy muttered a "g'mornin' " as he shuffled to the kitchen unit. The warmth of the stove soaked through the room, pushing back the feeling of intrusion.

"Can I help?" the boy asked, timidly setting the fallen bowl and spoon in the sink.

Jeremy shrugged and then hooked his thumb toward the cupboard. "You can set the table, I suppose."

They finished preparing breakfast in silence, carefully stepping around each other, avoiding contact. Silence persisted as they sat down at the table. The boy hunched rigidly in his chair, his gaze fixed on his plate, a posture so familiar to Jeremy that he ached at the sight.

"I guess I'm in a lot of trouble," the boy muttered. He glanced up, eyes pleading.

Jeremy gave him a noncommittal shrug. "A stiff lecture from the ranger," he told him, trying to sound stern but failing. "What'd you wander off for, anyway?"

"I don't know," the boy said with a shrug. "I didn't mean to. I just wanted to get away from the people. You know?"

Jeremy nodded.

"I mean, it just isn't fair. We waited two years for a camping permit, and then there's all them people, making all this noise. One guy even had a radio. All he got was static, but he wouldn't turn it off."

"Most people are too used to noise," Jeremy explained. "They're not comfortable with silence. It can be more frightening than the dark." He shuddered at the memory of his first few weeks at the lab, how the silence had all but engulfed him before he'd come to terms with it.

"Yeah, but there's still noise. Quiet noise."

Jeremy nodded, studying the young face, the blue eyes where shadows of hidden things drifted. His glasses slipped down his nose, but even in a blur, he found the boy's eyes haunting.

The boy's glance made timid forays around the room. Jeremy squirmed. What could he talk about? What were twelve-year-olds into these days, anyway? He hadn't been very much in touch when he was that age; how could he talk to one now?

"So what do you do in school?" Jeremy asked, feeling pleased to have a suitable topic, but chagrined at the hoarse tone of his voice.

"Not much," the boy answered with a shrug.

Jeremy sighed with frustration. "What's your favorite subject?"

Again a shrug. "P.E., I guess. I like soccer. I don't like history."

"Me neither." Jeremy offered a short grin, shifting in his chair and stretching out his legs. "Art was always my favorite subject, though." He waved his fork toward the sketches on the walls.

"You made these?" the boy responded with a touch of awe. "The ones in the Visitors' Center, too? My mom bought one—the one with two eagles."

Jeremy nodded, feeling pleased.

"Do you draw people?"

Jeremy shook his head. "Not very well."

"Could you draw me?"

Jeremy stared at him for a moment, trying to think of a good excuse. "Uh, no." *I could never get those eyes right.* "There isn't time. Uh, how about a tour of the lab?"

"The place with the computer?"

"It's a research lab. I study the weather up here. Come on. I'll give you the grand tour, such as it is."

Jeremy could've busied himself with his work and left Kevin to his own devices until Matt arrived. Instead he showed Kevin the computer with its gray boxes and black boxes, and the instrument field sprouting its detectors and samplers and monitors. Kevin began to fidget, shifting his weight from one foot to the other and picking at his fingernails.

"Pretty bland, isn't it." Jeremy sighed. "I'm not very good at explaining this stuff." He gazed at the far mountains and the morning fog still curling through the deep valleys. "How'd you like to see MABLE?"

"Mabel?"

"Up there." Jeremy jerked his thumb toward the peak.

The trail was steep and rugged, working its way around to the south side of the mountain, through a switchback and up, almost to the peak, to where MABLE's antenna perched, looking like a lost umbrella snagged on the rocks.

"What's that?" Kevin asked, leaning on his knees to catch his breath.

"That's MABLE. Minimal Array Built for Low-energy Environments. Sort of a joke," Jeremy explained. "Careful. Don't get too close to the edge there." The twenty-meter dish was mounted on a ridge above the scooped-out bowl of a glacial tarn, the broken rock sharp and jagged. The lake below reflected the pure, depthless blue of the Colorado sky with icy clarity. A series of similar lakes, like a string of beads, descended the mountain's flank.

"What does it do?" Kevin ran his hand across the wire mesh.

Jeremy smiled. "I listen to the stars with it."

"Oh, sure."

"Honest. What we can see with our eyes, or even the biggest telescopes, is only a small fraction of what's really out there."

He waved his hand across the sky. Kevin squinted up. The wind keened in the mesh of MABLE's dish and across her mooring cables, an eerie and alien song.

"Like quasars and stuff?"

Jeremy nodded. "Mostly 'stuff.' Ever hear of the 'music of the spheres'?"

"Huh?"

"Plato. Plato thought that the sun and planets and stars were imbedded in crystal spheres that turned around the Earth, and when all the spheres turned in absolute perfection, they produced a harmonious, perfect sound. In a way, he was right. The whole universe is singing, if you know how to listen."

They stood at the rim of MABLE's perch for a while, gusts of wind punching at their backs, nudging them toward the edge. Jeremy pointed out the eagle's nest, and they watched one of the birds take off, find a thermal, and glide in a slow, rising spiral until it was nothing more than a black speck, lost in an eye's blink. Kevin swayed dizzily, and Jeremy reached out to steady him.

Returning to the lab, Jeremy tuned the receiver to one of the hydrogen emission bands. "Listen, Kevin. That's the whole galaxy talking to you," Jeremy whispered. He watched the boy's eyes. For a moment, it seemed they shared the hub of the universe and really could hear the music of the spheres.

"What else can you hear?" Kevin asked. "Aliens?"

Jeremy smiled. "No. But I've found a signal that I haven't been able to explain yet. It could be a star or ion cloud or a birdie that's fooled my filtering programs—a birdie is something that originated on Earth. I don't know." He picked up last night's stripchart, still ribboned across the floor.

Kevin studied the chart, his finger tracing the thin lines. Questions came to his eyes like bubbles on a pond. "What are these?" Kevin pointed at the marks along the edge of the strip.

"Time marks—so I can figure exactly when the signal was received. And these numbers are azimuth and altitude settings, so I know where MABLE was pointing."

More questions. Jeremy leaned back in his chair, gesturing expansively. The conversation slowly segued from astronomy to more Earth-bound matters.

"I'll be in junior high this year," Kevin said suddenly, his gaze hard on Jeremy's face as if measuring his trust. "I'm sorta scared. I mean, like last year, we were on top. This year, we're back down at the bottom, and it's all different. The bigger kids pick on you.''

Jeremy nodded, remembering. He tried to make his face express encouragement.

"Everyone makes such a big deal about girls. I don't even know what to say to them.''

"I know how you feel." Jeremy leaned forward conspiratorially. "The first time I asked a girl to a dance, I stood about six feet away from her and literally whispered. She must have been able to read lips to understand what I was saying. Or maybe she was psychic.''

Kevin smiled at last and relaxed. Jeremy felt curiously relieved to see the shadows clear from his eyes.

"Anyway,'' he continued, "you're still too young to have to worry about it. Now is the time to enjoy yourself. Have some fun. I wish I had when I was your age.''

"Yeah, my mom says the same thing. But it isn't easy—''

The staccato beep of a horn startled them both. Kevin looked up at Jeremy, and melancholy again shadowed his eyes. *Don't be like me, Kevin,* Jeremy thought. *Don't end up stuck on some mountain, afraid to face people. Break out now, before it's too late.* He thought it, but he said nothing. He set his hand on the boy's shoulder as they headed outside.

"Go get your pack.''

Kevin nodded solemnly and headed for the cabin, eyes on his shoe tips. Jeremy watched Parker wheel the Forest Service jeep in a broad circle around the clearing to park next to Jeremy's pickup. A woman sat in the passenger's seat, one he knew had to be Kevin's mother. They had the same eyes. She scrambled out of the jeep and ran toward Kevin as he emerged from the cabin. But she stopped short and, arms stiff at her side, fingers twitching, refrained from hugging him.

"See? I told you he'd be all right,'' Parker called as he climbed from behind the wheel, a short, plumpish man in his late forties. His uniform always seemed two sizes too big and perpetually wrinkled. "Higgins, here, only eats kids in the winter, after he runs out of nuts and berries.'' He laughed, winking at Jeremy.

Jeremy glared back.

"Kevin, why?'' his mother asked, reaching out to brush the hair from his eyes.

Kevin shrugged. "I dunno," he murmured, and his glance flicked toward Jeremy.

The four of them stood there in an awkward tableau. Prompted by his mother, Kevin mumbled apologies and thank-yous. Jeremy ached. He wanted to say something, but Parker had already launched into his standard lost-kid lecture. "Do you know how much it costs to search . . ."

Kevin just stood there. Jeremy wanted to reach out to him, but the boy was too far away. Only once could he even catch his glance. Those eyes offered so much, hid so much. Perhaps he should've drawn the boy's portrait. He could've at least tried.

The jeep lurched forward, spitting gravel against Jeremy's pant legs. Kevin turned in his seat to wave just as the jeep entered the shadows of the trees. Jeremy watched until they were well out of sight and the dust had resettled, until the sound of the engine had melted into the natural buzz and murmur of the forest.

The cabin smelled of cold bacon grease. Jeremy stacked the dishes in the sink and left them there.

Floating. Drifting. Cold and empty black.

A presence. An image. Face hidden in shadow. Angles and contours not quite human.

Reaching out. Drifting apart. Now closer. Never quite touching. Face hidden.

Close now. So close. Fingertips aching, almost touching. Turning into the light. Shadows lifting. So close.

Falling! The sudden wrench of gravity. Jeremy gasped, arms flailing. One hand struck the wall. He awoke.

Dream images scattered like a flock of birds. Rubbing his hand, he huddled in the bunk, in the half-light of dawn, trying to catch the elusive fragments.

Daylight bleached the images to gossamer shadows. But the memory of the dream stayed with him, tugging at the edges of his thoughts. He still felt the chill emptiness, the aching need to touch the other's hand. He tried to sketch it. If only he could draw people.

After two weeks, the comfortable litter of his semihermitage had overcome the hotel-room neatness. The place was truly *his* again. He had toyed with the idea of deliberately messing up the cabin, but that wouldn't have worked. Clutter had to happen naturally, one dropped sock, one dirty cup left on the table at a time.

In the afternoon, he climbed up to the instrument field to make repairs and calibrate the winter-season instruments. The air was chill, and on the slopes below, the aspen were displaying their fall colors. Soon winter's snows would close him in. He found himself dreading the coming isolation.

The laboring drone of an engine intruded on the raw silence, and then the bray of a horn. Jeremy clenched his jaw tight and kept on working, even after he heard Matt Parker hailing him. He waited until the ranger was halfway up the narrow path before he set aside his wrench and stood to return the greeting.

"Haven't seen you lately," Parker explained. "I thought I'd bring up your mail."

Jeremy nodded. Anytime Parker didn't hear from him for more than three or four days, the ranger felt obliged to check up on him. Jeremy thought he should be grateful, but did Parker have to do it in person? Reluctantly, he offered the ranger a cup of coffee, and the two of them made their way back down the mountain to the lab.

Parker tossed the mail in a staggered heap on the desk. A small white envelope slipped out from beneath a gaudy sweepstakes offer. *What?* Jeremy wondered as he grabbed two mugs and the pot of coffee. The ranger squinted at the sketch pad Jeremy had left on the desk. A few faint pencil lines indicated a space-suited astronaut, and over his shoulder, *something*.

"What's that going to be?"

Jeremy shrugged. "Nothing." He snatched up the pad and leaned it against the wall behind him. "You wouldn't be interested, anyway."

Parker nodded and glanced around the room at the equipment. "You sure you ain't got a TV up here? You ain't picking up satellite signals with that fancy gadget up there?" He waved in the general direction of the peak.

Jeremy frowned and didn't answer. He glanced at the small white envelope, at the corner with the stamp and postmark. *Who do I know in Illinois?*

"How do you stand it alone up here?"

"I'm comfortable."

"Comfortable," Parker repeated with a snort. "Stagnant. You don't like people, so you hide from them."

"It's not that I don't like people. I'm just more comfortable dealing with them at a distance." Jeremy tapped his fingers on the pile of mail, the enigmatic envelope.

Parker leaned forward. "I know how it is. I was a shy kid, too, but I fought it. I grew out of it. Don't you think it's about time you did, too?"

Jeremy thought, *If you're an example of the results, I'd rather be a hermit forever.* "I tried. It just got worse. It didn't work." *But this isn't working, either.*

"Look, Higgins." Parker leaned back, twisting sideways to drape one arm over the back of his chair. "You ever need someone to talk to, I'm here. You hear what I'm saying?" Jeremy nodded. He heard. Parker might listen. But he would also file a report. Not out of malice, but duty, and a misintended sense of responsibility. *He's not a bad guy,* Jeremy thought, *just a jerk.*

Jeremy didn't even watch Parker leave. Pouring himself a fresh cup of coffee, he sat down at his desk. Mail was a luxury. He could handle people indirectly like this, even enjoy it. Deliberately he sorted the pile, stacking magazines and a mail-order book to one side, and dealing junk mail, bills, and business mail into their respective piles. At last he was left with only that one envelope. The address, written in a precise, clumsy cursive, slanted up and then down across the envelope. Sipping at his coffee, he savored the mystery as well as the anticipation. Curiosity an itch at the nape of his neck, he slit it open and pulled out a piece of ruled paper.

As he read, a smile blossomed gradually, then burst into a short laugh. He sighed and read the letter again.

Dear Mr. Higgins,

My mom said I should write to thank you for helping me when I got lost, so I am. I liked visiting you. I like the way you listened to me.

I am in school now. Are you lonely? I would like to be your friend.

Sincerely,
Kevin Cummings

P.S. I'm doing a science report about MABLE.

Jeremy read the letter a third time. The sparse details left him feeling hungry for more, as if he'd eaten one potato chip.

Robert phoned three days later, his call relayed through the ranger's station to Jeremy's radio. The disjointed quality of the radio link, even the lack of privacy, never bothered Jeremy. He felt protected by it.

"It looks good so far," Robert reported, his voice edged with static leaking into the seams of the relay. "Warwick thinks it's definitely extraterrestrial, but he's not saying what. We're still checking for verification, and we've requested IRAS photos of the sector. . . . Uh . . . Over?"

"What's the IRS got to do with it?" Matt Parker's voice cut in before Jeremy could switch to *send*. "There a tax on little green men?"

"I-R-A-S," Jeremy responded tersely. "It's an infrared telescope orbiting Earth." *Meathead.* "Robert, what about the SETI people? What do they say? Over."

"What's a 'seti'?"

". . . very cautious." Jeremy glanced over at his sketch pad propped against the In basket on his desk. "Smith claims it's only our own trash, reflected off an ion cloud or something."

"Can't be," Jeremy cut in. *The angle of the astronaut's arm isn't quite right, and the helmet needs to be rounder.* "It isn't on a diurnal cycle." A few pencil strokes blocked out the alien, defining size and position but little else. *Maybe tentacles. Or would that be trite?*

"That still doesn't mean it's an intelligent source. You know the guidelines. We're looking for something with a narrow frequency range, a pure tone, maybe, or mathematically significant."

"Plenty of people disagree with the guidelines. I mean, do you really think an alien mind will make sense of sixteen hundred seventy-nine blips and bleeps?" Jeremy's glance wandered to Kevin's letter tacked to the bulletin board. *How'd your science project come out?* he wondered. "Alien is alien; we can't expect *them* to think the same. Over."

"We can't let our imaginations take over, either. Anyway, it's—"

"Hey," Matt interrupted. "What's going on? Is Higgins seeing flying saucers or something?"

"No!" Jeremy and Robert chorused, though Jeremy knew he couldn't be heard. *Stick to flipping switches, will you?*

". . . he isn't," Robert continued. "Jer, it's a moot point until we get the thing verified. Over. No, wait. I'll know more by next week. Why don't you come down on the . . . let's see, the twenty-third? My turn to buy lunch. Over."

"Good idea," Parker added. "I'll drag him off that mountain myself, if I have to."

Jeremy shuddered.

Muted conversations and the clinking of china and tableware wove a web around the table they shared. Jeremy had trouble sorting out Robert's voice from the surrounding noise. The orange and yellow decor of the restaurant seemed harsh, even alien, and he couldn't seem to focus on the plastic panels and the too-green artificial plants. He kept his gaze on the table, his hands shredding the brown paper napkin in his lap. He'd had to repeat his order three times before the waitress could hear him. Now he sat with elbows held close to his sides, picking at the salad in front of him. In the booth behind him, three children bickered. The web tightened about him.

"Seems you have something, after all," Robert was saying. Jeremy winced at the loud enthusiasm in his voice and glanced around the restaurant to see if others had heard. Behind him, the parents were wearily telling their children to be quiet, without much effect.

"The photos from IRAS show what might be a brown dwarf within your target area, roughly thirteen parsecs away. About forty-one light-years. And we have possible verification, of a sort. Fellow in Australia reported a similar signal, same source, same cycle. Different time, of course. But we have your records to prove you found it first. You'll be famous, Jer old boy." He said the last part loud enough for half the restaurant to hear. Jeremy cringed. "We still have to be careful, though." He rubbed his hands together eagerly. "The real trick will be decoding. That's going to take time—maybe years."

The web, almost a physical barrier, closed even tighter now, pressing against his back, and barely allowing him to reach for his water glass. "The signal stopped," he muttered without looking up.

"What? Gone?"

Jeremy hunched closer to his plate. Under the table, he crossed his legs, and crossed them again at the ankles. "Stopped. It doesn't exist anymore. Last Thursday, it just quit. Flat-lined, like an EKG. No fade-out, nothing. And I haven't picked it up since."

"Did you check—"

"Of course I did. MABLE's fine." Over the top of Jeremy's

glasses, he saw Robert frown. "But this proves it had to be artificial."

"Jeremy, you didn't just make all this up, did you?" Robert's voice was almost a mumble.

"I wouldn't!" Jeremy protested. He faced Robert's suspicion eye to eye. "You know me. I . . . No!" He shook his head and slumped in his seat, his gaze returning to his plate.

"But why would it just stop?"

Jeremy shrugged. He glanced up as far as the second button of Robert's shirt. "Who knows? Maybe they got tired of waiting and quit, or they ran out of money. Maybe the bureaucrats made them shut it off. Maybe they don't care anymore, or maybe they're just gone."

The family behind him was leaving. Jeremy glanced at the children as they passed; the oldest was about Kevin's age.

Robert responded with a large sigh. "What happened? They blow themselves up?"

The waitress came with their orders, and Jeremy was silent, leaning away from her as she set his plate before him. He wanted the salt, but it was beyond his barrier. *I should write back to Kevin*, he thought as he concentrated on cutting his steak.

"That's not what I said. Something happened, and they're no longer capable or interested in transmitting. Look at us. How many ways could we commit technological suicide? Not just the nuclear stuff. Environmental. Economic. It's so easy. A little less caution, a little more aggression. A good dose of apathy. Boredom. Blooey!" He dropped his fork and spread his fingers to convey an explosion. His gaze snagged Robert's eyes. "You just give up. You quit caring and get sloppy. It's so easy when you're all alone. When you don't know if anyone else cares."

"Come on, Jer. You're talking like something really happened. We haven't even figured out what your signal means yet."

"Pretend—just pretend that something did." Jeremy pressed his hands against the edge of the table. "Imagine waiting, and coming so close. Only a few decades more, and we could get a message back to them. Nothing complicated. Just a simple 'Hello. We're here.' Do you know how much that would mean to someone who's lonely?" Jeremy paused. *What could I say to Kevin? Do I have anything worth saying?* "I mean, a whole race wondering if they're alone?"

Robert stared hard at Jeremy for a moment. "You've been up on that mountain too long, old friend."

Jeremy glanced off at the rest of the diners, though they blurred into a montage of color and shape without meaning. "Maybe that's the point," he whispered, then shook himself, shrugging off gray thoughts. "I feel as if I've let them down somehow." *How can I help someone else when I've failed myself?*

"*If* there was ever anyone out there to begin with. Besides, it's not like they're in Kansas. Forty-one light-years. You were too late before you were even born."

Jeremy picked at the edge of his placemat. "I keep wondering if we'll do the same thing someday. Just give up."

Robert shrugged. "Who knows? We keep hanging on—by our fingernails if we have to. The human race is a pretty stubborn entity."

"It's easier to hang on if you know there's someone else pulling for you." Jeremy hooked his gaze deliberately on Robert's eyes. *Do you hear what I'm really saying?*

Robert turned to look for the waitress. "Oh, miss, could I have some ketchup?"

Jeremy fled the city, tailgating a semi on the highway, jerking his truck around curves. Breathing in shallow gasps as if the air held a foul odor, he rubbed his hand across his face as if he could scrub away the touch of neon and smog, the cloying presence of too many people. The residue of the city tore away in the icy wind from the open window of the pickup, leaving him exposed to the raw isolation of the wilderness.

With grim relief, he watched the sun fold into the horizon. He flexed his fingers, aching from too tight a grip on the steering wheel, and took a deep breath to clear his lungs. He assaulted the narrow jeep road with fierce determination, perhaps even panic.

In his cabin, he built up the fire in the woodstove and set the coffeepot to boil. He inhaled the smell of the day-old coffee and pulled the darkness around him, letting the quiet soak through him. And still he trembled.

In the pure darkness of midnight, he climbed the peak. Ducking under the cupped ear of MABLE's dish, he ran his hand along its edge. He stood at the lip overlooking the tarn. The stars seemed close enough to touch—he had only to reach for them.

If he were to receive a message tonight—a real, certifiable, no-doubt-about-it message—and send an answer, he would be an old man, probably dead, before it could be received and answered. What good was a conversation that spanned generations between comments? Was there even anything out there worth listening for? It would be so easy to give up. He looked down at the pools of shadow below him.

So easy.

Just stop caring.

No one cares.

He arched his head back, hands on his hips for balance.

"Where are you?" he shouted at a deaf sky, needing the sound of his voice. "Why did you quit on me?"

He could almost sense the turning of the Earth beneath him. He thought that he should be able to hear it, like the grinding of a mill wheel or the rumble of massive machinery. Perhaps it was there, just beyond his hearing. If he listened hard enough, and held absolutely still . . .

But there was only silence. Not even the wind keened in MABLE's dish. Overhead the stars wheeled soundlessly, their light brittle and sterile in the iced air.

No moons; just stars. Stars and dark and silence. Below, the glassy stillness of the lakes reflected more stars. The lights of the campsites and mountain towns made constellations of their own, so that the horizon was lost and the sky appeared to curve down and under him.

The solidity of the Earth peeled away, leaving him, it seemed, on a pinnacle, the point of a needle. Floating. Stars above. Stars below. Drifting. No up; no down. Just he and the stars and the silence pressing upon him.

Falling!

Jeremy staggered back. His heel struck a rock. Flinging out his arms, he caught only air.

The dark caved in over him. He clawed at the night and touched only emptiness. And far overhead—oh, how impossibly far—the stars jeered.

Silent stars.

He screamed.

Closing his eyes to the vertiginous night, Jeremy rolled over. Stones shifted beneath him and clattered down the steep slope into the lake. His hands scraped against the raw granite but his feet lashed at nothing.

Trembling, he pulled himself away from the edge. On hands

and knees, feeling through the darkness, he scrabbled down the path until he perceived the dark-upon-dark bulk of the lab.

He ran.

Inside, he slammed the door against the night, and turned on every light. But the dark only closed in more, pressing blackness against the windowpanes, shutting out the stars. Looking out the window, he stared only at his own reflection. He jerked the curtains closed. Silence drifted in under the door, through cracks and vents, winding about him like a physical thing. He turned up the gain on MABLE's receiver. But the empty hiss of hydrogen was a mockery. He suddenly hated it. He'd reached out, risking humiliation, and had been abandoned. He pulled MABLE's plug.

Why are you here? he scolded himself, curling into a corner, hugging his knees to his chest.

I listen.

To what?

Stars. Lost children. It's what I do best. Someone has to listen.

Fool! Who listens to you?

Who? He stared at the radio, willing it to speak. Parker? He would only laugh. Laugh and then file a report: "Higgins flipped out last night."

Robert, then? No. Robert had never really listened to anything he said. Jeremy could almost hear him. "Jeremy, it's two in the morning. I need a cup of coffee." Besides, the call would have to go through Parker.

Jeremy shook his head slowly.

His desperate gaze found the sketch pad, the alien's face still blank. And, from this perspective, Kevin's letter just beyond.

I would like to be your friend.

As if written in a bolder hand or a darker ink, the words captured his attention.

Your friend.

His gaze shifted from letter to sketch, to letter and back again. Crawling across the floor to grab up the pad, he fumbled for a pencil without taking his eyes from that blank oval and the fragile image he now perceived there.

He drew. He erased—why had he never learned to draw faces? He drew again. Erased again. Took a deep breath and held it, trying to still the trembling of his hand. He drew.

*   *   *

A shaft of light peeked between the slit of the curtains, shyly begging entry. Jeremy stretched, yawned, and reached around to rub at the back of his right shoulder where knotted muscles tingled. Then he moved to the window and pulled aside the curtains. Night's shadow slipped like an ebbing tide down the mountainside.

Jeremy smiled, a thin smile of relief and fatigue, as he propped the sketch pad on the windowsill. Most of the features were still no more than light pencil scratchings. He would leave the face unfinished, for the eye of the beholder to complete. But the eyes were done and inked. A light wash of blue made them the focal point of the picture.

Gentle, melancholy eyes, where shadows of hidden things drifted, pleading for someone to listen. Eyes that offered so much. Offered friendship and waited. Waited for an answer.

MY YEAR WITH THE ALIENS
LISA GOLDSTEIN

We've both been Lisa Goldstein fans since she came on the scene with her American Book Award-winning novel *The Red Magician*. She's one of the most thoughtful and accomplished of the writers who have established themselves in the '80s (as evidenced by her nominations for the World Fantasy Award and the John W. Campbell Award for best new writer). Her latest novel, *A Mask for the General,* was published in hardcover by Spectra in 1987 and will be out in paperback in October. She has just been nominated for a Nebula Award for her short story, "Cassandra's Photographs." Lisa lives in Oakland, California with her husband, computer seller supreme, Doug Asherman.

"My Year with the Aliens," a richly-textured tale of alien contact set in the future, is one of the very best stories Lisa has written to date (which is saying something).

We had just taken the telescope from the storehouse when the yearly supply ship landed. My idea had been that we could use the telescope to look at the aliens' encampment. Of course I knew that the aliens were probably too far away to see, but I was running out of things for the kids to do. So the arrival of the supply ship was welcome, as a diversion if nothing else.

Stevie was the first one to see the ship. "Hey, look," he said, pointing at the sky. We all looked at the smoke trail the ship made as it automatically corrected its course to come down on the landing pad.

Erin ran for the telescope. "Fantastic," she said, looking through it. "You can see the landing gear come out and everything."

"Let me see," Stevie said.

"Why?" Erin said, not moving from the telescope.

"Because I saw the ship first."

"So?"

Stevie, who was the youngest kid on Carlson, six years old, pulled on the lace scarf Erin wore at her waist. She pushed him away, still looking through the telescope. "John," he said to me, whining. "Make her give it to me. She's hoarding. It's my turn."

"Come on," I said. "Let's go down to the landing pad."

The kids stood around uneasily. "Shouldn't we tell our parents it's here first?" Roberta asked.

Last week I had had sex with Roberta on a hay bale in one of the barns, but I had refused her second offer a few days after that. Since then she had challenged my leadership at every opportunity, and even though I hadn't wanted to be a leader in the first place, I knew that I couldn't let her challenges go unanswered. Besides, it was spring on Carlson, and I felt more restless than I'd ever felt in my life. I wanted to move, to do something. I didn't have time to wait and ask the parents, who were in the communal dining room at the monthly criticism/self-criticism session. "No, why?" I said. "They're busy. I don't think we should disturb them."

Stevie jumped up and down. "Yeah," he said. "Let's go." He ran for his bicycle, and the other kids followed him.

We rode our bikes south to the landing pad. It felt good to be out, to be doing something, and I felt even better because I knew that I really should have been inside with the parents at the monthly session. At seventeen I was treated in most things as an adult. But I had discovered a sort of loophole in the whole process of criticism/self-criticism: if you didn't go, you weren't around to be criticized. And I had no desire to listen to my parents and their friends telling me how I had screwed up.

We rode past the square artificial lakes we had filled with fish from Earth, past the pastures for the cows, the fields of wheat, the orchards of apple and plum trees. On the outskirts of the village we passed Crazy Elkonnen's house, with its small, forbidden, privately-owned garden. I rode a little faster when we came to his house and I made it to the landing pad first.

The ship had already landed by the time I got there. I slowed down when I saw it. Everything in our part of the world was so familiar to me that when I saw something new it looked unreal, almost two-dimensional. The other kids came up behind me and we got off our bikes and went closer.

The ship seemed larger than I remembered from last year. I pressed my palm against the grid and the door opened. We had never seen the supply ship before the parents had gotten to it, and we stood awhile taking it in. Our supply lists sent back to Earth had been separated into two sections, and whoever had stocked the ship must have understood the division, because everything was neatly packed on industrial shelving in two different parts of the ship.

The closest pile, the largest and least interesting to us, contained supplies our parents had asked for. Beams, glass, and fluorescent tubing for a greenhouse. Sewage treatment parts. A new sprinkler system. What looked like hundreds of identical workshirts and denim pants, the only clothes I can remember my parents wearing. Boxes of medicine, of education and entertainment videos.

We ran past that pile and over to the next, the things we kids had asked for. Lace gloves, soft kid boots, silk shirts, and bolts of silk. More than once our parents had told us that our clothes were hopelessly decadent, but whoever stocked the ship back in the United States must have decided that the clothes could pass. After all, they were made for the most part in China, which was still an ally, not like decadent Russia. This time when I picked up a shirt so light it seemed to be made entirely of spiderwebs I saw a tag sewn into it: PEOPLE'S REPUBLIC OF THE UNITED STATES. So they were making these decadent clothes even in the PRUS now, a good sign, I thought. I'd always known my parents' generation was behind the times; not surprising, really, since they'd spent 150 years in cold sleep after leaving Earth. Only non-living material could survive the instantaneous jumps the supply ships made.

Erin and Jeremy were fighting over a purple silk scarf. "John," Erin said. "He got the blue scarf last time."

"Roberta got that," Jeremy said. "I only got it after her."

"Yeah," Erin said. "A day after."

"Erin gets it the first week," I said, "and then Jeremy gets it for a week. And then it goes in the storehouse." Everybody except Jeremy seemed to think that was fair.

I looked quickly through the pile of clothing for the leather pants I had asked for, but they weren't there. Why did they consider leather decadent back on Earth but not silk? As I stood up, disappointed, I saw two large cardboard boxes stored separately from both the first and second groups. Curious, I went over and opened one of them. Inside was a video camera.

Now I noticed the envelope taped to the outside flap. I opened it and took out several sheets of folded paper:

Dear Comrades,

We have received your letter, sent with the last supply ship, about the forced landing of the Sorg. As you no doubt know, our discussions with the Sorg are at a very delicate point right now. While we trust you to use your own judgment on what the best way to deal with them might be, we cannot emphasize too strongly that it is important to be extremely careful and circumspect in your dealings with them. We the undersigned, a committee made up of biologists, physicists, anthropologists, diplomats, and Party functionaries, have found in our negotiations so far the following guidelines to be of use:

1. We do not yet completely understand the Sorg's political system, though some of us are of the opinion that it is similar in nature to our own socialist government. There are, however, many points of Party doctrine they do not seem to understand. It is not necessary to explain to the Sorg the principles of socialist thought. However, if they seem curious about our culture, try to answer their questions simply and accurately.

2. The Sorg are complete vegetarians and become squeamish when they see meat or fish being eaten.

3. Try to keep a record of any encounter with the Sorg, singly or in groups. Record the date and time of day, the weather, the circumstances, and a complete description of the encounter. Keep one copy of this record for yourselves and send another copy back via the supply ships. . . .

There was more of this drivel, pages of it. The cameras (there were two of them, apparently) had been sent to help us record our encounters with the aliens: "In all our negotiating sessions with the Sorg they have not minded the use of cameras. However, if they seem to take exception to the cameras, do not use them again. Send the film back to us via the supply ships."

I folded the message and put it back in the envelope. I could hardly wait to see how the parents were going to react. It was obvious even to me that the committee from the PRUS hadn't the faintest idea what was going on here.

The five Sorg had been on their way to Earth to join the negotiations when their ship malfunctioned and they made for the nearest inhabited world, which happened to be ours. One of the things they were on their way to negotiate about was the secret of live faster-than-light travel, how they managed to survive the interstellar jumps that had killed everyone who volunteered for them back on Earth. It was very important that the PRUS get this information before Russia or India, though I confess that just why this was important eluded me. The parents understood it, anyway.

The Sorg had sent a supply ship to their home planet for replacement parts as soon as they landed. The ship jumped back a few weeks later and they got to work. Comrade Morton, who had studied a little anthropology on Earth, went to their camp and delivered an invitation to them to come visit us, but he said that, although the Sorg were unfailingly polite, they refused because it would take time away from working on the ship. I had seen them only once, very briefly, when they visited our village right after they landed.

I looked at the two boxes again. The kids had stopped playing with the clothes. An idea started to form. "Two cameras," I said. I carefully tore the envelope off the first box and pasted it onto the second one. "Isn't that a bit decadent? When one camera would do?" I lifted the opened box and carried it outside.

I wasn't the oldest of the second generation but I think I was the oldest of the kids who had stayed outside that day, and for some reason everyone looked up to me as a leader. I had—and still have—no idea why. Just a few years ago I had been the fattest kid on the planet, the subject of at least one cruel joke a day. Then, in my sixteenth year I had grown six inches and lost all the fat, and suddenly everyone wanted to be my friend. All the boys waited on my every word, and all the girls wanted to take me to bed. And I never refused any of the girls, even though I must say that going to bed with them never satisfied me. After all, we had all slept in the same communal room until adolescence, when we were separated into a boys' dormitory and a girls' dormitory. *Like breeding stock,* I'd thought at the time. I dreamed of meeting a woman whom I hadn't seen crawling in diapers as a baby, or crying at a bad grade in school, or sweating out in the fields. I watched the videos that came on the supply ship over and over, even the educational films where a woman demonstrated the new milking machines or tractor parts, studying the unfamiliar gestures, the lift of an arm, the toss of a head. If I could only meet one of them, I thought—knowing all the while that it was impossible—my life would be fulfilled. The feeling of restlessness that had plagued me for the past year would go away.

And at the same time I knew that not even an exotic off-planet woman would make the restlessness stop. I wanted something—I can even say now I yearned for something, as embarrassing and old-fashioned as that word sounds—but I didn't know what. I would lie awake every night, tossing and turning until the boy in the bunk above me would say, "Would you for God's sake stop beating off and get to sleep?" And I'd say something stupid like, "Next time I'm in a criticism session with you I'll tell them you mentioned God." "Oh, shut up, John," he'd say.

But I became much less restless in the months after I took the camera. I don't think the camera was what I had been searching for, waiting for, all through my adolescence, but it gave me something to look forward to during the day. And I needed something to look forward to, since a little while after the supply ship landed I was excused from work to start my vocational tests.

I sat in a room with two other kids my own age, filling out questionnaires that would help determine my future. I answered page after page of questions on agriculture, child care, mechanics, animal husbandry, medicine. And all the while I sat there, the only noise in the room the rustling of paper and the scratching of pencils, I thought about how absurd it all was. I didn't want any of the options presented to me. I wanted to be a video maker.

No one on the planet had a place to store things, since private property was supposed to be unknown to us, and even might have been unknown to the first generation. But there were plenty of hiding places in the village, and after I finished my questionnaire for the day I went to the latest one—an unused barn, the hollow of a tree—and got the camera. At first I was afraid that Roberta would tell her parents what I'd done, or that someone would notice that the message had mentioned two cameras, but after a few days passed and nothing happened I relaxed.

My first feature was called *The Pioneers*. That's what the parents still called themselves, and the word had become a great joke with the second generation. I took footage of them marching off to the fields, working, marching back at night. While everyone was asleep I broke one of the massive overhead fans in the dining room, and when it had been taken down for repairs I had a perfect hole in the roof through which I could shoot the monthly meetings and criticism/self-criticism sessions. I spliced all this together, sped it up a little, and added a popular song in the background. We had our first showing on the television in the rec room, with one of the kids watching anxiously down the hall for the parents. It was a great hit.

For my next feature I filmed Crazy Elkonnen from a distance, using a zoom lens. I followed him as he bent over his pathetic little plot of dirt, hoeing it, weeding it, watering it. Every so often he stood up painfully, pressed his hand to his back, and looked out at the horizon. The first few times he did this I thought he was looking right at me, and my mouth went dry and my hands shook so badly I could see the scene jump later when I edited the film.

I did not want a confrontation with Crazy Elkonnen. The planet he had been on before coming to Carlson, Eclipse, had had total crop failure the third year of settlement. Usually when this happens, the colonists go back into the ship, back to cold sleep, and head for Earth. But for some reason no one left Eclipse. Later on, Earth people speculated that the water was drugged, or the air. Finally, when nearly everyone had died of malnutrition, five people managed to get to the ship. One of them died almost immediately after being thawed out on Earth.

Elkonnen wanted to go to another planet right away. He was held back because of the suspicious circumstances on Eclipse, and because of something people considered even more damaging. The Revolution had been fought while his ship made its slow way back to Earth, and the Party questioned the strength of his political beliefs. But he passed all his psychological tests and the examination by the Party, and he got a berth on the same ship as the parents. Once on Carlson, however, he reverted to his old capitalist habits. What he couldn't make or grow himself he took from the storehouse, secretly, as though ashamed. No one had the heart to criticize him.

When I was a child I heard his story not from one of the parents but from Jeremy, who added the rumor I was to hear again three or four times. Crazy Elkonnen had survived the famine by eating human flesh. I became convinced that he had developed a taste for cannibalism, and I knew he was only waiting his chance before he got one of us alone and reverted to what he had been on Eclipse. I organized some of the kids to keep watch over him, but they lost interest after about a month. It took years for my fear of the man to go away, and the fear came back whenever I passed him on one of the paths in the village.

After I shot enough footage of Elkonnen I edited it and called it *A Warning to Us All*. It was my second success. I stored it in the barn with the other tape.

By now my ambitions had grown enormously and I wanted to direct a play. I viewed everything in the meager library of videos the parents had brought with them from Earth, and finally decided on Bertolt Brecht's *Threepenny Opera*. The other kids were wildly excited by the idea, but it took them weeks to get down to memorizing the dialogue. Then they had to make costumes, despite my protests that the costumes came after the rehearsal. The girls had never worn dresses before, and they spent a lot of time putting them on and taking them off. I thought they looked dumb.

I used the time to read everything we had in the library on Brecht, and I found out a lot I hadn't known before. *Threepenny Opera*, for example, does not take place in Brecht's time, as I had thought, but two centuries earlier.

We rehearsed in a fallow field on the other side of the automatic sewage-treatment plant. People came to the plant so rarely that we knew no one would find us there. It was hot now, summer, and whenever the wind blew from the plant we could smell the sewage.

The rehearsals went well for the first few weeks. We had to skip a day because of an unseasonable rainfall, and the next day we could hear the singing worms in the fields around us. It was that day, too, in the middle of the wedding scene in the stable, that the kids simply stopped rehearsal. I thought Rick had forgotten his lines again and I looked in my book to prompt him. When I looked up he was staring at something behind me across the field. "Oh, shit," he said.

I still remember the complex of emotions I felt in the second it took me to turn around. I felt guilt, because I thought we had been discovered by one of the parents. But at the same time I was hoping that guilt was all I would have to feel, because Rick looked as if he was seeing something—or someone—unfamiliar to him, and in our village of eighty people that was impossible unless—

One of the Sorg stepped onto the field, staring at the ground and walking right toward us.

I had seen the aliens only briefly, when they came to visit us, so this one's appearance was still unfamiliar enough to be startling. He (she? I never found out) was bright blue, almost turquoise, probably the brightest thing on the planet. He looked human enough so that the differences were all the more shocking: the hard skin, like cartilage; the subtle wrongness of the facial bones. Tiny bumps stood out all over what I could see of the skin, and his belly protruded as though he had swallowed a cannonball. (Later that night that belly would be the subject of much ribald speculation in the boys' dorm.) He wore what looked like a copy of the parents' workshirt and pants, tailored to fit him.

The alien, still not looking up, picked his way across the field. He was almost on top of us but he didn't seem to have noticed us yet. We watched in something like shock, looking much the way we'd looked the time I'd bet Tom five of my work hours he couldn't cross the half-finished Unity Bridge. The bridge had given way beneath him and he'd fallen into the icy Unity River. I'd had to dive into the water fully clothed after him, and it looked like this time I was going to have to save everyone's asses too. I wished—as I had wished a hundred times before, though never with so much intensity—that I had never been made the unofficial leader of the second generation. "Uh, hello," I said. "Comrade."

The alien looked up, a little surprised, I thought, though probably I was reading something into his expression. "Hello, Comrades," he said. His voice, like his appearance, had subtle differences, with undertones of what sounded like a violin being played.

I cleared my throat. In all my seventeen years I had never had to talk with an adult I hadn't known since I was born, and I was finding out just how difficult it could be. I thought of all the ways I could torture the kids later on for not helping me out. But then I realized how much worse it could be if the kids joined in, because Stevie said, "Are you going to kill all of us?"

"Stevie!" Roberta said.

"No," the alien said. "We aren't going to kill you."

"What's your name?" Stevie said, unrepentant.

"Say 'Comrade,' Stevie," Roberta said.

"My name is Rurani," the Sorg said. The *r* was trilled in a way I could never imitate, as much as I tried later. "What's yours, Comrade?"

"Steve," Stevie said. "Are you here to watch our play?"

"I'm interested in studying the singing worms," Rurani said.

"I'm a biologist, and the rest of the crew doesn't need me to help fix the ship."

No one could think of anything to say to that either. I was trying not to let my surprise show. Of all the things on the planet he could have picked to study, he had chosen something I'd never given any thought to at all.

"Please," he said. "Don't let me stop you from what you're doing."

"No, of course not," I said, trying to regain control. "My name's John, by the way."

He nodded. It looked funny to see him do it, and I wondered if nodding was something he'd picked up from us, or from people on videos. He stood there awhile longer, and then, as if he sensed that we couldn't get back to the rehearsal with him standing right there, he said goodbye politely and left. We watched in silence as he went past the sewage-treatment plant. He walked as though he had too many joints, or they were in the wrong places. "God," Rick said after he was out of earshot. No one corrected him.

We were too conscious of that strange blue figure in the background, bending over and straightening, to continue rehearsal. The kids talked a little, softly, as though they were afraid they would be overheard. I didn't really pay much attention. I thought that if I could film Rurani, somehow capture on tape that furred violin voice and that strangely-shaped face, then my future would be assured. I could go back to Earth triumphant, not as a colonist from the sticks but as the first video maker ever to do a documentary about an alien being. Of course, in the 150 years it would take me to get back, video technology would change immeasurably. But maybe I could—

Suddenly I realized that I couldn't let the parents find out about the meeting. I made all the kids, about twenty-five of them, sit on the field in a circle. I talked to them reasonably, explaining that if they told the parents about the alien they would be asked a lot of questions about what they had been doing here, and that some punishment would be meted out. The same went for talking to the kids who hadn't been invited along, the ones who were always doing extra schoolwork or fieldwork, not the sort to get involved in something as disreputable as taping a play. I downplayed my role in taking the camera in the first place. As we sat there I thought how much like a criticism/self-criticism session we looked, though unlike the leader of one of those sessions I let only certain people talk.

"Do you understand?" I asked. I tried to look at each of them in turn, but it was Roberta I looked at longest. Twilight had come quickly, as it always does on Carlson, and I couldn't make out her expression. I thought I saw her nod.

But that night she went to her parents and told them we had talked to the alien. Somehow I wasn't at all surprised.

The parents canceled school the next day and called a meeting in the dining room. They pushed the tables against the walls and set up the chairs in a circle. Everyone but Elkonnen was there. I couldn't help but think that while they called it a meeting, it looked disturbingly like a criticism/self-criticism session. Had Roberta told her parents about the camera, too? What would my punishment be?

The schedule put my mother in charge of meetings for that month, but she disqualified herself because her son was directly involved. Comrade Morton, a short, fat man who had delivered the message to the aliens, opened the meeting. "We have received a report," Morton said, "that some people in our colony talked to one of the Sorg and did not report this conversation to this month's leaders, Comrade Walter and Comrade Jesse. We would like the comrades who were involved in this conversation to step forward, please."

I knew what was required of me in my position as leader. The huge fans, fixed now, whirred overhead. I raised my hand.

Morton turned to me in an odd, mechanical movement, like an automatic sprinkler. He looked disapproving. All the adults were looking disapproving, and I knew then that I was lost. None of them would be able to understand.

Our parents thought of themselves as being both ferociously practical, because they had built and farmed and irrigated Carlson, and wildly impractical, because on Earth they had been the intellectuals. When they got drunk on the bad wine they made they would reminisce about a nightclub called Betty's and sing songs we never heard at any other time. At those times I watched them as closely as they were supposed to watch the Sorg, trying to figure out what their other life had been like. For their part, they could not understand us at all. They didn't see that while they had given up their life in New York City to come to Carlson, we had never had a choice. We would live and die without seeing the big cities they had been glad to leave behind. They thought that being practical and impractical at the same time made them infinitely complex, never realizing that we, the second generation, could see through them easily. We were sure that there was more to life than what they knew. We wanted more for ourselves, wanted things we barely knew the words for: glamour, frivolity, excitement.

"How long have you been meeting with the Sorg?" Morton asked.

"Just once," I said. "Yesterday."

"And why didn't you inform Comrade Walter or Comrade Jesse about this meeting?"

Here it came. "Because then I would have had to inform them about—other things," I said.

Morton stopped for a moment, surprised. No one had told him, then. "What other things?" he asked.

"That I was using a camera I had taken from the supply ship."

Three or four people asked to be recognized. One told me how selfish I had been in hoarding the camera. Another said, "Wait a minute. You mean there was another camera? There was another camera?" over and over again, until Morton recognized Comrade Jesse. She surprised me by saying that since there was no private property in the village I hadn't really done anything wrong. Five or six more people wanted to be recognized. One of them asked what I was doing with the camera.

"Taping a play," I said. *"Threepenny Opera."*

That earned me a few points. I saw parents nodding in approval all around the circle. They loved Brecht, though judging from the videos sent on the supply ships he wasn't as much in vogue as he used to be.

"How long had you been doing this filming?" Morton asked.

"A couple of weeks."

"And who was in this play?" Morton asked.

I didn't want to give anyone away, but I wasn't really facing a moral dilemma. They would turn themselves in sooner or later—that's how these things worked. "Oh, you know," I said. "Kids."

"So you took these kids away from their studies and their work to film this play?" Morton asked.

"I didn't have any work," I said. "I was doing vocational testing."

"But what about the others?"

I shrugged. "I didn't think they'd come if they hadn't finished their other work," I said.

More people asked to be recognized, including one of the schoolteachers. I was told that schoolwork had been falling off in the past three weeks, that kids had been coming to class half-asleep. I was called selfish again. Finally they reached a consensus. I was asked to apologize for not telling anyone about the camera, and I apologized. No one made me promise to put it in the storehouse, though.

That let me off the hook for a while, and Morton turned to Roberta. "Will you please describe the conversation between the Sorg and Comrade John?" he said.

"Well," Roberta said, "he said hello. John, I mean. And then the alien said hello. Rurani. And Stevie asked him what he was doing, and the alien said that he was studying the worms, and that we should go back to what we were doing. And that was about it."

"The singing worms?" Morton asked.

"Yeah," Roberta said.

"I wonder why," Morton said. "I mean why that, and not anything else."

"There aren't any singing worms on Earth," Erin's father said.

"But the aliens aren't from Earth," my mother said. "Probably everything on Carlson is just as unfamiliar to this alien—what did you say his name was—Rurani?"

Five or six people started to talk at once, and Morton made no attempt to control them. They speculated about alien biology, alien music, alien hobbies. This was the parents at their worst, or, as they would say, their best. Meetings, including the one I had filmed from the hole in the roof, usually ended this way.

Unfortunately, an hour later Morton managed to regain control of the meeting enough to ask what should be done with us. Everyone who was involved with the play was asked to step forward, and they were given ten extra hours of work, to be spread out over the next month. Everyone but me. Because of the camera I got twenty hours. For the first time I spoke in my defense, asking if for my work hours I could continue making my video of *Threepenny Opera*. My request was denied. I was also asked to go back to the field where we had started shooting, to see if the alien would come speak to me again. This time Morton and my mother would come along.

But Rurani didn't show up the next day, or the day after that, and a week later the parents lost interest. Things went back to normal, or back to normal for everyone except me. I was angry. What was wrong with taping a play? We could certainly stand a little culture in this desolate place, couldn't we? I remembered an old-fashioned word I had read once—*godforsaken*—and I repeated it to myself as I attacked the weeds in the fields or got up early to milk the cows. I took a perverse pleasure in thinking that I was the first person on the planet ever to speak that word aloud.

Amy was working in the supply store when I went to check out the weeding machine. "Fieldwork again?" she asked as I signed the book.

"Yeah," I said. "They're out to get me. All I ever wanted was to bring a little culture—"

She stopped me. I think by this time everyone had grown a little tired of my speeches. "I'll trade you," she said.

"Yeah?" I said. "I'll take it. What's so hard about the supply store?"

"Guess who's checked out a television?" she said. I couldn't guess. "Crazy Elkonnen."

"You're kidding," I said. "Does he have electricity?"

She laughed, though I hadn't meant to be funny. "Apparently he does," she said. "He's had the set for a month now. And guess who has to go and get it back? I've put it off every day this week. Still want to trade?"

"No, thanks," I said, and headed for the bean field. Things could be a lot worse.

I forgot the conversation with Amy almost as soon as I left the supply house. I had something else on my mind. It had rained the night before, and that meant the singing worms would be back, and maybe, just maybe, Rurani would be back too. I weeded a few rows and then stopped, looking at the fields around me.

From all sides I heard the liquid harmonies of the worms. I had never paid attention to them before, up until Erin's father had mentioned at the meeting that there were no singing worms on Earth. Then I started to find them fascinating. The first generation might know about all kinds of things I could barely imagine— from big cities to nightclubs—but when it came to the worms we were equal. And it didn't hurt that Rurani was interested in them. I had even looked them up in the library in case Rurani came back, so that I would have something to talk to him about. But the only thing I could find was a fragment of a study Morton had started ten years ago and then apparently abandoned.

I turned the machine around and weeded another row. And then I saw him, one field over, bending and straightening just like he had the last time. Without hesitation I turned off the machine and walked over to talk to him.

"Hello, Comrade Rurani," I said.

"Hello, Comrade John," he said.

Now that I was here, the enormity of what I wanted to do embarrassed me. Had I truly thought that this strange being, with whom I had exchanged maybe ten words of conversation, would agree to let me tape him? "Um," I said. "Did you find any worms?"

"Yes, I did," he said.

"They're interesting, aren't they?" I said. "Did you know there aren't any on Earth?"

"No," he said. "I didn't know that. We have none on my planet either."

For the first time I noticed that his accent was different from ours, was closer to that of the people on the videos. He must have learned English from current videos for the negotiations, and of course the language had changed in 170 years. I felt even more self-conscious, and awkward, too. Not because he was an alien, though that did make me uncomfortable. But I would have felt just as shy with anyone from off-planet.

I followed him as he walked through the field, trying desperately to think of something to say. "Is that why you're studying them?"

"I'm studying them because they interest me," he said, not taking his eyes off the muddy ground. "Don't you have something that interests you?"

"Sure," I said. "I want to make videos. I have ideas for about eight or ten more. Some of them I'd like to write myself—I know just how I'd do it. But, see, I'm limited as long as I stay on this planet. I'd have to go back to Earth, use their technology, their actors, because no one here has the slightest idea how to act. . . ."

I had never told any of this to anyone. I don't even know why I was telling him, except that maybe I thought he could understand, that he had some kind of superior wisdom. But his answer, after a silence of several seconds, was disappointing. "How can you go back to Earth?" he asked. "You'll never get a ship to take you back, and even if you do it will be a hundred and fifty years before you land on Earth."

I couldn't help it. "You can take me with you," I said. "You have faster-than-light travel. I can go with you when you leave."

He moved away from me, only a few inches, but I knew I'd been rebuffed. The message about the Sorg I'd read on the supply ship had said that they move away to show that they want the subject changed. "We are not allowed to talk about faster-than-light travel," he said. "We may discuss it only with the negotiators on Earth."

"I wasn't talking about faster-than-light travel," I said. "I don't care about that at all. All I want is to get a ride on your ship, and then I can—"

Rurani turned and walked away. By his standards he wasn't being impolite, and yet when I went back to the weeding machine I felt more discouraged than I ever had before. All around me I could hear the worms singing loudly.

I didn't see him for a few days, though I looked for him in the bean field whenever I passed it. In my mind I rehearsed conversations with him, ways I could get him to take me to Earth, and the conversations always ended with his promise. On my second-to-last day of extra work I was walking to the field, thinking about the alien and Earth and the woman, long dead now, who had played Polly in the video of *Threepenny Opera*, and not paying any attention at all to my surroundings. A harsh voice said, "Hey, boy. Look up."

I looked. Crazy Elkonnen stood a few feet up the path.

My first impulse, I'm ashamed to say, was to run. But I knew I couldn't do that. I stared back at him, trying to look defiant, hoping he couldn't hear my heartbeat.

"I want to talk to you," he said, moving closer to me. His breath smelled vile, and I wondered when he'd last checked out toothpaste from the supply house. His voice sounded hoarse. I couldn't remember when I'd heard him talk to me, or to anyone. "You think I'm funny, don't you?" he said. "You laugh at me, I've seen you. Crazy Elkonnen, you call me. Don't you?"

"N-no," I said.

"No, *sir*," he said correcting me.

"No, sir," I said. I wondered what "sir" meant.

"You do, though," he said, coming closer to me. It was all I could do not to move away. "But you never think about what things might be like for me, do you? Well, do you?"

"No," I said. "No, sir."

"You bet you don't," he said. "Here I was, just back from Eclipse—a hellhole, boy, you better pray nothing like that ever happens to you—finally get back to the United States, the place I'd most wanted to be in all the universe, and what do I find?

The whole place has been taken over by Communists." He made it sound like a dirty word. "By Communists! My father fought a war to keep us safe from Communists, did you know that, boy?"

I tried not to show surprise. No, I hadn't known that, and neither, I'll bet, had the Party members who'd examined him. They probably wouldn't have let him back into space if they had.

"So the first thing I think is, I've got to get away," he said. "I think, maybe things'll be better on another planet. I can adapt, sure, I can adapt. I study Marx, Lenin, all those guys. I even get so I believe it, or I tell myself I believe it. And I make it, and I meet my fellow crewmates, I'm real polite, and you know what? Every damn person knows everyone else. They're all from New fucking York. I'm the odd man out, see? The odd man out. So I think, *What tne hell, I can adapt. I'll wait, I'll get to the planet, I'm skillful with my hands, always been skillful with my hands, and they'll love me.* Except they don't. Years go by. It never changes. Your mother? Your mother, the one every-one says is so smart? Your mother's a snotty bitch. Wouldn't give me the time of day. The time of day," he said again, emphasizing every word.

"Years go by," he said. "And then the aliens land. And you know what? They like me. I'm an alien too, in a manner of speaking. That guy you talked to, Rurani? We're buddies, me and Rurani. We're good friends. No one understands me, but Rurani does. You bet Rurani does."

He went on like that for quite a while. Obviously he'd wanted to say these things to someone for a long time. I couldn't listen. I knew that people don't belong to other people, that no one can own another person, but I'd always thought of Rurani as mine. As far as I knew I was the only person he'd ever talked to except for Stevie, and Stevie didn't count. Elkonnen was lying, he had to be. Rurani would never talk to someone as coarse as this man. But what if he had? If Elkonnen had wanted to hurt me for whatever grievances, real or imagined, he could not have found a better way.

"You just think I'm funny, right?" he said. "A funny guy. Never thought I'd make friends with your pet alien, did you? I'm just there to be laughed at. Crazy Elkonnen. Crazy Elkonnen, a warning to us all."

Everything fell together then, and I almost groaned out loud. Elkonnen had found my video. He'd found my video, and that's why he'd checked out the television. And he'd had the television for a month, so he'd watched it a dozen times, at least.

He must have seen me tense. He stepped even closer, looking gleeful. "That's right, boy, I found your video," he said. "I knew you were making it, saw you point that damn camera at me, and it was only a matter of time before I found it. And you know what I'm going to do about it?"

I shook my head.

"First I thought, I'll tell the boy's parents," he said. "But then I saw your other video, and I realized you had no respect for your parents. Fact is, I have no respect for your parents, so that's one thing we agree on, boy. And then I thought, *Well, who does he respect? He respects Rurani, that's who.* So I figured, why, I'll just tell Rurani what you did. Show him what you're capable of. And I'll bet he'll never talk to you again. I'll bet that. We're buddies, Rurani and me."

"No," I said, involuntarily. "No, you can't—"

"I can't?" he said. "You just watch me, boy." And he walked away.

I don't remember the rest of the day at all. I must have weeded, must have eaten dinner and done something in the evening, but my mind was in turmoil. If Elkonnen said anything to Rurani, I would have no chance at all of persuading him to take me to Earth. And the Sorg were my last hope, my only hope. I knew I could persuade Rurani if only I could talk to him. I wouldn't even have to mention faster-than-light travel.

On my last day of extra work, to my great relief, I saw Rurani at the end of the bean field. "Hi, Comrade," I said.

"Hello, Comrade John," he said.

Now what? I tried to think of the best way to turn the conversation to what I wanted, to ask again if I could come with him when he left for Earth. And after a moment I realized I had another problem. Crazy Elkonnen was walking slowly down the path to the bean field.

Had Elkonnen talked to Rurani? I knew that I had to discredit Elkonnen before he discredited me, a tactic I had learned in the criticism/self-criticism sessions. I couldn't let him come between me and my only chance for Earth. "See that man down there?" I said to Rurani.

Rurani nodded.

"He was on another planet before he came here," I said. "A planet called Eclipse. And there was a terrible famine on Eclipse, lots of people died. You know how they say Elkonnen survived?"

Rurani shook his head.

"By eating other people," I said. "He was a cannibal."

Rurani tensed. I saw that he wanted to move away, to change the subject, but that he was forcing himself to stay near me. "Is this what people do?" he said slowly. "Do they eat each other?"

I realized, too late, what I had done. *Oh shit,* I thought. The Sorg didn't even eat animals. A group of people that ate each other would be even more repulsive to them than it was to us. They would never give us faster-than-light travel now. By trying to make it to Earth, by focusing on my own narrow dreams, I had closed the door on everyone's dreams—the Americans', the Russians', the Indians', everyone's.

"No," I said quickly. "No, I made that up because I was mad at him. It's not a true story. He didn't really eat anyone."

For a moment I thought I had done it. But then Rurani stood up and walked away. I watched him go and went back to weeding. All day I hoped that he would come back later, the way he had before, and we could talk about something else.

But Rurani never came back. The next day we heard a noise that the second generation had never heard, and the first generation had heard only deep in their bones while fast asleep. Rurani's ship was taking off. All over the village people dropped what they were doing and ran to see it, a chip of bright metal mounted on a plume of smoke ten times bigger than that of the supply ships. Someone got the telescope out of the storehouse and we tracked it for as long as we could. Then, abruptly, it vanished.

"It's near Earth now," Morton said, awed. "They're seeing Earth, this very second."

"Amazing," Walter said.

Everyone, it seemed, wanted to stop work for the day and talk, as though this were the anniversary of the landing or of the Revolution, the two holidays we celebrated. Everyone except me. I went away angrily, feeling somehow betrayed. But betrayed by whom? Elkonnen? Rurani?

Had Elkonnen told Rurani about my cruelty to him, and had Rurani left me behind for that reason? Or did he believe that Elkonnen was a cannibal and not want anything to do with any of us? When I remembered my conversations with Rurani, brief as they were, I turned hot with embarrassment. In my mind I saw myself running after him, worm dangling from my hand, desperate to curry favor. Always before I had thought of myself as popular, strong, in control, and this new picture of myself was very disturbing. Even Stevie could have done a better job of talking to him. What could Rurani possibly have thought of me?

I spent the next few months asking myself those questions

over and over again, obsessively. The rains started, and the singing of the stupid worms seemed to come from every direction, mocking me. How could I have ever thought they were interesting?

The results of my vocational tests came in and I started learning mechanical repair under Jesse. But the questions left me no room to concentrate on anything else, and Jesse had to explain the simplest things to me again and again. She was very good about it, patient, uncomplaining, but I didn't care. I would stay on Carlson the rest of my life, and the worst thing about it was that I would never know why. I would never know if I could have said something to make Rurani understand what I wanted, or even if he'd been capable of understanding.

Time passed. We celebrated my eighteenth birthday, and the twentieth anniversary of the ship's landing. Slowly I stopped feeling so sorry for myself. I talked to Jesse more, and she showed me some of her inventions, brightly painted scraps of metal she'd put together that walked or jumped or flipped over when you wound them up. There was some frivolity left in the first generation, after all.

About this time I realized that Elkonnen might know the answers to some of my questions. It had taken me so long to figure this out, I guess, because I hated the whole idea of talking to him. I started forcing myself to wave to him whenever he passed. At first he looked surprised, suspicious, but after a while I got him to wave back. Then I started calling to him, saying, "Hello, Comrade!" I saw he didn't like the word *comrade,* so after that I just said hello. And then finally, one day, he stopped to talk.

"You want something from me, boy?" he said. His breath was as bad as ever.

"Me? No," I said. "Actually I just wanted to talk. You must have seen some really interesting things, living before the Revolution and everything."

"You just stop making fun of me," he said, and walked away.

But the next time I waved to him he came over. "Been thinking about what you said, boy," he said. "You got a point. I'm the only man in the universe who remembers what it was like before the Revolution. I ought to tell it to somebody so they can write it down. So it doesn't get forgotten. Oral history, they used to call that. Do they still do that?"

"Sure," I said. "Only we can tape it. I can make a video."

He actually laughed. "I might've known," he said. "You and that damn camera. You want to do that, boy?"

"Sure," I said.

I got the camera from my hiding place and we started taping. We met every day after that, after I'd finished my work with Jesse. Some of what he said was tremendously exciting, almost unbelievable. "Everyone had a car in those days, everyone, rich or poor. You get in your car and you can go anyplace you like, anywhere at all, and no one would stop you. Move clear across the country if you like, quit your job one day and start another one the next. None of this vocational-testing shit." But some of it was so boring I had to force myself not to yawn, like the time he went on for fifteen minutes about soap. "You could go into any store you wanted and there'd be eight, ten different kinds of soap. You had a real choice in those days, you bet. That's what capitalism was, it meant having a choice. You could buy any one of those soaps you wanted." He got angry when I asked him why you'd need that many.

After I'd been meeting with Elkonnen for about a month I realized that the kids had stopped looking up to me. Some of them even teased me. "Better watch it," Rick said once. "If he asks you to his house for dinner, better not go. Because you know what'll happen. You'll be the dinner." The other kids laughed wildly.

The funny thing was that I didn't care. I found out I didn't miss being a leader at all. I felt as though I had more friends than I had ever had before, though in fact I had only two: Elkonnen and Jesse. Because in a strange kind of way Elkonnen and I had become friends. I got him to go see Marilyn, our dentist, and Marilyn pulled two teeth that she later told me must have been hurting him for years. I told my parents how lonely he was, and when my mother waved to him one day you could have lit a match from the energy in his smile. I became the only person on the planet besides him who knew that his first name was George.

His strangeness, his alienness, was part of what attracted me to him. He pulled me out of myself in a way no one at a criticism/self-criticism session had ever done. And yet by his very solitariness he showed me how important a community is. One day after I'd finished taping I found myself heading not to my hiding place but to the supply store to check in the camera. I was the only person who ever checked it out again anyway.

In a lot of ways, I think, he was the key to the parents' life on Carlson. Although he believed, or needed to believe, that his life had been better before the Revolution, he couldn't help but mention once or twice how poor most of the people had been, including his own family. Through him I could see why the Revolution had been fought. I still thought of the parents as boring and narrow-minded, but I no longer blamed them as much as I had. I learned that the questions were more complex than I'd thought, that no one, not the parents or Elkonnen or even me, had all the answers.

But no matter how close we got, Elkonnen never answered my questions about the Sorg. He liked me, I think, and he was lonely enough to talk to anyone who'd talk to him first, but he never forgave me for that first video I'd made of him. He'd smile slyly and say, "That Rurani, now, he was a gentleman. He treated me right. Not like you Communists." But he wouldn't say whether he'd told Rurani about my video. I think that was his revenge.

I was beginning to think that I would never find out, when the supply ship landed in the spring. On it was a nearly frantic letter from the negotiating team. "The Sorg now seem to believe for some reason that humans practice cannibalism," the letter said. "We have denied this repeatedly, but we do not think they believe us. They are threatening to end the negotiations and return home.

"We think that they may have picked up this outlandish idea when they stopped to repair their ship on Carlson. We know, of course, that you would never give them this idea directly. But it is possible that they misinterpreted something you said. If you can remember anything that might shed some light on this subject, anything at all, please send it along with your report and supply list."

I hadn't gone out to the supply ship with the parents, so I didn't know anything about this letter until Amy told me. "Maybe your friend Elkonnen said something to Rurani," she said. "Do you think he'd do something like that? Maybe you'd better ask him."

I couldn't answer. I felt as if someone had hit me squarely in the solar plexus and knocked all the breath out of me. *I've ruined our chances*, I kept thinking. *I've ruined all our chances.* A stupid kid from a backwater planet who had never done anything of the slightest consequence had somehow managed to tip the scales against all of humanity, to throw away faster-than-light travel for everyone. I walked away from Amy without saying anything, like a Sorg. "John?" she called after me. "John, are you all right?"

I felt physically sick for the next few days. The worst part was that I couldn't ever tell anyone what had happened. I didn't have enough work hours left in my life for the kind of punishment I'd get if people knew what I'd done. I stopped talking to Jesse and Elkonnen, and spent a lot of time drafting letters in my head to the PRUS. But if the PRUS knew the true story, then sooner or later so would everyone on Carlson. Every scenario I could imagine ended badly.

When the parents called a meeting, I knew I had to go or they would become suspicious. It was a typical chaotic meeting, with everyone hotly denying that he or she had given the aliens such a ridiculous idea. Without any prompting from me, Elkonnen came and took a seat at the very back, outside the circle. I watched him closely throughout the meeting, feeling the start of renewed hope. Maybe he had said something to Rurani after all and I was off the hook. Maybe he'd come to the meeting because he wanted to speak. But he never stopped scowling, and at the end of the meeting, while the parents drafted an angry letter to send back with the supply ship, he got up and left.

I ran after him. "Elkonnen!" I said. "George!" He stopped and turned to me.

"Listen," I said. "Did you ever—you know—when you talked to Rurani did you ever say anything about—"

"About cannibalism?" he said. "Hell no, boy." He pushed me hard enough to throw me off balance. He was smiling now, a fierce, almost evil smile that made me shudder. At that moment I could easily imagine him eating the colonists on Eclipse. "And do you know why? No? Well, I'll tell you. Because I never talked to Rurani at all. Never. I just told you all that bullshit to worry you, boy. Looks like I did a pretty good job, didn't I?"

I stepped back.

"But I bet I know who did tell him," he said, coming after me. "I bet it was you, boy. Am I right? You told Rurani, didn't you, boy?"

"No," I said. "No. I didn't." I was whispering, as if the people still at the meeting could hear me.

"Whatever you like, boy," Elkonnen said. "Don't worry—I won't tell anyone. I keep myself to myself, you must have noticed that about me. Don't even know why I went to that stupid meeting. But if I were you I'd tell someone. It's not good to keep stuff bottled in like that. But hell, I don't mean to give you advice.'' And he walked away.

I did a lot of thinking that night, after everyone in the dorm room fell asleep. I understood that in his own strange way Elkonnen had made me a gift of his advice in exchange for everything I'd done for him. If you don't tell anyone, he was saying, you'll become like me. It was this, finally, that made me understand what I had to do. As he had done before, he had somehow drawn out the best part of me, the part I could be proud of. Whatever happened, I knew I would always be grateful to him. Halfway through the long sleepless night I realized how I could phrase my letter, and I got out of bed and went to the school to use the computer.

In the letter I told the PRUS that I had had several intimate conversations with one of the negotiators, Rurani. In one of these conversations, I said, I may have unwittingly led him to his unfortunate conclusion about the human race. I mentioned that there were many other things I could probably explain, that I would be invaluable as a member of the negotiation team. Unfortunately, I added, I was on Carlson and not on Earth. But if the negotiators could persuade the Sorg to come to Carlson and pick me up instead of going back home, they might find that I could make their task a little easier.

I also told them I know how to use a camera.

O Z

LEWIS SHINER

Speaking of wildly talented young writers, Lewis Shiner is another one of the very best to develop over the past few years. His first novel, *Frontera,* was nominated for the Nebula Award and he has received a great deal of attention for his electrifying short fiction. His newest novel, *Deserted Cities of the Heart,* was just published in hardcover by our sister company, Foundation Books (Doubleday), and will be published in paperback by Spectra in 1989. Lew lives in Austin, Texas with his wife.

It would take longer to attempt to describe "Oz" than it takes to read it. Take a deep breath. Brace yourself. Enjoy.

They fucking ripped the joint. Ozzie bit the head off a white lab rat during "CIA Killers" and Toad threw a sixteen-inch floor tom into the audience. Three girls rushed Ozzie during "Bay of Piggies," one of them with no shirt on. The cops had to empty the place with tear gas.

The goddamn reporters were mobbed outside. "Twenty-five years," one of them shouted. "How does it feel?"

"Piss off," Ozzie said. He was pushing fifty, still skinny and barely strong enough to last through a two-hour set. How the hell was he supposed to feel? "I was acquitted, remember? You know who did it. They all went to jail. All hundred and fifty of them. So leave me the fuck alone."

"But why rock and roll?" another one shouted.

Because I was going nuts. Framed, beaten, tried, but never forgiven. Fuck you all, he thought. *You got the greatest era of peace in the history of the world. No more assassinations, America out of Vietnam before it even got ugly, manned colonies on Mars. All because you got rid of those 150 bloodsucking bastards, in Attica now, the ones that had lived.*

But what about me?

"Why not?" Ozzie said.

"Lee!" another one shouted. "Lee, over here!"

"It's not Lee anymore," Ozzie snarled. "It's Ozzie Oswald, nice and legal, got it?"

Then he was into the limousine, soundproof, bulletproof, the kind Kennedy should have had. He laughed at the crowd and held up his middle fingers. *If I had it to do over,* he thought, *I would have killed him myself. What do you think about that?*

The limo took him off, laughing, into the night.

DEAD
MEN ON TV
PAT MURPHY

Speaking of speaking of wildly talented young writers, no listing of "the best of the newer arrivals" would be complete without Pat Murphy. Her short fiction, which appears in all of the major genre magazines, draws non-stop accolades and her most recent novel, *The Falling Woman,* drew non-stop Nebula Award recommendations. Pat's a graduate of the 1978 Clarion Writers' Workshop. She works at San Francisco's Exploratorium, one of the most enjoyable museums in the world.

"Dead Men on TV" is a poignant, heart-stirring contemporary story. It is state-of-the-art Pat Murphy.

stay up late each night, watching my dead father on TV. Tonight, he's in *Angels of the Deep*, a World War II movie about the crew of a submarine. My father plays Vinny, a tough New York kid with a chip on his shoulder. He was about twenty when the movie was made; he's darkly handsome, and an air of danger and desperation surrounds him.

I've seen the movie half-a-dozen times before, but I turn on the TV and curl up in my favorite easy chair with a glass of bourbon and a cigarette. The cream-colored velvet that covers the easy chair's broad arm is marked with cigarette burns and dark rings from other glasses of bourbon on other late nights. The maid told me that the stains won't come out, and I told her that I don't care. I don't mind the stains. The rings and burns give me a record of many late nights by the TV. They give me a feeling of continuity, a sense of history: I belong here. The television light flickers in the darkened room, warming me like a fire. My father's voice speaks to me from the set.

"Can't you feel it?" my father says to another sailor. His voice is hoarse; his shoulders are hunched forward, as if he were trying to make himself smaller. "It's all around us—dark water pushing down. Trying to get in." He shivers, wrapping his arms around his body, and for a moment his eyes meet mine. He speaks to me. "I've got to get out, Laura. I've got to."

On the TV screen, a man named Al shakes Vinny, telling him to snap out of it. Al dies later in the movie, but I know that the man who played Al is still alive. I saw his picture in the newspaper the other day: he was playing in a celebrity golf tournament. In the movie, he dies and my father lives. But out here, my father is dead and Al is alive. It seems strange to be watching Al shaking my dead father, knowing that Al is alive and my father is dead.

"I've got to get out," my father moans.

He can't get out. For the next hour and a half, he'll be stuck in the submarine with the water pressing in. I watch without sympathy as my father cowers in his bunk.

Late at night I watch the movies, knowing that most of the men and women who move across the TV screen are dead. In my living room, they tell jokes and laugh, dance to big-band tunes played by dead musicians, lie and cheat and betray one another, argue and make love. And despite all that, they are dead. It seems strange to watch dead people on TV. Are they all being punished? What did the others do, who did they hurt, who must forgive them?

I never believed in heaven or hell or life after death until the day after my father's funeral. I was sitting alone in my father's house, and I turned on the television. My father's face stared out at me. He was surrounded by stone walls and darkness. It took me a moment to recognize the scene from *The Pharaoh's Tomb*. My father plays an archaeologist who is trapped in the tomb by a gang of criminals who want to steal the ancient artifacts.

"We're trapped in here," said a woman's voice. She was on the edge of hysteria.

"There's got to be an escape route," he said. "We'll find it. There's got to be a way out."

My father was right there on my TV screen, even though I knew he was dead. He spoke to me from the TV screen.

I figure it this way. The movie camera steals a person's soul. Just a little bit of the soul with each picture it takes. But if a person is in a great many movies—well then, his whole soul is sucked up into the camera and caught in the movies.

The way I figure it, I have my father's soul in a box.

The Grocery-on-Wheels truck delivers my supplies: *TV Guide*, bourbon, eggs for breakfast, cold cuts for lunch, steak to grill for dinner, a few canned soups, fresh vegetables for variety. I cook for myself these days. I don't eat much. The last cook disapproved of my drinking and pestered me to eat more, go out more. So I fired her and now I cook for myself, eating only when my body demands fuel.

As a child, I was overweight: a round-faced little girl who, in all the photos, wears a sullen expression. Now I am thin. My wristbones are enormous. I can count my ribs. My face is angular, and I can see the bones beneath the skin. I order my clothes from mail-order catalogs and they are always too large for me, but I don't mind. I wear them anyway, belting the pants tightly to keep them from falling.

After I put away the groceries, I don my bikini and lie by the pool, leafing through the *TV Guide*. My father left me this ranch house and the trust fund that supports me. The gardener tends the yard and the pool. The maid cleans the house. I keep my father's soul alive by watching his old movies. He's all I have left.

I was five years old when my mother died. I remember she had soft hands and dark curly hair. I have pictures of her: a soft-bodied woman tending to fat, with a round face and dark eyes.

She came to California from Georgia, a soft-spoken country girl with a slight southern drawl. She was working as a secretary at MGM, and she met my father there. At the time, my father was still taking bit parts in cut-rate monster movies and westerns.

The year I was born, my father landed his first big role— Vinny in *Angels of the Deep*. That movie was a hit, and he went on from there with a few more war movies. Then he played a hard-boiled detective in a series of movies, and made a name for himself.

My mother started drinking heavily. Every afternoon she would sit by the pool, a glass of bourbon by her side. Some nights, my father wouldn't come home. The next day, my mother would start drinking early in the morning, lying in a lounge chair in her black one-piece swimsuit, dark circles beneath her dark eyes. I remember sticky kisses that stank of bourbon. I remember her telling me, "Your father's a no-good louse."

Bourbon and sleeping pills killed her. The coroner called it accidental death: she left no suicide note. But I know better. She killed herself; my father drove her to it. After that, my father was home even less. And when he was home, he seemed to look through me, as if I weren't real. I hated that.

I don't hate my father for the things he did to me. He didn't do anything much to me. I hate him for the things he didn't do. He didn't love me, he didn't want me, he didn't care about me—and that's what I can't forgive.

He sent me to private boarding schools, where I waited desperately for summer break. Then, during summer break, he sent me to camp. I lived in dormitories and cabins, cared for by teachers and counselors and housemothers. And I saw more of my father on the movie screen than I ever did in life.

He married again—three more times. Each marriage ended in divorce. But he had no more children. One was enough. One was too much. I don't think he ever wanted a daughter.

It's one in the morning, and I'm watching a videotape of *The Darkness Underground*. My father plays an impoverished coal miner, working the mine in a company town.

The living room is illuminated by the light from the TV screen. I love the light the TV casts—it makes everything seem unreal, fantastic, as if the living room had no substance. The couch and end table are dim outlines, barely visible. In this light, I'm not real. Only the world on the TV set is real.

The videotape is old: colored snow flickers on the screen. I watch the videotapes only when I have no choice; I'd much rather watch a broadcast and know that many people are watching my father. But the tapes have some advantages.

"I hate this life," my father says. He slams his fist down on the rough wooden table. "I hate it. I know why the fox gnaws off its leg to escape a trap."

"Don't," says the woman who plays his wife. I think her name is Mary. She dries her hands on her apron and hurries to his side.

I stop the tape, run it back, then play it again. "I hate this life," he says. Then he catches sight of me and stares from the television. "Laura, listen to me. Please." His face fills the screen. His skin is mottled with red and yellow snow that dances across his cheeks like flames. He slams his fist into the table. This time, I stop the tape before the woman can rush to comfort him.

I play the scene over and over, watching him strike the table and cry out in anger and frustration, unable to escape. "I can't stand this life," he says. "Laura . . ." His eyes watch me from the screen.

At last I let the movie run to the end. My father leads the miners in a strike. They triumph against the company, but my father dies. It's a good movie, especially the cave-in that kills my father. I play that over a few times.

At my mother's funeral, I walked beside my father, holding his hand. I've seen pictures of us standing at the grave. My father looks handsome in a black suit; I'm wearing a black dress, black gloves, and a broad-brimmed black hat. The only spot of white is my face: round, pale, and mournful, with black smudges for eyes. I remember that the dew from the grass in the graveyard beaded up on my new patent leather shoes. The droplets caught the sun and sparkled like diamonds. Newspaper reporters took pictures of us, but I would not look at the photographers; I was watching my shoes. When we left the photographers behind, my father stopped holding my hand.

We rode back home in a big black car that stank of dying flowers. I sat on one side of the big backseat, and he sat on the other. His eyes were rimmed with red and his breath smelled of whiskey.

I can't watch my mother on TV; she was never in the movies. I wonder what happened to her soul when she died. Is there a heaven for people who were never in the movies?

On Sunday afternoon, the two o'clock movie is *Summer Heat*. I've seen it before: my father plays a prisoner in San Quentin who was framed for a crime he did not commit.

At about one-thirty, I pull the drapes so that the room is dark and I switch on the TV. Instead of a picture, I get jagged lines, like lightning across the screen. I thump the side of the TV and the lightning jerks, but the picture does not return. The sound is a hash of white noise.

It's the maid's day off. I'm alone in the house and panic sets in quickly. I have to see the movie. I always watch my father's movies. I smack the set again and again, bruising my hand. I switch desperately from channel to channel. Nothing.

I look under "Television Repair" in the telephone book. In shop after shop, the phone rings unanswered. Sunday afternoon and no one is at work.

Finally, at a place called Pete's Repair-It, a man answers the phone. "Pete's Repair-It. Pete speaking."

"Thank God you're there," I say quickly. "My television's broken and I have to have it fixed."

"Sure," says the man. "Drop it by on Monday and I'll have a look."

"You don't understand," I say shakily. "It has to be fixed this afternoon. My father will be on at two and . . ." I glance at the clock. "It's quarter to two now. I'll pay extra."

"Sorry, ma'am," he says politely. "The shop's closed to-day. I just stopped by to—"

Then I break down. "You have to help me," I plead. "You just have to. My father's going to be on TV at two and I have to see him." I start crying and I can barely speak.

"Hang on," he mutters. "Just calm down. What's the matter with the set?"

Between sniffles, I describe the TV's behavior. He gets my address and promises that he will come right away. I pace, watching the clock. At five to two, I hear a van in the drive-way. I meet the man halfway down the walk. He's a broadly built man, middle-aged, with glasses and curly brown hair. Over the pocket of his red shirt, his name is embroidered: PETE. He carries a toolbox.

"Please hurry," I beg him.

I watch him work: removing the back of the TV and inspecting the tangle of wires inside. "Would you like something to drink?" I ask awkwardly.

"Sure. Have you got a beer?"

I shake my head. "How about bourbon and lemonade? That's what I'm drinking."

"All right," he says. "I'll try it."

He is whistling softly as I come out of the kitchen. "You could probably get yourself a new TV for the price of this house call," he says.

I nod. "Maybe I'd better get another. So I'll have one as a spare."

He chats as he works, talking about what's wrong with the set, about how much a new set might cost me, but I pay little attention. I am watching the clock, waiting for the moment I can watch the movie. Finally, at two-thirty, he plugs in the set and the picture snaps into focus. "Thank you," I say. "Oh, thank you."

I curl up happily on the couch. On the TV screen, my father paces to and fro in his little cell. "I don't belong here," he says.

His cellmate, a wiry man with a thin face and cold eyes, lies back on his bunk and laughs. "You and every other con in the joint."

"You don't understand." The screen shows a close-up of my father's face, his tortured eyes, his square chin rough with stubble. "I'm innocent."

"This is a great movie," I say to Pete.

"You've seen this before?" He picks up his drink and sits beside me on the couch.

"Of course," I say. "Five times before."

"Sure, you're innocent," my father's cellmate is saying. "You and everyone else. We're all innocent." The wiry man takes a drag on his cigarette, then blows the smoke at the ceiling. "But we're all stuck here together."

"If you've seen it before, then what was the big hurry to get the set fixed?" Pete growls. He is staring at me with puzzlement and frank curiosity. "You got me out here on a Sunday with a sob story about your father being on TV, and . . ."

"That's my father," I say quickly, pointing to the TV, where my father is lighting a cigarette.

"He's your dad?" Pete stares at the set. "I grew up watching his movies."

"So did I," I say. "I watch all his movies. All of them."

For a moment, Pete glances from the screen to my face and back again. "Yeah, I can see it," he says. "You look like his daughter."

I'm startled. "You think so?"

"Of course," he says. "Especially the eyes. You got the same eyes. I should have recognized you."

I notice that his glass is empty and I offer him another bourbon and lemonade. He accepts. I feel strangely comfortable watching the movie with him.

"He died about a year ago," I say. "But I watch all his movies. That keeps him with me."

"What a great guy he must have been." Pete hesitates a moment, then says soberly, "You must miss him a lot." He puts one arm around my shoulders as if to comfort me. I lean against his shoulder.

"Not really," I say. "These days, I've got him right where I want him. He can't get away."

Pete frowns. "What do you mean?"

"He's right here," I say. "I watch him every night." I laugh and Pete smiles uncertainly. But he stays for another drink. And another. We both get a little drunk.

I seduce the TV repairman by the light of the television, that flickering uncertain light where nothing is quite real. My father watches from the screen.

The late movie is a musical. My father plays a gambler who falls in love with a society lady. Dead men and women sing songs about love, and Pete's snores blend with the music, a rumbling bass voice. A vigorous chorus startles Pete; he wakes and blinks at me myopically.

"You okay?" he mumbles. He scratches his head sleepily, waiting for my reply.

"I just can't sleep," I say. "It's okay."

He struggles to a sitting position on the couch. "It's my snoring," he mutters gloomily. "I'm keeping you awake."

"No," I say. "Not at all. I just don't sleep much."

He sighs and pushes a hand through his hair. Half the curls stand on end. The curly hair on his chest matches the hair on his head. "My ex-wife always complained that I snored like a freight train."

I study him with new interest. Knowing that he has an ex-wife who complained about his snoring somehow makes him more real. He is naked and that suits him better than the shirt embroidered with PETE'S REPAIR-IT.

On the TV, three dead women in tight, sequined dresses sing about summer nights, moonlight, and love.

"What happened to your ex-wife?" I ask.

"She found someone who didn't snore and moved to Phoenix, Arizona."

"Do you hate her?"

"Naw. I figure living in Phoenix is punishment enough." He shrugs. "She's got what she wanted, but she still isn't happy. Some people just don't know how to be happy." He yawns and lumbers to his feet. "Want some hot milk to make you sleep?" Without waiting for my answer, he heads for the kitchen; I trail behind him. I watch him pour milk into a saucepan and rummage in the cupboards, a naked hairy man taking charge of my kitchen. "You got any brown sugar? It's better with brown, but I guess white'll do." He heats the milk to near boiling, sweetens it with sugar, and sprinkles cinnamon on top. Then he fills two mugs and leads me back to the living room. "My mom used to make this when I couldn't sleep," he says, giving me a mug.

The milk is sweet and soothing. I have never tasted anything so good. On the television, my father is dancing with the leading lady. Her head is resting on his shoulder and they look very good together.

"I hate my father," I tell Pete.

"Yeah?" He stares at the couple on TV and shrugs. "Why bother? He's dead."

I shrug, watching my father's face on the TV.

"Come on," Pete says. "Lie down and sleep." I lie beside him on the couch and he wraps his arms around me.

I dream myself into my father's movie. My father's arm encircles my waist and we waltz together beneath crystal chandeliers.

The ballroom's French doors open onto a clear summer night, but the room is cold and damp. The air stinks of decay, a charnel-house stench of rotting flesh and dying flowers.

My father and I spin together, and I catch a glimpse of the band. The bandleader is freshly dead; his body is bloated, the skin puffy and discolored. The dead musicians are in various stages of decay. A trumpet player presses the trumpet's mouthpiece to bare teeth; his head is a skull, precariously balanced on the column of vertebrae that rises from the collar of his tuxedo. The bass player plucks the strings with skeletal hands.

"Relax," my father says to me. He has held up better than the band, but his corneas have turned milky white, and the hand that holds mine feels suspiciously soft, as if it has begun rotting from the inside. "Isn't this where you've always wanted to be?"

At small tables around the dance floor, well-dressed men and women talk and laugh, but the laughter sounds like chattering teeth and rattling bones. A blond woman has lost clumps of hair and her sequined evening dress hangs limply on her shoulders, no flesh to fill it out.

"You can stay here with me," my father says. His eyes are sunken; his smile is the expressionless grimace of a skull. "I was never a good father. I can make it up to you now."

I try to pull away, but he clings to me, clutching at me with soft decaying hands, staring with cloudy sightless eyes. I tear myself free and run from him, toward the open doors.

On the TV screen, a woman in an evening gown is running away across the dance floor. My father stares after her. A lock of dark hair has fallen into his eyes. He looks handsome and charming. The dance floor is filled with beautiful men and women.

I slip from Pete's arms and unplug the TV before I can change my mind. The old television is too heavy to lift, so I drag it across the living room. The wooden legs make a horrible scraping sound on the Italian tiles in the entryway, and Pete wakes up.

"What are you doing?" he mumbles.

"Give me a hand," I say.

Half-asleep, he helps me push the set down the hall and out the back door into the yard. He stops in the doorway, watching sleepily as I drag the set down the concrete walk toward the pool. Near the pool, I tip it off the path. It lies on its back in the damp grass, the screen reflecting the patio lights and the moon.

The VCR is light by comparison. I heap the videotapes on top of the TV. Then I clear the upstairs closets of my father's clothing: white suits, tuxedos, a trench coat, a drawerful of blue jeans. A tweedy jacket carries his smell even now: a hint of tobacco, a whiff of aftershave, a touch of whiskey. I stand in the wet grass for a moment, holding the jacket and fingering the rough fabric. Then I drape it over my shoulders to keep off the wind. Pete watches, shaking his head.

In the garage, I find the can of gasoline that the gardener keeps there for the power mower. I am generous, dousing the clothes repeatedly.

A single match, and the heap of clothing erupts with flames. It is like the Fourth of July, like orgasm, like the moment when the monster dies, like the happy ending when the credits roll. Pete is pulling me away from the fire, shouting something. I struggle away from him for long enough to strip the jacket from my shoulders and hurl it into the flames.

I stand in the circle of Pete's arms, leaning against his shoulder. The air smells of gasoline, flames, and wet grass. I watch the flames and listen to the distant sound of sirens. It's good to be free.

ONCE
IN A LULLABY

FRED BALS

Here's yet another first professional sale by a writer who seems to exhibit too much talent to have come from nowhere. Fred Bals works as a business writer and lives in Merrimack, New Hampshire with his wife Peggy.

"Once in a Lullaby" is a wonderfully-told detective story with the extra kick that comes with the fantastic fiction territory. Fred noted that he wrote this story shortly after the death of John D. MacDonald and intended it as a tribute to his memory.

It was Cullens who started talking about weird cases the night I told them about the ruby slippers. Some of us were in the habit of sharing a few Friday drinks back then. Regulars included Sid Neely, Max Cullens, Terry Mahoney, and me. Neely had a reputation as a hot claims investigator, but also had too much mouth for my taste. Mahoney hadn't been able to talk about much for the last couple of months except how his latest wife had left him. Cullens was all right in my book. There were some other people at the table who I didn't know well enough to peg a last name on.

But I probably could have told you about any of them and been close enough to the truth. We were all divorced—most of us more than once—all past the age when anyone would mistake us for kids, and all looking at empty rooms, TV dinners, and drinking alone on any given Friday night. Instead, we went to the 12-14 Club and swapped lies and war stories. On good nights, we would help close the place. On the bad nights we'd go home early to our TV dinners and solitary beers.

All bars have personalities, shaped by the regulars who drink there. Some bars are for lushes, some for lovers. The 12-14 Club is a bar for cops and private investigators. It's run by Ned Barrabe, a retired cop and retired PI who has had more than his share of bad breaks.

A few years back, a kid on crack holding more firepower

than nerve took off most of Ned's left hand with a Bulldog .44 during what should have been a routine traffic stop. When he left the hospital, Ned pulled the pin and took his pension rather than working limited duty. He picked up his investigator's license and opened an office in Anaheim. On his third case, he went to the Disneyland parking lot and delivered a packet of motel-room photos to a wife who wanted the hard proof.

At some point, you learn you're never going to be able to predict how clients will react when they see a picture of their spouse in bed with someone else. Even when they're expecting it. Even when they think they want it to be true. I've seen laughter, tears, and everything in between when I've handed over the dirty truth.

Ned's client met her moment of truth by kicking him in the crotch. Then she went back to her car and drove over the photos. Ned was still holding the pictures in his right hand when she did it.

After he left the hospital that time, Ned took what was left of both hands and opened the 12-14. He does a good business, considering how long it takes to get anything more complicated than a beer from him.

The talk around the table at the 12-14 that night had centered on the break-in at the Hollywood Movie Museum. Some theories were tossed around the table about who had hit the place. There was general agreement that it was a pro job, probably done for some collector who couldn't lay his hands on whatever he wanted any other way. I hadn't had anything to say about it one way or the other.

For some reason, the break-in got Max Cullens talking about a woman he had followed for a week who he claimed had turned out to be a ghost. Halfway through it, I realized Max had stolen the plot from a story I had read years ago in some magazine. But I let him finish without saying anything. I thought his story was better than the original.

Then Neely told us about tracking a missing wife who he discovered was also the husband's sister. As I expected, Neely really wanted to talk about the good times he had shown the wife/sister in bed after he caught up with her. Too much mouth, as I said. After filling in the gory details, Neely let us know he beat up the husband/brother. The worst thing about the story was that it was probably true.

Neely's story put a damper on the table. I was washing out the bad taste it had left in my mouth when Max asked, "How about you, Johnny? What was the strangest case you ever worked?"

"I guess I've led a boring life compared to you two," I answered. "About the strangest thing that ever happened to me was getting a check that didn't bounce from a client. And it's only happened once."

The laugh went around the table, and even Mahoney took his face out of his drink long enough to flash a smile. "Ain't it the truth," someone said.

"Come on, Johnny D.," Neely said, trying to needle me. He didn't like me much, either. "A good-looking guy like you? I bet you have a few stories you could tell if you wanted to."

I glanced at my watch. It was around nine o'clock. Probably be another couple of hours before the woman I was expecting would show up.

"So what's the story, Mr. D.?" Neely started in on me again.

"I'll tell you a story," I said. "But you won't believe it."

"So what makes that different from any of your other stories?" Neely asked.

I thought about getting Neely outside, coldcocking him, and stuffing him into a dumpster. His ugly story had put me in the mood. But I let the thought pass and went back to sipping my beer.

"Yeah, like I said, you won't believe it," I repeated. "But you should listen anyway. Maybe I can tell one of you how to find your dreams. Want to hear about it?"

"So tell us," Cullens answered for the table.

"It started like most of my cases started back then," I began.

It started like most of my cases started back then. Wallace Emerson's secretary called and asked if I could see him that afternoon. Emerson is a judge now, but he was still an attorney in those days. One of the good ones. He tossed a lot of business my way. I ran down witnesses for him, checked depositions, did all that Perry Mason jazz for him. He paid good money for the work too—25 percent over my usual fee with a bonus added on sometimes. I was always glad to get the call from him.

So I made sure I was on time for the appointment, and his secretary brought me straight into Emerson's office when I arrived.

"Sit down, Johnny," he said. "It's good to see you again. How have you been?"

"Fine, Counselor," I answered as I sat in the chair across from his desk. "Good to see you, too. What have you got for me this time?"

Emerson smiled. "What I have is a little out of the ordinary. I think you might enjoy it. Have you ever been to an auction?"

"Pawn shops are more my speed, Counselor. But if you want me to go to an auction, I'm on my way."

Emerson pushed a catalog across his desk. "Take a look at this, Johnny. You may have heard that the Metro-Goldwyn-Mayer studios are moving to another location."

"Yeah," I said and began thumbing through the catalog. It had pictures and descriptions of clothes, movie props, and equipment.

"Then you may also know there will be an auction this Sunday to sell off the paraphernalia they no longer wish to keep. I want you to buy one of those items."

I stopped on a page circled in red and started laughing. "You want me to buy these? You know, Mr. Emerson, somehow I never thought of you as a movie buff."

"The ruby slippers worn by Judy Garland in *The Wizard of Oz*, yes. You are to buy them. But not for me."

"For a client?" I asked.

"In a manner of speaking. I received a telegram requesting my assistance with this. Naturally, I called the attorney who had contacted me to confirm that his message wasn't a hoax. I found he has a client who wants those slippers very much. And apparently, who is willing to pay dearly for them."

"Sounds like an interesting way to spend a Sunday. Count me in, Counselor. How do you want me to work it?"

"It's simple enough," Emerson replied as he brought out an envelope. "I've made the arrangements to have you attend under my sponsorship. The auction is closed to the general public and you have to prove a certain, ah, substantiality in order to garner an invitation. That has been taken care of and you have been assigned bidding number thirty-three." He opened the envelope and put on his glasses.

"I will give you these instructions as they were given to me. First, it was emphasized to me repeatedly—and, I might say, rather offensively—that these instructions are *not* to be deviated from under any circumstances.

"Thus, the auction begins at two P.M. The hall will be opened to allow review of the items at twelve o'clock sharp. You are to arrive at the studio early enough to allow time to examine the ruby slippers and see the guarantees of their provenance."

"Provenance?" I asked.

"Proof of their origin. In this case it will be paperwork assuring that these are, in fact, the actual slippers worn by Garland in the movie. I don't expect any problems with this, as the catalog specifically notes such paperwork. But I have been told that you are to withdraw if there is any question at all about the slippers' legitimacy.

"This brings me to the second point," he continued. "Evidently a number of slippers were made up for the movie. As many as eight, I understand. Two pairs have disappeared over the years. The six others will be on the block this Sunday. You are to examine and bid *only* on the pair of slippers labeled 1218-B in the catalog. The slippers, and I quote from the instructions, 'used by Dorothy for her return from Oz to Kansas.' "

"These people have more orders than the Normandy Invasion."

"Indeed," Emerson said sourly. "The collector's mind, I suppose. Nevertheless, both you and I will be well compensated for following the orders to the letter. *Quite* well, I might add. In any case, you are to purchase the 1218-B pair of slippers."

"What's my limit?" I asked. "What's my top bid for them?"

"There is no limit. You are to make whatever bid is necessary in order to secure them."

"Uh, Counselor, I'm not telling you how to do this, and like I said, I've never been to an auction before. But like *you* said, 'the collector's mind,' right? There's sure to be a lot of collectors at something like this, and the bidding may get hot and heavy. I don't want to put this guy into money troubles, no matter how much he thinks he wants these slippers. I need some limit on how much I can bid. When do you want me to bail out if the bidding goes too high? At a grand? Two?"

Emerson settled back into his chair, took off his glasses, and smiled at me. I realized the smile didn't extend to his eyes and knew how a witness must feel when Attorney Wallace Emerson had him in the hot seat. "Your concern is commendable," he said. "However, if you look at the catalog again, you will see the miniumum bid on 1218-B is a thousand dollars. So you will spend at least that. But in fact, I expressed a similar concern to my colleague about setting some dollar limit when I spoke to him. This was before he had the moneys transferred to a bank here in Los Angeles."

"And?" I asked.

"I will put it this way. If the bidding approaches three million dollars, you are to immediately call my home for additional authorization."

"Three million! Are these people crazy?"

"Perhaps." Emerson sighed. "I don't know. And ultimately it doesn't matter, I suppose. The money is in the bank. Insanity becomes eccentricity at a certain level of wealth. Look at the example set by Mr. Hughes. Now, when you have the slippers, put them into this box and bring them to me as early as possible Monday morning.'' He lifted out a small wooden box from behind his desk and handed it to me. ''I've been told that the slippers will fit snugly into it.''

The box was intricately carved, with a rainbow, the Scarecrow, Dorothy, and the rest of the Oz characters on the cover. I opened it up to find the interior lined with blue velvet. There were two spaces where the slippers could be fitted into the velvet.

''Nice,'' I said. ''Okay, I'll have them in here for you on Monday. At whatever it costs.''

''At whatever cost,'' he agreed. ''One *can* hope that the cost won't be excessive. But, again, we are simply the messengers in this instance. No matter what your personal opinions might be, have the slippers here on Monday. And I will see to it that they are delivered to my colleague's client.''

We talked about my fee, and I left with the catalog, the bank paperwork, and the Oz box. I was going to be well paid for this job; enough not to have to work for the next month if I didn't want to. I drove home whistling, with the Oz box sitting on the seat next to me, wondering how much Emerson was charging. Wondering what I would buy if I had three million dollars.

I dreamed about lions and tigers and bears that night.

On Sunday I drove to the MGM lot, arriving at a quarter to twelve. I flashed my invitation to the guard at the gates, asked for directions to the auction, and found a parking space. They were just opening up the doors when I arrived. There was already a crowd.

The auction was being held in an old soundstage that looked big enough to hangar a DC-11. Between the stuff they were going to auction off and the crowd, they were going to need every inch of space they had. I picked up my bidding sign—a piece of white cardboard with the number thirty-three written on it—and went looking for lot 1218-B (*Ruby slippers worn by Judy Garland in the 1939 production of* The Wizard of Oz. *Pair #2 of 6*).

I'm not a big movie fan, but I'm like everyone else. I've seen a lot of them, in the theaters and on TV. Walking through that soundstage was like having all the dreams you'd ever had spread out in front of you. I saw bits and pieces of a dozen movies I had watched over the years. Mad scientists' laboratories, dresses worn by actresses I had fantasies about when I was a kid, giant boulders you could pick up with one hand.

Martian flying saucers, glittering chandeliers, paintings of people who never existed, ugly Victorian furniture. Tuxedos, saddles, tommy guns, and harpoons. All for sale if you had the right money.

I found the table where the ruby slippers were on display. There was a kid behind the table who was handling questions. I caught her eye and waved her over to me.

"I'm Dann," I said. "I want to check the provenance on 1218-B before I bid." I figured that was the only chance I was ever going to get to use the word. And, who knows, maybe I'd impress the kid, who was a knockout.

I didn't. "Oh yes, Mr. Dann," she answered without giving me a second glance. "I was told you were going to be here. Just a moment." She brought a lockbox from under the table and took out some papers. "Here you are, sir."

I took the papers, walked away from the crowd surrounding the table, and found a quiet corner. The kid started to say something—probably about me walking off with the papers—but evidently decided just to keep an eye on me.

The papers looked fine, although I wouldn't have known the difference if I were holding forgeries. They were a running record the property master for *The Wizard of Oz* had kept to track the slippers: "6/19/38, 5:30 A.M. Checked out to Miss Garland. Returned at 9:00 P.M. 6/23/38, 2:30 P.M. Checked out to Von Rospach. Returned at 4:00 P.M." I looked for the date that Emerson had wanted me to verify, the date when they had filmed the final scene on the Oz stage, and found it. Garland had checked out the 1218-B slippers.

Satisfied, I brought the papers back to the kid. The crowd had thinned out, and it was easier to see what was on the table.

"Everything all right, Mr. Dann?" she asked.

"Looks fine," I answered and scanned the table for my ruby slippers. As Emerson had told me to expect, there were six pairs of shoes. The ones I wanted were at the top of the table.

"They're beautiful, aren't they?" the kid said. "I would love to own them. I loved that movie so much. I must have seen it a hundred times on TV."

They looked like those shoes kids used to wear for dance recitals. About the only thing that could be said for the 1218-B slippers was that they looked in better shape than the other five pairs. A tommy gun Cagney had used, now *that* I could see buying.

"Yep, they're just great," I lied. "Beautiful. Beautiful." I couldn't think of anything else, so I said it again, "Beautiful."

"Are you going to buy them, Mr. Dann?" she asked.

"Maybe, if I'm lucky and the price is right, honey," I answered.

I could see her struggling with the "honey." I forget that women don't like to be called that anymore. Maybe they never did. I don't know. Anyway, she didn't say anything, probably worried I'd turn out to be a big shot who could ruin her career. And looking the way she did, she obviously had a career. Or wanted one. *Everybody* wants to be in the movies in L.A. Sometimes it looks like everyone is.

She turned away to help someone else. I went back to strolling around and looking at the sights, both the props and the Beautiful People. At one-thirty, I found a chair and waited for the auction to begin.

It took about an hour for the ruby slippers to hit the block. Cagney's tommy gun sold for $7,500, and I had to sit on my fingers through the bidding. The 1218-A slippers—which were pretty beat-up—were taken for $650. I had my sign ready when they brought out the 1218-B ruby slippers, but as soon as the auctioneer finished his description and asked for the opening bid, the place erupted—if you call a flurry of sign-waving an eruption. The shoes went from a grand to $3,500 within seconds. I got the nod at $4,000, but the bidding went right past me, going up in $500 and $1,000 leaps.

It went to six yards before I put another bid in. Things started to quiet when it reached ten. By that time the only bidders left were me and a little guy who looked old enough to have played in the original movie. Maybe he was a grown-up Munchkin. He pushed the bidding to eleven thousand, so I came back with eleven-five.

Everyone turned to the Munchkin. He brought up his sign and shook four fingers at the auctioneer. Fourteen thousand dollars. I hadn't known you could go over a grand at a time. If this was a Ping-Pong game, then I guess that was the Munchkin's hard serve to shut me down for good. Hoping he didn't have a *four*-mill bankroll, I decided to try the finger business too. I waved my sign and waggled one finger for a bid of fifteen thousand. The auctioneer called it out and looked at the Munchkin. He waited a couple of seconds, then smiled and shook his head.

"To number thirty-three for fifteen thousand dollars," the auctioneer called as the audience applauded. I was pretty proud of myself, considering I had just spent fifteen thousand of someone else's money.

I went up to the table and worked out the payment deal. I was walking out of the hall before the bidding started on the next pair of slippers.

I stored the slippers in the Oz box, which I had left in my car. Emerson was right about that, too: the slippers fitted into it perfectly. I drove off the lot and went home.

That night I dreamed the Wicked Witch of the West tried to shoot me with Cagney's tommy gun. I put her away with a right hook.

That should have been the end of it for me, but it was just the beginning. I called Emerson's office at nine on Monday and found out from his secretary that he had been taken to the hospital on Saturday night. He wanted to see me.

"They call it a minor coronary incident," Emerson told me from his bed when I arrived. "Not serious enough to be considered a heart attack. Annoying enough to keep me here for a few days, I'm afraid. I will need some more of your time, Johnny."

"I've got nothing important going this week, Counselor," I answered. "What can I do?"

"You brought the slippers?"

I had them in the Oz box. Emerson opened it and looked in. "So these are the fabulous shoes. It seems our friend is in quite a fever to lay his hands upon them. I was originally asked to bring them to Kansas City tonight. I agreed, although I thought it was just adding more ridiculous expense onto an already costly exercise. There is absolutely no reason why the slippers couldn't be shipped by insured air express. In any case, I can't answer that obligation now. My doctor refuses to release me any earlier than Wednesday. I might override his objections, but unfortunately my wife concurs with him. And my wife is one of the few people on Earth whose opinion I'm unable to sway. How do you feel about taking a plane trip to Kansas? Naturally, all your expenses will be paid in addition to your daily fee."

"Why not?" I said. "I'd like to meet our slipper collector."

"Good. The feeling is apparently mutual. When I informed my colleague of my disability, his client asked for you in my place. I assured them that the slippers would be as safe with you as they would have been with me."

"Don't tell me," I said. "They have instructions about how I have to carry them. I have to balance the box on my head for the plane trip or something, right?"

"Nothing like that." Emerson laughed. "You're simply to carry it on board the plane. There will be a car waiting for you in

Kansas City. The client has offered to have you stay in his house overnight, or longer if you wish."

Emerson told me the ticket would be waiting for me at L.A. International. I'd be taking a six o'clock flight direct to Kansas City. I went home to pack.

It's easy to forget what winter means to the rest of the country when you live in sunny L.A. Kansas City was covered with snow. The pilot told us it was twenty-nine degrees outside. More snow was expected. A little under a three-hour trip by air from Los Angeles and it might as well have been another planet as far as the weather was concerned. L.A. *is* another planet to people in Kansas, I guess.

I had been smart enough to bring along my raincoat with the heavy lining, the warmest piece of clothing I owned. As the plane taxied to the terminal I reached for my suitcase and brought out the coat, ignoring the stewardess's canned speech to stay in my seat. By the time we stopped at the gate, I was already into the first-class section. I left with the first group of passengers as soon as the cabin door was opened.

I heard my name paged as I walked into the waiting area. I shuffled around a moist family reunion and found a white courtesy phone in the hallway. While I waited for an answer, I wondered whether airports hired actors and actresses to stage homecomings. It always looked like the same people. Maybe they went around the country putting on their act. Nobody had ever been waiting for me when I got off a plane.

On the other hand, maybe my luck was going to change. "Mr. Dann?" a voice asked on the phone. "Your driver is at the information desk downstairs."

I discovered my driver was a woman when I arrived at the desk. An Oriental woman in her twenties, looking cute and sexy in a chauffeur's uniform. She was at least four inches taller than I am, putting her close to six feet. She had black hair tucked under her chauffeur's cap and laughing, black eyes. I decided I was in love. I wanted her to tell me to forget the slippers and go with her to a motel room where we would do things I had never dreamed of.

My luck hadn't changed that much. "Mr. Dann?" she asked. "Hi, my name is Liralen. Dottie asked me to come out and get you. You have the slippers? Oh, I see you have the box. Good. Dottie is *so* excited. Is that your only bag? Do you need to pick up any other luggage? We should try to leave as soon as we can.

It's quite a trip to the house and we're expecting a snowstorm tonight. Oh, I'm sorry. I hope your flight was pleasant. I didn't mean to be rude.''

Her barrage of words seemed to have ended, so I decided to try to say something. "The trip was fine, thanks. And call me Johnny, okay? You're going to take me to whoever bought these?" I nodded at the Oz box tucked under my arm.

"Yes," she answered. "Hi, Johnny. I'm Dottie's, ah, *companion* is as good a word as any, I guess. Or chief bottle-washer. If you don't have any other luggage, we should be going. They're predicting heavy snow, and we have a long drive ahead of us.''

"I just brought the one bag," I replied. "Let's get moving.''

Liralen had a gray Rolls-Royce—the big, old Silver Ghost model—sitting in the No Parking zone outside. She smiled at the bundled-up cop standing next to the car, received a wink in return, and opened the passenger door for me. The Rolls's interior was bigger than my living room. I tossed my suitcase inside and had begun to get in when I saw the built-in flower vase on the car's running board. The vase was filled with fresh roses.

"Must have to replace those every five minutes in this weather," I said.

Liralen smiled. "You're right, they don't last for more than one trip. But I like the idea of putting out flowers. I carried these in the car and put them out for you before I went inside.''

"First time anyone has given me flowers," I said. "Thanks.''

She grinned at me again and I got into the car. Liralen went around to the driver's side and drove us away from the terminal.

There isn't much I can say about Kansas except it's as flat as last week's soda. The view was probably prettier in the summer. All I could see now was snow stretching off in every direction. And more was coming. Fat, heavy-looking snowflakes were dancing in the Rolls's headlights as we left K.C. and took a highway west.

I leaned forward in my seat and asked Liralen where we were going.

"Galen," she answered. "It's tiny. You can't even find it on the map. That's why I came in rather than telling you to rent a car. Between no directions and the storm, you would have ended up lost. Dottie owns it.''

"Owns what?''

"Galen.''

"Your boss *owns* the town?"

"I guess so, since it was her father's. I never asked her, come to think of it. I just took it for granted that she did. After all, it has her name. Or at least it used to have her name. No, it still does, I suppose. She doesn't."

I was beginning to think that Liralen was more dotty than "Dottie" was probably going to be, but I was having fun playing Burns to her Allen. If I had a cigar I would have lit it.

"Wait a second," I tried again. "Why doesn't she have her name anymore? Did she lose it?"

"No, silly." She giggled. "She had a judge change it. He didn't want to, but Dottie made him do it. Dottie always gets what she wants."

"I guess she does, at that," I said as I looked at the Oz box. "So what did Dottie have her name changed to?"

"Oh, it wasn't much of a change," Liralen began. "Just a let—" The Rolls took a sudden swerve. "Damn!" she cried. "The road is starting to ice up. I'm sorry, Johnny. Usually I *love* to talk while I'm driving the Gray Lady. But I want to get us home as fast as I can. I have a bad feeling about this storm. I think it's going to be a big one. I need to concentrate on my driving. Do you mind if we don't talk until we get to the house?"

I looked over her shoulder and saw the speedometer needle leaning on the eighty mark. I thought about telling her to slow down, but she was handling the big car better than I could have myself.

"Sure," I said and leaned back in my seat. "No problem. I'm one of those people who doesn't like to talk when they're driving, anyway. I think I'll catch some sleep. Plane trips tire me out."

"Thanks, Johnny. I'll put on some music if you like. Dottie had a stereo installed in the Lady." She giggled again. "What a fight *that* was with the Rolls-Royce people. You would have thought we were asking them to paint flames on the hood."

"Fine," I said. "As long as it isn't rock. I'm not much for that stuff. No offense meant."

"None taken. I bet I can guess what you like." A moment later music started filling the Rolls and the other Lady's voice came up over the piano lead.

"You've got it now, kid," I said and closed my eyes, listening to Billie play with the lyrics of "God Bless the Child" while the Gray Lady took us over the Kansas plains.

"Say good night, Gracie," I murmured sleepily.

"Good night, Gracie," Liralen replied.

I woke up as we were making the turn into a driveway. The snow was falling heavily now. Nothing had been plowed. The only way I could guess how Liralen had known where to drive was by following the slight depression the road made between drifts.

"Awake?" she asked as she heard me shift in the seat. "Good. You timed it right. We're here."

I leaned forward to look out the windshield. "Looks like you were right about the storm. Have I been out long?"

"Well, let's see. You started snoring about three minutes after I put on the music." She glanced at the dashboard clock. "And that was about two hours ago."

I looked at the clock and saw that the time was a little after eleven. "Two hours? You sure we're still in Kansas?"

"The last time I looked. It took me longer to get here than I was counting on. We have a full-scale blizzard on our hands. It's a good thing we have the Lady or we probably wouldn't have made it back tonight."

"You should have woken me up," I said.

"Why? So we both could worry? Or was the big, strong man going to take over the driving for little Liralen?"

"Sorry," I said. "I didn't mean anything by it. Just thought you might have wanted the company. Little Liralen drives like Andretti as far as I'm concerned. And you're taller than I am, anyway."

"Apology unneeded, but thank you. Compliment accepted gratefully, if not gracefully," she replied. "I'm sorry, Johnny. I get grumpy when I'm hungry. And I'm *starving*." We rounded a curve in the driveway. "But we're home now, thank heavens. Welcome to Galen's Castle in beautiful Galen, Kansas."

Galen's Castle wasn't really a castle. It was an old, beautiful mansion sitting in the middle of nowhere like a dowager aunt visiting poor relations in the sticks.

"Accommodations seem acceptable," I said as Liralen opened the car door for me. "But I thought you said there was a town around here."

"Galen is about twenty minutes away," she answered. "Dottie's father liked his privacy. We went through the town while you were asleep." She led me up the steps and opened the front door. "Go in and dry yourself out. Leave your bag in the front hall and I'll take care of it later. I expect Dottie will be in the library waiting for us. Go through the hall, take a left, and go all the way to the end. Tell Dottie I'll be there in a moment. I want to put the Lady in the barn while I still can.''

She turned around and left me, bouncing down the steps like a kid. I went inside and hung up my coat. I was looking at a rug that would have taken everything I owned to buy when I heard a woman's voice calling.

"A second," I yelled back, and pulled off my muddy shoes for the rug's sake. "I'm coming."

I walked past a gauntlet of portraits—Galen ancestors, according to the plaques on the frames—all looking outraged at my invasion of their territory. The doors to the library were open. There weren't any lights on inside. A fire was burning in a gigantic fireplace that I could have walked into upright. Bookshelves covered the walls from floor to ceiling. Patterns of light and shadows danced over the covers of thousands of books.

She was waiting for me. In the weak light cast by the fireplace, I could see that my mysterious slipper buyer had reached the frozen age where it was no longer possible to guess it with any accuracy. Past seventy is what I would have put in a report. Past eighty would have been an even bet. Whatever clock God had wound for her was still ticking away strongly.

She was sitting in a wing-back chair, a tiny woman, overwhelmed by the chair. She was wearing a high-necked blouse with a cameo brooch at her neck. A shawl covered her legs. Her white hair was pulled into a neat bun.

"I'm Johnny Dann, ma'am," I said. "I've brought what you wanted from California."

She switched on a lamp on the table beside her chair. "I apologize for letting you walk into the dark, Mr. Dann," she said in a surprisingly young voice. "I forget when Liralen isn't here." As her face came out of the dimness, I saw why she forgot about lights. She had the unfocused eyes of the blind. "Would you bring the slippers to me, please?"

I carefully put the Oz box into her hands. She smiled as her fingers traced the patterns on the lid. "I made this when I was eleven," she said. "A long time ago. A long time to wait." She started to open the lid and asked, "I suppose you think I'm a silly old woman, Mr. Dann? I understand that you paid fifteen thousand dollars for these on my behalf."

"It's your money, ma'am. Spend it any way you want. I'm just the delivery boy. And you can call me Johnny."

"Johnny, then. And please do me the same favor and stop all

your 'ma'aming.' It makes me think I'm even more decrepit than I'm sure I appear. I don't want to feel that way tonight.''

She opened the lid of the Oz box. ''Fifteen thousand? Fah! Fifteen hundred thousand or fifteen million dollars, I would have found a way to pay anything if I had needed to. I would have had them stolen if I had needed to. What price would you put on a world?''

A world? I didn't know what she was talking about. But I had a growing suspicion she was as loony as a bull goose. I began to wonder how early Liralen could take me back to the airport tomorrow.

''Well, you had the luck to pay only fifteen grand for them,'' I answered, after groping around for something to say. ''And I guess I had the luck not to have to steal them for you.''

She brought the slippers out of the box, her face tinged with ruby as they glowed in the firelight. ''Ah, yes,'' she murmured. Her fingers danced over every inch of the slippers as she turned them in her hands. ''Would you describe them to me please, Johnny?'' she asked in a soft voice.

''Ummmm. I don't know. Didn't you, uh, could you . . .''

''The movie? Oh, yes. These,'' she put one of the ruby slippers back into the box and gestured to her eyes, ''worked quite well until a few years ago. I saw *The Wizard* many times. I remember it better than I remember this room. I want to know what *you* see.''

What the hell, I thought, *she's paying me for my time*. I went into a report. ''Okay. A pair of shoes, somewhere between a size four and five, I'd guess.'' I moved in to get a closer view. ''A pair of low-cut woman's shoes. Short heels. Made out of some type of cloth or leather. A bow on the front upper part of each shoe. Dark red. Sequins covering the shoes. Makes them look like the paint job kids used to put on a hot car, if you know what I mean. What do they call it? Ah, yeah. Metal flake.''

I took the slipper from her hand and examined the inside. ''Padding in the instep of the left shoe.'' I pulled the other one out of the box. ''In both shoes,'' I corrected. ''Sweat stains on the padding. Something written in ink inside both shoes that's been blotted out by the stains. Obviously been worn.''

''By . . . ?'' she prompted.

''No way of telling from the shoes. But these say,'' I pulled the papers from my jacket before I realized she couldn't see what I was doing, ''uh, the papers—the *provenance*—you asked me to check say they were worn by Judy Garland in 1938 while filming—''

"*The Wizard of Oz.*"

"*The Wizard of Oz.* And were worn by her during the final scene on the Emerald City set where Garland—"

"Dorothy," she corrected sharply.

"Okay, Garland *as* Dorothy," I compromised, "uses the slippers to return—"

"To Kansas."

"To Kansas," I agreed, hoping our Ping-Pong conversation was over.

"The ruby slippers." She sighed tiredly. "The *right* ruby slippers. I can do it now. Finally. I know I can."

I think she forgot I was there for a moment, lost in whatever dream I had brought to her with the ruby slippers. She finally came back from wherever she had gone and said, "Thank you so much, Johnny. I'm sure you don't understand, and wouldn't believe me even if you did understand, but you have quite literally saved my life by bringing these slippers."

A loony tune, but a nice loony tune. Crazy or not, I liked her. "My pleasure," I said honestly. "If they're what you wanted, then I'm glad I could help you get them. Anyway, it was a change from the usual sort of case I work on."

"Stolen diamonds, car chases, and beautiful blondes, no doubt," Liralen said as she entered the library. Her hat and uniform were covered by melting snow.

She crossed over to Dottie and hugged her. "Hello, boss," she said. "The Lady is tucked safely away, we're home with the ruby slippers, and I think we're snowed in until June. All's right with the world. What's for dinner?"

"Get away from me, for heaven's sake, girl," Dottie answered in a mock-severe voice. "You'll give us both pneumonia. Go upstairs and get out of those wet things first. I'll break out Father's brandy. Tonight is for celebration if any a time ever was."

Liralen winked at me. "A hell-trip through the worst blizzard in years and what do I get? Abuse and orders. Not even a hello. And for what, I ask you? A pittance. Not even half a pittance. A pit! That's what I get, a pit!"

"Indeed." Dottie smiled. I could tell it was a well-worn routine between the two of them. "That's what you get for living with the crazy witch of Galen's Castle. Go change, please, child. I really don't want you to catch cold. We'll wait for you to come back before we open the brandy."

Liralen took off her chauffeur's cap and shook her head. An

explosion of black hair fell around her shoulders. "For your father's brandy I'll be back in two shakes of a lamb's tail. And I think I'll stop in the kitchen and bring the lamb with me. I'm starving to death, Dottie."

"As a matter of fact, I put some things out for us in the kitchen. Bring them back with you."

"Food!" Liralen cried happily. "Sustenance! Manna from heaven! Maybe a taco! Oh boy, I'm on my way then." She rushed out of the library, pausing in midstep to give me a fast kiss on the cheek. "I return upon the moment, if not sooner."

"Nice kid," I said to Dottie, my cheek still blazing from her kiss. I figured it was because she was relieved about being home. I didn't want to think about whether I wanted it to be true or not. "Too bad she's so shy."

"A quiet personality has never been one of Liralen's attributes," Dottie answered. "But she helps shake me out of my moodiness. I half-think that's why she does it. Johnny, the brandy is in the cabinet next to the window. Could you bring it out with three snifters, please?"

I stopped at the fireplace first and tossed in a couple of logs. "It sounds as if the snow is changing to freezing rain," Dottie said as I opened the cabinet. I glanced out the window.

"Yeah," I answered. "Liralen wasn't kidding. This is a bad one. I don't know whether I'll be able to fly out tomorrow."

"It doesn't matter. You're welcome to stay with us as long as you like. Tell me, Johnny, was Liralen right?"

"About what?" I asked as I brought the bottle and glasses back to the table and sat down. "My God, the label says this booze is over a hundred years old!"

"That 'booze' is brandy, sir," she said archly. "I'll thank you to treat it with some respect. There are fewer than thirty bottles of this vintage left in the entire United States. I understand a man in New York City owns the remaining ones. But I still have a few myself.

"I was asking," she continued, "about your job. What did Liralen say, 'diamonds, cars, and blondes'? Is that what a detective's life is filled with?"

"More like skip-tracing, repos, and divorces. Real life isn't much like the movies."

"Only when we decide to make it that way," she said with a smile. "I've never met a real detective before. Tell me what skip-tracing is, please?"

So I told her about the credit jumpers, check-kiting artists, dips, snitches, and hot-wire clowns. The sad ones and the bad ones. The hard guys and the more dangerous ones who want you to think they're hard. All the ones who make up a PI's life. Liralen came back after a time with some food on a tray. She was dressed in a floor-length caftan made of white silk that shimmered in the firelight. She sat on the floor next to the old lady, her arms wrapped around her knees, and listened to me talk. We opened up the brandy, and each sip tasted like liquid gold.

The chiming of a grandfather clock finally broke me out of my monologue. "One o'clock?" I said in surprise. "This brandy has put my tongue on hinges, Dottie. You should have shut me up. You must want to go to bed."

"I don't sleep very much anymore, Johnny. And I thought your stories were fascinating. But I'm sure you and Liralen are tired. Why don't you show Johnny to his room, dear," she said to Liralen. "And then go to bed yourself. I want to stay up a little longer."

Liralen shifted on the floor and looked at Dottie and then at me. "If he doesn't mind, I think I'll let Johnny find his room for himself. It's all ready, and I brought his bag upstairs when I came in. I'd like to sit and talk with you for a while, Dottie. I've caught my second wind."

"Fine by me," I answered. "I do like my sleep. Just tell me where my room is and what time I should be up for breakfast."

"First feed is at eight-thirty," Liralen replied. "First and only feed, for that matter. If you're not in the kitchen by eight-thirty-five we throw it to the dogs. At eight-forty we turn the dogs loose on you if you're not awake. And they're hungry critters."

"Guess I'll set my alarm clock, then. Where do I find my room?"

"Back through the hall and up the stairs. Third door on the left. The lights are on."

"Good night to both of you, then," I said. "I'll see you tomorrow, or later today, I guess."

"Sleep tight, Johnny," Liralen said, remaining seated and crushing my hopes for a good-night kiss. Maybe she regretted giving me the other one. I decided to stop thinking about it. I liked her too much to foul things up with a pass.

"Good night, Mr. Dann," Dottie said formally, holding out her hand. "I want to thank you again for all you've done."

I took Dottie's hand and bent over it, something I had never done before with any woman. "And again, it was my pleasure, Miss . . ." I stopped, remembering that Liralen had said Dottie had changed her name.

A bright fierceness burned out from those eyes that should have been empty. "Gale," she answered. "My name is Dorothy Gale."

"Then good night, Miss Gale," I said. "And take care."

As I was leaving the library, I turned back to ask Liralen something. I stood silently in the doorway and watched as the younger woman gently took off the old lady's shoes. She reached into the Oz box, took out the ruby slippers, and placed them on Dorothy Gale's feet.

And both their faces shone with a light that overwhelmed the fading firelight. I turned away without saying anything and went up to my room.

Dorothy Gale? I woke up the next morning still hearing the name. While I dressed, I decided to see if I could confirm the childhood memory that had inched its way into my dreams. I turned right at the foot of the stairs and went back to the library instead of trying to find the kitchen. It was only eight, so my breakfast was probably still safe from the dogs.

The book was there, of course. All the books in the series were there in first-edition hardcovers. I took the copy of Baum's *The Wonderful Wizard of Oz* from the shelf and thumbed through it. But I couldn't find the name I was looking for. Dorothy Gale. Late of Kansas. Honorary resident of the Emerald City. *The* Dorothy. So much for memory.

"We only serve in the library during late evenings, Johnny," *my* Dorothy Gale said as she came up behind me. "I think you'll have better luck in the kitchen if you want breakfast."

"Damn, Dottie, you scared me," I said, so startled that I dropped the book on the floor. "Sorry. Pardon my language. I didn't hear you come in. I just wanted to check on something."

"I take it you found what you were looking for?" she asked as she leaned over and picked the book up from the floor. She rubbed her fingers over the book's spine. "Hmmm, we're in the 'B' section. And this is my copy of *The Wizard*. Were you gathering more evidence that I'm a crazy old woman?"

"Galen to Gale. I couldn't figure out why. I thought I finally had it. I thought Dorothy's last name was Gale. But I couldn't find it." I took the book from her and replaced it on the shelf.

She laughed. "Your instincts were right. You just went to

the wrong source. Dorothy's last name *was* Gale. It was in the movie, but it wasn't in that book. Thus, your theory is proved, Mr. Holmes. The woman is mad.''

"Look, you can change your name to Dorothy Cowardly Lion for all it means to me. Really. You're someone with a lot of money who doesn't have to worry about what people think of you. You're a big fan of the Oz stuff, and your name was already close. So you dropped a letter to make it an exact match. That's maybe a little strange, but I've heard stranger. There's a guy from New Jersey who had plastic surgery so he could look like Elvis Presley. Now, that's crazy.''

"We'd have to know his reasons, wouldn't we, in order to say that?'' she asked. "All right, Johnny. I'll stop teasing you about it. You've been very kind, and really haven't given me any reason to feel that you think I am crazy. Why don't we get you some breakfast and we'll talk.''

I followed her out of the library, watching her as she led me to the kitchen. She was wearing the ruby slippers; their heels clacked against the hardwood floor. I wondered how she had been able to come up behind me without my hearing something. I wondered if she had slept at all last night. I was wondering about something else, too.

The kitchen was formidable, twice the size of the library. I sat at a table as Dottie poured me some coffee and brought out a covered plate from an oven. "I've been keeping this warm for you,'' she said. The plate was filled with buttermilk pancakes.

I glanced at a clock on the wall. "Am I late?'' I asked. "I thought Liralen said breakfast was around eight-thirty.''

"We've been up for a few hours. Farm folk, you know. Well, not really, but I suppose it rubs off after a time. I think there may be a Kansas law stating that you can't sleep past four-thirty.''

"I'll stay in L.A., then,'' I answered, my mouth half-filled with pancakes. "They have a law there saying you can't get out of bed till noon. Where's Liralen?''

"She took a shovel and went out to clear a path to the barn. She said she was going to try to clear part of the pond, too. I think she wants to go skating.''

I finished my pancakes, still watching Dottie, and refused a second helping. She poured another cup of coffee for me and I took it to the window. "I can't believe how much snow is out there,'' I said. "It's incredible.''

"The radio said we have over two feet,'' Dottie answered.

"Even worse, the wind is starting to pick up and the snow is drifting. The roads are terrible. I'm afraid you're going to have to put up with us for at least another day, Johnny. Kansas City airport is closed. The radio said they should be opening again sometime tomorrow."

"Suits me," I said as I turned back to her and carefully put my empty coffee cup on the table. "At least you'll have enough time to give me some answers."

"Answers? To what?"

I leaned over the table and hit the cup with my open hand. It should have ended up in Dottie's lap. She reached out and plucked it from the air as it was flying toward her.

"Like to that, for starters, lady," I said. "Nice catch, by the way. Last night you went to a lot of trouble to convince me you were blind. And I have to admit, you're good, you fooled me. But your act kind of faded in the morning light. I don't care how familiar you are with that book. It had a dustcover on it. No raised lettering. How did you know what I was looking at? I want to know what's going on. What sort of scam are you and the kid trying to run on me? Or was it Emerson you wanted to set up? And what's it all got to do with the slippers?"

She looked at the cup in her hand. "I can't see all that well yet. Everything looked like blobs of light this morning, almost the reverse of what happened when I began to lose my sight."

"Yeah, sure," I said. "Last night you were totally blind. Then you can see blobs of light. Now you see well enough to catch a cup one-handed. How come?"

She looked at me with the same fierceness I had imagined I had seen last night. Except this time her eyes *were* seeing me. "I don't know 'how come,' damn you, and I'll thank you to keep a civil tongue in your head when you're at my table. But I can tell you why. It's because of the ruby slippers."

"The slippers? Come on, Dottie. They're from a movie, not a faith healer. What would the slippers have to do with it?"

"I *don't know*," she shouted, getting to her feet. "What do you want me to say? It's not what I expected. But I didn't know what to expect. All I know is what I want!"

We stood there glaring at each other across the table. "Okay," I finally said. "What do you want?"

"What do I want?" She said it as if it were the first time she had ever spoken the question aloud. "What do I want?"

There were tears streaking down her cheeks. "I want to go

home," she said and raced out of the kitchen, faster than a blind woman should have been able to move.

I picked the cup off the floor, poured myself some more coffee, and sat down at the table. The tough-guy act hadn't worked too well. Johnny Dann, terror of kittens and old ladies.

After I finished the coffee, I went out to the hall and found a closet. My shoes and coat were in it. Even better, I found a man's heavy overcoat and a pair of winter boots. The coat was all right, but the boots were a couple of sizes too large. I stuffed a pair of socks into the boots' toes, put on the coat, and went outside.

Liralen had been busy. A path had been shoveled through the snow to the barn, and another path went down into a little valley. The driveway was still filled with snow.

I followed the second path and came to a frozen pond. Liralen was sweeping the ice with a broom when I arrived. She had shoveled away the snow from about half the pond's length.

"Lot of work," I said as she glanced at me.

"If you want to play, you have to pay," she answered and went back to her sweeping.

My boots skidded as I walked out onto the ice. Liralen was wearing a ski jacket and jeans. She had her hair tucked up out of sight again, this time in a wool hat. The ends of a long, multicolored scarf dangled down to her ankles. A pair of ice skates with their laces tied together hung over one shoulder.

"Your boss says she's getting back her sight."

"She told me this morning."

"You believe her?"

She looked at me again. "What's to believe, Mr. Dann? I've lived with Dottie for the past five years. The glaucoma was already taking over her eyes when I moved in with her. She went completely blind two years ago. Now she's starting to see again. It's supposed to be impossible, but she can see. I don't have to believe her. I can see it for myself. And so can you."

Mr. Dann. I wondered what had happened to "Johnny."

"You don't sound too happy about it," I said.

She threw the broom into a snowdrift and sat down on the ice. She tore off her boots and started lacing up her skates. "No?" she said. "Well, maybe I'm worried about what she's planning. Maybe I'm scared about what's going to happen to her if it doesn't work. Or maybe I'm just jealous and I'm worried about what's going to happen to me if it *does* work. You're the big-shot private eye. You figure it out. Give me your arm."

I held out my arm and she got to her feet. She let go and

glided away over the ice. I stood there until she came back and started a slow circle around me. "Hey," I said. "Last night I was the hero with the ruby slippers. Now you're mad at me. What have I done?"

She made another loop around me, staying just out of reach. I kept turning around to follow her. "You're making me dizzy," I said. "Are you going to give me an answer?"

She stopped and put her hands on her hips. "I'm mad because Dottie and I had a fight this morning. She wants to tell you about it. I don't think you're going to understand. You don't have enough imagination to understand. You're going to cause trouble. I wish I could take you to the airport right now."

"Tell me about what?"

She dug a toe into the ice, spun around, and shot away. "Ask her!" she shouted over her shoulder. "Investigate! Isn't that what you're supposed to do?"

With both women not talking to me—or to each other, apparently—there wasn't much for me to investigate. I went back to the library, built a new fire, and retrieved the copy of *The Wonderful Wizard of Oz* from the shelf. It's a small book; I finished it within an hour. I couldn't remember whether I had read it when I was a kid. I found out that the movie, which I did remember fairly well, followed the book's plot. But it had also changed a number of things.

"Would you like some coffee or tea, Johnny?" Dottie stood in the doorway holding a tray. Liralen was behind her.

She wasn't anywhere near seventy years old anymore. She looked . . . I don't know. Maybe forty now, at the most. I knew it had to be impossible, but it was her. She was wearing her hair down. It had dark streaks of brown shot through the gray. Her eyes were clear.

"Coffee, please," I mumbled as I looked at her. Dottie and Liralen walked into the room. Liralen watched us nervously as Dottie poured a cup of coffee for me and tea for herself and the girl.

As Dottie sat down, I pointed to the ruby slippers on her feet. "Those are supposed to be silver shoes, according to the book."

"You've been doing your homework, Johnny," she answered. "You're right, of course. But the silver shoes never really existed. The ruby slippers are real. It's strange how things affect us when we're children. I loved the books passionately when I was a child. But the first time I saw the movie it was as if it all became real for me. I suppose the color had something to do with it. It was the first color movie I had ever seen. When Dorothy walked into Oz, I went there too.''

She clasped her hands over her head. ''Ah, this feels so good. I can't begin to tell you how good this is. Do you have any idea what it's like not to be able to stretch? To be so stiff you can't move your arms past your shoulders?''

I didn't answer. ''I went back home that night and reread every Oz book I owned,'' she continued. ''I was too old for them then, much too old. But I believed in the story better than I had when I was little. I believed so well I saw a glimpse of something. Something like—''

I held up my hand. ''Wait,'' I interrupted. ''That's enough. I've had it. Last night I met a woman who was seventy years old. A woman who was blind. I said this morning that you might have been able to fool me about the blindness. But there's no way on Earth you could have made yourself up to look the way you did without my guessing. I've known too many actresses to believe it. The only thing that makes sense is that you have the woman I met hidden away somewhere. Maybe you're her sister or something. But in five minutes I'm going to start tearing this place apart until I find her. Or you can give me some answers right now. But no more stories. I don't want to hear about the damn slippers or movies or books anymore.''

''I told you so,'' Liralen murmured in a singsong lilt.

''And you shut up,'' I said to her. ''You told me to investigate, I'll investigate. Maybe you're going to be sorry you told me that.''

''You're a fool,'' Liralen said angrily. ''You can't believe your own eyes? I don't know why Dottie is bothering to do this. She could have waited until you were gone.''

''Enough, both of you!'' Dottie said. ''I won't have any more fighting.'' Liralen looked down at the floor, suddenly abashed. ''Johnny, look at me,'' Dottie commanded. ''Look at me and tell me I'm not the same person you met last night.''

It *was* her. I knew that already. I had been blowing smoke about the double hidden somewhere. Strike two for the tough-guy act. But what in hell was going on?

''All right,'' I conceded. ''You're right. I don't know how, but you're thirty years younger than you were last night. You can see now. You said this morning that the slippers had something to do with it. Tell me how.''

''I told you the truth this morning. I don't know. Perhaps

because I wanted it to happen. Perhaps because it needs to happen before I can go—''

"Home?" I asked, interrupting her again. "You said you wanted to go home this morning."

"Yes," she answered. "Home. To Oz."

"To Oz," I repeated stupidly. "Yeah, sure. That makes sense. A pair of movie slippers are going to take you to Never-Never Land."

"Wrong dream, Johnny," she cried. "Perhaps you need fairy dust to find your way to that one. Or 'take the second star to your right and straight on till morning.' But I know—*I know*—there's a path to that dream too. There's a path to every dream if you want to find it badly enough. I'm taking the path to Oz."

"With those?" I pointed to the slippers again.

Dottie stood up and clicked the slippers' heels together. "Yes. With these. They're what I needed. Do you know what a magical totem is for, Johnny? It's what a shaman, a witch doctor, uses to focus his belief so he can work his magic. The ruby slippers are doing the same thing for me. That's why I had to have them."

I could see her becoming younger in front of my eyes. She was no older than twenty now. The dress she was wearing was beginning to bag in some places, stretch in others, as if trying to reshape itself to her changing frame. Her hair was almost completely brown.

"And what happens now?" I asked.

She looked down at herself. "I don't know. But I think it's going to happen soon." She ran over to me and gave me a hug. She went to Liralen and hugged her too. "Oh, children. Please be happy for me. Please believe. I've wanted this for so long. I've been so afraid." She ran to the door. "I have to change my clothes again." She giggled. "For the third time today. Would you two please make up and be happy?"

The teenager, who looked younger than Liralen, ran out the door. I went to the bar, found some scotch, and poured myself a stiff shot. "You want one of these?" I asked Liralen.

"Definitely," she answered.

"Still mad at me?" I asked as I handed her the drink and poured another one for myself.

"No, not anymore. Do you believe it now?"

"I don't want to. But seems like I have to. I just watched her become twenty years younger right in front of me. And there's nothing wrong with *my* eyes. You really think she's going to Oz?''

She turned away and looked out the window. "Yes, I really think she is. And leave me behind."

I looked past her out into the snow. "Well, that I don't believe. Maybe she's talked herself into getting younger somehow. I don't know, maybe she's hypnotized us all. But she's not going anywhere in this weather. The wind is really picking up, isn't it? How did you get involved in all this, kid? How long have you known what she was planning?"

She looked at my reflection in the window and smiled. "You should stop calling me 'kid.' It makes you sound like an old man. You're not so old. And pretty good-looking for such a stubborn turkey."

"Yeah? Well, we're two of a kind, then. So what's the story about you and Dottie?"

A blast of wind rattled the house and startled Liralen. She stumbled backward and I put my arms around her to stop her from falling. She looked at me over her shoulder. I kept holding on to her. Then I put my drink on the windowsill and kissed her.

"A stubborn turkey," she murmured again. "And a slow one. Before I got mad at you, I thought I was going to have to do a strip-tease act or something to make you notice me."

"Be quiet," I said and kissed her again. "Dottie told us to make up."

Another blast of wind shook the house, and we simultaneously turned to the window. "Johnny!" Liralen shouted over the howl of the wind. "Look outside! Do you see it?"

I saw it all right. The funnel was white instead of black, but it was still a tornado. It was headed straight for the house.

"I thought you couldn't have those in the winter," I said, backing away from the window.

"You can't. It's not supposed to be possible. Johnny, what's happening?" She started for the door. "Dottie. It's Dottie, Johnny!" She ran out of the room, yelling for Dottie.

I gave one more glance to the monster twister bearing down on me like a freight train, then started after Liralen.

My ears were popping as I reached the stairs. I could hear Liralen shouting for Dottie on the second floor. The windows began to burst as I rushed upstairs. The whole house started to shake. I was trying to think of everything I had heard about how to survive a tornado. All I could remember was that you were supposed to hide in a basement. As usual, I was going in the wrong direction.

Dottie's room was at the top of the stairs. Liralen was standing in the doorway. I came up beside her and looked inside the room.

Dorothy Gale was standing in the middle of the room, smiling. She had her hands clasped together and was intently watching the far wall of her room. She was eleven, maybe twelve years old. She had put on denim overalls. Her hair fell past her shoulders, and there was one streak of white in the deep, rich brown of it. Her bare arms were covered with freckles.

"Time, children," she shouted to us over the wind. "Goodbye. I love you both."

"Dottie, please, no," Liralen cried. "It's a tornado, you'll be killed. Come with us."

The wall burst outward. I held on to Liralen and braced myself in the doorway as the room filled with snow and debris. The child still stood there, untouched by the winds howling around her. She turned to face the gaping hole in the wall and tapped the heels of the ruby slippers together.

The winds died. There was a glow coming from outside, coming from the hole in the bedroom wall. An opening began to form in the emerald glow. An entrance. Paved with yellow bricks.

"Dottie, no." Liralen sobbed as she struggled against me. "Come back. Don't leave without me." She broke away from me and rushed toward the child. The opening in the wall started to waver, broken plaster again starting to show through the emerald glow.

"Stop, Liralen!" I shouted. "It won't work for you." She froze in place and looked back at me. "It's her dream," I continued, not knowing how it was true. "She has to go by herself." I went to Liralen and put my arms around her. "I'm sorry," I said. "But you have to believe me. Let her go by herself."

As I held Liralen, the emerald glow strengthened again. The road reappeared. The child turned back to look at us, her feet already on the yellow bricks. "He's right. I can't take you with me, Liralen. I didn't plan for it, never dreamed of it. It's too late now. I'm so sorry. Goodbye, dear. Johnny, take care of you both. Find your own path. I saw it last night in you. Take Liralen with you. Make her part of your dream. Believe it can be done. Remember me."

"Goodbye, Dorothy," I said as I kept my arms locked around Liralen. I was crying too. "I'm glad you found your way home. Take care of yourself."

She turned away from us and walked the yellow brick road. She disappeared when she passed through the shining opening. A second later the opening disappeared too. Liralen and I were left alone in the room. The winds and the tornado had vanished. There wasn't any hole in the wall.

I took Liralen through the snow to Galen, and we stayed in a motel that night. I comforted her as well as I could. I went back to the house the next day and took the Gray Lady to the airport. Before I left, I cleared away the frozen roses that were still in the vases.

Liralen stayed behind to handle the problems we knew were going to come from Dorothy Gale's disappearance. There were problems, but they were finally straightened out. Liralen was the sole beneficiary of Dottie's estate. She's living in the old mansion on the Kansas plains now. We write letters to each other, and on the nights I can't sleep I pick up the phone and call her. We talk about our dreams.

"We talk about our dreams," I finished. "And I've never told the story to anyone before now."

No one said anything until Neely drawled out, "I think you've caught Alzheimer's, Dann." He waved at the waitress. "I don't know about the rest of you, but I didn't come here to listen to fairy tales. I want a drink and then I want to get laid."

"Jesus, Neely," Cullens growled. "Shut up, why don't you."

Neely bared his teeth in a grin as pleasant as a shark's. "Yeah, Maxie? You don't like it? Too bad. So what are we going to do about it?"

Cullens started to stand, reaching for Neely's throat. I stood up too and waved him off. "Forget it, Max," I said. "It was just a story. If Sid didn't like it, it's no skin off of me. I'm going to the bathroom. Someone order another beer for me."

Max dropped back into his chair. "The hell with it then, and the hell with you too, Neely. I liked the story, Johnny. Thanks for telling it. This round is on me, gentlemen, and then I'm going home."

Everyone relaxed. Neely yawned and studied his fingernails, avoiding looking at Max. The waitress started taking down orders. I headed for the bathroom. I made up my mind before I reached the door.

I kept on going and walked into the tiny storage room where Barrabe's handyman, Clarence, was sitting on a stack of beer cases.

"Hello, Clarence," I said. "What do you have back here that will burn?"

"Mr. D.," he answered. "Good to see you. Something to burn, you say?"

"Yeah. In a bottle."

"Hmmm. In a bottle." Clarence rolled the matchstick he was chewing to the other side of his mouth. "Well, let's see. We have some of that stuff behind you. Last restaurant I worked in used it to set fancy desserts on fire. That suitable?"

I pulled the bottle off the shelf and studied it. "Probably," I said. "Find out in a second." I looked around some more and found a rag. "Need a wick, too," I said as I ripped a strip off the rag. "This should do."

"Mr. D.," Clarence said nervously. "A man might say you were thinking about making one of those Molotov cocktail things."

"Not thinking," I replied. "I'll be back in a couple of minutes."

I walked out the back entrance and found Neely's yellow Corvette in the parking lot. Its top didn't reach higher than my waist. I pulled the cork out of the bottle and spilled some of the booze over the rag. Then I stuffed the strip down the bottle's neck and kicked in the Corvette's window on the driver's side. The window took two hard shots before caving in. Safety glass.

I flipped open my lighter and lit a cigarette first. Then I lit the strip, which caught with a blue-yellowish flame. I threw the bottle hard enough to shatter it inside the car. The booze exploded. I backed away, smoking my cigarette, and studied the fire.

"Neely's?" Ned Barrabe asked as he walked up behind me.

"Yeah. Clarence call you?"

"Umm. Thought I'd better see what you were planning to do with my fine liquor."

The 'vette's plastic seats were melting and the upholstery had caught fire. "Seems to be going along nicely. Good stuff. Think I'll head back in."

"Johnny," Ned called as I went into the club. "Neely is carrying a piece."

"Put the bottle on my tab," I said without turning around.

I walked back to the table. "Sid," I announced without sitting down, "I just set your car on fire."

Everyone looked at me. "That some sort of joke, Dann?" Neely asked.

"Nope. Burning pretty good the last time I looked. You might want to check it out."

"What the hell?" he shouted and rushed outside. The few

other people left in the club followed him out. Max grinned at me before he left. I sat down at the table. Ned had followed me in and was dialing the telephone.

I found a half-full bottle and poured the beer into my glass. I looked at my watch again. *She should be here anytime now*, I thought.

The doors slammed open and Neely rushed back in. He had his gun in his hand. Pointed at me.

"Dann!" he shouted. "I don't know whether you're crazy or drunk and I don't care. But you're going to pay. Get up."

I didn't move, didn't bother to look at Neely.

"Get up. Now!" he shouted again.

I took another bottle and refilled my glass.

"You think you can get away with this?" Neely asked, nearly screaming now. "Look at me! I'm telling you for the last time, get up. Or so help me God, I'll ice you right here."

"Sid," Ned said in a murderously quiet voice. We both turned to look at him. He had a sawed-off riot gun propped on the bar, aimed at Neely. He had done something to the trigger guard to accommodate his ruined hands. "Put it away and get out of here. I've called the fire department. Go out and take care of your car."

The gun swung between Ned and me. "No way, Barrabe. I'm taking him."

Ned shook his head. "One more time, Sid. Last chance. Put it away and leave. Five seconds."

The gun wavered for a second and then dropped to Neely's side. His face fell like a kid's who thought he was being spanked for no reason. "Are you nuts, too? He torches my car and I'm supposed to let him go? I haven't even made the first payment on it yet."

"You work for an insurance company. Let them worry about it. And nobody here did anything to your car. It's a rough neighborhood. We have a lot of bad kids around. Not the first time it's happened. That's what I'm going to say. That's what anyone who wants to drink in here again is going to say." Ned directed the last sentence to the crowd of people who had gathered in the door behind Neely.

"I don't like people waving firearms on my premises," he continued to Neely. "And I don't like you anyway, Sid. You're not welcome in my bar. You want to find out how much you're not welcome?"

Neely's mouth worked as if he were going to argue, but the

riot gun was still pointing at his middle. He holstered his gun, turned around, and pushed his way past the people at the entrance.

"Remember what I said," Ned told the people at the door. "And I just closed for the night. Get your nightcaps someplace else." He put the shotgun away, came out from behind the bar, and started to close the door. I saw her as she came through the stragglers and tried to get past Ned. "You hard of hearing, lady?" he asked. "I said we're closed."

"I'm with him," she said, pointing the package she was carrying at me. Ned turned around and I nodded.

She came to the table and sat down. Ned locked the door, went back to the bar, and came back with two more beers. "I'll have to have the lock repaired on the back door," he said. "Someone busted it. I'll have Clarence check and see if anything is missing."

"Like a bottle?" I reached into my wallet for my hideaway hundred and pushed the bill across the table.

Ned took the money and stuffed it in his front pocket. "I don't know anything about a bottle. I'll take this for the body-guard duty." He leaned down and looked into my eyes. "But don't *ever* do something like that again in my bar, Johnny D. Get killed on your own time if you want, but not on mine. We understand each other?"

"Understood, Mr. Barrabe. And thanks for the cover."

"My pleasure. I'm going to talk to the fire marshal. Maybe I can take care of it if I get to him early enough. The hundred might help, but I don't know. I'd think about taking a trip until the heat's off, Johnny. Even if I can fix it with the marshal, Neely's not going to forget."

"Funny you should say that," I answered. "I was planning to get out of town for a while anyway."

"Yeah?" he said. "Good. You two stay here and finish your beers. Let Neely find a ride before you leave."

Ned left. I looked at the woman sitting across from me. She was wearing a trench coat and a felt hat modeled after one of the old-time fedoras. As usual, the black hair was tucked away out of sight. "You're looking good, kid," I said. "Everything go all right?"

"Like clockwork," Liralen answered. "No problems. They said it was a piece of cake. Lester said to tell you he took some other stuff as a bonus for the job. He'll give us a few months before moving anything."

"Lester does good work. He'll probably end up dealing it all back to the insurance company. That's the way it usually goes."

"And how about this?" she asked as she put the package on the table. "Aren't they going to ask him where it went?"

"It won't matter." I took out a pocketknife and started cutting away the cords wrapped around the package. "Keep your eye out for Ned, will you, kid?" I asked. "I've already pushed him hard enough tonight."

"What was that all about, Johnny?"

I told her while I unwrapped the package. "Just a piece of business that I wanted to take care of before we left," I finished. "Seemed like the right time to do it." I pulled the paper off and uncovered the statue.

"Well, there it is, Johnny D.," Liralen said, grinning as she saw the look of wonder on my face. "Worth ten thousand of Dottie's dollars?"

"Every penny," I answered as I examined it. "Just the way it looked in the movie. Heavier than I thought it would be, though." I picked up the paper but left the statue uncovered, wanting to look at it for a while longer. "Okay, kid," I said. "That's it, then. Ready to go?"

Liralen finished her beer in one gulp. "Sure, Johnny," she answered as she wiped the foam mustache off her lip. "But where are we going?"

"San Francisco to start. We'll see after that."

She put her hand on my arm and stopped me as we left the club. "Johnny, are you sure?" she asked. "Can you take me with you? Will it work?"

I held up the statue of the black bird I was carrying. "We'll do it. Believe it. This was all I needed. This and you, kid." I wrapped the paper around the Maltese Falcon and laughed.

"After all," I said as I put my arm around Liralen. "This is the stuff dreams are made of."

MY IMAGINARY PARENTS

T.L. PARKINSON

"My Imaginary Parents" is a captivating story filled with magic and longing about a young boy from an unhappy home.

T.L. Parkinson has published stories in several volumes of the *Shadows* anthology series along with *After Midnight.* He has recently completed his first novel.

Billy dreaded Saturday night. He always hoped it would be different, but every week it was the same—only worse.

His parents belonged to a dance club that met on Saturday nights. The family ate at five o'clock so that Mom and Dad would have time to get ready. This bothered Billy's digestion, because his stomach was used to eating dinner at seven o'clock six days a week.

As soon as the plates were cleared, Billy felt the tension grow in his head, like a storm front that begins as a quiet dark line on the horizon and smothers you with snow before you know it.

Billy wanted to hide. If he went into his room and hid under the covers, they would drag him out. If he played with his dolls, which distracted him from the moody feelings, they would scold him because he was seven years old and seven years old was much too old (for a boy) still to be playing with dolls.

There was a lot he didn't understand; but on Saturday nights the confusion became immense, like a nightmare come from some dusty corner to swallow him. The air was full of it, as thick as the soot that blew up the chimney and settled on his face when he was playing in the tiny backyard with the chainlink fence.

Mom and Dad were now in the bedroom, getting ready. Billy was watching TV. Lucy and Ethel were up to their usual pranks.

Billy pretended he was part of their crazy world—but the program ended too soon. Then a gun show came on that he didn't understand and didn't like.

He turned off the set and started to read a book he had gotten from the school library. The sounds from the bedroom grew louder—Billy pulled pillows over his ears. He could still hear Mom laughing, Dad giggling like a girl—they made sounds they never made when they were around him. It sounded strange, muffled there under the pillows, but almost fun.

What they were doing was preparing to go out and leave him behind, leave him to the awful thing that happened on Saturday nights.

Billy lay on his side and propped up the book. The couch smelled plasticky—Mom had put something on it to keep it from spotting. The couch was new, and Billy had only recently been allowed to sit on it. He had carefully taken off his shoes, and tried to move around as little as possible.

Mom ran out of the small bedroom, got a red and green dress from the hall closet, and ran back in. She wore a white towel around her hair, and a blue towel around her middle, which she held up as though she were afraid someone would see her. Billy wondered why she did this; they had all seen her, plenty of times.

The door was open just a crack. Dad walked across the crack, and Billy could see that he had only one leg of his pants on, and that he hopped like a crippled sailor. Then Dad shut the door, hard.

A cloud of perfume hung over everything. Billy wanted with all his might to be somewhere far away, and he tried to imagine it. But the dark cloud of smells and feelings kept bringing him back.

The house had a small living room with a picture window that looked onto a postage stamp of snowy ground, and a shiny red Buick in the driveway that Dad had cleaned this afternoon. (It was starting to spit snow again.) There was the big bedroom where Mom and Dad slept, and a smaller room with two bunk beds, where Billy and his brother, Tom (six years older), slept.

Then there was the room hardly bigger than a closet that dad called his study. There was a huge painting of a naked woman with black hair overhanging a moth-eaten couch. The woman was really Marilyn Monroe, but Dad had changed her hair to black, like Mom's. Dad was an artist, and the room was his private place.

Mom and Dad now were in the kitchen, having a highball before they left. They came from the kitchen a few minutes later, faces red and eyes glittering.

Mom wore a low-cut dress with a white flower nestling between her breasts. Dad's hair was as brightly polished as his shoes, and he wore a dark suit with a purple tie, and cuff links of women's breasts with hands around them. They had been a joke gift from Melvin, a longtime friend of Dad's.

Oh boy, now it comes. They are going to leave. Billy sat back on the new couch, pushing his legs hard against the coffee table, until it rocked. He pushed his hands between the cushions and found the doll he had hidden there.

Mom kissed him goodbye, a long wet kiss which would linger on his cheek long after she had left. Dad said a gruff goodbye that sounded a little angry.

Did he know about the doll?

They were out the door in a cold wind. The footprints they made through the yard were as dark as a night sky without clouds.

Billy stood at the door long after the car was out of sight, waving furiously into dead air.

Eventually he had to turn around, and there was brother Tom, waiting, waiting for everything to be clear, for Billy to go to bed, so that he could do what he did every Saturday night.

Billy had been in bed for hours. He kept waking fitfully; the aluminum window rattled in a gusty wind, and there was a constant flow of cold air across his face which made his nose run.

Tom had not come to bed yet. Billy had checked twice, hoping that Tom would give it up, whatever it was that he was doing. The mysterious thing that Billy had better never mention.

Billy fell asleep again. When he woke next time the clock said two-thirty, and he could tell that Tom was now in bed, because in the blue light from the snow piled in the window box Billy could see the heavy curve of the upper bunk that meant it was occupied.

The front door slammed sometime later, and Billy was almost asleep again when the hall light bothered his eyes open.

Everything sounded funny, far away, like voices down a paper tube. Dad called out Tom's name; Tom slid from the bunk and went into the hall.

Mom's voice moaned like the cold wind; Billy couldn't make out the words. Tom didn't say anything. Dad choked, sputtered like a car on a cold morning, and then went out the front door. He always went out for a walk when he was angry.

Billy wondered what had made Dad so angry.

Mom had started to cry. Pain flew through the air like

snowballs with rocks in them. "I'm sorry, I'm sorry," Tom said, each time fainter, until his words were lost in a groan.

Billy tried not to listen. His head was swimming, and he felt like he had to throw up. A ringing grew in his ears until he could barely hear anything, which was a relief. It was as though he were suddenly far away from everything, in a plane or on a mountaintop, looking down.

Billy crept from bed and looked through the door. Mom still had her coat on, snow on the shoulders, her hair mussed, her eyes red, and her shoulders hunched forward. The white flower that she had worn between her breasts was gone.

She cradled a blue and green dress as though it were a child. She and Tom stood before an open closet, which was where Tom spent most of his Saturday nights after Billy went to bed.

The dress was torn under the arms—Tom had gained a lot of weight in the past two years; hormonal problems, the doctor said, whatever that was. He could no longer fit into Mom's clothes without ripping them.

Billy wondered why he did it, when he knew he would be caught. Billy also wondered why it bothered his parents so much; the feeling was worse than when his grandfather had almost killed Billy's cousin when he had caught him doing something awful in the barn; the boy had been in the hospital for weeks, and still was not completely right.

Billy wondered if wearing Mom's clothes was like trying to kill somebody.

Then Mom reached out to Tom, who stood as still as a statue. She said something from smudged red lips, silently. Tom shrugged away from her, and she followed, as though pulled by an invisible string. She grabbed for his shoulder, but her hand passed right through. She let her hand fall; it fell through Tom's chest in a slicing motion.

Billy closed the door as slowly as his panic would allow, then climbed back into his cold bed. He breathed used air under his sheets until his heart began to beat more slowly.

Billy felt big, heavy, like he was being crushed by something, but the something was himself. He lay very still and hoped for the feeling to go away.

A few minutes later, Tom climbed into bed; Tom barely made a whisper, he was as light as air.

In the lower bunk, Billy, afraid or unable to move, had a sudden thought, which moved swiftly, terribly.

What if this is not my real family?

*   *   *

Dad took away Billy's dolls soon after, and gave him a Lionel train set to keep him occupied. Dad was clever with his hands, so he made papier-mâché mountains for the trains to pass through, a bridge over real water, and toy soldiers hiding behind clumps of plastic trees.

Billy did not say much to Dad about the train setup, but he pretended to be interested so Dad wouldn't get mad and have to take a walk.

He missed his dolls terribly, especially the teenage boy doll who was shaped the way Billy would like to be when he was older. The doll reminded him of the older boy down the street who always cut the lawn with his shirt off. Billy sneaked a couple of the toy soldiers from the basement where they kept the trains, but the stiff little green figures were not the same.

One day when everyone was out of the house, Billy melted them on the stove. He had a terrible time cleaning up the green plastic mess—and had to wait an hour for it to cool down so he could peel it off the burners.

He just made it, stuffing the paper towels and the ruined sponge into the trashcan as Mom came through the door and slammed a bag of groceries down on the Formica counter top.

She mumbled something about an argument with a neighbor; she was always arguing with the neighbors, who gave her advice—but no one, no one, was going to give her advice about how to raise her children.

Billy felt a little proud of his Mom's stubbornness; and was also a little frightened by it.

She patted him on the head, sniffed the air (the plastic smell had not cleared out), and looked at him oddly.

Dad burst through the back door just when Billy thought she was going to say something about the smell.

Dad was all fired up about *his* parents, who were cheating him out of money. When Dad took Mom into the living room, Billy opened the kitchen window and let in the cold wind.

Billy had heard this argument many times, but he half-listened anyway. Dad said they were his parents, and he had to respect them, even if he didn't like them. She said she was angry that he let Grandma and Grandpop take advantage of him. The old folks had plenty of money; we need the money. Look at this house. He always said he would do something about it, but never did.

Dad worked for his father in a contracting business, and Grandma pulled the purse strings.

Tom came home late. They had started dinner without him. He looked terrible, like he had lost his best friend.

"How did it go with the doctor?" Dad asked in a rough voice, as though the words hurt coming out.

When Tom started to say something, there was no sound; but tears sprang into his eyes, and he ran into the hall closet and shut the door.

Mom got up to see what was wrong with Tom, but Dad grabbed her arm and made her sit back down.

Billy started to get that funny feeling in his head again. He looked down at his plate, at his hands, and listened. Slowly, everything grew quiet, as quiet as the middle of a field of snow before anyone sets foot on it.

When he looked up, he could see the backs of the chairs through Mom and Dad.

"Billy," a voice said out of nowhere, stilling his racing heart, "we are getting closer now. Be patient. Everything is going to be all right."

Just like that, everything was different. In a flash, like lightning, like a car crash, like anything that strikes and changes something in an instant.

Billy figured it out the same day Tom came home crying. Billy had had a long talk with the voices in his head. He had always had conversations with imaginary people, but with no one in particular. Now there were only two people in his mind, like tree shadows, growing larger as the winter sun grew weaker. The same two voices, real voices, achingly familiar, kept coming back again and again.

They told him Mom and Dad and Tom weren't his real family. They were ghosts, who had not paid their earthly debts and were being denied entrance to heaven. They had kidnapped him when he was a baby, because ghosts need something from the living to fill their emptiness and make them feel alive—they need an audience.

And there is no better audience than a captive audience: a stolen child.

"We're your real parents. We've been searching for you for years. But we're still far far away. You must be patient, and we will come to rescue you, slowly, over time."

"How much time?" Billy asked.

"There's no way to say," the voices said, "but it will depend on you."

And they would say no more.

Dad had never been much of a talker. He tried several times to talk to Billy in the next couple of weeks; but Billy kept making excuses. Finally, Dad insisted.

"Sit down," unreal Dad said one windy evening, and Billy sat on the green plastic footstool. Dad leaned forward in his easy chair. He fidgeted with his large red hands; his face, also red, seemed about to burst.

"I know you're too young to understand," Dad said quickly, "but when you grow up you'll see that all families have problems, and ours are no worse than anyone else's." All Billy could do was stare at the big chafed hands, and imagine them on Mom's ghostly shoulders.

Billy nodded, trying to look Dad right in the eye; but he found he couldn't do it for long without feeling queasy.

"Billy, have you been feeling all right?" Dad asked, also looking over Billy's shoulders.

Billy said dreamily, "I feel all right—really."

Dad kept talking, but Billy wasn't paying much attention. The words got fainter and fainter. He kept nodding as though he understood, and this seemed to satisfy Dad.

Billy was looking past Dad through the window. The moon rose over snow, light was coming up and going down, and there were swirling vapors in which Billy could almost, but not quite, see two forms moving toward him.

Startled, Billy looked back at Dad, who was silent and red, the words painfully bunched up in his chest. Billy felt some of the bunching up in his own chest, and Dad started to seem a little more real.

"Don't confuse pity with love," Billy's real parents told him, in his head. "He isn't really real."

Billy got up and walked away, saying he had some homework to do.

He felt a sharp pain in his heart, as though an icicle were moving through it.

He was going through an introverted stage; that is what Tom's doctor called it, when they took him one day when Tom had to get a hormone shot, and sneaked in a quick question about Billy.

Billy had been playing with the train set a little, when Dad was around. Dad seemed pleased and over the next week stopped staring at Billy in that confused way, and started paying more attention to Mom.

This left Billy out in the cold again, without attention, but he didn't mind. For the first time he was glad they had each other, and Tom, who dressed up like Mom: at least then they would leave him alone, and he might be able to slip away.

If he started feeling bad, he would turn on the TV but not really watch it. He was really watching the pictures in his mind, squinting his eyes hard and trying to make them come clear.

After a while he could see them, the people whose voices promised so much.

Mother was a tall woman with black hair just beginning to turn gray at the temples. She had long fingers and played the piano. She had olive-colored eyes with laugh lines about them. She spoke in a warm, even voice that calmed Billy's nerves like the sound of the sea on a spring day. Father was taller than Mother (who was tall for a woman), with big shoulders and a tuft of hair showing above his loose-fitting shirt. His voice was deep, as deep as the sound of distant traffic. He didn't talk much, but when he did it felt right; and when he held Billy in his arms, pressed against the broad chest, Billy knew that nothing could ever hurt him again. Father was like the sound of a bell on a cold clear morning.

They were coming closer, through the ice, as the days grew shorter and the temperature plunged below zero every night. There was always snow now, and ice beneath the snow.

It seemed that everything was cold; the house groaned and creaked at night, and the furnace was always humming its sleepy song.

And Billy knew, in the middle of all this cold, in this house, he was the only thing alive.

Billy marked off the days of winter on his calendar.

He saw his real parents in the cloudy bathroom mirror in the morning when he brushed his teeth. They smiled from the frosty windows at school. They sailed through the flickering lights on the backs of his eyelids when he was about to fall asleep.

Another day, of seemingly unending cold, and then another. But each day, although sometimes the waiting was unbearable, each day marked with a black X brought him closer to his rescue, and escape.

Billy wished away the time.

The voices told him to be patient, not to do anything yet—his ghostly family might hurt him, have him put away if he told them what was going on.

"Now that we've found you we won't let you slip away from us again."

So Billy waited as patiently as he could through the long winter, and kept as still as a stone about what he knew.

On the day of the final snowfall, a wet snow that sparkled in the bright sun, Billy went to bed with a bad cold. He was tired; no one was coming to rescue him. He would be stuck here forever. The voices had fooled him, just like Tom fooled him when he went down to his secret lab with his pimply-faced friend and dissected frogs; they always said they would let Billy see, but they never did:

"You can come in when you're a little older, brother. Look at that, the formula worked!"

Billy wondered, with his covers pulled tightly over his face, if he would ever be old enough. Sleep passed over him like the hand of a magician.

The window blew open. A breeze filled with lilac, a warm spring breeze, woke him, lifted the covers.

He walked to the window. Two figures moved just out of sight; their voices were strong and urgent.

And they told him what he must do.

It was Saturday night, the night of the first day that his real parents had come. Billy was terribly eager to meet them, to touch them, to have their arms about him.

Billy watched the ghostly family going through the motions. Mom and Dad got ready, Mom wearing her low-cut dress and then deciding to do something about it at the last minute, closing it with a rhinestone pin; Dad's face all flushed with eagerness. Tom, who was still overweight but not as badly, waiting in his room, reading aviation magazines on the top bunk.

Mom and Dad said goodbye, hurried out the front door, Tom rustled in the closet all night long, and Mom and Dad came home. No fight this time; Tom was more careful, making sure he didn't tear the dresses, and hung them up neatly.

By three o'clock they all were fast asleep, except for Billy.

He had gotten the stuff ready in the afternoon, some rags, and kerosene.

Mother and Father said the cardboard house would go up in a flash, and then they would meet him at the end of the street, under the black branches of the big elm tree.

He stuffed the kerosene-soaked rags around the radiator, under Mom and Dad's closed bedroom door, and on his own bunk underneath the snoring Tom.

He felt a little sad about Tom.

He got some of the big kitchen matches ghostly Mom had forbidden him to touch, which were hidden in a teddy bear cookie jar on the top shelf.

Billy liked the smell of kerosene. It reminded him of his grandparents' cabin in the woods, where they used oil lamps instead of electric ones. The smell made him feel warm inside, and he thought of deer and pine forests and sunlight streaming through trees.

He liked the way the rags burst into life when he threw the matches. The bunk bed caught fire right away, and then the door to Mom and Dad's bedroom became a wall of flame. The living room flickered like a candle—new shadows were everywhere, dancing and holding hands.

As an afterthought, he went into Dad's study and threw a burning rag under the painting of the naked woman. Mother and Father were hollering for him to get out quick, he was a real boy not a ghost and the fire would hurt him, but he had to do it; he had always hated that room, especially.

As he passed the open closet, he tripped on the red and green dress Mom had worn tonight; she had been too drunk to hang it up. Billy grabbed it and ran.

He just made it outside. The house was burning nicely as he stepped barefooted into the shiny blue night. The door slammed behind him. A hot wind licked his back.

When Billy got to the street, he turned around. A big red hand of flame reached out to him.

He was so close, and it was only a second before he turned away. But had he seen the three of them, ghosts making shapes in the roaring fire, running through the rush of flames, below the black smoke that coiled like a snake?

And had he heard Mom scream, "Where's Billy?" before everything grew still?

The elm tree was farther away than it looked. Billy walked toward that snowy umbrella, black holding white, where two figures stood with open arms.

Watching and waiting.

BIBLE STORIES FOR ADULTS NO. 17: THE DELUGE

JAMES MORROW

"Bible Stories for Adults, No. 17: The Deluge" is the kind of story that helps define the parameters we were working with in this anthology. This story is like *nothing* we've seen in a very long time and quite frankly, it will probably offend some of you. It is also absolutely brilliant.

Brilliant work comes often from Jim Morrow. His most recent novel, *This Is the Way the World Ends*, was a Nebula Award nominee, the runner-up for the John W. Campbell Memorial Award, and the BBC's selection for the best science fiction novel published in England during 1987. His short fiction has appeared in *Isaac Asimov's Science Fiction Magazine* and *The Magazine of Fantasy and Science Fiction,* and he has sold a story to the *Twilight Zone* television series. He currently lives in State College, Pennsylvania with his wife and daughter, where he is completing his fourth novel, a fantasy about the coming of Jesus Christ's sister to contemporary Atlantic City.

Take your cup down to the Caspian, dip, and drink. It did not always taste of salt. Yahweh's watery slaughter may have purified the earth, but it left his seas a ruin, brackish with pagan blood and the tears of wicked orphans.

Sheila and her generation know the deluge is coming. Yahweh speaks to them through their sins. A thief cuts a purse, and the shekels clank together, pealing out a call to repentance. A priest kneels before a graven image of Dagon, and the statue opens its marble jaws, issuing not its own warnings but Yahweh's. A harlot threads herself with a thorny vine, tearing out unwanted flesh, and a divine voice rises from the bleeding fetus. You are a corrupt race, Yahweh says, abominable in my sight. My rains will scrub you from the earth.

Yahweh is as good as his word. The storm breaks. Creeks become rivers, rivers cataracts. Lakes blossom into broiling, wrathful seas.

Yes, Sheila is thoroughly foul in those days, her apple home to many worms, the scroll of her sins as long as the Araxas. She is gluttonous and unkempt. She sells her body. Her abortions number eleven. *I should have made it twelve*, she realizes as the deluge begins. But it is too late, she had already gone through with it—the labor more agonizing than any abortion, her breasts left pulpy and deformed—and soon the boy was seven, athletic, clever, fair of face, but today the swift feet are clamped in the cleft of an olive-tree root, the clever hands are still, the fair face lies buried in water.

A mother, Sheila has heard, should be a boat to her child, buoying him up during floods, bearing him through storms, and yet it is Sam who rescues her. She is hoisting his corpse aloft, hoping to drain the death from his lungs, when suddenly his little canoe floats by. A scooped-out log, nothing more, but still his favorite toy. He liked to paddle it across the Araxas and catch turtles in the marsh.

Sheila climbs aboard, leaving Sam's meat to the sharks.

CAPTAIN'S LOG.
10 JUNE 1057
AFTER CREATION

The beasts eat too much. At present rates of consumption, we'll be out of provisions in a mere eight weeks.

For the herbivores: 4,540 pounds of oats a day, 6,780 pounds of hay, 2,460 of vegetables, and 3,250 of fruit.

For the carnivores: 17,620 pounds of yak and caribou meat a day. And we may lose the whole supply if we don't find a way to freeze it.

Yahweh's displeasure pours down in great swirling sheets, as if the world is trapped beneath a waterfall. Sheila paddles without passion, no goal in mind, no reason to live. Fierce winds churn the sea. Lightning fractures the sky. The floodwaters thicken with disintegrating sinners, afloat on their backs, their gelatinous eyes locked in pleading stares, as if begging God for a second chance.

The world reeks. Sheila gags on the vapors. Is the decay of the wicked, she wonders, more odoriferous than that of the just? When she dies, will her stink drive even flies and vultures away?

Sheila wants to die, but her flesh argues otherwise, making her lift her mouth toward heaven and swallow the quenching downpour. The hunger will be harder to solve: it hurts, a scorpion stinging her belly, so painful that Sheila resolves to add cannibalism to her repertoire. But then, in the bottom of the canoe, she spies two huddled turtles, confused, fearful. She eats one raw, beginning with the head, chewing the leathery flesh, drinking the salty blood.

A dark mountainous shape cruises out of the blur. A sea monster, she decides, angry, sharp-toothed, ravenous . . . Yahweh incarnate, eager to rid the earth of Sheila. Fine. Good. Amen. Painfully she lifts her paddle, heavy as a millstone, and strokes through a congestion of drowned princes and waterlogged horses, straight for the hulking deity.

Now God is atop her, a headlong collision, cracking her canoe like a crocodile's tail slapping an egg. The floodwaters cover her, a frigid darkness flows through her, and with her last breath she lobs a sphere of mucus into Yahweh's gloomy and featureless face.

CAPTAIN'S LOG. 20 JUNE 1057 A.C.
▰▰▰▰▰▰▰▰▰▰▰▰▰▰▰▰▰▰▰

Yahweh said nothing about survivors. Yet this morning we came upon two.

The *Testudo marginata* posed no problem. We have plenty of turtles, all 225 species in fact, *Testudinidae, Chelydridae, Platysternidae, Kinosternidae, Chelonidae,* you name it. Unclean beasts, inedible, useless. We left the *marginata* to the flood. Soon it will swim itself to death.

The *Homo sapiens* was a different matter. Frightened, delirious, she clung to her broken canoe like a sloth embracing a tree. "Yahweh was explicit," said Ham, leaning over *Eden II*'s rail, calling into the gushing rain. "Everyone not in this family deserves death."

"She is one of the tainted generation," added his wife. "A whore. Abandon her."

"No," countered Japheth. "We must throw her a line, as any men of virtue would do."

His young bride had no opinion.

As for Shem and Tamar, the harlot's arrival became yet another occasion for them to bicker. "Japheth is right," insisted Shem. "Bring her among us, Father."

"Let Yahweh have his way with her," retorted Tamar. "Let the flood fulfill its purpose."

"What do *you* think?" I asked Reumah.

Smiling softly, my wife pointed to the dinghy.

I ordered the little boat lowered. Japheth and Shem rode it to the surface of the lurching sea, prying the harlot from her canoe, hauling her over the transom. After much struggle, we got her aboard *Eden II*, laying her unconscious bulk on the foredeck. She was a lewd walrus, fat and dissipated. A necklace of rat skulls dangled from her squat neck. When Japheth pushed on her chest, water fountained out, and a cough ripped through her like a yak's roar.

"Who are you?" I demanded.

She fixed me with a dazed stare and fainted. We carried her below, setting her among the pigs like the unclean thing she is. Reumah stripped away our visitor's soggy garments, and I winced to behold her pocked and twisted flesh.

"Sinner or not, Yahweh has seen fit to spare

her," said my wife, wrapping a dry robe around
the harlot. "We are the instruments of his
amnesty."

"Perhaps," I said, snapping the word like a
whip.

The final decision rests with me, of course, not
with my sons or their wives. Is the harlot a test?
Would a true God-follower sink this human flot-
sam without a moment's hesitation?

Even asleep, our visitor is vile, her hair a lice
farm, her breath a polluting wind.

Sheila awakens to the snorty gossip of pigs. A great bowl of
darkness envelops her, dank and dripping like a basket submerged in a swamp. Her nostrils burn with a hundred varieties of
stench. She believes that Yahweh has swallowed her, that she is
imprisoned in his maw.

Slowly a light seeps into her eyes. Before her, a wooden gate
creaks as it pivots on leather hinges. A young man approaches,
proferring a wineskin and a cooked leg of mutton.

"Are we inside God?" Sheila demands, propping her thick
torso on her elbows. Someone has given her dry clothes. The
effort of speaking tires her, and she lies back in the swine-
scented straw. "Is this Yahweh?"

"The last of his creation," the young man replies. "My
parents, brothers, our wives, the birds, beasts—and myself,
Japheth. Here. Eat." Japheth presses the mutton to her lips.
"Seven of each clean animal, that was our quota. In a month we
shall run out. Enjoy it while you can."

"I want to die." Once again, Sheila's abundant flesh has a
different idea, devouring the mutton, guzzling the wine.

"If you wanted to die," says Japheth, "you would not have
gripped that canoe so tightly. Welcome aboard."

"Aboard?" says Sheila. Japheth is most handsome. His crisp
black beard excites her lust. "We're on a boat?"

Japheth nods. "*Eden II*. Gopher wood, stem to stern. This
is the world now, nothing else remains. Yahweh means for you
to be here."

"I doubt that." Sheila knows her arrival is a freak. She has merely been overlooked. No one means for her to be here, least of all God.

"My father built it," the young man explains. "He is six hundred years old."

"Impressive," says Sheila, grimacing. She has seen the type, a crotchety, withered patriarch, tripping over his beard. Those final five hundred years do nothing for a man, save to make his skin leathery and his worm boneless.

"You're a whore, aren't you?"

The boat pitches and rolls, unmooring Sheila's stomach. She lifts the wineskin to her lips and fills her pouchy cheeks. "Also a drunkard, thief, self-abortionist"—her grin stretches well into the toothless regions—"and sexual deviant." With her palm she cradles her left breast, heaving it to one side.

Japheth gasps and backs away.

Another day, perhaps, they will lie together. For now, Sheila is exhausted, stunned by wine. She rests her reeling head on the straw and sleeps.

CAPTAIN'S LOG.
25 JUNE 1057 A.C.

We have harvested a glacier, bringing thirty tons of ice aboard. For the moment, our meat will not become carrion; our leopards, wolves, and carnosaurs will thrive.

I once saw some idolators deal with an outcast. They tethered his ankles to an ox, his wrists to another ox. They drove the first beast north, the second south.

Half of me believes we must admit this woman. Indeed, if we kill her, do we not become the same people Yahweh saw fit to destroy? If we so sin, do we not contaminate the very race we are meant to sire? In my sons' loins rests the whole of the future. We are the keepers of our kind. Yahweh picked us for the purity of our seed, not the infallibility of our justice. It is hardly our place to condemn.

My other half begs that I cast her into the flood. A harlot, Japheth assures me. A dipsomaniac, robber, and fetus killer. She should have died with the rest of them. We must not allow her degenerate womb back into the world, lest it bear fruit.

Again Sheila awakens to swine sounds, refreshed and at peace. She no longer wishes to die.

This afternoon a different brother enters the pig cage. He gives his name as Shem, and he is even better-looking than Japheth. He bears a glass of tea in which float three diaphanous pebbles. "Ice," he explains. "Clotted water."

Sheila drinks. The frigid tea buffs the grime from her tongue and throat. Ice: a remarkable material, she decides. These people know how to live.

"Do you have a pisspot?" Sheila asks, and Shem guides her to a tiny stall enclosed by reed walls. After she has relieved herself, Shem gives her a tour, leading her up and down the ladders that connect the interior decks. *Eden II* leaks like a defective tent, a steady, disquieting *plop-plop*.

The place is a zoo. Mammals, reptiles, birds, two by two. Sheila beholds tiny black beasts with too many legs and long cylindrical ones with too few. Grunts, growls, howls, roars, brays, and caws rattle the ship's wet timbers.

Sheila likes Shem, but not this floating menagerie, this crazy voyage. The whole arrangement infuriates her. Cobras live here. Wasps, their stingers poised to spew poisons. Young tyrannosaurs and baby allosaurs, eager to devour the gazelles on the deck above. Tarantulas, rats, crabs, weasels, armadillos, snapping turtles, boar-pigs, bacteria, viruses: Yahweh has spared them all.

My friends were no worse than a tarantula, Sheila thinks. My neighbors were as important as weasels. My child mattered more than anthrax.

CAPTAIN'S LOG.
14 JULY 1057 A.C.

The rains have stopped. We drift aimlessly. Reumah is seasick. Even with the ice, our provisions are running out. We cannot keep feeding ourselves, much less a million species.

Tonight we discussed our passenger. Predictably, Japheth and Shem spoke for acquittal, while Ham argued the whore must die.

"A necessary evil?" I asked Ham.

"No kind of evil," he replied. "You kill a rabid dog lest its disease spread. This woman's body holds the eggs of future thieves, perverts, and idolators. We must not allow her to infect the new order. We must check this plague while we have the chance."

"We have no right," said Japheth.

"If God can pass a harsh judgment on millions of evildoers," said Ham, "then surely I can do the same for one."

"You are not God," said Japheth.

Nor am I—but I am the master of this ship, the leader of this little tribe. I turned to Ham and said, "I know you speak the truth. We must choose ultimate good over immediate mercy."

Ham agreed to be her executioner. Soon he will dispose of the whore, using the same obsidian knife with which, once we sight land, we are bound to slit and drain our surplus lambs, gratitude's blood.

They have put Sheila to work. She and Ham must maintain

the reptiles. The *Pythoninae* will not eat unless they kill the meal themselves. Sheila spends the whole afternoon competing with the cats, snaring ship rats, hurling them by their tails into the python pens.

Ham is the handsomest son yet, but Sheila does not like him. There is something low and slithery about Ham. It seems fitting that he tends vipers and asps.

"What do you think of Yahweh?" she says.

Instead of answering, Ham leers.

"When a father is abusive," Sheila persists, "the child typically responds not only by denying the abuse occurred, but by redoubling his efforts to be loved."

Silence from Ham. He fondles her with his eyes.

Sheila will not quit. "When I destroyed my unwanted children, it was murder. When Yahweh did the same, it was eugenics. Do you approve of the universe, Ham?"

Ham tosses the python's mate a rat.

CAPTAIN'S LOG.
17 JULY 1057 A.C.

We have run aground. Shem has named the place of our imprisonment Ararat. This morning we sent out a *Corvus corax*, but it did not return. I doubt we'll ever see it again. Two ravens remain, but I refuse to break up a pair. Next time we'll try a *Columbidae*.

In an hour the harlot will die. Ham will open her up, spilling her dirty blood, her filthy organs. Together we shall cast her carcass into the flood.

Why did Yahweh say nothing about survivors?

Silently Ham slithers into the pig cage, crouching over Sheila like an incubus, resting the cool blade against her windpipe.

Sheila is ready. Japheth has told her the whole plot. A sudden move, and Ham's universe is awry, Sheila above, her attacker below, she armed, he defenseless. She wriggles her layered flesh, pressing Ham into the straw. Her scraggly hair tickles his cheeks.

A rape is required. Sheila is good at rape; some of her best customers would settle for nothing less. Deftly she steers the knife amid Ham's garments, unstitching them, peeling him like an orange. "Harden," she commands, fondling his pods, running a practiced hand along his worm. "Harden or die."

Ham shudders and sweats. Terror flutes his lips, but before he can cry out Sheila slides the knife across his throat like a bow across a fiddle, delicately dividing the skin, drawing out tiny beads of blood.

Sheila is a professional. She can stiffen eunuchs, homosexuals, men with knives at their jugulars. Lifting her robe, she lowers herself onto Ham's erection, enjoying his pleasureless passion, reveling in her impalement. A few minutes of graceful undulation, and the worm spurts, filling her with Ham's perfect and upright seed.

"I want to see your brothers," she tells him.

"What?" Ham touches his throat, reopening his fine, subtle wound.

"Shem and Japheth also have their parts to play."

CAPTAIN'S LOG. 24 JULY 1057 A.C.

Our dinghy is missing. Maybe the whore cut it loose before she was executed. No matter. This morning I launched a dove, and it has returned with a twig of some kind in its beak. Soon our sandals will touch dry land.

My sons elected to spare me the sight of the whore's corpse. Fine. I have beheld enough dead sinners in my six centuries.

Tonight we shall sing, dance, and give thanks to Yahweh. Tonight we shall bleed our best lamb.

The world is healing. Cool, smooth winds rouse Sheila's hair, sunlight strokes her face. Straight ahead, white robust clouds sail across a clear sky.

A speck hovers in the distance, and Sheila fixes on it as she navigates the boundless flood. This sign has appeared none too soon. The stores from *Eden II* will not last through the week, especially with Sheila's appetite at such a pitch.

Five weeks in the dinghy, and still her period has not come. "And Ham's child is just the beginning," she mutters, tossing a wry smile toward the clay pot. So far, the ice shows no sign of melting; Shem and Japheth's virtuous fertilizer, siphoned under goad of lust and threat of death, remains frozen. Sheila has plundered enough seed to fill all creation with babies. If things go according to plan, Yahweh will have to stage another flood.

The speck grows, resolves into a bird. A *Corvus corax*, as the old man would have called it.

Sheila will admit that her designs are grand and even pompous. But are they impossible? She aims to found a proud and impertinent nation, a people driven to decipher ice and solve the sun, each of them with as little use for obedience as she, and they will sail the watery world until they find the perfect continent, a land of eternal light and silken grass, and they will call it what any race must call its home, Formosa, beautiful.

The raven swoops down, landing atop the jar of sperm, and Sheila feels a surge of gladness as, reaching out, she takes a branch from its sharp and tawny beak.

BEYOND THE SEVENTH SPHERE

AARON SCHUTZ

Maintaining the historical motif (though two stories could not be more different from one another), here's a riveting story of the distant past. It is also the fifth and final time in this volume we will present an author's first professionally published story. It certainly wasn't our intent to find this many talented new writers, though it has been a joyful experience. We wish each and every one of these writers great success with their careers. Hopefully, ten years from now someone will pick up this volume of *Full Spectrum* and say, "so *this* was where it began."

Aaron Schutz is a recent graduate from the University of Oregon with a BA in Ancient History and is currently enrolled in the New York University Graduate Writing Program.

The castle of the Portuguese kings was a sprawling artifice of stone set on the peak of a tall steep hill in Lisbon, the last great port of the Christian world in the East. Atop its immense walls, soldiers leaned lazily on their spears and gazed out over the villas of the nobility and past the dusky slums to the myriad sails tossing gently in the wind like petals of the white rose, on to the glittering waters of the sea, extending so far that they imagined they saw the final edge of the world itself.

Miguel left his father's castle through the crowded south gate—slowly, as if he were uncertain of his goal, though in his heart his determination was almost palpable as the hardness of a diamond. He was a small man, and young, though he felt that the wrinkles of concentration forever in his brow marked him clearly as a veteran and venerable scholar. His natural hair was shiny black, but the night before he had bleached it out to a pale blond, almost white, along with the small mustache and beard he had grown in the months of hiding. He was still certain that every face that met his would immediately recognize him as the renegade third son of the king. He prayed silently to God as he went, and the weight of the Bible in his pack bumped comfortingly against his spine.

His clothes were coarse, though well made: merchant's clothing. They were not the rags of a few weeks before, nor royal linen, nor the white novitiate robes he missed most dearly. A gold crucifix, blessed and presented to him by the pope, hung from a thin chain around his neck.

I am still a man of God, he thought, *though I may not carry my piety on my back.* The pope himself had declared Miguel's excommunication from the Church, yet his crucifix did not burn him, had not darkened to a damning black; through constant handling it shone even brighter than before.

Miguel walked beside the cobblestone Main Way, avoiding the bustling traffic of carts and workmen, moving through the area of villas that surrounded the castle like a coif. From the street he could see only walls, plastered brick, and remember the lush gardens beyond as he had seen them as a child from the great castle walls.

After forcing his way through a crowded tunnel gate, he entered the slums, and the villa walls disappeared. As the Way curved down, narrow side streets twisted and vanished into shadow on both sides. The vendors, banned from the upper areas, crowded into the spaces under the porticoes of ancient crumbling buildings; low doorways opened into small shops and restaurants. Over the summer heat and the filth lay the smell of fish, mixed with hundreds of other odors. The crowds seethed in currents and he followed those who headed down.

The Way was filled with voices—shouting, crying, as if the air itself lived.

Miguel knew little of this part of the city, and paid constant attention to the heavy weight of his purse, secreted carefully in his tunic. When younger he had come here occasionally, escorted by a train of soldiers and his tutors, surrounded by a bubble of the atmosphere of the castle. Now, the environment was stronger than he, pulling him in, yet leaving him strangely separate. He remembered his studies in Rome. Then, he had been immersed in the wonder of God—as he was now, but in a different way. He felt naked to God, not insulated by Him.

He met the wharves, much later, and the stench of sea brine mixed with the greater stench of fish. Ships of many types bumped at the wooden docks and floated out in the bay, sails furled on immense masts that towered and dipped against the horizon. He passed workers straining at cables and crates, some white, some black—drawn from the pagan depths of Africa: ragged men, yet with strength, and not, he was certain by the look in their eyes and their bellowing obscenities, the strength of

God. Everywhere, sea gulls flew and cried and alighted for some morsel before launching themselves again, and Miguel took this as a good omen, a comforting sight. *I too am a sea gull!* he wished to cry to the heavens.

After asking directions many times, following false leads for miles, Miguel finally found the inn he sought. It squatted in the shadow between two large warehouses down a side street just off the water. A sign with a battered ship painted on it read: THE STURDY KEEL. He felt very tired, his body not well recovered from his months of hiding; the sky had begun to darken as the sun fell below the horizon.

Inside, the bar was brightly lit by lanterns hanging above, and the room faded into rowdy darkness away from it, filled with tables and men. Miguel asked the bartender quietly for the owner, and, after being led into a back room, he handed a stooped old man the note given to him by a castle steward, along with a good number of gold coins. "An old friend from the Moorish wars," the steward had said. "You can trust him." The old man eyed Miguel, and had one of his retainers test the coin, but finally nodded, having said nothing, and showed him to a small room on the second floor.

Miguel prayed far into the night before falling into the rough bed.

He dreamed he flew again.

Days passed, and many captains came to see him, lured by the odor of gold: English, Italian, Spanish, Portuguese. "For the right price," many would say, "I would go anywhere!" Yet all left, increduluous, when he told of his destination:

"I wish passage to the edge of the world."

Every evening Miguel sat quietly at a table in a corner of the main room, shunned by the others. Occasionally, talk wafted through the air to him of the madman who wished to visit the edge of the world.

He spent most of his time in the room he had rented, sleeping through the day. He spoke with ship captains in the evening, and then spent the rest of the long night in vigil, on his knees with his Bible in his hands, sending his earnest prayers up through the seven spheres of the sky to his God, who swam in the depths beyond. He wished to visit a chapel, but he was no longer of the Church, and was afraid. Only at the touch of dawn at his window did he finally slump into bed.

On the sixth night, Miguel despaired. Very few came to see

him now; there had been only two the night before, and though, unlike the others, they had offered to take him, the innkeeper warned him off. "No better than pirates, them."

Miguel declared to his God that if a ship did not come his way on the morrow, he would purchase a small vessel and attempt the journey alone.

Early the next evening, however, as he sat deep in thought, steeling himself against the fear that welled up inside him, a man sat down in the chair opposite his. He was tall, with golden bowl-cut hair, dark skin blending with the shadow of the room. His eyes were gray, cloudy agate, and his rough vest fairly exploded with brightness: a streaked rainbow pattern of red and yellow and orange and more. He smiled, yellow gap-toothed.

"I am Keelag," he said in guttural, strangely accented Portuguese. "I am the master of the *Torque*. They tell me," he pointed to the bar, "that you wish to charter a vessel."

"Yes," said Miguel tiredly. "I will pay one hundred gold coins to the master who will accept my terms. That is not a poor fee." He looked up into the man's eyes. "I wish passage to the edge of the world," he said.

Keelag was silent for a long moment. Then, "Ahh," he said, "and when shall we leave?"

"You would go?" said Miguel.

Keelag's face, which had become impassive, broke into a broad smile, and then he broke into booming laughter, as if he had just told a tremendous joke. Finally, through tears, he said, "I had heard of your destination. If you are mad, then perhaps so am I. The depths below, to my crew, are the home of the sun; they do not fear them. We have been to the edge before. If you truly have the price, I think I would not mind seeing it again before my death."

When Miguel spoke to the innkeeper, the old man said only, "I know little of him, but what I know is good. I would trust him, I think. Perhaps you have no choice in the matter, yes?" and he smiled.

In the morning, Keelag returned to the inn and guided Miguel to his ship through the labyrinth of the wharves.

"Isn't she beautiful?" said Keelag, sweeping his arms out as if to encompass the vessel.

The *Torque* was unlike any ship Miguel had ever seen. It was long and narrow, pointed at the prow and at the stern, where it came up in a crest above the steering bars of the double rudders.

Low in the water, it looked more a longboat than a ship. Two masts fingered up from the center and near the foredeck.

An ancient, wrinkled black man sat by the gangplank, the muscles in his arms like bundles of soft cords. Feet dangling over on the hull, he watched them with obsidian eyes. He too wore a rainbow vest, though its pattern was different from Keelag's. Keelag said, "This is Maza. You might call him my first mate."

Keelag pulled Miguel on board, and Maza turned, his gaze following them.

"There's nothing like her in the world," Keelag said. "A Venetian nobleman built her for a vacationer. He was fascinated by the ancient Greeks, had it built on the model of one of their small warships: a penteconter. She's not really, though. The noble wanted to take her out on the sea for long hauls, and so she draws a lot more than she should. Got her cheap because the noble was bored with her. I've ridden her through the worst the sea has to offer." He showed Miguel the row of twenty benches that ran along either side of the ship, and opened one of the hatches that covered the oarholes. "She's too heavy to be fast on oars alone," he said, smiling, "but under oar and sail, in a good wind, isn't a ship in port that can catch her."

Miguel looked around the ship and noticed how worn and scarred the wood was. Keelag showed him to the cabin at the stern that would be his: smaller even than his room at the inn.

"She'll do," said Miguel.

He stood a few moments on the rocking deck then, shaking a little, staring out over the platter of the bay. He turned away and stared into Maza's strange eyes. *Perhaps I am insane*, he thought. He strode off the ship.

He returned to the inn to pray. During the next few days he bought and had sent to the *Torque* two huge bolts of fine heavy linen, a great bundle of oaken poles, and assorted other lumber found in the city markets. He also sent on board heavy thread, needles, and cordage. Then, two days before leavetaking, as he returned to the inn, he spied the white robes of a burly novitiate standing just within the doorway. The Church had found him, he was certain of it. He turned and ran, weaving through the crowds to where the *Torque* floated at dock.

The ship swarmed with rainbow-vested black men, moving supplies and equipment on board. At the stern, Miguel grabbed

Keelag's arm as he spoke with a crewman in a liquid, guttural language.

"We must leave now!" Miguel said, panting.

Keelag turned. "What is this?"

"We have to leave," Miguel said. "They've found me. They'll be here soon, I'm sure of it."

Keelag frowned. "We can't leave for at least a day."

"We must!" said Miguel, shaking and frantic. "What'll I do? They'll come and search. They'll watch the ship, after—I'll never get back on."

"Calm down," said Keelag, and he smiled. "On my ship, strangers find only what I wish them to find." He turned back to the black man and spoke to him again in that strange language. The man moved his hands in assent, watching Miguel. "Go with him," Keelag said.

Miguel followed the man down to the foot of the central mast. He looked up and saw that the rest of the crew were watching him as they worked; not directly, not staring, and yet watching him closely all the same.

At the foot of the mast, the dark man did something to the decking, and a hatch slid out of place, exposing a dark space within.

It smelled of seaweed and oils as Miguel eased his way down. It was cold, close to the hull, the sea. As the hatch slid back and blackness encompassed him, he realized that they were under no compulsion ever to let him out again. Keelag had not even cared who his pursuers were; it had not mattered. Miguel wanted to scream and pound on the now unidentifiable hatch.

The space was small, but large enough for two men, four if they were crammed. He sat against the curve of the mast and put his faith in God.

Minutes later, he heard the men of the Church arrive. He couldn't make out any words, but he heard them searching, occasionally smashing. He wondered if he knew any of them. Probably one of the Jesuit fathers would be in charge: Father Montello or Father Chari. He had loved them, still loved them. How could they be wrong when they were so good? *And yet I have been touched by God*, he thought. *I am certain*, though he was not; still, he must know, he must! He had always sought knowledge, watched the stars as a child and wondered at their beauty. But more than anything, he had wondered at the greatness of God.

He squirmed around and put his arms around the smooth

coldness of the mast, shivering. His compulsion fought his fear and called him still to the edge of the world.

Late that night, years later to Miguel in the stuffy darkness, the trapdoor slid back and Keelag's face smiled gap-toothed at him in starlight. He handed down food and a jug. "The Church, eh," Keelag whispered, and chuckled. "Tomorrow," he said. "Until we leave, you stay here."

"Yes," said Miguel hoarsely, and took a great gulp of wine. The hatch slid shut. Miguel ate ravenously and drank most of the wine. He felt strange then: not happy, not sad, floating. In the darkness, the line between sleep and consciousness was indistinct.

He dreamed he *flew*, catching the wind from below as he passed the curving waterfall edge of the world, slung beneath the linen wings of his immense kite. Then, somehow, the sweeping kite became his arms; he became a sea gull, crying out as he flew above strange cities, lands where seas of the damned screamed in torment and rivers of lava flowed. He flew up past the star angels, whose hair was like silver and diamonds intertwined, faces too white to see. Up he flew, through heat and coldness, through oil and air, through all the seven shells of the sky, till he exploded out like an arrow from a great bow into the ether.

For a long time, there was nothing; a universe of emptiness. Then, looking up, he gazed into a face with tremendous eyes that he forgot even as he watched. He wanted to speak, but could not.

Miguel awoke when the sea wind and sunlight poured down upon him. Hands reached from above, pulling him from his cave, and helped him to stand. Maza sat at the rear of the ship, beating a rhythm on a short wide drum. On the benches, rainbow-vested black men shiny with sweat strained at the oars in time to the drum, laughing and shouting unintelligibly to one another. In the distance behind the stern the land was visible only as a thin gray line, a bead welding the sky to the sea.

"I'm hungry," he said to the two men who held him. They cocked their heads, watching him. "Can't they even speak a civilized language?" Miguel demanded of Keelag, who had said nothing.

Keelag shook his head. "They find your northern languages crude and ugly. They don't want to sully their minds with such." He spoke their guttural language to one of the men, who left for the tiny cookhouse below the foredeck.

Miguel turned and walked shakily to the prow, picking his way carefully over the piled bales and crates, to gaze forward to the horizon. Then Keelag shouted behind him and the beat of the drum ceased as the ship slowed and stopped, to rock quietly with the slap of waves.

He turned as the crew left the benches after carefully securing the long oars. Two men climbed the masts to thrust cords through iron eyelets at the tops. The others manhandled long heavy bundles, poles wrapped in huge sheets of sailcloth, up to the masts. As they pulled the sails carefully up, Miguel watched in confusion, for they were unlike any he had seen before. Triangular, they jutted out a great distance from the masts, but only in one direction, to the rear. The jib puffed out beside him as it too was hoisted, and the *Torque* began to move with the crack of sailcloth cupping the wind.

Keelag glanced at Miguel and smiled, moving toward him. "We get away from port before they go up," Keelag said from below the foredeck. "The Church doesn't take kindly to the new and different. We have square sails for the Mediterranean, but there's no law on the open sea."

Suddenly, something occurred to Miguel. "You must lend me your Bible," he said. "I have left mine at the inn."

Keelag shrugged. "We don't have one."

"You have no Bible?"

Keelag merely shrugged again. "Don't like them," he said.

Miguel turned back to the prow, holding tight to the rail. The horizon was empty.

Miguel lay in the prow of the *Torque*, his head and one arm hanging over the side, wind blowing his spray-damp hair, reaching down unconsciously to the water as he watched broken foam cast away from the cut of the prow. In the angle of the golden dawn light, the foam was as white as cotton. *The purity of your being, Lord*, he prayed silently, *it shows in all things*. For that moment, he was certain.

Then, as the orange wheel of the sun broke free from the horizon, a piercing wail went up from the deck behind him. Three days on the sea, and it was like the first time; he was sure he would never get used to it. Turning, he watched the black men twist like oil through their morning rituals, light and darkness intermixed through their rainbow vests: a prayer of thanks for the return of their flaming god. *Animals*, Miguel thought. Mere pawns for his trip to the edge; yet what strange pawns God had chosen. Even as they danced, he felt they were watching him; they were always watching.

Keelag stood at the tiller, mouth wide, laughing in violent contentment. His tanned skin was pale in comparison to their shiny darkness, and his golden hair made him seem almost a pillar of the north, of the light of God and the Church. Early, Miguel had asked him, "Do you believe in God Almighty, and Jesus Christ His Son?" and he had answered, sadly almost, that he did not worship them. An atheist; the crew were merely pagans.

Miguel looked to the billowing sails, the heresy of their shape. He turned his gaze to the horizon. *I am coming*, he thought.

Night came. Again the crew made obeisance and Miguel drew his cloak around him from the cold and the wail, worse in darkness. As the weather was calm, Miguel slept on the foredeck, covered by a heavy oiled canvas. Later, the face of the moon kissed the lip of the horizon, and silver light after the stars was almost like morning. He couldn't sleep, and lay on his pallet at the prow, feeling the *Torque* slap into the sea again and again and again.

After a long time, he felt suddenly that something was different. For a second he was unsure what it was, and then he realized that the ship was empty of voices and the sound of men as he had never heard it before. He sat up and turned to face the obsidian eyes of the crew.

They crowded down together below him on the rowing benches and reclined on the crates secured between. Maza was in front, Keelag standing a little to the side with his seemingly eternal smile.

"How does it go, Your Majesty?" he said.

Miguel shrugged slowly. "So you knew?"

Keelag nodded. "There are plenty of heathens on the wharves, myself included. But there are few that the *Almighty Church* would have any interest in."

Miguel's gaze swept over the dark faces, and he felt alone. He thrust his hand into the wide collar of his blouse and grasped his crucifix. "What do you want?"

Keelag shrugged. "I want nothing. *They*," he indicated the crew, "wish to travel your life with you."

"What?"

"To them, we are all products of our youth. You are important to them; I don't understand why. They want to know you, and to know you, they must know your life." Keelag smiled wider. "Tell us a story," he said.

"You've been paid. Leave me alone!"

"It doesn't work like that," Keelag said reasonably. "We could take the rest of your money now. We have no need to visit the edge. You're lucky in that way, because I would as soon do that and dump you into the sea, but I am only captain of that which doesn't matter to them. It was Maza who sent me to you, though he could not explain to me why. It is in truth their ship, and they don't care about the money. They want to be paid in another coin. Besides," Keelag said with a chuckle, "isn't it your Christian duty to bring pagans and heretics to the word of God? If you truly feel yourself a man of God, though your Church has forsaken you, we should learn the great truth through your shining example."

Miguel was silent for a time. Keelag was in some sense correct, though to him it was only a jest. And he had little choice.

"Begin at the beginning," Keelag said softly.

"I was born on the thirtieth day of May, the year of our Lord 1384, in my father's castle in Lisbon," he said, and though he had been meaning to give only a curt sketch, to show them the power of God and yet hide his own soul deep within, a strange spirit took him and he began to speak in a flood of words as he lost hold of where he was and felt as if he were again a child. As he spoke, he heard Keelag begin also to speak in their guttural language, and it was almost as if he could hear the echo of his own words, though a part of him realized that he could, in truth, understand nothing.

My mother I never knew, he said. She died in childbirth. The last word from her lips was *Miguel*, so my father named me that.

I remember, long ago, a soldier lifting me above the battlements so that I could look out over the city and to the sea. . . . I asked him many questions about the walled-in checkerboard gardens and villas, the sprawling slums, and the ocean. But he knew little, though he held me there patiently for a long time. I must have been very small.

I have always wondered . . . about the world . . . many things. I can't explain. From the time I can remember, I loved the Mass in the cathedral. The Gregorian chants echoed from the huge ceiling and touched me as if to my soul. The archbishop would stand in his white robes at the pulpit, and speak of the world, of life . . . of God.

All answers lie in His being. Only through Him may we learn the true meaning, the true life. I have, I think, *always* known that my true calling was to God.

My tutor in Latin, in the Bible, was Father Montello. He was a small man, with a tremendous mustache that was his pride and joy sweeping out beneath a bulbous nose. He was not a cheery man, but full of the light of God. We met every afternoon in his small room in the cool cellar of the cathedral. We had great discussions and read to each other from the Bible. I learned the language of God, and much else. There was no subject that he did not know of, on which he would not converse. We would search together through the cathedral library for the answers to our many questions. Many times he would speak of the library at Rome, filling a great section of the labyrinthine catacombs, brought from the far corners of the world: Alexandria, Baghdad, Athens, Byzantium. . . . He warned me many times, though, of the voice of the Devil, the serpent-tongued. There were true answers and there were those that derived from the blackest pit.

From an early age, my world was the interior of the cathedral; I awoke every morning to the clear pealing of bells, but my need for knowledge was stifled in the small library. Slowly I became despondent, and petitioned the archbishop for a transfer to Rome. He was suspicious, but Father Montello and others with whom I worked were able to convince him that Asmodeus's talons were not in my heart, to their later shame.

At times, on this ship, I forget and think for a moment I am again on that wondrous journey to the Holy City. But then I was all anticipation, and held no court with the sea.

A guide met me at the docks, and I entered Rome through the Gate of Kings, past acres of gravestones inscribed with the names of the ancient consuls and praetors of the Empire. My guide led me to a small office in the building of the Mother Mary. I was introduced to the old cardinal Barnas, under whom I would study. He was the highest official of the books, and my guide made every attempt to impress me with the fortune I had received in his personal tutelage. Barnas was a very large man with a tremendous double chin, eyes like soft-boiled eggs, and a razor-thin nose sunken in the fat of his face. His only comment on seeing me, after allowing me to kiss his hand was, "You have much to learn, Miguel."

The next day he summoned me to his chambers and led me

down a narrow flight of stairs, waddling in his saillike robes, to the catacombs where the library was. "In times long past," he said, puffing, "the faithful dug these to keep them safe from persecution at the hands of the heathens of the Empire. Now they contain what remains of them and their descendants, what is important: memories, glimpses of the wonders of God and His Son." Below, shelves were carved into the cool dry tunnel walls, containing hundreds of thousands of scrolls and tomes and manuscripts. How Barnas loved his library—yet he loved books for what they were and not what they contained. He held out many volumes as we traversed the maze of knowledge—illuminated manuscripts of a beauty beyond belief and explanation; letters penned in the hands of ancient kings, preserved carefully behind heavy glass—for they would crumble at the merest touch. "To be a librarian," he said to me, "you must hold the book in the highest esteem, and your mind must become a labyrinth like the library itself. It is arranged in an order of chance, of time, of God, and as you become a model of the library, you shall become—in essence—a part of it, a piece of history."

Last, after more than an hour of wandering, he allowed me to peer down a long tunnel filled with many volumes. "These are the work of the damned, the heretics," he said. "We keep all books, for we are a *library*, and as God has allowed them to come into being, we must be willing to hold them. The secret, the truth of a great librarian, is to have knowledge without knowledge." He tapped his graying temple. "In here is contained the essence of every book in the tunnels; the library is of me as I am of the library. And yet I know nothing, I am truly innocent and filled only with the word of God. You are young yet, you must learn. This tunnel is your final task, the culmination of your education as a librarian if you are so intended by God." He then set me to memorizing a small section of the library.

This was not what I had expected, but the power of his vision overwhelmed mine. He disliked me. I knew that, as I knew he felt instantly I would never be a librarian. But he was a man of many systems, a God-fearing man, and he gave me the treatment he would have given any other. I wished to prove myself to him, and immersed myself in my studies. The art of a librarian, for in its own way it is an art, thought without thought—knowledge and innocence—seemed to me the perfect solution.

The streets of Rome wander my mind as characters in the play of another's making, the Forum a field for cows, only sad bits of stone remaining to mark the fulcrum of the greatest empire, destroyed by the power of God, streets filled with the robes of the Church, crowds of pilgrims seeking the benevolence of the pontiff. A few months after my arrival I stood in a crowd of other novitiates and received this crucifix from the hand of His Holiness himself. It is strange, but I cannot bring his face clearly into my mind, only the soft brown eyes gazing into mine as if he saw into my soul itself. The flames of doubt were already licking within me.

For months I strove to please Barnas, through the green of spring and into the heat of summer, but he gave me little encouragement. "The art of a librarian is its own reward," he said. "It is between God and your soul. I cannot give fulfillment as a mother gives milk, only God." I think I, also, knew in my heart from the beginning I would not succeed. It was because I needed to *know*; God had given me this instinct for knowledge which I could not control.

As autumn came to the Holy City, I began to wander the catacombs alone, furtively, lantern in hand but unlit till I reached the objects of my desire. In secret I began to search for knowledge, not as a true librarian, but for the essence itself. It was the tunnel of the heretics that drew me—though when I arrived it was almost as if I could hear the bat wings of the Devil fluttering as he slept heavily in the depths. Many times I was nearly caught, and extinguished my lantern to cower in darkness and listen to the rustle of passing robes, the slap of sandals, brushed by lantern light.

But what I found! The wonders! There were many papers that were obviously the ravings of the mad, but others were shocking in their clarity. One man recounted his experience of a visit to the edge of the world in a small sailing vessel. His prose was flooded with the shimmer of fish, the hooting calls of dolphins. He told of a great wind that blew unceasingly up from the edge, forcing him back stronger and stronger as he advanced.

The most incredible, however, was a sheaf of papers I found weeks later. Secured in a great leather satchel were many drawings in a spidery hand, and they held perhaps the greatest temptation of all.

They were charts, diagrams with long detailed instructions scrawled beneath. At first I didn't understand, but finally I realized what they were. Wings! They were wings for a man.

Everything was there. The weave of the linen, the shaping of the poles, the types of wood. And the *way* of flying too, how to use the wings. I knew in my heart it was blasphemy, but I returned again and again to that sheaf of wonder, reading it many times—I could not help myself. This was the realization of a dream we all must have, I think. The power to fly, to escape the grip of land and soil and stone.

I read the papers so many times that the lines and figures and flowing instructions became engraved in my mind.

There came a night when I was so engrossed in the papers that I did not notice the light of another lantern joining mine. He made no sound, and I only discovered him when I looked up to clear my eyes of the twisting figures. Barnas stood there beside me, a tremendous dark figure, face empty of emotion. "Come with me," he said after a time, and turned away. I followed him up to a private cell, where he left me till morning.

I was brought before a panel of cardinals, some of whom I knew by sight. They asked me many questions. Many I could not answer. It was Barnas, surprisingly, who spoke on my behalf.

I heard little, being lost in what I had done, but I remember a fragment. ". . . He has some talent and a mind, and, I think, a love of God. He must work out his confusion."

The panel decided to restrict me to a cell, and except for the Mass and to exercise, to think on what I had done.

But my mind would not be distracted. I saw the lines and ciphers of the wings in my dreams, in the grain of the walls of my room. I found myself collecting twigs from the autumnal walks to the priory, cutting fine linen from the lining of my cloak. At night, in the light of a candle, the wings, a small model of them, began to take form in my room, the lines delicate threads. It is as if there were two of me, a part that feels and wants, and a part that thinks and understands. Which is closer to God, I do not know.

Weeks later, I was called from exercise again to the close-smelling, carpeted, paneled room. Barnas stood there, silent, and held the wings in his great hands. I said nothing, but nodded when he indicated them with his eyes, unsurprised though I had thought them well hidden. The other cardinals watched. Barnas suddenly tossed them into the air, and they *flew* in a great smooth curving sweep till they struck the wall with a light tap and fluttered to the floor. I drew breath at the beauty of it, barely noticing the expressions of fear and revulsion in the faces of the old men at the long table before me. Many made the sign of the cross, and the whisper of fervent prayer filled the room. . . .

Perhaps I should have been put to death. It may be that they were loath to proclaim the son of the Portuguese king as a witch. But it had been done many times before, and for lesser crimes. No. I think again it was Barnas who came to my aid, though I cannot explain why. He must have had his reasons, yet I cannot imagine what they were. Perhaps he saw something in me that others could not.

I was returned to Portugal by merchant caravan over the Alps and the Pyrenees. In Lisbon, Father Montello attempted to speak with me, but I could not. My father and brothers and friends visited me, but I hardly knew them. Though I could not speak, I was capable of action, could take care of myself, and so I was sent to the north for penance. My life was given, as is often done in such cases, into the hands of God.

I settled in early spring into a small stone hut on the cliffs above the sea, a herd of goats my only companions. I spent many days praying for guidance. There were sea gulls, and I watched them for hours. I noticed that they rode the wind forced up by the cliff for long periods without moving their wings.

I soon walked down to the nearest town, and sold there such baubles as I had with me to purchase linen and poles and cordage. Returning to my home, I worked long days on the wings till, early in summer, I made my first flight, leaping from a small hill. I flew only a few tens of feet, and then crashed so as to force a week of work on the wings to repair them. Oh, but that moment was perhaps the greatest of my life! I had flown!

The rest of the summer I spent refining the wings, working from the figures in my mind, the spindly instructions of that long-dead heretic. My flights became longer and longer. Finally, I felt my expertise to be great enough, and leaped from the sea cliffs on a windy day, with the breakers roaring beneath me. At first I fell, and then, for the first time, as the sea gulls dipped and cried around me, I rose in the wind, going higher as I skimmed the edge of the cliff.

And it was that day, late in fall with the tendrils of winter reaching into the land, that Father Montello came to return me to Lisbon. What he must have thought, seeing this great white bird soaring above the cliffs! Yet he must have realized who was slung beneath those sweeping ribbed wings, for I heard shouting as he ran up the slope. I landed lightly, and waited for him to reach me.

He tore the wings from my grasp and, speaking in the holy tongue the words of exorcism, hurled them from the cliff. He turned back to me, making the sign of the cross, and bade me follow him. He had ceased to see me as a man, and perceived me only as a tool of the Devil. I would be excommunicated, burned as a witch, and my ashes spread to the four winds. I had not thought myself capable of it, but I struck him then, and again harder and again, until he lay at my feet. I secured him with cords he would work himself free of after a time, and ran.

Through the winter I lived as a thief, a madman. I lived in the woods, though I was ill trained by my earlier life to do so, and entered towns only to steal. I knew I should give myself unto the justice of the Church, to accept fitting punishment for my terrible crimes, but I was afraid.

Somehow I survived the winter: in itself a sign. I did not lose my faith or forget my prayer. In my heart I felt that the Church was wrong, that my direction came from God. Yet, without the Church there would be no correspondence with Him.

The signs of spring began to show. The birds returned; snow was gone from the ground and green shoots of life rose to seek the sun. I was drawn over my life in memories, as now. In my dreams I heard the hooting of dolphins, smelled the salt air, saw the curving edge of the world. I wished to fly again.

Then, on a warm April morning, I saw a sea gull in the sky. In a slow circling glide, it landed at my feet and pecked at some bread I had stolen the day before. Suddenly I knew. I saw His plan in my mind as I saw the ciphers of the wings. Only one power was greater than the power of the Church: the power of God. He would be my final judge, for I remembered the sea gulls rising on the wind from the cliff and the tale of the man who had visited the edge. I would fly on the rising wind through the seven spheres of the sky to meet Him. . . .

There is little more to tell. I returned in stealth to the Lisbon castle and sent word to my father. The castle steward came soon, and brought money and advice. I came to the wharves, and that is my story.

Miguel sat quietly then. He felt very small. The crew slowly moved away.

"Ahh . . ." said Keelag. "I begin to understand."

Miguel lay back and watched the stars till he fell into the sleep of stones.

He woke late the next morning. After washing his face in salt water and eating a breakfast of fruit and a hard biscuit, he stood at the prow, his mind as empty as the sky. Keelag walked up to stand beside him, silent for a while.

"Deep in Africa," he said suddenly in a strong voice over the rush of the sea, "where there is no winter and the jungle rules, lies the lake kingdom of Elysia. It is a beautiful place, the smooth wide water and cries and colors of the jungle still sharp and fresh as new dates in my mind. The tendrils of the Church reach only weakly there. Odd ships ply the waters of the immense lake, many with our triangular sails. I remember the eleventh night of the sun, with the dancing and singing and great burning of incense so that one felt as if one were made of the clearest glass. Ahh . . ." Keelag was silent for a moment.

"Before the coming of the missionaries, the Elysians thought little of the world outside. They heard tales of a great expanse of water far down what you call the Congo River, but the dangers of the jungle were great, and warlike tribes prowled the outskirts of Elysia. So the people of the lake explored what they deemed as inner space: charting the movements of the heavens—the seven spheres—and of their flaming god. Without the influence of the Church, they discovered many engines and devices of power. Pagan magic, you would say. Perhaps. I . . . do not know." Keelag paused, but Miguel made no motion as he stared stonily to the horizon, gripping the railing tight as the *Torque* bounced lightly in the grip of the wind.

"But as the missionaries arrived, the Elysians began to turn their minds' eyes outward. The old king would have none of it, and spent his last days on the roof of his palace, his eyes full of his beloved stars. The new king, however, Aes, was young and full of wonder at the news of the surrounding world. He wished to go himself, but his advisers would not allow it, and so he brought together the greatest scientists and shamans and sailors of his realm to charge them with his desire. He gave them a great chest full of the yellow metal so prized by the Europeans, and bade them purchase with it a passage to the fabled countries of the North. There, they were to use the remainder to procure a vessel, as Elysia had only lake boats, and for three years to travel the vastness of the world, recording their discoveries, their careful observations. 'We wish,' he said with great emotion, 'to know of this, our world, and await eagerly your return!'

"With them also he sent one who had been adopted into the family, and who was in some sense his brother, though he could never truly be one with those of Elysia. This one was to be their interpreter, being knowledgeable in the ways and language of his pale race.

"The celebration of our departure was the most wondrous I have seen in my brief time on this Earth. I still remember the flash of bright powders glowing in the air above the jungle as we slipped down the river and into the night. I still taste the hint of sweet liquor in my mouth at the memory. . . . And so we departed the lake. We came upon the *Torque*. We traveled, and met despair. We cannot return. Though they make pretense, we are truly beaten."

He turned to Miguel. "I have been around the world," he said, "many times, and on the other side, where Asia becomes the sea, the shoreline is smooth, following the curve at the edge of the world. It is almost as if there were once something more, but it was shorn away with an immense blade." He raised his arms. "The world is too small! I have been everywhere I wish to be, and there is nothing more. I feel as Alexander must have felt when he met the sea in Persia with his conquering army behind, and threw his sword into the sand in despair.

"You do understand? We cannot return. We cannot allow them to know their limits as we know them. It is too terrible. For ten years we have wandered, with nothing but ourselves and our ship. You see, *now* I understand. If you can fly from the edge of the world, if you can destroy the shells of the sky with your wings, then we are freed. Do you understand?" Keelag shouted.

Miguel still ignored him. He shook almost imperceptibly. Finally, he turned away from the prow and said, almost to empty air, "I must begin my work." He walked down to the goods lashed amidships and began to search for the supplies he had brought abroad.

The sky became yellow as a muddy river, later, the clouds graying to evanescent stones in the current. With the wailing of the crew behind him, Keelag came slowly up the center of the *Torque*, picking his way over the high-piled bales and crates. He came up on the foredeck as Miguel carefully packed away the beginnings of his wings. Miguel watched as Keelag stood to one side and regarded him.

"I don't know why I even bother to talk to you," Keelag said. He paused, shook his head slightly. "You seem to think that I'm ignorant and illiterate. You're mistaken. I know nothing of my true parents; I was found as a young child alone in the depths of Africa. The natives who found me brought me many miles to a missionary they had heard of. Perhaps they thought my pale skin great magic. This man's name was Father Ambrose, and he searched long for any sign of my parents, but found nothing. An island in a heathen sea, he determined to raise me himself on the grand Christian ethic. I could read in the holy tongue soon after I learned his native Portuguese, and learned other languages in my time with him. All the classics have passed before these eyes, and the Bible, ah, yes, of course the Bible.

"But I lived not in Portugal, but in the jungle's depths, and so I also spoke the tongue of the black men as my own, though the father sought to insulate me. Though I was different—far different than I ever imagined—the children accepted me easily, and so I lived in two cultures at once, but did not truly know them to be so.

"The father visited the low sprawling palace of the old king often in some forlorn hope, I believe, that he would convert him and so gain a hold over his great pagan nation. The king and his retainers found him interesting and amusing. As I grew past the sixth year, the father began to take me with him on his weekly pilgrimages to the palace. Partly because I spoke the Elysian tongue better than he, and was occasionally helpful in translation, but mostly because he enjoyed my company. He was very lonely, the only Christian for many miles. And the black people, in their quiet refusal to speak any tongue but their own, seemed like obstinate animals. He was a good man, in his own way. The king and much of the palace gave me the name I now wear in preference to the father's gruff choice from Kings. A rough translation would be *precocious one*." Keelag laughed quietly, staring out at nothing.

"Ahh . . . but in my tenth year, the father died. Hearing this, the old king quickly adopted me as his son, and set to teaching me the religion of the sun, the ways of the lake, and all that the son of a king should know. Yet he knew, as I did not for many years, that I was not truly one of his people and not a child of the sun. Though I was allowed to receive my vest of the colors of the light," he said, stroking the weave of his rainbow vest, "I was never truly initiated into her worship." He fell silent for a time. Miguel watched his silhouette against the fading sky.

"We are like ghosts to them," Keelag said softly. "They are truly pagans: to them each life is only one of many, a string of glistening beads. Many times at night, they speak of their past lives, short intense glimpses of another time in their dreams. But we . . . have only *this* one life. Their wise men, and Maza is perhaps the wisest, say that they can see the souls of others. We are pale not only in our skins. Maza has told me that my soul is as faint as a flickering candle, while theirs blaze like bonfires, filled with their many lives. They are not unlike their god.

"Maza has seen us go, in the many ports we have visited. He has seen us reach up into a shadowed doorway from our bodies, to be flung like a spark into the sky."

He turned to Miguel. "I have faith in the god of the black men, and yet she is not my god. What is your God in the ether to my flaming sun? Where shall we go then? To Heaven? Or perhaps to nothing. Why does He covet the uncountable candle flames of souls that seek Him in the depths beyond?

"I am nothing but a flicker in time. I am doomed, not by the color of my skin, but by the light of my soul. What is He that I should worship Him?"

Miguel said nothing. After a time, he returned to his wings. When they were safely secured, he came and stood beside Keelag. "I am terribly afraid," said Miguel. "I am sorry. This is not what I had expected at all. I have no Bible, and even the most familiar of psalms seem to flit from my mind like birds. The closer I come to the Father, the more distant He seems."

Keelag said slowly, "You have, at least, a search, a direction." He smiled gap-toothed at Miguel. "You must ask Him for me, though He must supply both the question and the answer. If He is God, He should be able to do as much. I am lost between worlds—have nothing of my own but these decks—and wood and sea are not enough."

Each morning, Miguel woke on the foredeck to the wailing of the dancing, rainbow-vested men and the brush of the sun. Much of the day he spent at work on his wings, but when his fingers and arms were too weary to handle the delicate materials carefully, he would wander the *Torque*, watching the ocean.

The crew seemed eternally busy as they cleaned the decks and checked the rigging, repairing the continual slow deterioration of a wooden ship. Through Keelag, he learned that the buckets occasionally dipped and then hoisted from the sea were tested for temperature as the black men searched to learn more of the patterns of the sea. Any strange beasts pulled up by sampling nets were carefully sketched by a squat man in whose thick fingers a lump of coal became a magical tool. Always as they traveled, they observed and recorded.

Long cords equipped with hooks trailed from the stern, baited with the flying fish collected every morning from the decks. Two of the largest men stood beside them, and hauled back at the sign of a bite. Occasionally Miguel would watch as they pulled in the great straining body of a sailfish or marlin or shark. When the fresh stores were depleted, they ate much fish, living on what they caught in their travel.

At the center of the *Torque*, the crew soon erected a strange device of glass and metal tubing, carefully set on gimbals. A kind of magical still, it somehow drew on the power of the sun. Into it was poured salt water, and soon, from a cloudy interior, fresh water began to emerge.

As the *Torque* gained distance from land, the sea seemed to fill with life. Packs of dolphins sped by, leaping and sparkling in the light. Keelag was forced to tack more than once to avoid vast floating platforms of oceanweed.

Miguel accompanied Maza and others of the crew to the first floating island they encountered, a few weeks after Lisbon, and it too teemed with life: small and skittering, the air above filled with a shifting cloud of birds, and sea gulls. "Ahh . . ." he breathed. The false land beneath his feet felt like a cushion of moss.

Once, a man in the rigging spied the spouts of whales in the distance and raised the alarm. The ship swarmed with men as they raced to lower the boats for a kill, till Keelag shouted above the din. Miguel asked him later what he had said. "No! No whales. We have not the time nor the space!" The cook complained that he needed oil for his fire, but Keelag merely shook his head. "No whales," he said quietly, "We sail for the edge of the *world*."

As they traveled, the days became warmer and the nights brighter, till the night was like a dawn forever and the day burned. Miguel asked Maza through Keelag why this was so, and Maza explained that because the world was like a great platter, the western edge, in summer, was close to the sun, and light spilled over from below.

Miguel spent much time praying, but it was as if he were wrapped in cotton: his prayers seemed unable to reach the terrible distance in the sky. He could not feel the Father, and could only be heartened by the memory of the certainty he had felt not long before, a feeling he came soon to suspect he had invented in himself. He did not know. He wished to hate the rainbow-vested men, but he could not. The wailing soon ceased to repel him. Occasionally he actually found himself wishing to join in their dance, and despised himself.

They encountered no storms; each day was almost painfully clear, with few clouds in the steel-blue sky. Many times at night, after the disappearance of the sun, Miguel could not sleep; he sat amidships, watching Maza and Keelag play a strange game similar to chess. Many carved figures, elephants and birds and men and women, were arranged on a matrix of squares. One side played light and one dark. Before he moved, each player shook a half-dome of glass bottomed with a wooden square dotted with many depressions, containing three white and three black marbles. With each pattern created beneath the glass came a change in the rules of the game. At first Miguel felt he understood, till the same pattern happened twice in a single game and the rule changes were dramatically different.

"It is not the pattern, but the sense of the pattern that matters," said Maza through Keelag. "I and you and the ship and the sea are integral parts. How could it be different? There are no rules, only a sense between the two players of what the pattern represents. Between good players, there is rarely disagreement or discussion. Any game must model life, which is real, and in life there are no rules that cannot in some sense be disregarded, bent, dissipated. There is no competition," Maza indicated Keelag and himself, "though invariably triumph in the dance, which is to be sought for but not always gained and which is naught but a stepping stone to another game."

Not certain he understood, still Miguel watched. He discovered after viewing many games that in the complex shift of rules, Maza's judgment was never questioned, and what in many cases seemed agreement was merely noncommittal agreement on Keelag's part: student and instructor in the dance. Once Miguel also tried to play, but was soon gripped with a terrible fear that he could not identify, and left, shaking.

At night, in his dreams, Miguel would cry, "Barnas! Father Montello! Where is the answer you have found?"

Sometimes he would dream he awoke to sit up and gaze upon the blazing souls of the crew.

The days fell behind them.

As the edge approached, Keelag became more and more

restless. For a time Miguel had spoken to him, but then Keelag had begun to fade into a strange state in between, an echo as Miguel spoke through him to Maza, to the crew. He said he did not know what would become of him if the *Torque* returned him to the jungle land. He had grown used to the sea; what he had was little, but it was more than he had had before.

The days passed, and Keelag began asking strange questions of Miguel as he worked on the wings. "All this," he said, and spread his arms as if to encompass everything, "it is beautiful, yes?" Miguel nodded in assent. "Ah . . ." said Keelag, "then would it not be beautiful had God not created it? The beauty resides in the thing and need not flow from its creator. Where is the need for your God in the scheme of things?" At first Miguel did not understand, and then he said that without God there would be no beauty. Another time Keelag asked, "His actions are so mysterious, His plan obscure. How can you be certain of your God, of His existence?" Miguel said only that His pattern was evident in all things, but did no more work on the wings that day.

Later, under the dimly lit shell of the night sky, Keelag said, "A leap to death is no direction to follow. You need not decide today, tomorrow, next year. Ah . . ." Keelag sat and leaned back against the rail. "You could travel with us, visit the many ports of the world, held safe from the hands of the Church. . . ."

Miguel said nothing. The next morning, however, he came to Keelag and told him to turn the *Torque* around, away from the edge. Keelag made no comment, nor did the crew.

At first Miguel was happy, relaxed, laughing with the crew, speaking in the few words he knew of their tongue. But he slept for the first time away from the sky in his tiny cabin at the stern. He found himself often staring beyond the stern to the horizon. As time passed, he became quiet and despondent. After four days, he ordered the ship turned again toward the edge.

"It is not enough to simply *travel*," Miguel said later. "And I cannot run forever."

A sailing vessel on the open sea is a world of its own, and so the *Torque* was a world traveling to the edge of the world. At times, Miguel wondered which world he would truly be leaping from. Much of what he had gained in his life on Earth was lost to him. His purpose had become an unfathomable tapestry of desire.

The wings were done, great sweeping things with a harness

slung beneath. Days before reaching the edge, he could see the mist rising like a great wall of white on the horizon.

Keelag and the crew had little time for him now, checking the sails carefully, replacing the rigging. They watched the current incessantly, measuring its increase. Finally, at night in light almost that of day, Keelag heeled the *Torque* around, and with light sail they approached slowly against the current. The wind opposing them was almost a gale.

A question occurred to Miguel, which began to gnaw within him until he finally had to drag Keelag and Maza aside to ask.

"If you have unending lives," he said, "then why do you strive so to live?"

In Keelag's voice, Maza said, "Some do not. Some, for example, live life through childhood again and again—killing themselves at an early age—but that is not a good way, and much is lost from earlier lives. We seek a path to . . . I know not what." He moved his hands. "If we do not prize this life, then how can we prize the next, and then what is life?"

Miguel had the wings moved carefully to the stern. As day came, the crew danced for the sun, and then unshipped the oars to resist the increasing current, the sails full in the wind. The air was filled with the beat of Maza's drum and the roar from the edge.

Then, a hundred yards away in the mist, from the stern, Miguel spied the edge of the world: a boiling, seething line that stretched away into the mist on both sides. Keelag shouted beside him and Maza's tempo increased. The rowers strained, and the ship came to a shifting halt.

"Now!" Keelag said.

Miguel carefully strapped himself into the fluttering wings in the lee of the *Torque*'s crest.

He looked into Keelag's eyes. "Don't fly too near the sun," Keelag said softly, and they both smiled. Miguel grasped him in a clumsy embrace. "Are you certain?" Keelag asked.

"No," said Miguel, and he launched himself from the lee into the force of the winds.

He went up like a circling leaf: a petal of the white rose— under the glittering gaze of the crew.

Keelag raised his fist to the sky. "Fly!" he shouted. Then softly, "Fly!"

MAGISTER RUDY

RICHARD GRANT

As genuinely impressed with the talent of the new professionals contributing to this volume, we are just slightly less than awed by the fact that Richard Grant only has two novels and a handful of published stories to his credit. Few writers at any level of experience can match Richard sentence-for-sentence. He's one of those all-too-rare people who can stop you cold with a turn of phrase. His first novel, *Saraband of Lost Time,* was runner-up for the Philip K. Dick Award. His second, *Rumors of Spring,* received coast-to-coast raves and was recently published (by us, thankfully) in paperback. He is currently completing his third, *View from the Oldest House,* which we will also proudly publish. Richard lives in Washington, DC with his wife Mary and their unforgettable son, Matthew.

"Magister Rudy" is nearly indescribable and any capsule description would do it a great injustice. But even if it weren't about *anything*, it would be worth reading for some of those wonderful Grant sentences.

R ed nose or no, it was not going to be an easy winter.

In the world, there were rumors of war. Ships crawled over black seas. Troops ran like insects in long, frightened columns. Great weapons poised, pencils of death, ticking off throw-weights and alert conditions.

In the village of Cloud Mountain, a kind of crystallization was in progress. Time ran more sluggishly, events tending to lump together, people moving slowly or standing in clots. The Regional Administrator insisted upon order. With an ivory-handled pen, he ran down lists of commodities for emergency distribution. Fuels, medical supplies, foodstuffs. Even water: it might come down to water. Not rationing, the Administrator insisted; only rational thought.

In the big field behind the Alternative School, down by the lake, Rudy Stanton was getting his ass kicked pretty frequently. He was scrawny as a stick, and tired of the whole growing-up business. Mornings like this, bright and ice-perfect, he'd just as soon have gone walking alone beside the water, watching the sun pulling clouds out of the trees above the mountain.

Tap on the whiteboard.
"The universe isn't made of hard things."
Thump on the desk.

"Contrary to appearances."

That's a laugh, thought Rudy. From what he could tell, the universe was composed of nothing *but* hard things, differing solely in how much discomfort they would cause when they hit you. Physical Sciences hit Rudy every afternoon at two-fifteen.

"It's an illusion to think in terms of particles, little planets rotating around their nuclear suns." The young instructor, with a blond mustache, stood just in front of his desk, his demonstration table—like, he was putting that authority symbol behind him. He wanted the students to relate.

"You ought to think in terms of *fields*," he urged them. "In terms of patterns. Dynamic patterns of being, of *presence*, constantly swirling and changing their relationships. That's what an equation is, you know. A relationship. What we think is solid, like desks, and walls, is just a certain kind of ordering of these relationships, these presences. You could think of a force field, in a science fiction movie. You know—you've got your prisoner in an invisible cage, only really it's surrounded by this force field, and when the prisoner tries to walk through it . . ."

The instructor did a slapstick *thump* on his forehead, bouncing off the imaginary wall.

"He *thinks* it's solid. But really it's just energy. And energy is just a presence, a field of being, arranged in a certain way. You could arrange it another way. You could turn the force field off. The prisoner could walk right away from it, then."

The instructor sashayed across the room, his arms swinging widely at his sides. *Free as a bird*.

Sure, thought Rudy. He was not smart enough, maybe, to understand everything in Physical Sciences, but he was smart enough to know that if something felt hard, it was hard. It would hurt when it hit you, and you could never just walk away.

Beside him, Brod Marmack, a big boy with large red fists, who had nearly eaten through his pencil, said under his breath: "What is this guy, some kind of fruit?"

His boots thumped the legs of the lab table, sending tremors into Rudy's arm.

He invented the game because he was small, and didn't do well in the others. It was just a way to waste time, a secret recreation. He could play it even while he was doing something else—while he was sitting in class, or standing out in the field waiting to get his balls kicked in—but it was better when he could concentrate, like when he was alone walking beside the lake, or lying in his room.

It began on a particular day. Out behind the Cloud Mountain Alternative School, there was a noncompetitive game in progress. The students from midlevels 2 and 3, boys and girls together, had been sent out across the big field, zigzagging more or less like a lightning bolt from the quaking aspens at the ridge down to the spruces by the water. Most of the spruces were dying or dead, and you could see the lake right through them, and the postcard village beyond. The object of the game was to pass a big yellow ball—something like maybe a surplus weather balloon, much too large for a player to handle alone—up the zigs and zags of the lightning bolt, until it was safely planted on the level ground of the ridge. Only, you had to stay more or less where they put you, so that whatever role you personally had in moving the ball along was going to be a small one. The idea, Rudy supposed, was to cooperate. So big deal. You jounced the ball along, helping the person beside you, until the mass was taken up by someone farther up the line. Mostly it was pretty boring. You stood there daydreaming, watching the waves slap bits of broken wood across the lake.

The trouble was, not everybody took boredom with equanimity. Some players were getting restless, waiting for the ball to bobble along, and were devising ingenious parallel entertainments. Uphill from Rudy, one zag away, Brod Marmack and a couple of friends had rigged a slingshot out of an aspen branch and something long and rubbery, Rudy did not like to think what. They were poking among the stalks of meadow flowers looking for just the right projectile. Rudy could read the situation like a cue card. Brod was going to try to puncture the weather balloon. Well, more power to him. This was a waste of time, as noncompetitive games mostly turned out to be: once you got the idea, it was just a matter of going through the motions, proving to somebody (though no adults were watching) that you had the proper attitude.

The big yellow ball cleared the corner of Rudy's zag. He heard some shouting beside him, but what Brod and the guys were doing seemed more interesting. The grounds were swept now and then of hard-edged debris, to discourage this sort of thing, but in a field like this you could always find something good hidden down in the dead leaves of amaranth, or whatever it was. Rudy hadn't gotten too much out of Life Sciences, either. The shouting got louder, and suddenly there was this gigantic yellow thing bearing down on him.

Up close, you lost the sense of *ball*. What you got instead was something like *surface*. Rudy put his hands up, but the ball had enough momentum to push his arms back and come to rest against his narrow chest. It felt dry and dirty and almost flat. Then Rudy collected his strength, and someone from down the hill came up to help, and the ball was moving again, first in the wrong direction, then—as Rudy did his bit for group synergy—obligingly headed up the line again.

Then the projectile hit.

It was not a rock. It was a piece of metal, shaped like a fat Magic Marker, and it had come wobbling side-to-side on its long axis (was that pitch, or yaw?) but generally flying true, so that the tip struck first. Only, the ball was already gone when it got there. The projectile struck Rudy's head, chipping a small notch for itself in the side of his skull.

He was not unconscious. He lay on the ground for a while, listening with a feeling of great detachment to the voices of the other kids in the field. They sounded far away, but Rudy knew that was a trick of perception, that they were really clustered around him, leaning down, doing ineffectual things to try to help him. All he needed, though, was a little time to recover. Time heals, and he could tell he wasn't hurt very badly. Actually the break in the monotony of the game was rather pleasant. He heard Brod shouting louder than anyone else, something about the little fucker got in the way, how did I know the stupid asshole was hiding behind the ball, and then Rudy felt like closing his eyes and just waiting for someone to come get him.

In the vision—he supposed you could call it that, since he was perfectly awake and it was certainly not a dream—in the vision he was standing up in the field and everyone was back in their places again. The ball was being thumped along, zig-by-zag advancing toward the ridge. Except that this time, in this version of the game, the whole thing had a funny slow-motion quality. The kids on the hillside were not acting so much like real people, but were really locked in to this whole noncompetitive project, everyone doing his or her synergistic best to further the common objective. The ball moved in an orderly manner from node to node. And that's what the kids all seemed like, Rudy thought: like just objects, in fixed positions—little clusters of power like the things on a pinball machine. He even imagined that he could see the power moving from them into the ball, then dissipating, flying off like water from a bicycle wheel as the ball went slower and began dropping downhill, until the next node gave it a little *joink* and the thing picked up energy again.

Only there was this problem. One of the nodes in the chain, a bright orange one—the nodes had lost some of their resemblance to kids, now—this orange node was radiating power in large quantity; it rolled off like sweat, running down the hill and getting in the way of things. The orderly movement of the ball up the line was blocked by this uncooperative energy, which seemed to grow greater and greater as the ball kept coming back and back again, pressed up the hill dumbly by the other little nodes in the chain, who were too stupid to see that the orange blob wasn't going anywhere and they might as well just quit for the day. Instead, the power backed up. The ball was moving quickly back and forth, jiggling between one side and the other, absorbing all this energy, which you could tell wasn't a good idea, and Rudy was pretty sure something unpleasant was going to happen.

"Would you like to go home now, Rudy?"

He nodded, yes, and opened his eyes.

"Good, that's good." The young Physical Sciences instructor leaned over him, checking out some kind of patch that had been placed against the side of his head, partly blocking the view out of one eye.

To Rudy's surprise, there was no one else in the field. He was lying under a dark wool blanket, and the sun was lower than it ought to have been.

"Your father was here," the instructor said.

There was something in his voice. Rudy tried to think what, or to get a better look at the young man's face, but all he saw was his own memory—an earnest smile, a blond mustache. He closed his eyes. He felt dizzy. The instructor continued: "Your father said to give you this. . . ." A pause, as though he were reading. "*Arnica 6X*. He said to let you rest, and you'd be able to go home when you woke up."

Rudy opened his eyes again. He blinked; he nodded. "Yeah," he said gamely. "I guess so. Only, I wasn't asleep really."

The instructor looked a little surprised when Rudy gathered himself and his blanket and sat up. His head throbbed, but it wasn't awful.

"It must be nice," the instructor ventured, with something in his voice again, something like asking but not asking a question— "It must be nice to have a doctor in the family."

Rudy said, "Yeah, I guess. Well. I guess I'll head on home."

The instructor nodded. "We'll see you tomorrow, then?"

More or less for the hell of it, Rudy made an insensible reply to that. He said, "The universe isn't made of hard things."

The game began that night, in earnest.

His father, Geoff, was sitting in the living room when Rudy came in a little after sunset. Rudy's nose was red, as always in the winter, but today there hadn't been anybody to tease him about it on the walk home. The streets of the village were almost empty, which had something to do with the Regional Administrator's insistence upon order, after the attack on the train. They did not get the paper, in Rudy's house, and very seldom did anything like watch TV. The setup for the game was thus almost perfect.

"So." Geoff smiled. "Feeling okay? It felt like there was a minor chipping injury, but mostly you were just bruised. Nothing that won't heal quickly. Do you want another dose of *Arnica*?"

"You're the doc, Doc," Rudy said: a family joke, a form of reassurance.

His father smiled and went back to his asanas. Five twenty-five, time to do yoga. Rudy expected a reminder along these lines to come any moment now, but Geoff only got himself in the candle position and stayed there, remarkably supple for a man of his age. You could not tell if he was breathing. Rudy supposed he himself was being given the night off, in recognition of his injury.

As he hit the stairs, his father's voice came after him: "You can spend a little extra time doing your program tonight, if you want to. It'll help your head get better."

"Whatever you say, Doc."

Then he was in his own room, pulling his clothes off. But halfway into his asana pants he decided—again, more or less for the hell of it—to blow off meditating altogether. That time lying in the field, evidently for longer than it had felt like, had accomplished pretty much the same thing: he felt cleaned out inside, and very alert. He wanted to think some more about the experience he had been calling, for convenience, the vision, but which was about to become the game. The Game, really. Capitalized for emphasis, and to set it apart from the usual run of experience. From the very beginning the Game was unique, because it was something you could do better alone.

At the Cloud Mountain Alternative School, the day began

with something called Devotions, which was supposed to be a "nondenominational interactive observance of the spirit of world religion," in the words of the Parents' Guide, but which usually turned out to be a sort of vaguely directed group discussion of current events. It was Rudy's chief source of information about goings-on in the wide world, and he was among the only students who regularly bothered to show up on time. Brod Marmack seldom arrived less than twenty minutes late. But after all, they couldn't very well sock you for skipping church, could they? And that's what Devotions was, in fact: a show of belief, in something, or in nothing, or in everything. In Alternatives, whatever they were.

"Today," said the morning's instructor, "I'd like to talk some about a very old idea."

The instructors changed according to some rotation; it was hard to figure out, and Rudy had expected to see the young Physical Sciences guy. But it was an honest-to-god Philosophy woman whom Rudy had almost never seen, since he had opted for Music instead during the elective module. His father hadn't approved of that, but had kept quiet about it. Rudy supposed that *approval* was not a major category with him. Still, you could tell. In Music they were getting into countertonalism this term, and composition as an expression of the collective consciousness, and Rudy was thinking maybe Philosophy wouldn't be a bad idea next time around. So this morning might have been interesting, if only he weren't so tired.

"The idea is this," the Philosophy woman said. "That a general in the field can do nothing more than change the order of a battle, while a saint on a mountaintop, or a hermit in his cell, can change the order of the world."

Rudy squinted to consider this, and to consider the woman who sat with her arm hitched up on the back of the chair, and long gray-brown hair tossed sideways in the other direction, in a posture that seemed to indicate a certain predisposition of thought: she had already chosen her position. She was at ease. Rudy fidgeted and touched the bruise on his head, which as Geoff had predicted was healing without any problem.

"That's so *true*," said the unmistakable voice of Myfanwy Morris, behind and to the left of him.

"How can you possibly say that?" demanded the woman from Philosophy.

You could imagine Myfanwy. She didn't expect a question like that; hadn't she been trying to agree with the teacher, as always? Now her eyes were open and blinking, as her gentle mind rolled back over what she had said, where she had gone wrong.

"Well, I mean," she said, "like the Resistance. All those attacks, and killing people—that's not going to stop the war. Is it?"

"You're talking about military tactics," the Philosophy woman said sharply, "when I am talking about the fundamental nature of reality. Listen, now: *A saint on a mountaintop . . .*"

"But everybody knows that," said Rudy.

He was as surprised as anybody else. Truly, he hadn't intended to say anything. He was tired from being up so late, thinking about the Game, and anyway as a matter of personal policy he never opened his mouth unnecessarily. It was just asking to have your teeth kicked in.

For some reason, though, the woman was smiling at him. "Everybody knows that," she repeated. "And what is it exactly that everybody knows?"

The seasonal color of Rudy's nose spread out to encompass his pale cheeks, his narrow neck, his earlobes. He said, "You know. How it's like an iceberg. And most of it—most of what there really is—isn't worldly stuff like bullets and battlefields. It's, like, ninety-nine percent of it is down where you can't see it, all folded up. Unexpressed possibilities. And so the saint can do more than the general, because he can access more of what's really down there. And I guess, maybe rearrange things."

The woman must have been new to the Alternative School, for this little recitation seemed to surprise her. She shifted a bit in her chair.

"You're not worried, then," she said, sounding actually curious, "about the breakdown in civic order? Or the possibility of war? Do you really believe that the ninety-nine percent of reality will protect you, if the one percent decides to destroy itself?"

"I don't know." Rudy glanced at the other kids around the room. Among the things he didn't know was why he had gotten himself into this. At least, thank God, Brod Marmack hadn't shown up.

"You don't *know?* Does that mean you don't care? Or just that you haven't stopped to think about what's happening around you?"

"I mean, I don't know. I don't know anything about the Resistance. I don't know about the war. I don't know about any of it."

He lowered his eyes. Off to the side, someone murmured:

"He's Dr. Stanton's kid."

The Philosophy woman must have heard this; she gave a very slight nod. "Well then," she said, addressing the room at large. "Let's take this idea a little further."

Rudy slipped down in his chair, easing himself back into the Game.

On the hillside, the nodes had begun to glow. They vibrated, just perceptibly, and no longer bore any resemblance to a bunch of kids. Pure energy, perhaps. But not quite that. Pure something, though. Rudy seemed to be watching them from somewhere at once inside and outside the field of play. He was a player himself, a participant, but also he was like a commentator, a separate observer. His role, he felt, was to explain what was happening on the hillside, to read the pattern of nodes and energies and interpret it for some unseen audience.

The mystery was, he actually did seem to understand it. And the greater mystery was, it actually did seem to be something real. When the glowing yellow object that had been the ball shimmered along the surface of the hill, moving from one nexus to another, Rudy really did feel that some meaning was being expressed, some important transaction occurring. When it reached the point of blockage and was turned away, forced back down the hill again, he felt a welling of emotion inside himself that was something like resentment—but the feeling also seemed to contain certain greater depths, certain possibilities. It had someting to do with the nature of the player nodes themselves, and something to do with what the yellow thing really was. Rudy wished he could pass through the membrane that kept him from entering the Game altogether: that he could reach out and pick up the golden sphere as though it were a big glass ball. And touch it, and gaze into its shining depths, and press his nose against its warmth.

"I'll murder your skinny ass," promised Brod Marmack, "if you tell them how you got hurt."

Rudy looked up from lab table in annoyance—not a usual part of his emotional repertoire, but things had been different lately.

Whom would he tell? As far as he knew, nobody was the least bit curious as to how he had come to be hit by a piece of metal during a noncompetitive game. They were concerned—if indeed there was a *they*, and if they were concerned at all—about whether Rudy's head was okay; and the good Dr. Stanton had seen to that. Besides, what the hell was Brod worried about? There was, as far as Rudy could tell, no system of punishment at the Alternative School. If you were caught doing something wrong (as Rudy had been caught skipping class, when he was younger, because he had a big cold sore on his lip and he didn't want the other kids to tease him), then somebody would sit you down and talk to you. It was time-consuming and basically stupid; but then, one must suppose that life itself was like that, for people like Brod Marmack.

"I haven't told anybody," he said, withholding the promise that Brod seemed to be looking for.

Brod pretended to ignore him. The young Physical Sciences instructor was nosing around the room, stepping with a casual air among the tables, like just one of the fellows, checking on how the experiment was coming along. Rudy glanced up as he passed, and the instructor smiled at him. Then he walked on. There was something in the smile, Rudy thought, as there had been something in the guy's voice back in the field, and it had better not have been pity.

He returned to the little array of equipment organized just so on his table. He could basically have finished the experiment anytime he wanted to, but then he would have to sit around waiting for all the other kids to get done. Next to him Brod Marmack's stuff was lying around in a crazy sort of order that may have been no order at all. Obviously, he hadn't a clue.

"Now remember," the instructor said, having returned to the front of the room, "what we want to do is, we want to bring about the change in phase-states in a way that consumes as little energy as possible. That's the problem, and we may find that there is no single solution. But remember, we're not talking about brute application of force. We're talking about getting things in the proper order. And remember" (you could hear the emphasis building), "what appears to be an absence of power is sometimes just an effective resistance."

Rudy felt like slipping into the Game, but he held himself back. It had gotten pretty absorbing, and it worried him—the way the brightly colored nodes stood out against the background, the way the field itself had turned a shiny black. Not an empty black, but full of color and movement, things swirling around that you couldn't quite see, or maybe you could barely glimpse them. Even now, just remembering it, he felt himself being pulled away, the lab table fading in front of him, becoming translucent, and with Brod Marmack in the very next chair this was not something you really wanted to happen.

"I'm just going to step out of the room for a few minutes," said the instructor. "We'll see how everyone is doing when I get back."

This was an old Alternative School ploy. It was to encourage cooperation, to allow students to get up and walk around and talk about the experiment, sharing ideas in ways that might be considered cheating, somewhere else. The actual effect was something different. There was a sense of everyone giving in to a sort of massive collective distraction.

"Have you got your curfew card yet?" said a girl up near the front of the room. She was talking to Myfanwy Morris. Myfanwy said something too quiet to hear, and the girl said, "No, but they might, if any more trains get hit. I mean, like suppose you were late getting out of Dance or something. Do you want them to throw you in jail?"

Rudy wondered about this. His own curfew card lay undisturbed in its gray, registered-mail envelope. Geoff had signed for the envelopes and placed them, unopened, on the mantel. His expression had been unreadable. After a few moments he had said, not to Rudy in particular, but to anyone who might have been there to hear him, "No. I just can't see it." And that had been that. Rudy had heard nothing more about the cards or about the other things his classmates seemed unable to quit talking about—the curfew, the Resistance, the coming war. He wondered if there was anything he ought to know.

"Absence of power," said Brod Marmack beside him. "Fucking A."

A group of boys had gathered around him, as always. One of them, elbowing in to see more closely whatever it was that Brod was doing, shoved Rudy a couple of inches forward, lab stool and all. They had formed a little circle, from which emitted snickers and some quiet murmurs of disbelief.

"I dare you," said one of the boys.

"Marmack, you're common as shit," said another.

The boy who had elbowed in next to Rudy turned quickly away, as though something had frightened him. As he stepped back, a hole appeared in the circle, and Rudy—out of no special interest or curiosity, but just because that's where the big vibes seemed to be coming from—found himself staring into the middle of things along with everybody else. Brod Marmack was bent slightly forward, head angled toward a place between his knees, where he had placed a wide-mouthed beaker. Rudy's eyes drifted down, his attention still somewhat diffused. It was not for several seconds that he realized he was staring at Brod Marmack's penis.

It was an ugly thing: thick and dark-skinned, with an amazing amount of hair bunched up at the base of it. What had made it hard to register, at first, was that it was fully tumescent. It was the largest thing of its kind that Rudy had ever seen, and Brod's fist was moving rapidly along it, up and down, alternately hiding and revealing it. Rudy realized, without really understanding, that Brod was planning to ejaculate into his experimental solution.

"God, look at Stanton," somebody said. "He's eating this up."

The little crowd of boys looked up from the show in Brod's lap. Rudy felt himself turning crimson—as though he, and not Brod, had been caught doing something shameful.

"He can't get *enough* of it," a boy declared.

Rudy looked away, tried to withdraw himself from the indecency, but somehow he had gotten caught up in it.

"Oh yeah?" Brod Marmack twisted around on his stool. His face was red as well, though a different red from Rudy's, and veins stood out on his neck. "Never seen it before, huh? Well take a good look, you little faggot."

Brod's dick was aimed at Rudy like a cannon. Rudy didn't want to look, but how can you not look at a weapon that's being pointed at you? Brod gave a series of angry pumps, and then the whole thing seemed to turn into gushy, foul-smelling liquid. Rudy thought he might throw up, but it was even worse than that. He just kept watching. A couple of drops, right at the beginning, had shot onto his pants.

The other boys started drifting away. Their expressions were neutral and resolutely private, as though each was making a silent denial that he had been a part of anything. His protective screen withdrawn, Brod stuffed himself hurriedly into his pants, returning the beaker and its corrupted contents to the table. There was something furtive or guilty, even meek, about his movements—even though, from what Rudy could tell, no one but himself was paying the slightest attention. It was as if some profound realignment had taken place: energies once focused had dissipated, a powerful signal faded into the background noise of the room. What this meant, Rudy had no idea. All he could think about was the sight of something ugly, and the strong smell of wasted potency.

The curfew began a week or so later, and for some reason Brod had not spoken or even made solid eye contact with Rudy from that time to this. It was an inexplicable thing. It was as though the two of them were no longer living on exactly the same plane of reality. Rudy was grateful, on several counts. Not first among them, but fairly high on the list, was the fact that it gave him one less thing to worry about, so he could devote his attention to the Game.

The Game had gotten more complicated. It was harder to follow, all at once, and you needed to concentrate. This meant in practice that Rudy could only get into it at certain times of the day—walking to and from school on the path by the lake, for example, or sitting alone in his room when he was supposed to be meditating. The fact was, Rudy had just about given up meditation altogether. He would join his father for asanas and pranayama, then slip up to his room and close his eyes in the chair beside the window, and the Game field would appear before him as sharp and clear as winter sun.

On the field, the nodes had become almost perfectly luminous: very bright, yet also immaterial. Their energy was both powerful and localized; it did not spill out to light the outer darkness. Each node seemed to be the expression of some self-sufficient essence or principle, maybe nothing more than pure thought. The node that was Rudy, or through which Rudy was watching the Game, was different from one time to the next—a different color, a different location—and lately, with excitement, he had begun to understand that his point of view was moving higher and higher up the hill. Sometimes he seemed to touch the golden ball, and sometimes to pass through it, to know for a moment something of its infinite depths. At other times the ball fell down behind him, lower on the hill, or else he had risen in those moments to a transcendent height, from which he could look down on everything. But he had to admit—as the experience got more intense, it also got harder to make sense of. Rudy could not even think about it, as he had before, in the time between sessions, because to think about the Game was to become part of it, to the exclusion of everything else. And there were days, looking back on the walk he had taken to school, or the hours he had sat alone in his room the previous night, when he could remember nothing. Nothing at all.

One of those days was in early February. Rudy was standing by the lake, down behind the Alternative School, where the path dipped close to the frozen water, when he flashed on the fact that he was lost. Not lost in the usual sense of not knowing where to go. More like lost in thought, or lost in time. He didn't know if it was morning or afternoon. It was twilight, he saw, and he had been walking somewhere, but he wasn't walking anywhere right now, and the cloud cover was so thick you couldn't tell, one way or another, which direction the sun was. He supposed he had been playing the Game, but he couldn't remember that either. His mind was utterly empty, and for several minutes he stood there that way, wondering and lost.

It was a silly dilemma, and he couldn't think of a good way around it. If, on the one hand, it was morning, he was no doubt late for Devotions by now, and soon if he kept standing here he would be late for Music. On the other hand, if it was afternoon (and from the quality of the twilight, he suspected this), he had better get his ass in gear or he was going to have to whip out his card at least once for some stupid patrolman, possibly stand still for a search of his bookbag, and explain to Geoff what the hell he had been doing out so late. Not, of course, that Geoff would absolutely *ask* him; but you know.

There were a couple of options, and the easiest one he was doing already: he was standing there to see what was going to happen. It was obviously getting dark or getting light, one or the other, and although it was happening slowly, after a while the direction of things would be unmistakable. In the meantime, Rudy felt pretty much like a jerk. Plus, he was getting cold from just standing around.

Since it seemed like a low-risk course of action, Rudy turned up the hill toward the Alternative School. At worst, he would have to retrace the couple of hundred steps up the hill, and he might still be able to beat the curfew. He was about halfway there—between the dead spruces by the lake and the quaking aspens on the ridge—when it all came back to him. He remembered leaving school a couple of hours before, and coming down the path, and slipping into the Game. But he remembered a lot of other stuff, everything running through his mind very quickly. He remembered that this was where it had started: where he had first gotten the vision, after Brod Marmack fired something with a slingshot. He remembered the sound of the young instructor's voice. He remembered Geoff's unreadable expression when he signed for the curfew letters. And he remembered people telling him things—lessons, which he seemed to be hearing again now, the words running over and over.

The universe is not made of hard things.

Rudy knew he ought to turn around and go home. The field was now getting perceptibly darker, and even though he knew the path by heart it was a long way around the lake to the postcard village—longer if you had to duck the patrolmen—and it always took forever after dark. Yet, something kept him standing there. Some feeling. A sensation that was not completely unfamiliar, though which right at the moment he did not have a name for.

The general in the field can change only the order of a battle, but the hermit in his cell can change the order of the world.

Rudy the fucking hermit. He thought of what a ridiculous person he was: no friends, no particular talents, no knowledge of what was going on in the world. Not just the curfew, the columns of soldiers, the ships crawling over black seas. A lot more than that. Everything, in fact. The things normal kids talked about. The games they played, competitive and otherwise. Football. Ice-skating. Climbing mountains. Jerking off.

At the end of the field, Rudy heard a noise that might have been an animal trying to get somewhere before the cold of night set in. There was a kind of labored breathing, and crunching of icy ground. Little by little these sounds elaborated themselves into a kind of pattern, and the pattern seemed to fit somewhere. The breathing came to resemble, for a few seconds at a time, a murmur of voices. The crunching fell silent and then started up again.

What appears to be an absence of power is sometimes just an effective resistance.

Rudy realized, without quite understanding, that there were two figures above him on the hill, in the shadow cast by the Alternative School. He knew also that where he stood, in the middle of the field, the figures might turn their heads and notice him, and—again without really understanding—he figured it would be a good thing not to let this happen. The closest bit of cover was the line of aspens at the ridge, and in smooth quick strides he made for them, even though this brought him closer to the figures behind the school. It was like some problem in Physical Sciences: two processes going on at the same time, and you had to figure out how they were related.

He made it to the trees without being seen. Nonetheless, you might say he got there too late. Because by the time he slipped into the shadows, he had recognized—with the first light of understanding just beginning to dawn—who the two figures were, standing behind the school. One was the young Physical Sciences instructor. The other was Brod Marmack.

Their voices were not distinct—being kept deliberately low— but by edging his way through the darkness inside the treeline,

Rudy could make out a phrase or two. The faint light of understanding grew brighter.

". . . more this month." This was the young instructor. You could almost see his mustache from here, gone white with frozen breath. He said another thing, and then, "Tell them I'm sorry."

"They don't give a fuck whether you're sorry."

It was not like Brod to keep his voice down for long. The instructor made shushing noises, and the next couple of sentences were indecipherable. Rudy was as close as he could get now unless he could figure out some way to be invisible. Perhaps if he were a saint and this were a mountaintop, he wouldn't be having so much trouble.

"I'll fake it," Brod said, or seemed to say. It could have been *make it*, or *take it*. So much of perception depends on the observer—on what's already present, inside your head.

There was a new thing: a box. It must have been heavy, because when Brod lifted it he gave a grunt, and he had to adjust his grip. As he shifted the box, Rudy heard scraping noises, and something already present in his head made him think this was the sound of metal rubbing metal in the cold.

It *was* cold. Rudy was shivering there among the trees, and maybe the weird state of mind he was in was an early sign of hypothermia. Maybe he wasn't getting enough blood to the brain or something. But since flashing on the fact that he was standing on the path, in the twilight, nothing had made a whole lot of sense. And yet at the same time he thought he was beginning to understand something; that after standing around like a jerk for so long, totally out of it, he was finally getting the picture.

"Yeah, well, I'm going," said Brod. "I'll tell them what you said."

The young instructor said something—*goodbye*, Rudy supposed—and Brod said *What?* Only he said it without words, with his whole body. His head jerked around, and Rudy could see his eyes flash like tiny explosions in the darkness. Suddenly he seemed to make a lot of motions at the same time, the way athletes are able to do, and Rudy had always had trouble following such things. The box struck the dirt and split open. Rudy felt himself pressed to the ground, Brod landing on top of him, a knife being held against his throat, but he could not remember the specific, physical events that had led up to this. He saw the funny look in the young instructor's eye, and he thought maybe he knew what that was all about now.

"You stupid little shit," said Brod. He was full of smells,

dark animal odors, and they drifted all over Rudy. "You little asshole. I'm going to cut your tongue out, and then I'm going to stuff your balls in your mouth."

"Get off him," said the instructor.

Brod looked up, puzzled, disappointed, a doglike gesture.

"There's no need for that," the instructor said. Patiently, as in a classroom. "Mr. Stanton is an intelligent young man. Let's try to explain it to him. I'm sure we can make him understand."

"*I* can make him understand," Brod grumbled, but he rolled off, and he put the knife away. Rudy could breathe well again and he was no longer worried about hypothermia.

"It's all a matter of how things are arranged," the instructor was saying. "Nothing is permanent, nothing is truly solid. The equations, the relationships, are shifting every day. We have to remember that. We have to apply the appropriate force to take advantage of it. We don't have to be prisoners: we can stand up and walk out of our cells."

Rudy felt as though he were falling through the net of words. He felt them around him, and tried to catch hold, but despite himself his mind was swimming free. He was hearing other things, other levels of meaning. His head began to ache, the site of his bruise, and he felt like even *that* was full of significance.

A little while later, they let him stand up. He was afraid of a hundred things, but they were allowing him to go. The invisible walls had fallen away, and he was walking down the hill toward the lake. After a few steps, alone in the black field, he hesitated.

The instructor was watching him, and Brod. They were just standing there when Rudy turned back, as though they had been waiting for this. He was no more than twenty feet away.

"I'm glad you understand," the instructor said after him.

"Sure," said Rudy. There was light from somewhere, and it shone on the pieces of metal that had spilled from the box. Each one was shaped like a fat Magic Marker. Each one was just like the thing that had missed the ball and made a notch in Rudy's skull.

"If you tell *anybody*—" This was Brod, of course; the last thing Rudy heard. "If you tell *anybody*, I'm going to murder your skinny ass."

In the postcard village, they arrested him. His curfew card was stamped 6:00 P.M., and now it was almost eight. There was also the matter of blood on his neck, torn clothing, the evidence of a fight. They searched his bookbag and asked him many questions; then they took him to a well-lighted room, where they put him in a chair beside a window.

The Game had never been like this before. Rudy had never been able to follow it, to concentrate and let himself enter the field of play, but at the same time remain aware of what was happening around him. It was a funny sort of awareness—drifty, you might say, or distant—as though he could no more easily reach out and touch Geoff, when they brought his father in to see him, than he could reach out and touch the golden ball that moved slowly, majestically, between the nodes on the hill. Each was about equally remote. And yet each was real, he knew that too. It was all a matter of relationships. The way you chose to arrange what was already present.

"My son doesn't know anything about the Resistance," Geoff told them. "I've kept him away from all that. For that matter, I don't know all that much myself."

They said they believed him. They said they just wanted to keep Rudy in custody, for his own protection. Something had happened to Rudy, everyone could see that. It might be helpful to know what it was.

"I'm a doctor," said Geoff, "a homeopath. I can take care of him perfectly well. If you'll let me treat him, I'm sure he'll be willing to help you."

They said they understood that. But at present they thought it best if no medication was given. There was a question of evidence, of testimony. It was important to consider certain points of law.

Geoff's face was as much of a mask as ever, but Rudy understood now what the mask was doing there. His father said, "Perhaps I was wrong. But I have only wanted to protect him from this."

The nodes on the field glowed more brightly than ever. They had attained a new level of purity, a new phase-state. Geoff was there for a while and then he was gone. Rudy was taken to another room. It was a jail cell. Without a break, the Game continued. Better than that: it progressed. Everything was vibrating very rapidly, so rapidly that Rudy understood he was not really perceiving it, it was too fast for that. He was simply aware of it, in a direct manner. He himself, as a part of the Game, and as a player, was at the point of making an important transition. He was at the point of becoming a Master.

Now and then, in sports, you want to get back to basics. You want to review first principles. Rudy remembered that the object of the Game had been to get the ball to the top of the hill. He remembered how a certain node, an orange node, had been blocking it. He remembered the conflict, the resistance, energy backing up. It seemed so trivial now—a little dance of metaphors. The Game had gotten inconceivably larger, infinitely more subtle. It was about many things; it had a multitude of objects; you could interpret it any way you wished, but you could never reduce it to the language of conflict, or politics, or war. Those things did not have enough dimensions to contain it. The black field stretched out to the edges of Rudy's imagination and was still expanding. And it was full, teeming with nodes of light like something alive. That was the Game, now: a whole separate realm of existence. An alternative world.

And yet, it occurred to Rudy, you *could* push the ball to the top of the hill, if you wanted to. In fact, you could do so easily, without disturbing the pattern of things, the arrangement, now that you understood how really insignificant it was. If you wanted to, you could eliminate the orange node altogether. Or you could transmute it; you could turn it into something else, another potency, another color. If you were a Master, you could do pretty much any damned thing you liked.

Somewhere around him there was movement, coarse physical activity. The field hummed a bit. Energies shifted. Rudy tried to focus on what was happening, but he found that this upset things, that it caused the ball to roll downhill again. So he did something in his mind, floated to another phase-state of awareness, and from there, impassive, he watched Brod Marmack being shoved into the room.

"That lousy little fuck-head. Just leave me alone with him and I'll show you grounds for arrest. I'll teach that little shit to sing on me."

Rudy noted with interest that they were not attempting to correct this misimpression. They were not troubling to tell Brod that Rudy had not sung, that in fact he had not even talked.

"The little prick—we should've never let him out of there."

They were keeping remarkably quiet about this, Rudy thought. They were letting Brod go on, letting him rave and stalk back and forth across the room. At times he came very close to the single bunk, where the Game proceeded, where Rudy sat crosslegged, striving for some final mastery. They did not interfere when, at one point, Brod swung out an elbow and caught Rudy with admirable precision on the site of his injury. The boy's body responded to this; it was a purely autonomic response, an excitation of the limbic brain. Still, they took note of it. Rudy knew this in a direct way, and did not respond. He did not want to agitate the field by thinking about it. It was part of the game they were playing—but the Game was infinitely greater.

"Just give me half a chance," Brod told them, "and I'll murder him."

They believed him. Rudy believed him too.

On the other hand, that wasn't all of it. Brod had surprised him before, and Rudy was surprised again now at the depths that all this anger was concealing. Somewhere in there was the young instructor, and there were others. So Brod had his own game too. Shadowy forms lurked behind his blustery words: people, bullets, battles yet to come. Rudy saw these things, and if he did not entirely understand them, he understood something of their essence, their inner potency. He saw that there was a kind of blockage, which Brod was trying to maintain, and which *they* were trying to break through. They were trying to take the hill, and Brod was trying to stop them. That was the pattern. It did not seem, from where Rudy sat, all that terribly interesting. Perhaps, after all, he should thank Geoff for that.

"Just leave me alone with the little prick," Brod said, because by saying that he could avoid saying something else. He was in pain from the beatings they had given him, and this anger was what he had left. He was making his stand here. Rudy was surprised at how he felt about it.

Before him, shimmering, rose the yellow ball. The nodes had become almost transparent, their brilliant lights gone white with just a hint of attenuation. Everything was open; all possible paths were clear. It was pretty obvious that a big thing, the final thing, was going to happen.

Brod screamed. They were striking him again. They were shouting things at Rudy. "One of you is going to break," they said, "and until you do you're just going to stay right here in this cell." Rudy thought they were probably right—that somebody *was* going to break. It was probably going to be Brod, who was badly injured. How much time had passed, in that other world? How much time was left to him?

Abruptly, they were alone. Rudy and Brod. No doubt the others were out there, somewhere, watching through hidden eyes, but from where Brod sat you could not be sure of that. There was silence, and a powerful sense of being alone. Brod must have felt it, for he lowered his head into his hands and cried.

Then, without warning, as he had always done things, he changed again, or perhaps he was just following the zags of his own lightning bolt. He turned on Rudy, shouting words that were no longer perfectly distinct: the old threats, but heavily underscored with a new and darker meaning. His mouth formed sentences like This is what you've been asking for, and We'll see how long you last, you little faggot.

Rudy did not exactly hear these things, though it all seemed clear enough. Brod was going to kill him. In order to prevent him from doing so, he must have thought—based on his notion that Rudy was an informant—that the others would come and they would kill Brod instead. The battle would end in a stalemate; the hill would not have been taken. Something like that. Rudy was getting tired, himself, and it seemed time to have it over.

Brod came at him with his large fists. There were only two paces between them, but time and space were different in the Game, and Rudy did not hurry his move. He reached out carefully, keeping his balance, and took the yellow light into his hand as though it were a big glass ball. He drew it closer, until he could see the words that floated there, like the motto on a coin.

What appears to be an absence of power is sometimes just an effective resistance.

That was it, then. Rudy relaxed; he felt his body change in some way; felt Brod's fist reach his face and discover there this new thing, this alternate substance.

"What the fuck," said the other boy.

Rudy watched the nodes in the Game attentively. They quivered, as though the field itself were shaking, and Rudy thought this might be some reaction to the several sets of feet that were pounding into the room. The node that had once, in a certain plane of meaning, seemed to be representative of Brod glowed with a particular urgency, like a warning light on a panel, and Rudy reached out to it with the greatest possible delicacy. As he touched it, the light flared and vanished. The other lights, the ones that had been set against it, contesting over the yellow ball, flickered for a moment, like frightened fireflies. Rudy placed a finger on each of them in turn. The field was becoming much clearer now. There was nothing close to him but the gleaming ball. Again he lifted it, and again he saw words floating there.

The hermit in his cell, he read, *can change the order of the world.*

Rudy looked around the little room, which was small and

bright. At the same time—the way Brod had been two things at once, and the young instructor, and Rudy himself—the room was also boundless, and very dark. It was like a sea, a night-black sea, and the glowing nodes around him were like the mast lights of ships, blown by a rising storm. Or again, it was a battlefield, black with smoke, and the nodes were bloodred fires. Rudy gave an involuntary shiver. He was terrified of the great scale of things, and the darkness. It would be wrong, he saw, to put all the lights out. There must be an alternative solution.

He felt that somewhere there had been a mistake, that some pattern or arrangement had been misinterpreted. The lightning bolt of energy that flowed across the field, passing from player to player, had gotten all twisted up. There was conflict, needless resistance. The Game wasn't supposed to be competitive.

Or maybe that wasn't right. Or maybe it wasn't the whole story. Maybe the Game was a stupid idea to begin with. Maybe the conflict had been an inevitable outcome, a perfectly natural way to pass the time. You couldn't just hang out on a hill and pass a ball around. Maybe the Game itself had been the problem— the whole order of things, the field and the nodes and the yellow ball, the stuff that had been present from the beginning.

It was like a test. Not a test in Physical Sciences, where you knew there had to be an answer. It was more like Music, or even Devotions, where the whole thing depended on how you felt at the time. Rudy felt dizzy, like he was sick, like he was tossing in choppy water. But that was a surface problem: a wave effect. The tip of an iceberg. Underneath it, down deep, he knew it would be calmer. He knew he could get down there, if he only let go.

Until now, the Game had seemed to have a meaning. There had been a kind of relationship between that world and this, between the field behind the Alternative School and the terrifying field of Rudy's vision. That relationship, like all relationships, had changed now. The Game had no meaning anymore, or none in the world of ordinary schoolkids. So Rudy, who never had felt perfectly at home there, let that world go: every reference, every metaphor. He floated down through the depths, through the inhuman lattice of possibilities, where at last the inner order of things was clear.

It was cold, and the loneliness rang like metal striking stones, and Rudy was exhausted by the time he had moved all the pieces into a new arrangement. He wasn't sure his answer was the best one, or if it was good enough to pass the test, but he sensed that time was running out on him.

He broke through the surface again, into the warmth. The field grew brighter. The light came from a golden sphere suspended just above his eyes: a crystal ship, a container of meaning, ready to receive him. As he reached for it, he felt his eyes quiver, and he was afraid for a moment that the warmth, the beauty—even the Game itself—was fading away. But he steadied himself, and the balance returned.

There was one more message.

The universe, said the yellow ball, *is not made of hard things.*

Rudy awoke on the single bunk of a jail cell. He was alone there. He blinked: the sun was in his face. For a few moments, while his eyes adjusted to the light, he stared down at his own hands and arms as though they belonged to someone else. They were obviously his, though—pale and scrawny, lightly freckled at the wrist. At last, growing restless, he stood up and stretched.

It seemed like something Rudy had always known, that he could walk through the wall. It was, after all, only a question of relationships. He felt different this morning; he sensed that things were arranged in some new way. Maybe the weather was changing, the spring arriving early. Maybe the lake would melt, and the sky would turn the water from black to blue. Rudy made his way around it, following the path that skirted the field, behind the Alternative School. He moved quickly, without much effort; which was nice, because it left his mind clear. There were a lot of things to look at this morning—the sky, the mountain, the thick green spruces, the game in progress on the hill. There were a lot of kids there, and a young instructor. At first Rudy thought they might have seen him, that he would have to leave the path and join them. But the instructor just kept watching the trees that cut off the view of the postcard village, and the kids kept shouting in some spirit of collective freedom, running higher and higher on the hill. Rudy thought the yellow ball was gone, but then he saw it, suspended just above his eyes: sparkling like glass, pulling clouds out of the trees above the mountain.

THE
THING ITSELF

MICHAEL BLUMLEIN

TO HETTY

Here's one more stunning story of relationships before we close. It's as powerful a tale as you will read anywhere else in this anthology.

Michael Blumlein has sold work to a number of magazines, including *The Mississippi Review, Omni,* and *Twilight Zone.* His first novel, *The Movement of Mountains,* was published to very favorable review attention in 1987. His second, *A Native in the Land,* is forthcoming. Michael lives in San Francisco where he is a physician and faculty member of the University of California School of Medicine.

This is a story about love. It is about Laurie and Elliot, two people who meet in their late twenties. Laurie is a nurse and an outdoorswoman. She jogs and she hikes. She has had experiences with men, none of them long. She prefers her enlistments short and definable.

Elliot is a doctor. He has cystic fibrosis, a disease of the lungs and pancreas. He is a dedicated and conscientious worker and a wit. A vivid imagination is his handle on survival.

There are lessons in this story. Particular ones, and universal. A video is forthcoming. And later, a syndicated column. Love, after all, is not so hard. It is not a city, or a thought. When attended to with foresight and maturity, love is as straightforward as boiling an egg.

I. THE ROLL OF THE DICE

Laurie met Elliot while she was working in the intensive care unit. It was in the early morning hours after the fire that had swept through the college women's dormitory, and all medical personnel had been mobilized. The blackened bodies of coeds hadn't yet been removed from the crowded corridors. They lined the walls, silent lumps under crumpled white sheets. The smell was horrible. Families raged and grieved, while nurses, doctors, administrators, and orderlies performed their grim tasks. The proportions of the tragedy stripped away artifice. The normally meticulous women forgot about their makeup, their lipstick and eyeliner. Mascara trickled in tears down their cheeks. The carefully groomed administrators had no time to shave, and tiny splinters of hair stuck out from their chins and cheeks. For a short while these people came together in a way unknown to them by the light of bright and ordered day.

Laurie found Elliot in the ICU. They had communicated several times before, under purely routine circumstances. The lids of his eyes seemed to close as he leaned over the girl in the bed. He placed his stethoscope on her chest and shook his head.

"Take a break," Laurie said. "You've been here all night."

Elliot pretended not to hear. His forehead was nearly touching the singed skin of the girl. He tried to hold back his tears.

Laurie stood silently next to the bed. Her stethoscope was draped over her neck; her hands squeezed the side rail. She watched Elliot, who seemed so sad and alive. She reached across the dying girl and took his hand.

"C'mon, let's have a cup of coffee."

Elliot let her lead him to the nurses' lounge, where they sat on a cheap plastic couch. It was split down the middle, and the foam showed through. Elliot held his face in his hands, staring at the floor. Laurie bent the spigot of the coffee machine, filling two cups with lukewarm coffee. Her eyes were bloodshot; the gray bags beneath them made her look twice her age. She had been a nurse for five years, and this had been the worst night of her life. Unconsciously, she put her hand on Elliot's neck and began to rub.

Elliot let her, not expecting to relax. He was too tired to sleep. He put the coffee cup on the table and touched Laurie's leg. He turned sideways on the couch, crossed his legs in a yoga position, and stretched out his back. Laurie rubbed it. She leaned closer and pulled him against her. Snaking her hands between the buttons at the front of his shirt, she touched his chest.

Elliot took her to the on-call room and locked the door. He made a few lame jokes about doctors and nurses. She laughed a little too loud. When they made love, it was slow, then very quick. Elliot was funny and gentle. Laurie was surprised at how easy it was. She got hot fast and reached a sharp climax. Elliot came too, and in moments was asleep. His breathing was rapid and coarse for a long time. Laurie stayed awake. She was amazed. A verse from somewhere played in her mind:

> The dead come knocking
> The dead come knocking
> And love, sweet love,
> It lets them in.

II. CHOOSING THE RIGHT SPECIES

Tall men aroused in Laurie feelings she preferred to avoid. She was five foot three, and Elliot, if anything, was half an inch shorter. This suited Laurie just fine. When they moved in together, they kept things—books, pots, linens—close to the ground. They left the top shelves in the kitchen empty, and made sure their two full-length mirrors were hung low on the doors.

A month after getting the apartment, Elliot came down with pneumonia. He was put in the hospital and ended up staying for three weeks. During this time Laurie got a taste of a different life. She visited him daily, twice when she could. They did crosswords together, read to each other, shared meals. Elliot craved starches—noodles and spaghetti—because of his body's poor ability to digest protein. Laurie brought in food and ate with him. She got a little fat. She stopped jogging because she didn't have time, and saw more of his nurses than her own friends.

On the whole, though, she was happy. She had a man, and the man loved her. He needed her. It made her feel good.

Elliot's pneumonia slowly improved. His breathing became easier, and the oxygen was taken away. Soon he was able to say more than one or two sentences without getting out of breath.

"Imagination," he told Laurie, "is the source of my strength. When I stop inventing, I will die."

He was twenty-nine, and had already lived years beyond others with his disease. His future was not bright.

"Fiction is power," he went on. "Out of it grows fact. Avoidance is sometimes more direct than study."

Elliot loved the sound of words and the shelter they brought. When he had the breath, he could talk for hours. He told Laurie stories.

One day they were lying together in his hospital bed, Elliot in his issued gown, Laurie in a skirt and blouse. The nurses allowed the intimacy because Laurie was one of them, because Elliot was a doctor. They allowed it because they were sympathetic; they understood the nature of health and recovery.

The back of the bed was raised so that Elliot could breathe easier. Laurie was nestled by his side, one hand draped across his stomach. She was half-asleep, timing her breathing to the cadence of Elliot's voice.

"Like the Pope," he was saying, "I believe in angels. Not good and bad ones, as he supposes. Reflective ones. Mirrors in the shapes of Möbius strips. A kind of personal and mathematical afterlife. Are you listening?"

She nodded sleepily.

"It is not simply belief," he went on. "There are certain proofs. . . ." He paused, looking down at the hand on his stomach. It was finely veined, strong, and the arm, the soft belly of the biceps, was beautiful as it disappeared into the sleeve of her blouse. He became aware of her breasts pressed against his side.

"There is a restaurant," he said. "I have visited it more than once. Its atmosphere is unique; its elegance, legendary. The special there is an ambrosial delight not to be found elsewhere. Not were you to search a lifetime." He put a hand on her breast and spoke authoritatively. "Mother's milk. Not milk and honey, not the milk of human kindness, not even the milky tears of dew at dawn. Simply, purely, pleasingly, Mother's milk. The brew of Mammalia. The sustenance of our kind."

She smiled dreamily. Encouraged, Elliot went on.

"Here," he swept out an arm, "on our very premises we house a wide variety of creatures. The multitudinous reflections of God's eye are yours to choose from. In cages in the basement we have rabbit, chipmunk, gopher, and beaver. Our shrew milk is heavenly, though scant. An agile child has been trained to gather it: her tiny, supple fingers deftly milk the precious fluid into thimbles, which you may purchase as souvenirs.

"In a corral adjoining the flank of the restaurant lie our

marsupials, the wombats and koalas, the kangaroos. Beyond, in our rolling grasslands, dotted with oak and madrone, irrigated by fifteen miles of flexible conduit, waters from artesian wells, graze elephant, ass, moose, zebra, yak, giraffe, and llama. Anteaters forage there, and armadillos. It is still summer, and the young of these creatures are not yet weaned. There is milk in abundance, thick milk, thin, sweet and bitter. Some is white as snow, some yellow, other gray as ash. We have a team of starving children, adept at identification, trained to run quickly and carefully. They keep low, and draw upon udders with acrobatic skill and finesse. For each cup of milk delivered to our kitchen they receive a handful of coin; every third cup nets them a day of rest. They are strong-hearted and eager to please. Choose your mammal and feed a child."

He paused to gather his breath.

Laurie yawned, stretched. "You haven't mentioned the carnivores," she said.

"We offer a complete listing. The cost, as you might expect, is higher. The risks are greater, the mothers not so obliging. Extraction is more labor-intensive, requiring from two to five brave souls. We don't use tranquilizer guns, as it would taint the milk. A mothering carnivore, be it badger, weasel, lion, bear, or wolf, is a touchy animal. Her glands are guarded items, the product a precious commodity. But a sip of cheetah milk . . ." He sighed, licking his lips, "it puts hair on your chest."

"I don't need more hair," said Laurie. She touched a scratch mark on her calf. "I have to shave too much as it is, and I hate it."

"Then you should definitely skip the carnivores. Besides, the milk has a tendency to be harsh. Causes the mouth to pucker." He pursed his lips and blew her a kiss.

"Ethical considerations require that the last class go unnamed. Strictly speaking, we are not even supposed to have the milk available. Gathering it has been declared an objectification of the provider. Many who are not in need of the income consider it degrading. Others claim that its collection and availability carry sexual overtones that should not be confused with food. Notwithstanding these objections, it is a most popular item."

"Men, I presume, favor it more than women."

"Surprisingly not. Women choose it as often."

"It's in your mind, Elliot."

He laughed. "I'm a piece of fiction."

"You're a good man. What will I do without you?"

"Don't be maudlin." He started to say more but was interrupted by the beginnings of a cough. It started deep in his chest
and rumbled up like thunder. His face suffused with blood, and
his whole body shook. It seemed like he was tearing his insides
out.

"Should I call the nurse?"

He didn't answer, working his lungs until finally he brought
something up. He spit it into some Kleenex, then reached over
and turned on the oxygen. He stuck the plastic prongs in his
nose.

Laurie watched. She waited. Her initial apprehension gradually faded, but a knot of tension stayed in her stomach. She was
still learning this man's routine. This life.

"I'm worried about you," she said at length.

"It's okay," he said, panting. His forehead was beaded with
sweat. "I . . . have to . . . get . . . the phlegm up."

"It's always like this?"

He nodded. They held hands and listened to the oxygen
bubbling quietly up beside the bed. Gradually his breathing
calmed. Laurie asked him about dying.

"Everyone dies," he said.

"But you have CF."

"I don't think about it. Only when I'm sick."

She looked at him quizzically. "I don't believe you."

He stared at her, then looked away. "I think about it. What's
the difference?"

"The difference is I'm involved. I just found you. I don't
want you to die."

"I won't die."

She was not convinced.

"I won't," he repeated. "I promise. Listen . . ." He took
her hand. "There's one more item. One more kind of milk."

"Stop," she said.

"No. Listen. It's the last. The purest. It's a vapor, it enters
through closed lips, condenses on the tongue. It's the sweetest
milk there is. Full of gentleness and comfort. The breath of an
angel."

"I don't believe in angels," she said stiffly. "This is about
dying, isn't it?" Tears brimmed her eyes. "You're going to die,
aren't you?"

"No." He shook his head. "It's just a story."

III. IMAGINATION AND GOOD HEALTH

Love requires health. Health is hypnotism, trust, science. It is persuasion and power, belief spread like a blanket, a bed. It is rational, irrational. Chemistry, words, light, and sound.

An agent can be employed. A drug, for example, a root. Or a shell, mud, bark, the husk of an insect. A scalpel can be the agent. The ace of cups. There are capsules the size of cherries, poultices that smell like tar. Horn of goat, spore of fungus, fender, headlight, bottle cap. A healer must not be narrow-minded.

He can tell a story.

Elliot is a healer, a doctor of medicine. He works in a windowless room with a desk and a table. A curtain can be drawn around the table for privacy. Patients who willingly lie naked for his examination use the curtain's screen to reclothe themselves. It is the shield behind which they recover their dignity.

On the wall above his desk is taped a card with the words: DO NO HARM. Out of sight on the back of it is a quote from a friend: "I've always said I don't mind nobody bullshittin' me, but if you're going to jive make it good. Make me believe it."

One afternoon a woman enters his office. She is overweight and wears pants whose zipper is broken. She has on a loose-fitting T-shirt and a bandanna that hides her hair. Settling in the chair beside his desk, she says, "I got burning."

Elliot is tired from a bad night. He stifles a yawn. "Burning?"

"All up in my head," she touches it, "and down my back. It draws on me. Cuts clear from back to front. My arms and legs too. My whole body burns."

Elliot thumbs through her chart, thick with multiple visits, multiple complaints. Even before knowing what she has, he wonders what she wants.

"How long have you had the burning?"

The woman calculates. "Two days, maybe three."

"Have you tried anything?"

"Rubbing alcohol."

He nods.

"Listerine."

He waits for more, but the woman is close-lipped. She stares at her lap, as though awaiting punishment.

"And did they help?"

"They soothed a little. I still got the burning."

Elliot is drowsy, and his mind is not working well. Burning makes him think of sparks, fire, sexual yearning. He knows if he is not careful, the thread will vanish and he will lose control.

He tells her to undress, and when she is ready he goes to examine her. She does not appear ill. In the midst of listening to her lungs, Elliot is struck by a fit of coughing. He retreats across the room, leaning against his desk until the paroxysm passes. Winded and slightly embarrassed, he completes the exam. He draws the curtain and tells her to dress.

At his desk he ponders his own health. It is slowly failing. He feels it when he tries a deep breath. Always he wants for air.

The woman seems healthy enough. He resents this, but also he is grateful. Her story is making him work and forget. When she is dressed and sitting, he has a sense again of her fear.

"The exam," he says carefully, "is normal."

"Then what's the burning?"

"It's a reaction to something. Maybe a virus. Or an allergy. It should be gone in a few days."

She looks at him, her face working to stay calm. Her eyes are everywhere but at his. "My mother died of cancer."

"This is not cancer."

"It ate her up. In the end the fever got her. Burned her till she couldn't eat. Couldn't breathe either."

"You do not have cancer." Elliot takes her by the wrist and forces her to look at him. "Do you understand?"

"I'm not going to die?"

"Not of this."

"Are you sure?"

"Listen to me. This is not cancer. You are not going to die."

She looks away, and then her eyes dart back, as if to make sure he is telling the truth.

"You believe me?"

She nods tentatively, then stands. "I feel better. The burning, it'll go away?"

"Yes. Call me next week."

She leaves, and Elliot settles in his chair. He feels charged by the encounter. On a scrap of paper he scribbles the words:

science: to know, and beneath them, *fiction: to shape*. Next to *fiction* he sketches a picture of a syringe and needle. He draws a colony of bacteria and an equation to estimate the blood flow through the heart. Above it, opposite the word *science*, he sketches the face of a man. He has a single eye, from whose pupil radiate tiny stars, half-moons, mythical animals in miniature. They rise above his head, where they circle in a cloud of barely discernible shapes. They look like the bacteria below, and, noting this, Elliot draws a bridge connecting the two. He smiles, then yawns. Cradling his arms on the desktop, he puts his head down.

Sometime later, a knock on the door stirs him. Heavy-lidded and still half-asleep, he swivels in his chair. Through the door walks a clown in full regalia—whiteface, painted smile, pink wig. On his forehead is penciled a blue eye.

Elliot stares. He rubs his eyes. There is another knock, and he turns to the door, grateful for the interruption. This time a skeleton hobbles in, all bones, ambulating without visible means of support. In its teeth is clenched a cigar; the smoke trails up and hangs in its eye sockets. The skeleton takes a position near the clown, who regards Elliot with a gay, fixed smile. He wrinkles his forehead, and the eye there blinks.

Elliot is speechless. His mind skirts over the day's events, searching for clues. Did he eat something bad? Was there a drug in his morning tea? Something in the air? The skeleton and clown seem to be waiting. There is another sound at the door, followed by a brief inrush of air. Elliot girds himself and turns. Standing in the doorway is a naked man, his face and torso vaguely familiar. Sweeping out from his back are wings.

Elliot numbly watches this last one enter, then gets up and shuts the door. This is a private matter, he is sure. It occurs to him that it might be his time to die.

The three gaze at him without detectable emotion. The clown speaks.

"Life is not simple, my friend. You've probably noticed. Boundaries constantly change. It is a difficult concept for the egocentric mind.

"A person, for example, starts as a single cell. The cell divides, migrates, differentiates. There is no 'fact' of existence."

"Who are you?" Elliot asks. His voice is shaky.

"Nor of nonexistence," the winged person continues. "Dead tissue is carried off by scavengers. Bones, by droplets of water. Death is hardly less complicated."

"Why are you here? Who are you?"

"There is no thing that does not change. There is no fact. There is only fiction."

"We are Humor, Death, Science," says the clown. "Your homunculi. A lovely triad, don't you think?"

"Think?"Elliot stammers. "Am I thinking?"

"Don't be cute." The skeleton waves its cigar. "I was told you were a nice fellow."

"Courteous," says the clown.

"Kind."

"A hard worker."

"Why are you here?" Elliot asks.

"A lesson in geography," rattles the skeleton. "Boundaries. The imagination."

"You scare me."

"We could not possibly harm you," murmurs the one with wings. "Love prevents us."

"Love, however, does not kill bacteria." The clown scribbles a formula in the air. "Science is chemistry. Subatomics is the nature of things."

"The end of things is the nature of things," says the skeleton. "Forgetfulness is such a blessing."

"The wind is a blessing," says the winged one. Of the three he seems the most human. 'Breath is the common origin. It is the source of inspiration."

"Which of the triad are you?"Elliot asks.

"I am Death," whispers the angel.

Elliot is now visibly shaken. He strains to think of something to say, to do. The tension rises in his body. When it hits his chest, he is seized by a fit of coughing. It is a bad one, lasting more than a minute. By the time it ends, he is breathless. His face is red, his head between his legs.

"Air," he whispers. "Air."

IV. DOING THINGS TOGETHER

At the foot of Elliot and Laurie's bed is a twenty-four-inch Sony color television. The remote control device lies between them on the sheet. They are watching the Miss America Beauty Pageant.

Elliot is bored with the contestants, putting up with their dime-store, egregious obsequiousness in order to catch a glimpse of the true star, the enigmatic Bert Parks. Parks is a kind of hero to Elliot. He seems to age so gracelessly, like no man on earth, from the lizardlike skin at his neck to the sleazy, hungry, haunted pits that pass for his eyes. His smile is a lurid caricature, evoking death camp assurances and promises. And his singing . . . his singing is mesmerizing.

A rhapsody to the beatific pucker of femininity, Parks's voice is a tribute to science. To mind over matter, imagination over true flesh. When Parks sings, Elliot nearly weeps. He thinks of drugs stronger than morphine, of direct stimulation of the neural centers of pain and pleasure. He is astounded by the man, by his determination, his self-denigration, his longevity. During the closing bars of the pageant's hymn, Elliot suddenly realizes that Parks is not human.

If he studies the man's image carefully, he can discern gaps between body parts. When one of the contestants passes behind him, Elliot catches a glimpse of the sequins on her dress through Parks's thyroid gland. When Parks turns to greet her, pink feathers (presumably from her headpiece) sprout from his eye sockets. It is a revelation. Bert Parks, the suave, polished, unctuous ringmaster, is an illusion.

Laurie is more interested in the girls. She is captivated by their glossy smiles and precise bodies. Their perfect nails and hair, and endless legs. Despite her humiliation at their grating optimism and choreographed gaiety, Laurie is envious. She imagines futures of attention and worth, of great personal magnetism and reward. She feels inadequate. Taking the remote control device in a hand, she punches off the TV.

"Am I pretty?" she asks Elliot.

"Exceptionally."

"No. Don't answer fast. I want you to think about it. I want the truth."

He cups his chin in his palm and looks her over. The wide, acne-pocked forehead. Weak chin, full breasts, short, fat legs.

"You are beautiful," he says.

She looks him in the eye. "You mean it?"

"I mean it. Beautiful. It's as simple as that."

Laurie smiles then, a broad, teary-eyed smile. "I love

you, Elliot. If I could, I'd give you my breath. I'd breathe for you.''

"Laurie," he says, taking her hands, "if I could, I'd sing for you. I'd sing words that you'd believe, and I'd put them in your brain in a place you'd never forget. . . .'' He pauses, then laughs. "If I could, Laurie, I'd be Bert Parks for you. I'd be immortal.''

V. WORKING IT OUT

Laurie works in the intensive care unit. Sometimes it is slow, sometimes busy. Of the six beds in the unit only one is filled tonight. In it is a thirty-year-old man who looks ninety. His eyes are yellow, his arms spindly, his face sallow. His belly is so swollen that he has not seen his feet in months. He can't lie flat because it is impossible to breathe, so he has to be propped up in bed. He doesn't sleep well but can't take pills because his liver is shot. He has terminal cirrhosis and has been in and out of a coma for days.

Presently he is in, which means that there is not much for Laurie to do. From time to time she checks his bottles, and every hour she takes his vital signs. Between these small tasks she sits at the nurses' station reading an outdoor magazine. Tonight she finds it boring and keeps reading the same passage over and over. She is thinking about Elliot.

All her life Laurie has depended on men. This she resents, and so for years has made a deal with herself. A secret, barely conscious deal: her men will have flaws. Her first lover was unreliable; her second, distant and moody. The one before Elliot indulged himself in a cause more than he did in Laurie. Elliot's flaw is his illness. It puts the two of them, she feels, on equal footing. He cannot leave her because he needs her. He depends on her. This gives her a sense of security. It makes her feel curiously independent and strong. She has casually forgotten the inevitability of his early death. She is unaware of how carefully she has chosen a situation that will soon cause her grief. Laurie herself lives in a world of periodic coma.

She has a cup of coffee, and then another. Between three and five are the worst hours of the morning, the hardest to stay awake. She starts to do her nails but stops because she doesn't really care. The girls are girls; she is a woman. The men can meet her on her own ground.

The coffee has its effect, and her head begins to buzz. Her hands get jittery, and she starts to have a few wild thoughts. From the bed of the cirrhotic she hears a sound. There is a curtain around him, and when she gets up to look behind it, he is gone. In his place is a man with wings.

Oh shit, Laurie thinks. *Something's wrong. Something's terribly wrong.* Then the nurse in her takes over.

She makes the man comfortable, fluffing up the pillow and straightening the sheets. His wings curl around, resting on his torso and upper thighs. He smiles up at her from a drawn face; he does not look well at all. She gives him a sip of water, and he thanks her with his eyes. She tells herself that she should report this to her supervisor, but as she turns to go he touches her with a wing. He makes her understand that he wants her to take a feather. As a gift. A token. Laurie refuses, but the man insists. It is all so very strange.

Finally she consents, choosing a small white primary near the tip. She tugs on it, but it sticks tight. She pulls harder, and harder still.

It comes loose with a pop, then a hiss. Laurie feels a soft stream of air against her face. It tastes faintly of milk.

She touches her lips with the tip of the feather. The hiss continues. She realizes she has acted willfully. It does not surprise her. All things must pass. She is a survivor. The man's time is up.

VI. SONG AND LAMENT

You promised you wouldn't die. You said it, and yet you bought life insurance every chance you got. At eighteen, twenty, twenty-five. Twenty-five years old! There is no insurance at twenty-five; at twenty-five some people open their eyes for the first time. Open them and see a world. Take the wrong turn sometimes, stumble maybe, but none would call it death. Disappointment, sure. A setback. But not death. How can we die before we even open our eyes?

But it was different for you. You were sick from the start. Your mother said she wouldn't have had you if she'd known. She was crying when she said that; it was after you died. She would have aborted, she said, if not with the help of someone with conscience, then in some back alley. With a stick, a hanger. With lye if she had to. However dangerous and terrible, she would have tried. Because life was too hard for you. Too damned hard.

You couldn't run or skip, couldn't move fast to save your life. Couldn't scale a peak and stand above the world, stretch out where there's nothing but sky. Or pause on an alpine trail, lupine clumped around the base of a gnarled juniper, wind in your face, snow in the air. Stop and sit on a piece of granite the size of an elephant. Share lunch. You couldn't breathe the mountain air, the fine, crystalline air. The oxygen was too thin, your lungs too choked with phlegm. You almost died when we drove across the Rockies.

But you said dying wasn't on your mind when you weren't sick. When you weren't laid out in bed, coughing, panting, struggling to bring up the phlegm. You said you didn't think about it, but how could you not? How could you not be afraid the next day might be just a little harder, your lungs more tired, your breath feebler? When you're sick like that, isn't every day a sick day, even when you're better? Don't the pills get old, and the treatments? Isn't there a part of you that waits for things to worsen, that expects to die?

But you said no, and showered me with fancy words and stories. With gentleness and patience. With love.

Sometimes you seemed a saint. Tough, vulnerable. Weakened, you were stronger. Resilient. Erotic.

You were the sexiest man I knew.

You didn't hike or swim. Didn't cook. You talked to me. You listened. You made jokes and made love.

You used to come home after work—after ten, twelve exhausting hours at the hospital—and boil a package of spaghetti for dinner. Spaghetti and butter. That was it. For dinner. No wonder you died.

You made me laugh, see? Taught me humor. Imagination. Things to ease the pain.

Like buying that guidebook of San Francisco with each street labeled according to its grade. Red was steep, yellow gentle, blue level. You plotted a course through the city, convinced me the modest hills were mountain peaks, the brightly painted Victorians sweet-smelling pine. Stray cats were skunk, dogs were wolf and deer. The reservoirs were alpine lakes, and you carried repellent to keep the mosquitoes down.

You were good at easing the pain, Elliot. The pain of less. The pain of having to lose you.

I remember the last morphine shot, the one that let you lie back, that let the knotted muscles in your chest and neck finally ease. The room was dark, your friends circled the bed like a hand. One by one they told the stories, they made a web of memories with you at the center. So that when they were done, you were remembered, and free to go. You slumped against me, heavy, loose at last, and asked, Can I die? Your voice was so feeble I scarcely heard. Can I die?

Yes, I whispered. Yes, yes, die now. You would have fought had I said no.

You smiled, and your mouth got slack. You gave a little shudder, and you died.

I did not weep. I felt anger and sadness. Your weight. I watched the moonlight on the floor. I heard wheels in the hall. The world had wings.

JOURNALS
OF THE
PLAGUE YEARS

NORMAN SPINRAD

And now for the big finish. Norman Spinrad has been giving the world brilliant speculative fiction for nearly three decades. His novels, which include *Bug Jack Barron*, *The Void Captain's Tale* and *Child of Fortune*, are among the most challenging, stimulating, and consistently innovative the genre has ever produced. His work has been translated into a dozen languages, and been nominated for many major awards, including the National Book Award. He has also been a sandal maker, a literary agent, a critic and columnist, and a radio talk show host. His most recent novel, *Little Heroes*, has just been published in paperback, and his new collection of novellas, *Other Americas*, will be published in September.

"Journals of the Plague Years" is vintage Spinrad, which means you should strap in for the ride of your life. It is a story of the near future focusing on an all-too-familiar disease, the way that disease has totally overthrown the morals and mores of our society, and the explosive consequences when a cure is discovered.

INTRODUCTION

I t was the worst of times, and it was the saddest of times, so what we must remember if we are to keep our perspective as we read these journals of the Plague Years is that the people who wrote them, indeed the entire population of what was then the United States of America and most of the world, were, by our standards, all quite mad.

The Plague virus, apparently originating somewhere in Africa, had spread first to male homosexuals and intravenous drug users. Inevitably it moved via bisexual contact into the population at large. A vaccine was developed and for a moment the Plague seemed defeated. But the organism mutated under this evolutionary pressure and a new strain swept the world. A new vaccine was developed, but the virus mutated again. Eventually the succession of vaccines selected for mutability itself, and the Plague virus, proliferated into dozens of strains.

Palliative treatments were developed—victims might survive for a decade or more—but there was no cure, and no vaccine that offered protection for long.

For twenty years, sex and death were inextricably entwined. For twenty years, men and women were constrained to deny themselves the ordinary pleasures of straightforward, unencumbered sex, or to succumb to the natural desires of the flesh and pay the awful price. For twenty years, the species faced its own extinction. For twenty years, Africa and most of Asia and Latin America were quarantined by the armed forces of America, Europe, Japan, and the Soviet Union. For twenty years, the people of the world stewed in their own frustrated sexual juices.

Small wonder then that the Plague Years were years of madness. Small wonder that the authors of these journals seem, from our happier perspective, driven creatures, and quite insane.

That each of them found somewhere the courage to carry on, that through their tormented and imperfect instrumentalities the long night was finally to see our dawn, *that* is the wonder, that is the triumph of the human spirit, the spirit that unites the era of the Plague Years with our own.

—Mustapha Kelly
Luna City, 2143

JOHN DAVID

I was gunfoddering in Baja when the marks began to appear again. The first time I saw the marks, they gave me six years if I could afford it, ten if I joined up and got myself the best.

Well what was a poor boy to do? Take my black card, let them stick me in a Quarantine Zone, and take my chances? Go underground and try to dodge the Sex Police until the Plague got me? Hell no, this poor boy did what about two million other poor boys did—he signed up for life in the American Foreign Legion, aka the Army of the Living Dead, while he was still in good enough shape to be accepted.

Now you hear a lot of bad stuff about the Legion. The wages suck. The food ain't much. We're a bunch of bloodthirsty killers too bugfuck to be allowed back in the United States fighting an endless imperialistic war against the whole Third World, and our combat life expectancy is about three years. Junkies. Dopers. Drooling sex maniacs. The scum of the universe.

For sure, all that is true. But unless you're a millionaire or supercrook, the Legion is the best deal you can do when they paint your blue card black and tell you you've Got It.

The deal is you get the latest that medical science has to offer and you get it free. The deal is you can do anything you want to the gorks as long as you don't screw up combat orders. The deal is that the Army of the Living Dead is coed and omnisexual and every last one of us has already Got It. We've all got our black cards already, we're under sentence of death, so we might as well enjoy one another on the way out. The deal is that the Legion is all the willing meat-sex you can handle, and plenty that you can't, you better believe it!

Like the recruiting slogan says, "A Short Life but a Happy One." We were the last free red-blooded American boys and girls. "Join the Army and Fuck the World," says the graffiti they scrawl on the walls about us.

Well that too, and so what?

Take the Baja campaign. The last census showed that the black card population of California was entitled to enlarged Quarantine Zones. Catalina and San Francisco were bursting at the seams and the state legislature couldn't agree on a convenient piece of territory. So it got booted up to the Federal Quarantine Agency.

Old Walter T., he looks at the map, and he sees you could maintain a Quarantine line across the top of the Baja Peninsula with maybe two thousand SP troops. Real convenient. Annex the mother to California and solve the problem.

So in we go, and down the length of Baja we cakewalk. No sweat. Two weeks of saturation air strikes to soften up the Mexes, a heavy armored division and two wings of gunships at the point, followed by fifteen thousand of us zombies to nail things down.

What you call a fun campaign, a far cry from the mess we got into in Cuba or that balls-up in Venezuela, let me tell you. Mexico was something like fifty percent Got It, their armed forces had been wiped out of existence in the Chihuaha campaign, and so it was just a matter of three weeks of leisurely pillage, rape, and plunder.

The Mexes? They got a sweet deal, considering. Those who were still alive by the time we had secured Baja down to La Paz could choose between deportation to what was left of Mexico or becoming black card citizens of the state of California, Americans like thee and me, brothers and sisters. Any one of them who had survived had Gotten It in every available orifice about 150 times by us zombies by then anyway.

Wanna moralize about it? Okay, then moralize this one, meatfucker:

The damn Plague started in Africa, didn't it? That's the Third World, ain't it? Africa, Latin America, Asia, except for China, Japan, and Iran, they're over 50 percent Got It, ain't they? And the It they Got keeps mutating like crazy in all that filth. And they keep trying to get through with infiltrators to give *us* the latest strain, don't they?

The Chinese and the Iranians, they *kill* their black-carders, don't they? The Japs, they deport them to Korea. And the Russians, they nuked themselves a cordon sanitaire all the way from the Caspian to the Chinese border.

Was I old Walter T., I'd say nuke the whole cesspit of infection out of existence. Use nerve gas. Fry the Third World clean from orbit. Whatever. They gave us the damn Plague, didn't they? Way we see it in the Army of the Living Dead, anything we do after that is only a little piece of what the gorks got coming!

Believe me, this poor boy wasn't shedding any tears for what we had done to the Mexes when the marks starting coming out just before the sack of Ensenada. Less still when they couldn't come up with a combo of pallies that worked anymore, and they shrugged and finally told me it looked like I had reached Condition Terminal in the ruins of La Paz. Like I said, when I first Got It, they gave me six years, ten in the Army of the Living Dead.

Now they gave me six months.

I shot up with about a hundred milligrams of liquid crystal, chugalugged a quart of tequila, and butt-fucked every gork I could find. Think I blew about ten of them away afterward, but by then, brothers and sisters, who the hell was counting?

WALTER T. BIGELOW

Oh yes, I know what they say about me behind my back, even on a cabinet level. Old Walter T., he was a virgin when he married Elaine, and he's never even had meat with his own pure Christian wife. Old Walter T., he's never even stuck it in a sex machine. Old Walter T., he's never even missed the pleasures of the flesh. Old Walter T., he'd still be the same sexless eunuch even if there had never been a Plague. Old Walter T., he's got holy water for blood.

How little they know of my torments.

How little they know of what it was like for me in high school. In the locker room. With all those naked male bodies. All the little tricks I had to learn to hide my erections. Knowing what I was. Knowing it was a sin. Unable to look my own father squarely in the eye.

Walter Bigelow found Christ at the age of seventeen and was Born Again, that's what the official biography says. Alas, it was only partly true. Oh yes, I dedicated my life to Jesus when I was seventeen. But it was a cold, logical decision. It seemed the only means of controlling my unwholesome urges, the only way I could avoid damnation.

I hated God then. I hated Him for making me what I was and condemning me to hellfire should I succumb to the temptations of my own God-given nature. I believed in God, but I hated Him. I believed in Jesus, but how could I believe that Jesus believed in me?

I was not granted Grace until I was twenty.

My college roommate Gus was a torment. He flaunted his naked body in what seemed like total innocence. He masturbated under the bedclothes at night while I longed to be there with him.

One morning he walked into the bathroom while I was toweling myself down after a shower. He was nude, with an enormous erection. I could not keep my flesh from responding in kind. He confessed his lust for me. I let him touch me. I found myself reaching for his manhood.

He offered to do anything. My powers of resistance were at a low point. We indulged in mutual masturbation. I would go no further.

For months we engaged in this onanistic act, Gus offering me every fleshly delight I had ever fantasized, I calling on Christ to save me.

Finally, a moment came when I could resist no longer. Gus knelt on the floor before me, running his hands over my body, cupping my buttocks. I was lost. His mouth reached out for me—

And at that moment God at last granted me His Grace.

As his head lowered, I saw the Devil's mark upon the back of his neck, small as yet, but unmistakable—Karposi's sarcoma.

Gus had the Plague.

He was about to give it to me.

I leaped backward. Gus was an instrument of the Devil sent

to damn my flesh to the Plague and my soul to everlasting torment.

And at last I understood. I saw that it was *the Devil*, not God, who had tormented me with these unwholesome urges. And God had let me suffer them as a test and a preparation. A test of my worthiness and a preparation for this moment of revelation of His Divine Mercy. For had He not chosen to show me the Sign that saved me from my own sinful nature at this eleventh hour?

That was when I was granted true Grace.

I sank to my knees and gave thanks to God. *That* was when I was Born Again. *That* was when I became a true Christian. That too was when I was shown my true calling, when the vision opened up before me.

God had allowed the Devil to inflict the Plague on man to test us, even as I had been tested, for to succumb to the temptations of the flesh was to succumb to the Plague and be dragged, rotting and screaming, to Hell.

This was the fate that Jesus had saved me from, for only the Sign He had shown me had preserved me from death and eternal damnation. My life, therefore, was truly His, and what I must use it for was to protect mankind from this Plague and its carriers, to save those I could as Jesus had saved me.

And He spoke to me in my heart. "Become a leader of men," Jesus told me. "Save them from themselves. Do My work in the world."

I promised Him that I would. I would do it in the only way I could conceive of, through politics.

I became a prelaw major. I entered law school. I graduated with honors. I found, courted, and married a pure Christian virgin, and soon thereafter impregnated Elaine with Billy, ran for the Virginia State Assembly, and was elected.

The rest of my life is, as they say, history.

LINDA LEWIN

I was just another horny spoiled little brat until I Got It, just like all my horny spoiled little friends in Berkeley. Upper-middle-class family with an upper-middle-class house in the hills. My own car for my sixteenth birthday, along with the latest model sex interface.

Oh yes, they did! My mom and dad were no Unholy Rollers, they were educated intellectual liberal Democrats, they read all the literature, they had been children of the Sexy Seventies, they were realists, they knew the score.

These are terrible times, they told me. We know you'll be tempted to have meat. You might get away with it for years. Or you might Get It the first time out. Don't risk it, Linda. We know how you feel, we remember when everyone did meat. We know this is unnatural. But we know the consequences, and so do you.

And they dragged me out on the porch and made me look out across the Bay at San Francisco. The Bay Bridge with its blown-out center span. The pig boats patrolling the shoreline. The gunships buzzing about the periphery like angry horseflies.

Meat City. That's where you'd end up, Linda. Nothing's worth that, now is it?

I nodded. But even then, I wondered.

I had grown up with the vision of the shining city across the Bay. Oh yes, I had also grown up knowing that the lovely hills and graceful buildings and sparkling night lights masked a charnel house of the Plague, black-carders all, 100 percent. We were told horror stories about it in sex hygiene classes starting in kindergarten.

But from about the fifth grade on, we told ourselves our own stories too. We whispered them in the ladies' room. We uploaded them onto bulletin boards. We downloaded them, printed them out, wiped them from memory so our parents wouldn't see them, masturbated over the printouts.

As porn went, it was crude, amateurish stuff. What could you expect from teenage virgins? And it was all the same. A teenager Gets It. And runs away to San Francisco. Or disappears into the underground. And, sentenced to death already, sets out to enjoy all the pleasures of the meat on the way out, in crude, lurid, sensational detail. And of course, the porn sheets all ended long before Condition Terminal was reached.

But I was a good little girl and I was a smart little girl and the sex interface my parents gave me was the best money could buy, not some cheap one-way hooker's model. It had everything. The vaginal insert was certified to five atmospheres, but it was only fifty microns thick, heated to blood temperature, and totally flexible. It had a neat little clit-hood programmed for five varieties of electric stimulation and six vibratory patterns. I could wear the thing under my jeans, finger the controls, and never fail to come, even in the dullest math class.

The guys said that the interior lining was the max, tight and soft and wet, the stim programs the best there were. But what did they know? Who among them had ever felt real meat?

Oh yes, it was a wonderful sex interface my parents gave me to protect me from the temptations of the meat.

And of course I hated the damned thing.

Worse still when the guy I was balling with it insisted on wearing *his* interface too. Yech! His penile sheath in my vaginal insert. Like two sex machines doing it to each other. I remember an awful thing I did to one wimp who really pissed me off. I took off my interface, made him take off his, inserted his penile sheath in my vaginal insert, activated both interfaces, and made him sit there with me watching the two things go at each other without us for a solid hour.

And then there came Rex.

What can I say about Rex? I was eighteen. He was a year younger. He was beautiful. We never made it through two interfaces. I'd wear mine or he'd wear his and we'd go at it for hours. It was wonderful. We swore eternal love. We took to telling each other meatporn stories as we did it. This was it, I knew it was, we were soul mates for life. Rex swore up and down that he had never done meat and so did I. So why not . . .

Finally we did.

We took off our interfaces and did meat together. We tried out everything in those meatporn stories and then some. Every orifice. Every variation. Every day for two months.

Well, to make the usual long sad story short and nasty, I had been telling the truth, but Rex hadn't. And I had to learn about it from my parents.

Your boyfriend Rex's Got It, they told me one bright sunny morning. He's been black-carded and they've dropped him in San Francisco. You and he never . . . you didn't . . . because if you did, we're going to have to turn you in, you know that, don't you?

Well of course I freaked. But it was a cold slow-motion freak, with everything running through my head too fast for me to panic. I had a whole month till my next ID exam. I knew damn well my card would come up black. What should I do? Let them drop me in San Francisco and go out in a blaze of meatfucking glory with Rex? Yeah, sure, with the lying son of a bitch who had killed me!

I thought fast. I lied up and down. I threw an outraged temper tantrum when my parents suggested maybe I should go in for an early check. I convinced them. Or maybe I just let them convince themselves.

I found myself an underground doc and checked myself out. Got It. I drifted into the Berkeley underground, not as difficult as you might think for a girl who was willing to give meat to the secret Living Dead for a few dollars and a few more connections. I learned about how they kept ahead of the Sex Police. I learned about the phony blue cards. And I made my plans.

When I had hooked enough to score one, I got myself a primo counterfeit. As long as I found myself a wizard every three months to update the data strip, it would show blue. I could stay free until I died, unless of course I got picked up by the SP and got my card run against the national data bank, in which case I would turn up null and it would all be over.

I hooked like crazy, three, four, five tricks a day. I piled up a bankroll and kept it in bills. The day before I was to report for my ID update, I got in my car to go to school, said the usual goodbye to my parents, and took off, headed south.

South to Santa Cruz. South to L.A. South to anywhere. Out along the broad highway to see what there was to see of California, of what was left of America, out along the broad highway toward the eventual inevitable—crazed, confused, terror-stricken, brave with fatal knowledge, determined only to have a long hot run till my time ran out.

DR. RICHARD BRUNO

They used to call it midlife crisis, male menopause, the seven-year itch, back when it wasn't a condition to which you were condemned for life at birth.

I was just about to turn forty. I had dim teenage memories of quite a meaty little sex life back at the beginning of the Ugly Eighties, before the Plague, before I married Marge. Oh yes, I had been quite a hot little cocksman before it all fell apart, a child of the last half-generation of the Sexual Revolution.

When I was Tod's age, fifteen, I had already had more real meat than the poor frustrated little guy was likely to get in his whole life. Now I had to watch my own son sneaking around to sleazy sex parlors to stick it into sex machines, and don't think I was above it myself from time to time.

Marge, well . . .

Marge was five years younger than I. Just young enough to never have known what the real thing was like, young enough to remember nothing but condoms and vaginal dams and the early interfaces. Oh yes, we had meat together in the early years, before it finally resulted in Tod. Poor Marge was terrified the whole time, unable to come. After Tod was born, she got herself an interface, and never made love again without it.

Marge still loved me, I think, and I still loved her, but the Plague Years had dried her up sexually, turned her prudish and sour. She wouldn't even let me buy Tod an interface so he could get it from a real girl, if only secondhand. His sixteenth birthday is more than time enough, she insisted shrilly every time we fought about it, which was frequently.

Naturally, or perhaps more accurately unnaturally, all my libidinal energies had long since been channeled into my work. It was the perfect sublimation.

I was a genetic synthesizer for the Sutcliffe Corporation in Palo Alto. I had already designed five different Plague vaccines for Sutcliffe that made them hundreds of millions each before the virus mutated into immunity. I was the fair-haired boy. I got many bonuses. I had my own private lab with little restraint on my budget. For a scientist, it should have been heaven.

It wasn't.

It was maddening. A new Plague strain would appear and rise to dominance. I'd strip off the antigen coat, clone it, insert its genome in a bacterium, and Sutcliffe would market a vaccine to those who could afford it, make hundreds of millions in six months. Then the next immune strain would appear, and it would be back to square one. I felt like a scientific Sisyphus, rolling the dead weight of the Plague uphill, only to have it roll back and crush my hopes every six months.

Was I taking my work a bit too personally? Of course I was. My "personal life" consisted of the occasional interface sex with Marge, which I had long since come to loathe, watching my son sneaking around to sex machine parlors, and the occasional trip there myself. My "personal life" had been stolen from me by the Plague, by the Enemy, so of course I took my work personally.

I was obsessed. My work *was* my personal life. And I had a vision.

Cassette vaccines had been around for decades. Strip down a benign virus, plug in sets of antigens off several target organisms, and hey, presto, antibodies to several diseases conferred in a single shot.

Why not apply the same technique to the Plague? Strip one strain down to the core, hang it with antigen coats from four or five strains at once, and confer multistrain immunity. Certainly not to every mutation, but if I could develop an algorithm that could predict mutations, if I could develop cassette vaccines that *stayed ahead* of the viral mutations, might I not somehow be able eventually to force the Plague to mutate out?

Oh yes, I took the battle personally, or so I admitted to myself at the time. Little did I know just how personal it was about to become.

JOHN DAVID

No sooner had we finished mopping up in La Paz than my unit was airlifted up to the former Mexican border as part of the force that would keep it sealed until the SPs could set up their cordon. Through the luck of the draw, we got the sweetest billet, holding the line between Tijuana and San Diego.

They kept us zombies south of the former border, you better believe they didn't want us in Dago, no way they would let us set foot on real American soil, but meatfucker, you wouldn't *believe* the scene in TJ!

Back before the Plague, the place had been one big whorehouse and drug supermarket anyway. For fifteen years it had been a haven for underground black-carders, Latino would-be infiltrators, black pally docs, dealers in every contraband item that existed, getting poorer and more desperate as the cordon around Mexico tightened.

Now TJ found itself in the process of becoming an American Quarantine Zone, and it was Bugfuck City. Mexicans trying to get into Dago on false passports and blue cards. Wanted Americans trying to get out to anywhere. False IDs going for outrageous prices. Pussy and ass and drugs and uncertified pharmaceuticals and armaments going for whatever the poor bastards left holding them could get.

And the law, such as it was, until the SPs could replace the Legion, was *us*, brothers and sisters. Unbelievable! We could buy anything—drugs, phony blue cards, six-year-old virgins, you name it—or just have what we wanted at gunpoint. And money hand over fist, I mean we looted everything with no law but us to stop us, and did heavy traffic in government arms on top of it.

Loaded with money, we stayed stoned and drunk and turned that town into our twenty-four-hour pigpen, you better believe it! No one more so than me, brothers and sisters, with those marks coming out, knowing this could be my last big night to party.

I scored half-a-dozen phony blue cards and corroborating papers to match. I stuffed my pockets with money. I shot up with every half-baked pally TJ had to peddle, and they had everything from Russian biologicals to ground-up nun's tits in holy water. If this was my Condition Terminal, I was determined to take as much of the world with me as I could before I went out. I meatfucked myself deaf, dumb, and blind and must've Given It to five hundred Mexes in the bargain.

Then they started phasing in the Sex Police. Well, as you might imagine, there was no love lost between the Army of the Living Dead and the SPs. Those uptight Unholy Rollers took any opportunity to snuff us. Looters were shot. Meatfuckers caught in the act were executed. And of course, brothers and sisters, the Army of the Living Dead gave as good as we got and then some.

We'd kill any of the bastards we caught on what remained of our shrinking turf. We'd get up kamikaze packs and go into their turf after them. When we were really loaded, we'd catch ourselves some SP assholes and gang-bang them senseless. Needless to say, we weren't into using interfaces.

Things got so out of hand that the Pentagon brought in regular airborne troops to round us up. That little action took more casualties in two days than the whole Baja campaign had in three weeks.

When they started dropping napalm from close-support fighters, it finally dawned on those of us still around that the meatfuckers had no intention of rounding us up and shipping us to the next theater. They were out to kill us all, and they were probably working themselves up to tactical nukes to do it.

Well, we weren't the Army of the Living Dead for nothing. I don't know where it started or who started it. It just seemed to happen all at once. Somehow all of us that were left stuffed our loot in our packs, armed ourselves with whatever we could lay hands on, and suddenly there was a human wave assault on the border.

It was the bloodiest ragged combat any of us ever saw, crazed zombies against gunships, fighters, and tanks. How many of the bastards did we get on the way? More than you might imagine, better believe it, we were stoned, drunk, in a berserker rage, and we were now the Living Dead twice over, with Double Nothing to lose, triple so for yours truly.

How many of us got through? A thousand? Five hundred? Something to keep you from oversleeping, citizens. Hundreds of us zombies, our packs stuffed with money, false IDs and ordnance, over the border into San Diego, hunted, dying, betrayed by even the Army, with nothing left for kicks but to take our vengeance on *you*, meatfuckers!

And I was one of them. The meanest and the craziest, it pleases me to believe. Betrayed, facing Condition Terminal, with nothing left to do with what little was left of my life but bop till I dropped and take as many of you as I could with me.

LINDA LEWIN

I drove aimlessly around California for months, down 101 or the Coast Highway to Los Angeles, down 5 to San Diego, up to L.A. again, up 5 to the Bay Area, back around again, like a squirrel in a cage, like one of those circuit-riding preachers in an old Western.

I Had It. My days were numbered. I needed cash—for gas, for food, for a flop in a motel, for what pallies I could score, for updating the data strip on my phony blue card. I hooked wherever I could, using my interface always, for I swore to myself that I would never do to anyone what Rex had done to me. I didn't want to go to Condition Terminal with *that* mark on my soul.

Bit by bit, inch by inch, I drifted into the underground. You'd be surprised how many black-carders there were surviving outside the Quarantine Zones on phony IDs, a secret America within America, hiding within plain sight of the SPs, living by our wits and our own code.

We found one another by some kind of second sight impossible to explain. Pally pushers. ID wizards. Hookers just like me.

And not like me.

There were bars where we met to trade in pallies and IDs and information. You met all kinds. Pally dealers and drug dealers. ID wizards. Hookers like me, male and female, selling interface sex to the solid citizens. And hookers of the other kind.

Hookers selling meat.

It was amazing how many blue-carders were willing to risk death for the real thing. It was amazing how innocent some of them were willing to be. At first I refused to believe the stories the meatwhores told in the bars, cackling evilly all the time. I refused to believe that they were knowingly spreading the Plague and laughing about it. I refused to believe that blue-carders could be so stupid.

But they were and they could. And after a while, I understood.

There were people who would pay fantastic prices for meatsex with another certified blue-carder. There were clandestine meatbars where they hung out, bars with ID readers. Pick up one of these fools, pop your phony card in a reader, and watch their eyes light up as the strip read out blue, no line to the national data banks here, not with the SPs raiding any such bar they could get a line on. And you got paid more for a quick meatfuck than you could earn in a week of interface hooking.

Sure I was tempted. There was more to it than the money. Didn't I long for meat myself? Wasn't that how I had Gotten It in the first place? Didn't these damn blue-card assholes deserve what they got?

Who knows, I might have ended up doing it in the end if I hadn't met Saint Max, Our Lady of the Flowers.

Saint Max was a black-carder. He carried his own ID reader around and he didn't worry about phony cards reading out blue.

Saint Max would give meat only to certified *black*-carders, and he would never refuse anyone, even the most rotted-out Terminals.

I was in an underground bar in Santa Monica when Saint Max walked in, and half-a-dozen people told me his story before I ever heard it from his lips. Saint Max was a legend of the California underground. The only real hero we had.

Max was a bisexual, male or female, it didn't matter to him, and he never took money. People fed him, bought him drinks, gave him the latest pallies, found him free flop, sent him on his way. "I am dependent on the kindness of strangers," Max used to say. And in return, any black-carder stranger could depend on kindness from him.

Max was old; in terms of how long he had survived with God knew how many Plague strains inside him, he was ancient. He had lived in the San Francisco Quarantine Zone before it was a Quarantine Zone. And he was a man with a mission. He had this crazy theory.

I heard it from him that night after I had bought him a meal and about half-a-dozen drinks.

"I'm a living reservoir of every Plague strain extant, my dear," he told me. "And I do my best to keep up with the latest mutations."

Max believed that all black-carders had a moral obligation to have as much meatsex with one another as possible. So as to speed the pace of evolution. In a large enough pool of cross-infected Plague victims the virus might mutate out into something benign. Or a multiimmunity might evolve and spread quickly. A pathogen that killed its host was, after all, a mal-adapted organism, and as long as it was killing us, so were we.

"Natural selection, my dear. In the long run, it's our species' only hope. In the long run, everyone is going to Get It, and it's going to get most of us. But if out of the billions who will die, evolution eventually selects for multiimmunity, or a benign Plague variant, the human race will survive. And for as long as all these pallies keep me going, I intended to serve the process."

It seemed crazy to me, and I told him so, exposing yourself to every Plague strain you could. Didn't that mean Condition Terminal would just come quicker?

Saint Max shrugged. "Here I am," he said. "No one's been exposed to as many Plague variants as me. Maybe it's already happened. Maybe I've got multiimmunity. Maybe I'm a mutant. Maybe there's already a benign strain inside me."

He smiled sadly. "We're all under sentence of death the moment we're born anyway, now aren't we, my dear? Even the poor blue-carders. It's only a matter of how, and when, and in the pursuit of what. And like old John Henry, I intend to die with my hammer in my hand. Think about it, Linda."

And I did. I offered Max a ride up the coast and he accepted and we ended up traveling one full slow cycle of my circuit together. I watched Max giving meat freely to one and all, to kids like me new to the underground, to thieves, and whores, and horrible Terminals on the way out. No one took Saint Max's crazy theory seriously. Everyone loved him.

And so did I. I paid my way with the usual interface sex, and Max let it be until we were finally back in Santa Monica and it was time to say goodbye. "You're young, Linda," he told me. "With good enough pallies, you have years ahead of you. Me, I know I'm reaching the end of the line. You've got the heart for it, my dear. This old faggot would go out a lot happier knowing that there was someone like you to carry on. Think about it, my dear, 'A Short Life but a Happy One,' as they say in the Army of the Living Dead. And don't think we're all not in it."

I thought about it. I thought about it for a long time. But I didn't do anything about it till I saw Max again, till Max lay dying.

WALTER T. BIGELOW

After two terms in the Virginia Assembly, I ran for Congress and was elected. Capitol Hill was in a state of uproar over the Plague. National policy was nonexistent. Some states were quarantining Plague victims, others were doing nothing. Some states were testing people at their borders, others were calling this a violation of the Constitution. Some representatives were calling for a national health identity card, others considered this a civil rights outrage. Christian groups were calling for a national quarantine policy. Plague victims' rights groups were calling for an end to all restrictions on their free movements. Dozens of test cases were moving ponderously toward the Supreme Court.

After two terms watching this congressional paralysis, God inspired me to conceive of the National Quarantine Amendment. I ran for the Senate on it, received the support of Christians and Plague victims alike, and was elected by a huge majority.

The amendment nationalized Plague policy. Each state was required to set up Quarantine Zones proportional in area and economic base to the percentage of victims in its territory, said division to be updated every two years. Every citizen outside a Zone must carry an updated blue card. In return for this, Plague victims were guaranteed full civil and voting rights within their Quarantine Zones, and free commerce in nonbiological products was assured.

It was fair. It was just. It was inspired by God. Under my leadership it sailed through Congress and was accepted by three-quarters of the states within two years after I led a strenuous nationwide campaign to pass it.

I was a national hero. It was a presidential year. I was told that I was assured my party's nomination, that my election to the presidency was all but certain.

LINDA LEWIN

Saint Max had suddenly collapsed into late Condition Terminal. Indeed he was at the point of death when I finally followed the trail of the sad story to a cabin on a seacliff not far from Big Sur. There he lay, skeletal, emaciated, his body covered with sarcomas, semicomatose.

But his eyes opened up when I walked in. "I've been waiting for you, my dear," he said. "I wasn't about to leave without saying goodbye to Our Lady."

"Our Lady? That's *you*, Max."

"*Was*, my dear."

"Oh, Max . . ." I cried, and burst into tears. "What can I do?"

"Nothing, my dear . . . Or everything." His eyes were hard and pitiless then, yet also somehow soft and imploring.

"Max . . ."

He nodded. "You could give me one last meatfuck goodbye," he told me. He smiled. "I would have preferred a boy, of course, but at least it would please my old mother to know that I mended my ways on my deathbed."

I looked at his feverish, disease-ravaged body. "You don't know what you're asking!" I cried.

"Oh yes I do, my dear. I'm asking you to do the bravest thing you've ever done in your life. I'm asking you to believe in the faith of a dying madman. On the other hand, I'm asking for nothing at all, since you've already Got It."

How could I not? Either way, he was right. The Plague would kill me sooner or later no matter what I did now. I would never even know by how much this act of kindness would shorten my life span. Or if it would at all. And Max was dying. He had lived his life bravely in the service of humanity, at least as he saw it. And I loved him more in that moment than I had ever loved anyone in my life. And what if he was right? What other hope did humanity have? How could I refuse him?

I couldn't.

I didn't.

Afterward, as I held him, he spoke to me one last time. "Now for my last wish," he said.

"Haven't I just given it to you?"

"You know you haven't."

"What then?"

"You know, my dear."

So I did. I had accepted it when I took his ravaged manhood inside my unprotected body. I knew that now. I knew that I had known it all along.

"Will you take up this torch from me?" he said, holding out his hand.

"Yes, Max, I will," I promised and reached for the phantom object.

"Then this old faggot can go out happy," he said. And died in my arms with a smile on his lips.

And I became Our Lady. Our Lady of the Living Dead, as they were to call me.

JOHN DAVID

San Diego was crawling with SPs, and they probably would have sent in commando units to hunt us down, if they weren't so terrified of what would happen if the citizens were to find out that hundreds of us zombies were loose and on the warpath in the good old US of A.

And we were, meatfuckers, better believe it! Wouldn't you? Sooner or later they were going to get us all, and if they didn't, the Plague would, and in my case, sooner than later. So we scattered. I don't know what the others did, but me, I stayed drunk and stoned, and meatfucked as many of the treacherous blue-carders as I could lay my hands on. And tracked down all the pally pushers I could find. I don't even know what half the stuff I shot up was, but something in the mix, or maybe the mix itself, seemed to slow the Plague. I didn't get any better, but I seemed to stabilize.

But the situation in Dago didn't, brothers and sisters. It became one close call after another. Finally I got caught by a couple of stupid SPs. Well, those Unholy Rollers were no match for a zombie with my combat smarts. While they were running one of my phony cards through the national data bank and coming up null, I managed to kill the meatfuckers.

I picked my IDs off the corpses, but now the national data bank had me marked as a zombie on the run, and when they found these stiffs, they'd fax my photo to every SP station in the fifty states. The Sex Police took a real dim view of SP killers, and nailing me would be priority one.

I had only one chance, not that it was max probability. I had to disappear into a Quarantine Zone. San Francisco was the biggest, hence the safest. Also the tastiest, or so I was told.

So I snatched a car and headed north. How I would break *into* a Zone, I'd have to figure out later. If, by some chance, I managed to avoid the SPs long enough to get there.

WALTER T. BIGELOW

Congress set up the Federal Quarantine Agency to administer the National Quarantine Amendment. It would have enormous power and enormous responsibility. It was the wisdom of Congress, with which I heartily concurred, that it be entirely insulated from party politics. The director would be chosen in the manner of Supreme Court justices—nominated by the president, approved by the Senate, serving for life, removable only by impeachment.

After the president signed the bill, he called me into his office and pleaded with me to accept the appointment. It was my amendment. I was the only political figure who had the confidence of both Plague victims and blue-carders.

All that, I knew, was true. What was also true was that many insiders blanched at the thought of a Bigelow presidency. This was the perfect political solution.

It was the most important decision of my life and the most difficult. Elaine had had her heart set on being First Lady. "You just *can't* let them take the presidency away from you like this," she insisted. Ministers and black-carder groups and politicians of my own party, some sincere, some otherwise, begged me to accept the lifetime directorship of the FQA. For weeks, they all badgered me while I procrastinated and prayed.

It seemed as if the voices of God and the Devil were speaking to me through my wife, party leaders, men of God, men of power, saints and sinners, battling for possession of my soul. But which was the voice of God and which the voice of Satan? Which way did my true duty lie? What did God want me to do?

Finally, I went on a solitary retreat into the Utah desert, into Zion National Park. I fasted. I prayed. I called on Jesus to speak to me.

And at length a voice did speak to me, in a vision. "You are the Moses I have chosen to lead My people out of the wilderness," it told me. "Have I not commanded you to become a leader of men? Those who would deny you power are the agents of the Adversary."

But then another stronger and sweeter voice spoke out of a great white light and I knew that this was truly Jesus and whose the first voice had really been.

"I saved you from the Plague and your own sinful desire in your hour of need," He told me. "I raised you up from the pit so that you might do God's will on Earth. As I gave up My life to save Man from sin, so must you give up worldly power to save the people from their dark natures. As God chose Me for My Calvary, so do I choose you for yours."

I returned from the desert to Washington and I obeyed. I put the thought of worldly glory behind me. There were those who snickered when I accepted this appointment. There were those who laughed when I told the nation that I had done it at the bidding of Jesus.

Even my wife told me I was a fool, and a breach was opened between us that I knew no way to heal. We became strangers to each other sharing the same marriage bed.

Oh yes, I paid dearly for my obedience to God's will. But while I may have lost my chance at worldly power and hardened my wife's heart against me, I remained steadfast and strong.

For God had saved me in that dormitory room with Gus and granted me Grace and salvation. And Jesus spoke truth to me in the desert in the presence of the Adversary and saved me again. And so in my heart I knew I had done right.

DR. RICHARD BRUNO

How could I have done such a thing? How could I, of all people, have been naïve enough to Get It from a meatwhore? As the ancient saying has it, a stiff dick knows no conscience, and they don't call a fool a stupid prick for nothing.

For my fortieth birthday, I got royally drunk and righteously stoned, and I demanded a special birthday present from Marge. Was it really too much to ask from one's own wife on the night of the rite de passage of my midlife crisis? Tender loving meat for my Fateful Fortieth? We were both blue-carders. Marge had hardly any sex life at all. The only times I had been unfaithful to her were with radiation-sterilized sex machines.

I was loaded and raving, but she was entirely irrational. She refused. When I attempted to get physical, she locked herself in the bedroom and told me to go stick it in one of my goddamn sex machines.

I reeled out into the streets, stoned out of my mind, aching with despair, with a raging fortieth-birthday hard-on. But I didn't slink off to the usual sex machine parlor, oh no; that was what Marge had told me to do, wasn't it?

Instead, I found myself one of those clandestine meatbars. To make the old long story modern and short, I picked up a whore. We inserted our cards in the bar's reader and of course they both came up blue. Off I went to her room and did every kind of meat I could think of and some that seemed to be her own inventions.

I staggered home, still loaded, and passed out on the couch. The Morning After . . .

Oh my God!

Beyond the inevitable horrid hangover and conjugal recriminations, I awoke to the full awfulness of what I had done. In my present sober and thoroughly detumescent state, I knew all too well how many phony blue cards were floating around the meatbars. Had I . . . ?

I ran the standard tests on myself in my own lab for six days. On the sixth day, they came up black. When I cultured the bastard, it turned out to be a Plague variant I had not yet seen.

By this time I had prepared myself for the inevitable. I had made my plans. As fortune would have it, I had ten weeks before my next ID update, ten weeks to achieve what medical science had failed to achieve in twenty years and more of trying.

But I had motivation. If I failed, in ten weeks I would lose my blue card, my job, my mission in life, my wife, my family, and with no one to blame but myself. At this point, I wasn't even thinking about the fact that I was under sentence of eventual death. What would happen in ten weeks was more than disaster enough to keep me working twenty hours a day, or so at least it seemed.

And, crazed creature that I was, I had a crazy idea, one that, in retrospect, I saw I had been moving toward all along.

My work on cassette vaccines was already well advanced, so might it not be possible to push it one step further, and synthesize an *automatic self-programming* cassette vaccine? It might be pushing the edge of the scientific possible, but it was my only hope. A crazy idea, yes, but was not madness just over the edge from inspiration?

I stripped a Plague virus down to the harmless core in the usual manner. But I didn't start hanging on the usual series of antigen coat variants. I started crafting a series of nanomanipulators out of RNA fragments, molecular "tentacles."

What I was after was an organism that would infect the same cells as the Plague. That would seize any strain of Plague virus it found, destroy the core, and wrap the empty antigen coat around itself, much as a hermit crab crawls inside a discarded seashell in order to protect its nakedness from the world.

In effect, a killed-virus vaccine that could still reproduce as an organism, an organism continually reprogramming its antigen coat to mimic lethal invaders, that would use the corpses of the Enemy to stimulate the production of antibodies to it, a living, self-programming cassette vaccine factory within my own body.

The theory was simple, cunning, and elegant. Actually synthesizing such a molecular dreadnaught was something else again . . .

LINDA LEWIN

The story of what happened on Saint Max's deathbed became a legend of the underground. And whereas Max had been old and had long since outlived any rational expectations of survival, I was young, I appeared healthy, and so what I was risking was readily apparent.

Like Saint Max, Our Lady gave the comfort of her meat to anyone who asked her. I gave freely of my body to young black-carders like myself, to rotting Terminals, to every underground black-carder between.

Perhaps because I was young, perhaps because I was the first convert to Saint Max's vision daring enough to put it into practice, perhaps because I was so much more naïvely earnest about it than he had been, perhaps because I appeared to be in such robust health, there were those who believed in it now, who believed in me, in the Faith of Our Lady. If Saint Max had been our Jesus, and I was our Paul, now there were disciples to spread the Faith, no more than scores, maybe, but at least more than Christianity's original twelve.

Spreading the Faith of Saint Max and Our Lady. Gaining converts with our hope and our bodies as we wandered up and down California. The Plague strains would spread faster now. Millions might die sooner who might have lingered longer. But were we not all under sentence of death anyway, blue-carders and black-carders alike?

Millions of lives might be shortened, but out of all that death, the species might survive. We would challenge the Plague head-on, in the only way we could—love against despair, sex against death. We would force the pace of evolution and/or die trying.

And while we lived, we would at least live free, we would live, and love, and fight for our species' survival as natural men and women. Better in fire than in ice.

WALTER T. BIGELOW

I had done as God commanded, I was doing His work, but the Devil continued to torment me. Elaine remained distant and cold, the Plague continued to spread despite my best efforts, and then, at length, Satan, not content with this, reached out and put his hand upon my Billy.

Billy, the son I had raised so carefully, the son who to my joy had Found the Light at the age of fourteen, began to act strangely, moping in his room at night, locking himself in the bathroom for suspiciously long intervals. I didn't need to be the director of the Federal Quarantine Agency to suspect what was happening; any good Christian father could read the signs.

I was prepared to find pornography when I searched his room one morning after he had left for school, but nothing could have prepared me for the vile nature of the filth I found. Photographs of men having meatsex with each other. With young boys. Photographs of naked young boys in the lewdest of poses. And, worse still, hideous cartoons of boys and girls having the most impossible and revolting intercourse with sex machines, automated monstrosities with grotesque vulvas, immense penile organs, done up to simulate animals, robots, tentacled aliens from outer space.

I reeled. My skin crawled. My stomach went cold. Worst of all, the Devil caused my weak flesh to become loathsomely aroused as all those terrible and tantalizing memories of Gus came rushing back between my legs to haunt me.

Revolted, appalled, shaking with outrage and confusion, I was forced to wait until the evening to confront him, and the Devil struck me a second blow in the office, for that was the day when the first reports of the Satanic cult of Our Lady of the Living Dead appeared in my electronic mailbox.

Of course I was aware that there were hundreds of thousands, perhaps millions, of black-carders living underground outside the Quarantine Zones on bogus blue cards, and spreading their filth among the innocent. We caught hundreds of them every week.

But this . . . this . . . this was Satan's masterstroke!

Out there in California was a woman, or perhaps several women, known as Our Lady of the Living Dead, clearly possessed by the Adversary and doing his work quite consciously, recruiting others into her Satanic cult, spreading his lies and the Plague in ever-wider circles.

Black-carders were openly offering their meat to their fellow black-carders, spreading multiple strains of Plague virus throughout the underground. Interrogations seemed to indicate that these slaves of Satan actually believed that they were the saviors of the species, that in some mystical manner they were speeding the course of evolution, that somehow out of their unholy and deadly couplings a strain of humanity would evolve that was immune to the Plague.

He is not the Prince of Liars for nothing. He had apparently quite convinced these poor doomed creatures of this one, cunningly using their despair-maddened lust and turning it against us all, giving them a truly devilish excuse to wallow in it until they died in the conviction that they were doing God's Work in the process.

And laughing at them and at me by causing his servant to wrap herself in the cognomen of the Mother of Jesus!

I gave the necessary orders. The stamping out of the cult of Our Lady was to be the SP's number one priority. Arrest these people. If any resisted, shoot to kill. Close as many meatbars as possible. And do it all as conspicuously as could be managed. Spread the fear of God's wrath and that of the SP among the denizens of the underground.

After a day like that, I was constrained to return home and confront Billy. There was denial, sobbing confession, promises of repentance, and strong penances set. I had done my patriotic duty and my fatherly duty. It had been hard, but I had done God's will and was as at peace as one could be under the terrible circumstances.

But Satan was still not finished with me. He seized Elaine, my good Christian wife, and caused her to launch into the most appalling tirade. "How can you be so hard-hearted?" she demanded. "Aren't things bad enough for young people growing up these days? At least you shouldn't try to keep Billy from a little safe masturbation."

"It's against God's law! Besides, you saw that revolting, unnatural—"

"Of course it's unnatural, Walter! What else can you expect when the most natural thing in the world is the one thing none of us can do anymore!"

"Elaine—"

"If you were a real man, Walter T. Bigelow, if you were a real Christian, if you were a real loving father, you'd take the poor boy to a sex machine parlor and show him how to get some harmless release!"

I could hardly believe my ears for a long moment. This could not be Elaine! But then I understood. This insinuating blasphemy was coming from her lips, but my poor wife was only an instrument. The voice saying these awful things through her had identified itself by the very act of causing a good Christian woman to mouth them.

"I know you . . ." I muttered.

"No you don't, Walter Bigelow, you don't know me at all!"

"Get thee behind me—"

"Have it your own way!" she shouted. And she locked herself in the bedroom, leaving me to spend a sleepless night in the living room, praying to Jesus, demanding to know why He had so forsaken me in the presence of the Enemy.

JOHN DAVID

I made my way up the coast toward San Francisco real slowly, spending nearly a month in Los Angeles, which was big, and sprawling, and a hell of a town for a zombie to party in. There were plenty of meatbars, my latest batch of pallies seemed to be holding up real well, I was looking' good, I had umpteen phony blue cards, and I was able to meatfuck myself near to exhaustion. It was almost too easy.

And then one night I found out why.

I let myself get picked up on the street by this sexy space case who told me she'd give me free meat if I was a *black*-carder, if you can believe that one. Well, she was beautiful, I was real stoned and in a kind of funny mood, so I shoved her into an alley, Gave It to her, and then announced my wonderful secret identity as a black-card-carrying zombie of the Army of the Living Dead, expecting to get my jollies watching her freak.

Only she didn't. She smiled at me. She fuckin' kissed me, and she told me I was doin' the Work of Our Lady whether I knew it or not.

Say what? Say who?

And she told me.

She told me that whether I knew it or not, I was a soldier in a different army now, an army called the Lovers of Our Lady. Whose mission it was to have meat with as many people as possible in order to save the species, if you can believe *that* one, brothers and sisters! That somehow by all of us Giving as many strains of It to each other as we could, we might end up with multiimmune humans.

Believe it when they tell you L.A. is full of all kinds of weirdos, brothers and sisters!

But soon the weirdness began getting ominous. All of a sudden the SPs were swarming all over the meatbars like flies on horseshit, running every last customer they caught through the national data bank no matter how long it took. The underground safe houses were no longer so safe. They were grabbing people at random on the streets and blowing away anyone who showed any resistance. I mean, suddenly the Sex Police were real agitated.

I never did find out whether they were hot after me and my fellow zombies or what, I mean after a few close calls, there was clearly no percentage in sticking around to find out. Especially since the pallies were starting to wear off once more and I was getting to lookin' obvious and ragged. San Francisco was beginning to look like my best bet again after all.

I snatched me another car and headed north again, staying away from the population centers, meatfucking my way slowly up the center of California, following a kind of secret underground circuit.

It was real easy, once I got the hang of it and picked up on the stories. That weirdo back in L.A. had given me a good steer. All I had to tell these assholes was that I was doin' the Work of Our Lady and they'd do me anything.

DR. RICHARD BRUNO

It was arduous, but my little dreadnaught was ready with five days to spare, and it was even more elegant than my original concept. Like the Plague itself, it infected via the usual sexual or intravenous vectors, colonizing semen, blood, and mucous membrane. Unlike the Plague, however, it did not interfere with T-cell activity or production. Lacking an antigen coat, it was "invisible" to the host immune system.

As a retrovirus, it would write itself into host genomes, so that when it expressed itself during cellular reproduction, it would invade two more cells, a process that would continue until all suitable host cells were infected.

If an invading retrovirus should be encountered during the expression phase, it would destroy the active core and wrap itself in the "dead" antigen coat. If the host already had antibodies to these antigens, that variant would die. If not, it would eventually write itself back into a host genome, shedding the antigen "shell" in the process.

Thus, when a retrovirus invaded the host, the host bloodstream would become saturated with empty invader antigen coats, to which the host immune system would eventually form antibodies, conferring immunity to the invader precisely in the manner of a "killed virus" vaccine.

It not only conferred immunity to all strains of the Plague virus, it would automatically immunize the host against *all* retroviruses. And, like the Plague, it would spread via sexual contact.

That was what my molecular analysis predicted. It remained only to test the dreadnaught. But there was a stringent law against introducing into human hosts a live, genetically tailored organism capable of reproduction outside the lab, even for test purposes. It would take congressional legislation to allow me to begin human tests, and even then it could be years before the dreadnaught received FDA certification.

And I had only five days. In five days, I was up for ID card updating. If I tested out black, which I would, I would lose my job and be dumped unceremoniously into the San Francisco Quarantine Zone, and all would be lost.

I had only one chance to keep my blue card long enough to see the whole process through. I myself would have to be my first test subject. If it didn't work, all was lost anyway. If it did—and I was convinced it would—no one ever need know that I had violated the FDA regulations.

So I injected myself with the dreadnaught culture. Three days later, my body was free of the Plague. I took some of my blood and exposed it to other Plague strains as well as a variety of other retroviruses. My dreadnaught killed them all.

I called Harlow Prinz, the president of Sutcliffe, and asked for a special meeting of the board of directors, at which I promised to present the greatest advance in medicine in the last fifty years and then some. I could all but hear him drooling.

The Nobel for medicine seemed a certainty.

And, seeing as how the dreadnaught would spread itself by sexual contact without the need for economically prohibitive mass inoculation, it could eliminate the Plague from the festering Third World as well, so a second Nobel, this one for peace, might not be beyond the bounds of possibility.

WALTER T. BIGELOW

Elaine refused to have interface sex with me at all. She refused to sleep in the same bedroom with me. She took to disparaging my manhood. Meals were undercooked, overcooked, slovenly prepared. Her housekeeping deteriorated. She kept insisting that I introduce Billy to the sex machine parlors and called my righteous refusal "un-Christian."

I no longer knew the woman I lived with. Elaine was now acting like a woman with a secret life, indeed like a woman hiding an adulterous relationship. Was it possible? How long had it been going on? Had she been making a fool of me all these years?

Of course I had the necessary resources to find out. I had her followed. But what the reports revealed was no human lover.

There were written accounts. There were still photos. There was even an ingeniously obtained clandestine video.

Elaine was a sex machine addict.

Almost every day when I was away at work, she visited one of several sex machine parlors, and stayed for at least an hour, engaging in machine sex perversions of which I had previously been unaware, which I had not even previously believed possible.

When I confronted her with the evidence, she defiantly admitted that she had been doing it secretly for years. "You just haven't been satisfying me, Walter."

"Adulteress!"

"*Adulteress?* Just the opposite! I've been doing it to *keep from becoming* an adulteress!"

"It's against God's law!"

"Show me anything in the scriptures against it!"

"It's the sin of Onan!"

"Good Lord, Walter, it's the Plague, can't you see that?"

"Of course I can see that! God is testing us, and you've failed Him."

"*I've* failed *Him*? Or has *He* failed *us*?

"Blasphemy!"

"Is it?" she insinuated "Can it be Jesus's God of Love who has taken natural love itself away from us and forced us into all these perversions? Look what's happened to us! Look what's happened to Billy! Where is God's Love in all that?"

"It's the Devil tormenting us, not God, Elaine!"

"That's what I'm telling you, Walter Bigelow! The Plague is the work of the Devil, not God. So anything that helps us survive Satan's torment—the interfaces, the sex machines—must be God's mercy. Jesus loves us, doesn't He? He can't want us to suffer any more than we have to!"

And then I knew for certain.

Not the Prince of Liars for nothing.

My Elaine had neither the evilness of spirit nor the cunning of mind to say these things to me. She was clearly possessed by the Devil.

Christian and husbandly duty coincided.

I placed Elaine under clandestine house arrest.

And began consulting exorcists.

DR. RICHARD BRUNO

They were all there—Harlow Prinz, the president of Sutcliffe, Warren Feinstein, the chairman of the board, and the entire board of directors. They all had dollar signs in their eyes as I began my presentation. They listened with rapt silence as I proceeded, a silence that grew rather ominous and eerie as I went on.

And the conclusion of my presentation fell into a deathly graveyard hush that seemed to go on forever. I finally had to break it myself.

"Uh . . . any questions?"

"This, ah, dreadnaught virus is a self-replicating organism? It will reproduce by itself outside the lab?"

"That's right."

"And it spreads like the Plague?"

"It can easily enough be made pandemic."

"Who has had access to this information?"

"Why, no one outside this room," I told them. "I did this one on my own."

Like a crystal suddenly dissolving back into solution, the hushed atmosphere shattered into a series of whispered cross-conversations. After a few minutes of this, Prinz snapped orders into his intercom.

"Security to lab twelve! Seal it off. No one in or out except on my personal orders. Get a decontamination team down there and execute Code Black procedures."

"*Code Black?*" I cried. "There's no Code Black in my lab! No pathogen release! No—"

"Shut up, Bruno! Haven't you done enough already?" Prinz shouted at me. "You've created an artificial human parasite, you imbecile! The FDA will crucify us!"

"*If* we report it . . ." Feinstein said slowly.

"Yes . . ." Prinz said.

"What are you going to do, Harlow?"

"I've already done it. We'll follow maximum Code Black procedure. Incinerate the contents of lab twelve, then pump it full of molten glass. We'll keep this an internal matter. It never happened."

"But what about *him?*"

"Indeed . . ." Prinz said slowly. "Security to the boardroom!" he snapped into his intercom.

"What the hell is going on?" I finally managed to demand.

"You've committed a very serious breach of FDA regulations, Dr. Bruno," Feinstein told me. "One that could have grave consequences for the company."

"But it's a monumental breakthrough!" I cried. "Haven't you heard a word I've said? It's a cure for all possible Plague variants! It'll save the country from—"

"It would destroy Sutcliffe, you cretin!" Prinz shouted. "Fifty-two percent of our gross derives from Plague vaccines, and another twenty-one percent from the sale of palliatives! And your damned dreadnaught is a *venereal disease*, man—it wouldn't even be a marketable product!"

"But surely the national interest—"

"I'm afraid you haven't considered the national interest at all, Dr. Bruno," Feinstein said much more smoothly. "The medical industry's share of GNP has been twenty-five percent for years, and the Plague is hard-wired into our economy; your dreadnaught would have precipitated a massive depression."

"And destroyed the whole raison d'etre of our policy vis-à-vis the Third World."

"Thereby shattering the Soviet-Chinese-American-Japanese entente and rekindling the Cold War."

"Leading to a nuclear Armageddon and the destruction of our entire species!"

What monstrous sophistry! What sheer insanity! What loathsome utterly self-interested bullshit! They *couldn't* be serious!

But just then two armed guards entered the boardroom, and their presence suddenly forced me to realize just how serious the board really was. They were already destroying the organism. From their own outrageously cold point of view, their hideous logic was quite correct. The dreadnaught virus *would* reduce the medical industry to an economic shadow of its former self. Sutcliffe *would* fold. And their jobs and their fortunes would be gone. . . .

"Dr. Bruno is not to be allowed to leave the premises or to

communicate with the outside,'' Prinz told the guards. They crossed the room to flank my chair with pistols at the ready.

"What are we going to do with him?"

How far would they really go to protect their own interests?

"Perhaps Dr. Bruno has met with an unfortunate accident in the lab . . ." Prinz said slowly.

My God, were they *deadly* serious?

"Surely you're not suggesting . . . ?" Feinstein exclaimed, quite aghast.

"The organism is being destroyed, we can wipe his research notes from the data banks, no one else knows, we can hardly afford to leave loose ends dangling," Prinz said. "You have any better ideas, Warren?"

"But—"

Did I panic? Did I become one of them? Was I acting out of ruthless self-interest myself, or following a higher imperative? Or all four? Who can say? All I knew then was that my life was on the line, that I had to talk my way out of that room, and the words came pouring out of me before I even thought them, or so it seemed.

"One million dollars a year," I blurted.

"What?"

"That's my price for silence. I want my salary raised to one million a year."

"That's preposterous!"

"Is it? You've said yourself that the survival of Sutcliffe is at stake. Cheap at twice the price!"

"Cheaper and safer to eliminate the problem permanently," Prinz said.

"Ye Gods, Harlow, you're talking about murder!" Feinstein cried. "Dr. Bruno's suggestion is much more . . . rational. He'd hardly be about to talk while we're paying him a million a year for his silence!"

"He's right, Harlow!"

"The other's too risky."

"I don't like it, we can't trust—"

"He'll have to agree to accept an appointment to the board," Feinstein said. "Meaning that he knowingly accepts legal responsibility for our actions. Besides, we're destroying the organism, aren't we? Who would believe him anyway?"

"Will you agree to Warren's terms?" Prinz asked me.

I nodded silently. In that moment, I would have agreed to *anything* that would let me get out of the building alive.

Only later, driving home, did I ponder the consequences of what I had agreed to, did I consider what on Earth I was going to do next. What could I possibly tell Marge and Tod? How could I explain our sudden enormous riches?

And what about my mission, my Hippocratic oath, my duty to suffering humanity? Those imperatives still existed, and the decision was still in my hands. For what the board fortunately did not know was that the dreadnaught virus had *not* been completely destroyed. The sovereign cure for the Plague was still alive and replicating in my body. I was immune to all possible Plague variants.

And that immunity was infectious.

JOHN DAVID

I made my way up the coast to the Bay Area, and there I was stymied, brothers and sisters. I kept on the move—San Jose, Oakland, Marin County, and back again in tight little circles. The SPs were everywhere, they were really paranoid, they were rounding up people at random on the street, and it wasn't only the likes of me they were after.

The Word had come down from the usual somewhere to put the heat on. The SPs around the meatbars were tighter than a ten-year-old's asshole. Everyone they rousted got their cards run through the national data bank, I mean there were roadblocks and traffic jams ten miles long. People were disappearing wholesale. And the poop in the underground was that they were doing all this to come down as hard as they knew how on anyone "doing the work of Our Lady."

And that was me, brothers and sisters. I mean, I was determined to meatfuck anything I could anyway, and calling myself a "Lover of Our Lady" was not only the best come-on line anyone had ever invented, it was ready access to the safe houses that were opening up everywhere in response to the heat, to cheap and even free pallies, to the whole black-carder underground. For sure, I'm not saying that I bought any of that bullshit about sacred duty to evolve immunity into the species, but I sure dished plenty of it out when it made life easy.

But why did I stick around the Bay Area in the middle of the worst Sex Police action in the country when sooner or later I figured to get caught in a sweep? When I did, and my phony blue card came up null, they'd run a make on my prints and come up with my Legion record, and then they'd for sure flush me down their toilet bowl, you better believe it!

Well, for one thing, the marks were coming out again, I was beginning to get moldy and obvious, and here at least I had some chance of disappearing into the underground. And for another, I was getting weak and feverish and maybe not thinking too clearly.

And there was San Francisco, clearly visible across the Bay. Where the SPs never went. The only safe place for a wanted zombie like me. The only place I could bop till I dropped. Sitting there staring me in the face. Somehow, getting there had become a goal in itself, something I just had to do before I went under. What else was left?

But there was an impenetrable line of razor wire and laser traps and crack SP troops across the Peninsula behind it and a bay full of pig boats patrolling its coastline and enough gunships buzzing around it day and night to take Brazil. All designed to keep the meatfuckers inside. But just as effective in keeping the likes of me out.

No one ever got out of San Francisco. And there was only one way in. Your card came up black, and the SPs loaded you into a chopper and dumped you inside from five feet up. But if the SP ever got its meathooks on me, they'd punch my ticket for sure, and not for San Francisco, you better believe it!

The only other way in was a loner kamikaze run on the blockade, and that was even more certain death. Oh yeah, I knew I was deep into Condition Terminal now, but *that* spaced out yet, I wasn't!

DR. RICHARD BRUNO

What I did, for the time being, was nothing. I banked my new riches in a separate account and told Marge nothing. I showed up at the lab every day and puttered around doing nothing.

I staggered around in a trance like a moral zombie, hating myself every waking moment of every awful day. I had successfully performed my life's mission. I had conquered the Enemy. I could have been the Savior of mankind. I *should* have been the Savior of mankind.

Instead, all I could do was hide the secret from my wife and collect my blood money.

Would I have done it on my own? Would morality finally have been enough? Would I have ultimately been faithful to the oath of Hippocrates? I would never know.

My son Tod took the decision out of my hands.

One night the Sex Police showed up at our house with Tod in custody. He had been caught in a raid on a meatbar. His card had come up blue against the national data bank and he had passed a spot genome test that I had never heard of before, so they really had nothing to hold him for.

But they read Marge and myself the riot act. This kid was caught peddling his ass in a meatbar, we don't know how long he's been doing it, he claims it was his first time. He's blue now, but you know what the odds are. Get the horny little bastard an interface and scare the the shit out of him, or he's gonna end up as Condition Terminal in San Francisco.

While Marge broke down and wept, I had my awkward man-to-man with Tod, poor little guy. "Do you realize what you've been risking?" I demanded.

He nodded miserably. "Yeah," he said, "but . . . but isn't it worth it?"

"Worth it!"

"Oh, Dad, you knew what it was like, flesh on flesh without all this damned metal and rubber! How could you expect me to live my whole life without ever having that?"

"It's your *life* we're talking about, Tod!"

"So what!" he cried defiantly. "We're all gonna die sooner or later anyway! I'd rather live a real life while I can than die an old coward without every knowing anything but interfaces and sex machines! I'd rather take my chances and be a man! I'd rather die brave than live like . . . like . . . like a pussy! Wouldn't you?"

What could I possibly say to that? What would *he* say if he knew my wonderful and awful secret? How could I even look my own son in the eye, let alone continue this lying lecture? What could I possibly do now?

Only one thing.

If I was still too much of a cowering creature to save the world at the expense of my own life, at least I could contrive to save my son, and without alerting the powers at Sutcliffe in the process. And at least covertly pass this awful burden off to someone else.

Tod's plight had shown me the way and given me the courage to act.

A stiff dick might ordinarily know no conscience. But mine was the exception that proved the rule. It *was* my conscience now. *Use me,* it demanded. *Use me and let a Plague of life loose in the world.*

LINDA LEWIN

"I may be a meatwhore, but I'm not a monster!" I told him indignantly. "What you're asking me to do is the most loathsome thing I've ever heard!"

He had approached me in a meatbar in Palo Alto.

I had been spending a lot of time in such places lately, for here the Work of Our Lady was doubly important. For here bitter and twisted black-carders came with their phony blue cards to take sexual vengeance on foolish blue-carders. Every time I could persuade one of these wretches to take their comfort in me, I saved someone from the Plague. And every time I could persuade him afterward to do the Work of Our Lady instead of infecting more blue-carders, the ranks of the Lovers of Our Lady grew.

But Richard, as he called himself, was something different, the lowest creature I had ever encountered even in a place like this.

He wanted me to have meat with him, and then, a week later, to have meat with his own teenage son! And I could name my own price.

"What's so terrible about that?" he said ingenuously. "Your card will come up blue, won't it?" But his sickly twisted grin told me all too well that he knew the truth. Or part of it.

I knew what a chance I was taking. He could be undercover SP. He could be anything. But if I just refused and walked away, he'd only find another meatwhore with a phony blue card more than willing to take his money to do this terrible thing.

"I'm *her*," I told him. "I'm Our Lady of the Living Dead."

He didn't even know who Our Lady was or the nature of the Work we were doing. So I told him.

"And that's why I won't do what you ask. I only have sex with black-carders. I've Got It. And I'll give the Plague to you and your son. And so would any meatwhore you're likely to find. Don't you really know that?"

"You don't understand," he insisted. "How could you? You can't give me the Plague, no one can. I'm immune."

"You're *what*?"

And he told me the most outrageous story. He told me that he was Dr. Richard Bruno of the Sutcliffe Corporation, that he had developed an organism that conferred immunity to all Plague variants. That he could infect me with it and make me a carrier. That's why he wanted me to have meat with his son, to pass this so-called dreadnaught virus to him.

"Your really expect a girl to believe a line like that?"

"You don't have to believe anything now," he told me. "Just have meat with me now; you've already Got It, so you have nothing to lose. A week later, meet me here, and I'll take you to a doctor. We'll do a full workup. If you test out blue, you'll know I'm telling the truth. I'll give you fifty thousand right now, and another fifty thousand after you've had meat with Tod. Even if I'm lying, you're still a hundred thousand richer, and you've lost nothing."

"But if you're lying to me, I'll have given you the Plague!" I told him. "I won't risk that."

"Why not? I'm the one taking the risk, not you."

"But—"

"You *do* know what I'll do if you refuse, don't you?" he said, leering at me. "I'll just offer someone with less scruples the same deal. Even if I'm just a lying lunatic, you won't have saved anyone from anything."

He had me there. I shrugged.

"I've got a room just around the corner," I told him.

DR. RICHARD BRUNO

It was the best sexual experience I've ever had in my life, or at any rate since my teenage years, back before the Plague. Flesh on flesh with no intervening interface or rubber, and with no fear of infection either, the pure simple naked act as it was meant to be. And while some part of me knew that it was adultery, an act of disloyalty to Marge, a better and higher part of me knew that it was an act of loyalty to a higher moral imperative—to Tod, to suffering humanity—and that only sharpened my pleasure.

But I did feel shame afterward and not for the adultery. For *this*, this pure simple act of what was once quite ordinary and natural pleasure, was what I had the power to bring back into the world, not just for me and for her and for Tod, but for everyone everywhere. This was my victory over the Enemy. And what was I doing with it?

Nothing. I was taking a million dollars a year's blood money to hold my silence and, admittedly, to preserve my own life.

But now that I had already taken the first step upon it, a way opened up before me. I could hold my silence and keep taking the money, but I could spread the dreadnaught virus far and wide, via this cult of Our Lady and my own clandestine action.

The moral imperatives of the oath of Hippocrates and the fondest desire of any man coincided. It was my duty to have meat with as many women as I could as quickly as possible.

LINDA LEWIN

I hadn't even dared to let myself *want* to believe it, but oh God, it was true!

The underground doctor to whom Richard Bruno had taken me ran antibody tests and viral protein tests and examined blood, mucus, and tissue samples through an electron microscope.

There was no doubt about it. I was free of all strains of the Plague. Indeed, there was not a retrovirus of any kind in my body.

"Do you know what this means?" I cried ecstatically on the street outside.

"Indeed I do. The long nightmare of the Plague Years is coming to an end. We're carriers of life—"

"And it's our duty to spread it!"

"First to my son. Then to as many others as quickly as

possible. We need to infect as many vectors as we can before
. . . in case . . . so that no matter what happens to us . . .''

I hugged him. I kissed him. In a way, in that moment, I
think I began to love him.

"When?" I asked him breathlessly.

"Tonight. I'll bring him to your room."

DR. RICHARD BRUNO

Tod was all hot sweaty excitement when I told him I was taking
him to a real human whore. "Oh Dad, Dad, thank you . . ." he
cried. But then he hesitated. "This girl . . . I mean, you're sure
she's . . . you know . . .''

Now *I* hesitated. Between telling him the easy lie that I had
found him a real blue-carder or telling him the whole improbable
truth. I sighed. I screwed up my courage. I had lived too long
with deception.

"It's really true?" Tod said when I had finished. "The
dreadnaught virus? What they did at Sutcliffe? All that money?"

I nodded. "Do you believe me, Tod?"

"Well yeah . . . I mean I want to, but . . . but why haven't
you told Mom? Why haven't you . . . you know, given it to
her?''

"Would she have trusted me?"

"I dunno . . . I guess not. . . .''

"Do *you* trust me?"

"I want to . . . I mean . . .'' He looked into my eyes for
long moments. "I guess I trust you enough to take the chance,"
he finally said. "I'm the one that did all the talking about being
brave, huh, Dad. . . .''

I hugged my son to me. And I took him to Linda Lewin's
room. He entered tremulously but he stayed almost two hours.

LINDA LEWIN

I longed to shout the glorious truth from the rooftops, but when

Richard told me the whole horrible story of what had happened at Sutcliffe, I had to agree that I should continue the Work of Our Lady as before, spread the dreadnaught virus as far and wide as possible among the unknowing before those who would stop us could find out what was happening. It was hard to believe that such greedy evil was possible, but the fact that I was cured and the world knew nothing about the dreadnaught proved the sad truth that it was.

Richard swore Tod to secrecy too, and together and separately the three of us began to spread the joyful infection around Palo Alto, telling no one.

Why did I stay in Palo Alto for two weeks instead of resuming my usual rounds up and down California, when in fact spreading the cure around the state as quickly as possible would have probably been wiser and more effective?

Perhaps I felt the need to be near the only two people who shared the glorious secret and the deadly danger of discovery. Perhaps I had fallen in love in a strange way with Richard, with this tormented, fearful, but oh so brave man.

More likely that I knew even then in my heart of hearts that this couldn't last, that sooner or later Sutcliffe would get wind of it and we would have to run. And when that happened, Richard and Tod would be helpless naifs without me. Only Our Lady would have the connections and road wisdom to even have a chance to keep them one step ahead of our pursuers.

DR. RICHARD BRUNO

Once again, what could I possibly tell Marge? The whole story, including the fact that my Hippocratic oath required me to have meat with as many anonymous women as I could? That I had our son similarly doing his duty to the species?

Obviously I had been inexorably forced step by step into such extreme levels of marital deception that there was no way I could now get her to believe the truth, let alone accept its tomcatting moral imperative.

Yet, tormented as I was by the monstrous series of deceptions I was forced to inflict upon my wife, I had to admit that I was enjoying it.

After all, no other men in all the world had the possibility of enjoying sex as Tod and I did. Meat on meat as it was meant to be, and not only free of fear of the Plague, but knowing that we were granting a great secret boon with our favors, that we were serving the highest good of our species in the bargain.

And I was cementing a unique relationship with my son. Tod and I became confidants on a level that few fathers and sons achieve. Swapping tales of our sexual exploits, but sharing the problem of how to recruit Marge to the cause too.

Or, at the very least, infect her with the dreadnaught. But Marge would never have meat with me. Nor would she willingly abandon monogamy. Sexually, psychologically, Marge was a child of the Plague Years, and even if she were to be convinced of the whole truth, she would never condone the need for my profuse infidelities, let alone agree to spread the dreadnaught in the meatbars herself.

In retrospect, of course, it was quite obvious that things could not really go on like this for long.

They didn't.

Tod got caught in an SP raid on a meatbar again.

But they didn't drag him home this time. Instead, the news came on the telephone, and it was Marge who chanced to take the call. Tod was being held at the Palo Alto SP headquarters. Other detainees had told the SP that he had been a regular. Black-carders had admitted having meat with him. He was undergoing testing now and his card was sure to come up black.

"Don't worry," I told her when she relayed this information in a state of numb, teary panic, "they'll have to let him go. He'll test out blue, I promise."

"You're crazy, Richard, that's plain impossible! You're out of your mind!"

"If you think I'm crazy now," I said, pouring her a big drink, "wait till I get drunk enough to tell you why!"

I gulped down two quick ones myself before I found the courage to begin, and kept drinking as I babbled out the whole story.

"Now let me give the dreadnaught to you," I woozed when I was finished, reaching out for her in a state of sloppy inebriation.

She shrieked, pulled away from me, ran around the living room screaming, "You animal! You're crazy! You've killed our son! Stay away from me! Stay away from me!"

How can I explain or excuse what happened next? I was drunk out of my mind, but another part of me was running on coldly logical automatic. If there could be such a thing as loving rape, now was the time for it. Marge was certain that I was a sinkhole of the Plague, and there was only one way I could ever convince her of the truth. I had to infect her with the dreadnaught, and I couldn't take no for an answer.

The short and nasty of it was that I meatraped my own wife, knowing I was doing the right thing even as she fought with all her strength against me, convinced that she was fighting to keep herself from certain infection with the Plague. It was brutal and horrible and I loathed myself for what I was doing even as I knew full well that it was ultimately right.

And left her there sobbing while I reeled off into the night to retrieve Tod from the SP.

I was in a drunken fury, I was a medical heavyweight, I demanded that they run a full battery of tests on Tod and myself, and I browbeat the tired SP timeserver who ran them unmercifully. When they all turned out blue, I threatened lawsuits and dire political recriminations if Tod were not released to my custody at once, and succeeded thereby in deflecting his attention from the ''anomalous organism'' he had noticed in our bloodstreams long enough to get us out the door.

But the ''anomalous organism'' would be noted in his report. And Sutcliffe would be keeping close tabs on my data file, and there were certainly people on their end who would put one and one and one together. It was only a question of how much time it would take.

And we couldn't stay around to find out. We had to run. Tod, myself, Linda, and Marge. But where? And how?

We drove to Linda's and had to wait outside for half an hour till the man she was with left.

LINDA LEWIN

''There's only one place we can go,'' I told Tod and Richard. ''Only one place we can hide where the SP can't come after us . . .''

''The San Francisco Quarantine Zone?'' Richard stammered.

I nodded. ''The SP won't go into San Francisco. There isn't a Fuck-Q alive who'd be willing to do it.''

''But . . . *San Francisco* . . . ?''

"Remember, *we* have nothing to fear from the Plague," I told them. "Besides . . . can you think of anywhere where what we three have is more needed?" ·

"But how can we even *get* inside the Zone?"

I had to think about that one for a good long while. I had never even heard of anyone trying to get past the SP *into* San Francisco. On the other hand, neither had the SP. . . .

"Our best bet would be by boat from Sausalito. We wait for a good foggy night, then cross the Golden Gate through the fogbank in a wooden rowboat, no motor noise, no radar profile. The patrol boats stick in close to San Francisco and they're watching the coastline, not the Bay. The helicopters won't be able to see us through the fog even if they are flying. . . ."

"Sounds like risky business," Richard said dubiously.

"Any better ideas?"

Richard shrugged. "Let's go collect Marge," he said.

DR. RICHARD BRUNO

The three of us piled into Linda's car—they'd be looking for mine once they were looking for anything—and drove back to our house.

Marge was still in a state of shock when we got there. Even when she saw Tod, even when he and Linda backed up my story, she still couldn't quite believe me. She started to come around a bit when I showed her the enormous balance in my secret account.

But when I told her we had to flee to San Francisco, she fell apart all over again. There was no time for further persuasion. Richard, Linda, and I were forced to wrestle her into the car by brute force, with my hand clamped over her mouth to prevent her from screaming.

We drove around the rim of the bay to Sausalito, bought a rowboat, rented motel rooms, and waited.

The fog didn't roll in good and thick until two nights later. During these two days, with Tod and Linda and myself talking to her almost nonstop, Marge slowly came to believe the truth.

But accepting the fact that all of us had a moral duty to spread the dreadnaught in the only way possible was a bit more than she could swallow. She could accept it intellectually, but she remained emotionally shattered.

"I believe you, Richard, truly I do," she admitted as the sun went down on our last day in Sausalito. "I can even admit that what you're doing is probably the right thing. But me, I just can't. . . ."

"I know," I told her, hugging her to me. "It's hard for me too. . . ." and I made tender love to her, meat on meat as it was meant to be, for what was to prove to be the last time.

That night a big bank of fog rolled in through the gap in the Golden Gate Bridge, a tall one too, that kept the gunships high above the San Francisco shoreline. It was now or never.

Tod hesitated on the pier.

"Scared?"

He nodded.

"Me too, Tod."

He clasped my hand. "I'm scared Dad," he said softly. "I mean, I know we don't have much of a chance of making it. . . . But if anything happens . . . I want you to know that I wouldn't have it any other way. . . . We had to do what we did. I love you, Dad. You're the bravest man I've ever known."

"And I'm proud to have you for a son," I said with tears in my eyes. "I only wish . . ."

"Don't say it, Dad."

I hugged him to me, and then we all piled into the boat, and Tod and I began to row.

The currents were tricky and kept pushing us east and the going was tougher than I had anticipated, but we steered for the lights of the city and made dogged progress.

We couldn't have been more than five hundred yards from the shore when a spotlight beam suddenly pinned us in a dazzling circle of pearly light. "Rowboat heave to! Rowboat heave to!"

So near and yet so far! If the SP caught us, we were finished. We had no choice but to row for it.

We pulled out of the spotlight and zigged and zagged toward the shore while a motor roared back and forth behind us and the spotlight flitted randomly over the flat waters. The fog was quite thick, and they had trouble picking us up again.

When they finally did we were within two hundred yards of the shore. And then they opened up with some kind of heavy machine-gun.

"We're sitting ducks in this boat!" Tod shouted. "Got to

swim for it!'' And he dived overboard and down into the darkness of the waters under a hail of bullets.

Everything seemed to happen at once. The boat tipped as Tod dived, Linda rolled over the side, Marge panicked and fell overboard, the boat turned turtle—

And we were all in the cold water, swimming as far as we could under water before surfacing for air, catching quick breaths, swimming for our lives beneath a random fusillade of bullets and a skittery searchlight beam.

There was no room for thought or even fear as I swam for my life with aching lungs, no time or space to feel the horror of what was happening. Until, gasping for air, exhausted and freezing, I clawed my way up a rocky beach.

Out across the dark waters, the searchlight still roamed and the machine-gun fire still flashed and chattered. Linda Lewin crawled up beside me, panting and coughing. We lay there, not moving, not talking, not thinking, for a long time, until the gunboat finally gave up and disappeared into the fog.

Then we got up and searched the beach for at least an hour.

Tod and Marge were nowhere to be found.

''Maybe they made it farther up the beach,'' Linda suggested wanly.

But I knew better. I could feel the void in my heart. They were gone. They were gone, and I had killed them as surely as if the hand on the machine-gun trigger had been mine.

''Richard—''

I pulled away from her comforting embrace.

''Richard—''

I turned away from her and let a cold black despair roll like a fog bank into my mind, erasing all thought, and filling me with itself, wondering whether it would ever roll out again.

And hoping in that endless bleak moment that it never would.

JOHN DAVID
▰▰▰▰▰▰▰▰▰▰

I suppose I knew it had to happen sooner or later, brothers and sisters, but at least I thought I'd be able to go down fighting and take some of the meatfuckers with me.

It didn't happen that way. They got me while I was asleep, would you believe it!

I was going downhill fast, I was feverish, weak, and I wasn't really thinking, I mean I was wandering the streets like an obvious zombie for real. I got picked up by some people whose faces I don't even remember who took me to an Our Lady safe house in Berkeley, where I passed out as soon as I hit the mattress.

Some meatfuckin' safe house!

I got woke up in the middle of the night by a gun butt in the back of the neck and another in my belly. They rounded everyone in the joint up and hauled us to the SP station. They ran everyone's cards against the national data bank.

Everyone but me. Me, they didn't have to bother, seeing as I was an obvious Condition Terminal and they had caught me with about a dozen assorted phony blue cards in my kit. Me, they just took my finger and retina prints and faxed 'em to Washington.

"Well, well, well," the SP lieutenant purred after no more than half an hour. "John David recently of the Legion, wanted for about ten thousand counts of murder, meatrape, and ID forgery, not to mention robbery, insurrection, border crashing, and treason. You're a bad boy, aren't you, John? But I'm real pleased to meet you. I get the feeling you're gonna get me a nice promotion. Tell you what, if you do, the night before they do you, your last meal's on me."

WALTER T. BIGELOW

Not content with possessing my wife, Satan pursued me to my office. First the blasphemous cult of Our Lady and then a series of anomalies in the San Francisco Bay Area that seemed to indicate that the national data bank had somehow been compromised.

It was common enough for phony blue cards to come up black against the national data bank. But it was unheard of for anyone caught with a forged blue card not to prove out black upon actual testing for the Plague, for of course it made absolutely no sense for someone with a valid blue card to use a forged one.

But it was happening around the Bay Area. There were almost a dozen cases.

And now this truly bizarre incident last night in the same locale. Four people in a rowboat had actually tried to run the Quarantine blockade *into* San Francisco! Two of them seemed to have actually made it.

When the bodies of the other two were fished out of the Bay, they proved to be Tod and Marge Bruno, the son and daughter of one Dr. Richard Bruno, a prominent genetic synthesizer with the Sutcliffe Corporation.

The local SP commandant was due for a promotion or at least a commendation.

He had run all three names through the national data bank. Tod Bruno had been caught in a meatbar sweep three days previously. Although many witnesses claimed he was an habitué, he had come out blue under a full spectrum of tests. The commandant had had the wit to dig deeper and found that some "anomalous organism" had been noted in the actual report.

Instinct had caused him to order the bodies of Tod and Marge Bruno to be given a thorough and complete autopsy down to the molecular level. And it was that report that put me on a plane for San Jose.

There was a strange "pseudovirus" written into both of their genomes. It shared many sequences with the Plague virus but resembled no known or extrapolated variant, and it had other sequences that could not have evolved naturally. The bodies had been dead too long to try to culture it.

An unknown "pseudovirus" in the bodies of the family of a prominent genetic synthesizer . . . It could only be one thing— an unreported Condition Black incident at Sutcliffe. And the ultimate handiwork of the Devil had been released—some kind of horrible artificial human parasite, a manmade Plague variant. We had two corpses that had been infected with it, and I was virtually certain that Bruno at least was also infected, and was alive somewhere in San Francisco.

What might happen in that cesspit of Satan was none of my affair, but Tod Bruno had been infected when he was picked up in a meatbar outside the Quarantine Zone, and he had passed through a full battery of tests and come out blue.

Meaning that this monstrous thing was invisible to all our standard Plague tests. What had the Devil wrought at the Sutcliffe Corporation?

As I flew westward, I had the unshakable conviction that I was flying toward some climactic confrontation with the Adversary, that the battle of Armageddon had already begun.

LINDA LEWIN

San Francisco was not what I had expected. I'm not sure what I had really expected, a foul Sodom of ruins and rotting zombies, maybe, but this was not it.

The streets were clean and the quaint buildings lovingly cared for. The famous old cable cars were still running and so were the buses. The restaurants were open, the bars were crowded, and there were cabarets and theaters. There were even friendly cops walking beats.

Food and various necessities were allowed in through the Daly City Quarantine Line and sterilized products allowed out, so the city did have an economy connected to the outside world. The place was poor, of course, but the people inside it held together to see themselves through. Food was expensive in the restaurants but artificially cheap in the markets. Housing was crowded, but the rents were kept low, and the indigent or homeless were put up in public buildings and abandoned BART stations.

Oh yes, there were many horrible Condition Terminals walking around, but many more people who could have easily melted into the underground life outside. And there was something quite touching about how all the temporarily healthy deferred to and showed such tender regard for the obvious Living Dead, something that reminded me of dear old Max.

Indeed his spirit seemed to hover over this doomed but fatalistically gay-spirited city. Of necessity, everyone was forced to be a Saint Max here, and although the Lovers of Our Lady did not exist as such, everyone here seemed to be doing the Work.

No one here had to worry about Getting It, or being carded, or picked up by the SP. All of that had already happened to all of them. So, while there were more open gays here than I had ever thought to see in my life, stranger still to say, there was less . . . perversion in San Francisco than anywhere else I had ever been.

No meatbars as such, for every bar was a meatbar. Hardly any sex machine parlors, for the people of San Francisco, already all under sentence of death, could give one another love freely, like what natural men and women must once have been. Even the obviously terminal had their needs tenderly cared for.

No place I had ever been seemed more like home.

Only the pall of Plague that hung over the city marred the sweetness of the atmosphere, and that seemed softened by the fogs, pinkened by the sunsets, lightened by the deathhouse gaiety and wistful philosophic melancholy with which the citizens confronted it. "Everyone's born under a death sentence anyway," went the popular saying. "Here at least we all know it. There is no tomorrow sooner or later, so why not live and love today?"

Uncertain of what to do next, I began doing the Work of Our Lady in the usual manner, offering myself to anyone and everyone, spreading the dreadnaught slowly, but unsure as to whether or when to spread the glorious news.

I would have been happy there—indeed the truth of it was that I *was* happy—even while I sorrowed for poor Richard.

Richard, though, was like a little child whom I had to lead around like a creature in a daze. All his energy and motivation seemed to have vanished with his wife and son. I could understand his grief and guilt, but this couldn't last forever.

"We've got work to do, Richard, glorious and important work," I kept telling him. "We've got to spread the dreadnaught among these people."

Mostly, he stared at me blankly. Sometimes he managed a feeble, "You do it."

After a few days of this, I decided that I could no longer wait for Richard to come around. I had to make the fateful decision on my own.

This spreading the dreadnaught by myself clandestinely was just too slow. If there were evil men out there intent on stopping the dreadnaught, they'd be tracking us down. I needed to infect thousands, tens of thousands, before they could act, and the only way that could happen would be if the people of San Francisco *knew* what they were spreading and set out to do it systematically.

First I began revealing myself as Our Lady to my lovers and in the bars, and there were enough people in San Francisco who had once done the Work on the outside—even some I had once known in my circuit-riding days—so that my claim gained credibility.

In one sense, the people of San Francisco had always been doing the Work of Our Lady, of Saint Max, but in another sense, the legend had never been central here. In San Francisco, the people did the Work of Our Lady to please one another and themselves, not because they believed they were serving the species' only hope.

But then I began recruiting an army of Lovers of Our Lady and I did it by proclaiming the glorious truth.

That the shattered man I sheltered in my rooms was a great scientist and an even greater hero. That he had developed the dreadnaught organism. That through him I had been infected with the gift of life. That I could infect anyone I had meat with with the cure, that anyone I had meat with would also become infectious. That the Plague Years, through Richard Bruno's instrumentality and at horrible personal cost to himself, were now coming to an end.

That all we had to do was what we were doing already—love one another.

There were more skeptics than believers at first, of course. ''Bring me your Terminals,'' I told them. ''Let them have meat with Our Lady. When they're cured, the whole city will see I'm telling the truth.''

WALTER T. BIGELOW

Satan himself seemed to be speaking through Harlow Prinz when I confronted him, laughing his final laugh, for what the president of Sutcliffe finally admitted under extreme duress was worse, far worse, than what I had originally feared.

Bruno had been working on some sort of Plague-killer virus. But he had been building it around a Plague variant and something went wrong. He had created instead a Plague variant that mutated randomly every time it reproduced. That was invisible not only to all current tests short of full-scale molecular analysis, but would *remain so* to anything that could be devised.

There *had* been a Condition Black, but only inside the lab, and there were plenty of reports to prove that Sutcliffe had followed proper procedure, as well as a mountain of legal briefs supporting the position that such internally contained Condition Blacks need not be reported to the SP.

''We had no idea Bruno was infected,'' Prinz claimed. ''Isn't that right, Warren?''

Warren Feinstein, Sutcliffe's chairman, who had sat there silently all the while with the most peculiar expression on his face, fidgeted nervously. "No . . . I mean yes . . . I mean how can we be so sure he *was* infected . . . ?"

"The man's wife and son were infected, now weren't they, Warren?" Prinz snapped. "You heard the director. Extreme measures must be taken at once to contain this thing!"

"But—"

"Wait a minute!" I cried. "Surely you're not suggesting the man . . . had *meatsex* with his wife and . . . and his *son* knowing he was infected?"

"Let's hope so," Prinz said. "At any rate, we have no choice but to act on that assumption."

"What?"

"Because if he didn't . . ." Prinz shuddered. "If he didn't, then we may all be doomed. Because if Tod and Marge Bruno *weren't* infected sexually, then this new virus has to be what we've always feared most—a Plague variant that doesn't need sexual or intravenous vectors, an ambient version that spreads through the air like the common cold."

"Oh my God."

"You have no alternative, Mr. Director," Prinz went on relentlessly. "You must obtain the necessary authority from the president and have San Francisco sterilized at once."

"Sterilized?"

"Nuked. Condition Black procedure, admittedly on a rather extreme scale."

"That's monstrous, Harlow!" Feinstein shouted. "This is going too far! We've got to—"

"Shut up, Warren!" Prinz snapped. "Consider the alternative!"

Feinstein slumped over in his chair.

"If this thing *is* ambient, we're all doomed anyway, so what's the difference?" Prinz said in Satan's cold, insinuating voice. "But if it isn't, and if Bruno's spreading it in San Francisco . . ."

"You can't just kill a million people on the supposition that—"

"Shut up, Warren!" Prinz snapped. "You can't afford to listen to this sentimental fool, Mr. Director. You've got to be strong. You've got to do your duty."

My duty? But where did that lie? If I had the San Francisco Quarantine Zone sterilized by a thermonuclear explosion, Bruno would be vaporized. And I had to have Bruno live for interrogation before I did any such thing, I realized. I had to know whether he had had meatsex with his wife and son. For if he had, then I would know the virus *wasn't* ambient, that there was hope. *Then* and only then could I have San Francisco sterilized with a clear conscience.

Then and only then would such an awful decision serve God and not the Devil.

I had to find someone willing to go into San Francisco and bring Bruno out. But where was I going to find someone crazy or self-sacrificing enough to do that?

JOHN DAVID

I was feeling pretty punk when two SPs dragged me into an interrogation room, handcuffed me to a chair bolted to the floor, and then split.

But I came around fast, you better believe it, when old Walter T. himself walked into the room and shut the door behind him!

The old meatfucker came right to the point.

"I've been looking for someone very special, and the computer spit your name out," he told me. "I've got a job for you. Interested?"

"You gotta be kidding. . . ."

"We're going to drop you in San Francisco. I want you to bring a man out."

"Say what?" Well shit, brothers and sisters, I could hardly believe my ears. I mean, even in my present Condition Terminal, my ears pricked up at *that* one. And old Walter T., he sure didn't miss it.

"Interested, aren't you? Here's the deal. . . ."

And he told me. An SP helicopter would drop me into San Francisco, where I was to snatch and hold this guy Richard Bruno. Every afternoon at three o'clock they'd have a chopper circle Golden Gate Park for an hour. When I had Bruno, I'd shoot off a Very pistol, and they'd pick me up.

"What do you want this guy for?" I demanded.

"You have no need to know," he told me.

I eyed him dubiously. "What makes you think I'll want to

come out?'' I mean, this dumb meatfucker was gonna throw me into my briar patch, but what could possibly make him believe I'd do his dirty work for him and deliver some poor bastard to the SP? Could he *really* be as stupid as he seemed? It didn't seem real likely.

''Because upon delivery of Bruno you'll be given a full pardon for all your capital crimes.''

''Hey, look at me, man, I've got maybe a month left anyway.''

'' You can go back into the Legion. As a captain.''

''As a captain?'' I snorted. ''Shit, why not a bird colonel?''

''Why not indeed?''

''You're really serious, aren't you?'' Jeez, what a tasty run I could have as a fuckin' brigade commander. But . . . ''But I'm a goner anyway. What difference is it gonna make?''

''The Legion is going into Brazil again even as we speak,'' he told me. ''We can pump you up with the best military pallies and all the coke and speed you can handle. And drop you into Brazil with colonel's wings at the head of a brigade twelve hours after you deliver Bruno. A short life, but a happy one.''

''Terrific,'' I said, studying old Walter T. carefully. This still didn't quite add up. He was holding something back, and I had a feeling I wasn't gonna like it. ''But what makes you so sure I wouldn't prefer to spend that short happy life in San Francisco?''

Now it was Walter T.'s turn to study *me* carefully, then shrug. ''Because unless you bring Bruno out, that could be a lot shorter than you think.''

''Huh?''

''We're going to drop you into San Francisco anyway, so I might as well tell you the truth,'' Bigelow said. ''I get the feeling nothing else is really going to motivate you, but *this* surely will.''

He told me, and it did.

Bruno was some kind of genetic synthesizer. He had screwed up real bad and created a new Plague variant that was invisible to all the standard tests and just might be able to spread through the air.

''So we need to know whether Bruno is infected with something that could be spreading around San Francisco right now, something that we can only hope to stop by . . . shall we say measures of the maximum extremity.''

Well, brothers and sisters, I didn't need any promotion to

bird colonel to figure out what he meant by *that*. "You mean nuke San Francisco, don't you?"

"Unless we have Bruno to examine and unless that examination reassures us that he hasn't been spreading this thing, we really have no alternative. . . . I'll give you two weeks. After that, well . . ."

"You nuke San Francisco with me inside it!"

Bigelow nodded. "I think I can trust you to do your honest best, now, can't I?" he said.

Well, what could I say to that? Only one thing, brothers and sisters. What I told old Walter T. next.

"I want the coke and the speed and the pallies *right now*. All I can carry."

"Very well," he said. "Why not? Anything you need."

"I don't have any choice, now, do I?"

"None whatever."

If I hadn't been cuffed to the chair, I would have ripped off the old meatfucker's arm and beaten him to death with it. But even then, I had to admire his style, if you know what I mean. Turn the bastard's card black, and old Walter T. would have been right at home with us, fellow zombies.

LINDA LEWIN

After the marks started to fade from terminal cases and black-carders started proving out blue on the simple tests the underground docs put together, the word began to spread faster, and so did the dreadnaught, and the Lovers of Our Lady began to spread the good news on their own in the streets and bars of San Francisco.

One day a delegation came to me and took me to a rambling old house high on a hill above Buena Vista Park that they called the House of Our Lady of Love Reborn. They installed me in quarters on the third floor and they brought Richard with me.

There I was surrounded by the Lovers of Our Lady. And so was Richard. He was surrounded by people who cared for him, who loved him, who knew what heroic deeds he had done, and at what terrible cost. Slowly, far too slowly, he began to react to his surroundings, to mutter haltingly of his guilt and despair. But he still refused to join in the Work, for he found the mere thought of sex loathsome, no matter who offered themselves to him, including myself.

And the Work itself, though proceeding apace, was going far too slowly. How long did we have before the outside world learned the truth? Months? Weeks? Days? And what would happen then? Indeed, might it be in the process of happening already?

What I needed to do was infect all of San Francisco with the dreadnaught, so that when the outside world finally intruded, it would be presented with the truth and its massive proof as a glorious fait accompli—an entire city, a Quarantine Zone once completely black, now entirely free of the Plague.

Once, long before most of the people here were born, San Francisco had experienced a magical few months that was called the Summer of Love, a legend that still lived in the myth of the city.

So I conceived the notion of a Week of Love, a celebration of the dreadnaught and a means of quickly spreading it to all, a carnival of sex, a citywide orgy, a festival of Our Lady of Love Reborn.

And perhaps via such a manifestation and celebration of what he had brought back into the world, Richard too might be reborn back into it. . . .

JOHN DAVID

The pallies they shot me up with before they dropped me in San Francisco didn't seem to do much good, but the speed and coke sure did, brothers and sisters. I might look like Condition Terminal on its last legs, but I was riding high and burning bright on the way out, you better believe it!

I expected San Francisco to be weird and wild, something like TJ before the SP moved in on us, but this was something else again, weird for sure, but not exactly this zombie's idea of *wild*.

The city was like something out of an old movie—clean, and neat, and like you know *quaint*, like some picture postcard of itself, and I found I could have just about any kind of meat with anyone I wanted to just by asking for it, even looking like I did.

There were plenty of terminal zombies like me walking around and plenty more outrageous faggots, but these people were like so damned sweet and kind and nicey-nice to us on the way out it made me want to puke. I mean all this peace and sympathy sex and love pissed me off so bad I just about *wanted* to see Wimp City nuked, if you know what I mean.

But not, of course, with me in it!

Bigelow had it covered. I had no choice at all. I had to get my crumbling ass in gear and get my mitts on Bruno, on my only ticket out.

DR. RICHARD BRUNO

I can hardly remember what it was like inside that place of darkness or even precisely how and when I began to emerge from it. First there was a soft warm light in my cold blackness, and then I slowly began to take notice of my surroundings.

I was living in an ancient Victorian house high on a hill in San Francisco, a place that was known as the house of Our Lady of Love Reborn. Linda Lewin was living there with me, and I knew that she had been caring for me through my long dark night. As had many others. For this was a house of love and hope. It was a kind of a brothel, and a kind of church, and what was being spread here was my dreadnaught virus. And all those who came and went here loved me.

"Dr. Feelgood," they all called me. Not the creature who had brought his wife and son to death, but the man who had brought love back into the world.

"You've grieved long enough, Richard; Marge and Tod are gone, and they deserve your grief," Linda told me. "But you've also done a wonderful thing, and that deserves your joy. Come join the party now. See what they died for. See what you've brought back into the world! This is the Festival of Our Lady of Love Reborn, but it's the Festival of Dr. Feelgood, too."

And she and the Lovers of Our Lady took me on a tour of San Francisco, on a tour of the carnival, on a tour through an erotic wonderland out of long-lost dreams.

The whole city was partying—in the bars and the parks and the streets. It was Mardi Gras, it was the feast of Dionysus, it was the Summer of Love, it was beautiful madness. Everyone was drunk and stoned and deliriously happy, and people were making love, sharing meat, openly everywhere—in apartments, in bars, right out on the streets.

They were celebrating Love Reborn in the very act of creating it. They were celebrating the end of the Plague Years as they brought it to an end with their joyful flesh.

"Do you understand, Richard?" Linda asked later, back at the house of Our Lady of Love Reborn. "Marge and Tod are dead and they never lived to see what they died for, and that's a sad thing, and you're right to mourn. But they didn't die in vain, they died to help you bring love back into the world, and if they're watching from somewhere, you can know they're smiling down on you. And if they're not, if there's no God or Heaven, well then, we're all we've got, and we can only take shelter in the living. Do you understand?"

"I'm not sure, Linda . . ." I murmured.

"Then let me help you to begin now," she said, holding me in her arms. "Come take shelter in me."

And, hesitantly at first, but with a growing strange peace in my heart, a warrior's peace, a peace that had become determination by the time we had finished our lovemaking, I did.

And afterward, I understood. Marge and Tod were gone and nothing I could do would bring them back, and that was a terrible thing. The Plague Years had in one way or another made monsters and madmen of us all, we had all been trapped into grievous mistakes, fearful, and frustrated, and loathsome acts, and nothing we did now could change that either. We had *all* been victims, and perhaps the lives of all of us who lived through the Plague Years could never be made whole.

But that dark night was ending and a new day was dawning, and we, and I, had to act to give it birth and protect it into its full maturity. My personal life had died back there in San Francisco Bay with Marge and Tod and I had nothing left but my duty to the Hippocratic oath.

And vengeance.

Nothing I could do would ever bring my family back or entirely erase my guilt in their deaths. But I could take my vengeance on Prinz, on Feinstein, on the Sutcliffe board, I could do my part in seeing to it that their worst fears were realized, that the dreadnaught virus they had sought to destroy spread far and wide, saving suffering humanity while it destroyed the Sutcliffe Corporation in the process.

Thus would my part in the twisted nightmare of the Plague Years end with the ultimate perverse yet joyful irony:

Just and loving vengeance.

So tomorrow I will go forth into San Francisco and join the Week of Love. And tonight I am sitting here in the House of Our Lady and writing my story in this journal, which is now concluding. When it is finished, it will be sent to the president, to the head of the Federal Quarantine Agency, to the news services, to the television networks. Before you let them act against us or tell you that this is all an evil lie, demand that they go in and test the populace or at least a good sample for Plague. That's all I ask. Know the truth for yourself. Tell others.

And I promise it will set all of you free.

JOHN DAVID

I had good photos of Bruno, but you ever try tracking down one guy in a city of a million? Especially in a city that seemed to have gone completely apeshit. Everyone seemed to be drunk or stoned. People were having meat *everywhere* right out in the open, in the streets, in the parks, in alleys. Half-dead as I was, they were still shoving their meat even at the likes of me, babbling a lot of crazy stuff about how they were saving me from the Plague, as if anything could help me now!

I was goin' out fast, I was a mess of sarcomas and secondary infections, weak, and feverish, and half out on my feet, taking enormous doses of speed and coke just to keep going. But, fast as I was going, I still knew that this city was gonna go faster, and with me in it, unless I could deliver Bruno to the SP. I mean, one way I had maybe three weeks left, the other only ten days.

An extra eleven days of life may not seem like such a big deal to *you*, brothers and sisters, but it sure as shit would if *you* were the one who knew that was the best you had left!

Anyway, it was enough to keep me focused on finding Bruno, even spaced and stoned and dying and staggering around in the biggest orgy the world had ever seen. And I started grilling random people on the street and being none too gentle about it.

I was so far gone I must have beaten the crap out of half-a-dozen of them before it got through to me that the "Dr. Feelgood" the whole damn city was babbling about was the very guy I was looking for. Dr. Richard Bruno, the son of a bitch who had maybe let loose the worst Plague variant ever and who for sure was gonna get all these assholes vaporized, and me with them; and they were somehow convinced the bastard was some kind of hero!

Well, after I copped to that, it wasn't much sweat tracking the famous Dr. Feelgood down. All I had to do was follow my nose and all the talk about him through the bars and streets until I ran into someone who told me he was partying in a certain bar in North Beach right now.

I got there just as he was walking out with a good-looking momma on his arm and a dreamy smile on his lips. As soon as I saw him, I went into motion, no time or energy left for tactics or thought.

"Okay, Bruno, you son of a bitch, you're comin' with me!" I shouted, grabbing him by his right arm and whipping it behind his back into a half-nelson bring-along.

Half-a-dozen guys started to move in, but, far gone as I was, I still had that covered. I already had my miniauto out and waving in their faces.

"This guy's comin' with me, assholes!" I screamed. "Anyone tries to stop me gets blown away!"

Then everything seemed to happen at once.

Some jerk got brave and slammed into my knees from behind.

I kicked blindly backward, fighting for balance.

Bruno yanked himself out of the half-nelson.

A circle of angry meat closed in.

I started firing without caring at what, whipping the miniauto in fanning fire at full rock and roll.

"Dr. Feelgood" got himself neatly stitched up the back from ass to shoulder by high-velocity slugs.

Bruno folded as everyone else came down on me like a ton of bricks.

Next thing I knew, I had had the shit thoroughly beaten out of me, and two guys were holding me up by the shoulders, and Bruno was down there on the sidewalk croaking and looking up at me.

"Why?" he whispered with blood drooling out of his mouth.

"Don't die, you stupid meatfucker!" I screamed at him. "You're my only ticket out of here!"

"Kill the bastard!"

"Tear him apart!"

I laughed and laughed and laughed. I mean, what else was there to do? "Go ahead and kill me, suckers!" I told them all. "I'm dead already and so are you, gonna nuke you till you glow blue!"

"Cut his heart out!"

Bruno looked up at me from the sidewalk with this weird sad little grin, almost peaceful, kind of, as his light went out.

"No . . ." he said. "No more . . . just and loving vengeance, don't you see . . . Marge . . . Tod . . . it's nobody's fault . . . take him . . . take him. . . ."

His voice started to fade. He coughed up more blood.

"Take him where, Richard?" a woman said, leaning over him.

"Take him to Our Lady . . ." Bruno whispered. "Let him take shelter in . . . in . . ."

His lips moved but no more sound came out. And that was the end of that.

Bruno was dead.

So was I.

And in ten days, so was San Francisco.

LINDA LEWIN

They brought Richard's body back to the house of Our Lady of Love Reborn and laid him out on a couch. Half-a-dozen Lovers of Our Lady were restraining a wild-eyed young terminal case and being none too gentle about it.

And they told me what had happened. And Richard's dying words.

Only then did I really look at his murderer. His body was a mass of sarcomas. His frame was skeletal. His eyes were red and wild.

"Why?" I asked him in a strange imploring voice that surprised even me.

"My ticket out of here before they drop the Big One Lady but it's all over now ain't it do your damnedest we're all dead zombies anyway brothers and sisters. . . ."

He wasn't making sense, nor would he, I knew then. This poor creature was no more responsible for his actions than Richard had been when Marge and Tod died. I had heard of this sort of thing before. Condition Terminals turning berserker on the way out, taking as many as they could with them. He too was a victim of the Plague, as were we all.

And I understood Richard's last words now too, perhaps better even than he had in the saying of them. His life had been in a sense over already, and all this poor creature had done was set his tormented soul free. I understood why he had forgiven his assassin, for in that act of forgiving, he had at last found forgiveness for himself for the deaths on his own hands, or so at least I prayed to whatever gods there be.

"What should we do with the bastard?"

"Kill him!"

"Tear his damn heart out!"

"No!" I found myself saying. "I'll do it for you, Richard," I whispered, and I took his murderer's hand. "He forgave you, and so must I."

"Go ahead and kill me, don't want your forgiveness, it don't mean shit, I'm a dead man already and so are you!"

"No, you're not," I told him gently. "Let me take you upstairs and give you the good news."

JOHN DAVID

And she did, though of course I didn't believe a word of it at the time, not even after Our Lady gave my disgusting dying flesh the gift of her meat. Not that I was exactly in any mental condition for deep conversation anyway.

But days later, when the sarcomas began to disappear and my head cleared, I knew that the whole damn story that Linda had told me over and over again was all true.

I mean, I had sure done my share of evil, but what those meatfuckers at Sutcliffe had done was enough to make a combat medic puke! I never had no use for Walter T. Bigelow—and less so after the number he had run on me—but I was willing to bet that the old meatfucker had believed what he told me about poor Bruno. Those Sutcliffe creeps must have fed him their line about

Bruno to get him to nuke the evidence of what they had done out of existence. And the dreadnaught virus along with it! Just to line their own pockets and save their own worthless asses!

And oh shit, Bigelow still believed it!

"What day is this?" I asked Linda when my head was finally clear enough to realize what all this meant and what was about to happen.

It was two days till the Big Flash.

"You've given me the good news, now I've gotta give you the bad news," I told her. And I did.

I had never seen Our Lady break down and cry before, but now she did. "Then poor Richard died for nothing. . . . And everyone here is doomed. . . . And no one will even know. . . . And the Plague will go on and on and on. . . ."

While she was moaning and sobbing, I did some fast thinking. I still had the Very pistol, and that SP chopper was going to circle Golden Gate Park at three for two more days. I had the means to bring it down, and if I could take it . . .

"You gotta find me a guy who can fly a helicopter," I said.

Our Lady stared at me blankly. I shook her by the shoulders. "Hey, you gotta snap out of it, Linda, and listen to me! I got a way to get us out of here before they drop the Big One!"

That brought her around, and I laid it out for her.

It was simple, really. We'd dress the helicopter pilot up in a trench coat and a slouch hat or something so no one could see he wasn't Bruno until I got us aboard the SP chopper.

"I'll take care of the rest," I promised. "Probably be just a pilot and a copilot, piece of cake. Then you come aboard, and we take off like a big-assed bird for the Marin side, ditch the chopper, and disappear. You saved my life, now I'll save yours."

LINDA LEWIN

"But what about *San Francisco?*" I said. "We can't just . . ."

John shrugged. "San Francisco is gonna be nuked out of existence anyway," he said. "Nothing we can do about that, our asses is all we can save."

"But all these people . . . and the dreadnaught virus . . ."

"Look at it this way—at least there'll be you and me left to spread it. . . ." He leered at me wolfishly. "I'll do my part to spread it far and wide, you better believe it, sister!"

"We just can't leave a whole city to die!"

"You got any better ideas?"

I stared at this poor savage creature, at this killing machine, at this ultimate victim of the Plague, and I thought and thought and thought, and finally I did.

"We'll capture the SP helicopter," I told him. "But we won't just escape. We'll fly down to Sutcliffe—"

"And do what?"

"Capture Harlow Prinz and Warren Feinstein. Take them to Bigelow."

"Huh?"

"Don't you see? When they tell Bigelow the truth—"

"Why the hell would they do that?"

I did my best to imitate John David's own fiercest leer. "I think I can leave that one up to you, now can't I?" I said.

He stared at me as his face slowly twisted into the mirror image of my own. "Yeah . . ." he said slowly. "I think I could enjoy that. . . ."

He frowned. "Only this is getting mighty dicey, sister. I mean, grabbing the chopper should be no sweat, and if all we was doing was putting it down in Marin and disappearing on foot, our chances would be pretty good. But faking the radio traffic long enough to fly the thing to Palo Alto and snatching the Sutcliffe creeps and getting them to Bigelow . . . Hey, the SP ain't the Legion, but they ain't that far out to lunch either. . . ."

"We've got to try it!"

"We wouldn't have a chance!"

"What if we had a diversion?" I blurted. "A big one . . ."

"A diversion?"

My blood ran cold as I said it. It was monstrous. Thousands might die. But the alternative was a million dead for no good cause. And monstrous as it was as a tactic, it was still the only just thing to do. Morally or practically, there really was no choice. It was the only chance we had to save the city, and the people had the right to know.

"What do you think would happen if everyone in San Francisco knew what you've just told me?" I said.

"That they were all going to be nuked in two days? Are you kidding? They'd go apeshit! They'd—"

"Storm the Quarantine Line en masse? Swarm out into the

Bay in hundreds of small boats? Try to get across the gaps in the bridges?''

"Jeez, it'd be just like TJ, only a thousand times bigger, the SP would have its hands full, we just might be able to. . . ."

He studied me with new eyes. "Hey, beneath all that sweetness and light, you're pretty hard-core, you know that, sister? I mean, using *a whole city* as a diversion . . .''

"These people have a right to know what's going to happen anyway, don't they, John?" I told him. "Wouldn't *you* want to know? This way, even if we fail, they get to go out fighting for something and knowing why. Better in fire than in ice.''

WALTER T. BIGELOW

Satan held me on the rack as I waited fruitlessly for David to extract Richard Bruno from San Francisco. Three and four times a day Harlow Prinz called me to demand in shriller and shriller tones that I have the city nuked. Was this the voice of God or the voice of the Devil? What did Jesus want me to do?

And then Satan put my back to the final wall.

Reports started coming in to the Daly City SP station, where I had ensconced myself, that a huge ragtag flotilla of small boats was leaving the San Francisco shoreline. Fighting had broken out all along the landward Quarantine Line.

It was becoming all too apparent that I could procrastinate no longer.

Mobs with bridging equipment were swarming onto the San Francisco ends of the Golden Gate and Oakland Bay bridges. The whole city was trying to break out of the Quarantine Zone, and they couldn't all be stopped by conventional means. Only a thermonuclear strike could prevent the new and far deadlier Plague strain from entering the general populace now.

I was forced to put in my long-delayed fateful call to the president of the United States. . . .

JOHN DAVID

I had wanted the Big Breakout to start sharply at three to make damn sure the SP chopper wasn't scared off, but Linda had told too many people, and the Lovers of Our Lady were out in the streets whipping things up for hours beforehand, and the action began to come down raggedly an hour early.

But the fighting was going on at the borders, not the center, and Golden Gate Park was just about empty. The SP chopper pilot must've been over the city already, or maybe he was the sort of righteous asshole who followed the last order no matter what.

For even with half the city already throwing itself against the Quarantine Line, the chopper appeared over the park right on the money at three sharp.

I fired off the Very pistol, and down it came. I stuck my miniauto conspicuously in our pilot's back and frog-marched him to the open chopper door.

As I had figured, there were only a pilot and a copilot in the cockpit. The moment we were inside, I jammed the muzzle of my piece into the back of the pilot's neck.

"Outside, assholes!" I ordered. "But strip first! One word out of either of you and I blow you away!"

"Hey—"

"What the —"

"I told you, no lip! Out of those uniforms! Move your asses!"

They took one look at the miniauto and another at me, and stripped down to boxer shorts and T-shirts muy pronto, you better believe it!

"Out, assholes. Better run till you drop, and don't look back!"

I booted them out of the chopper and fired a long burst over their heads as Linda climbed aboard, and they ran for the nearest bushes.

Then me and our pilot put on their uniforms, which I figured would come in mighty handy if we ever made it to Sutcliffe, and off we went.

The skies were empty as we headed south over the city at about three thousand feet, but things started getting hairy as we approached the Quarantine Line.

I could see ragged mobs of people moving toward the SP positions below, the SP troops were using heavy machine-guns and some light artillery, and the air beneath us was thick with gunpowder smoke, through which I could see sparkles, laser-straight tracers, occasional explosions.

All hell was breaking loose on the ground, and the airspace below us was full of helicopter gunships making low, slow strafing runs with cannon and rockets.

But all the thunder and lightning and confusion made it easier for us in the end, seeing as we were one chopper out of many.

"Bravo five three seven Charlie, what the hell are you doing up there?" a voice screeched at us over the radio.

"Don't answer!" I told our pilot. "Take her down into the traffic!"

When we had dropped down into the cloud of gunships, I screamed into my microphone, "Motherfucking black-carder faggot bastards!" And fired off a few rockets.

"Hey, those are *our* people down there!"

"And *our* asses up *here!* You just fly this thing, and let me worry about tactics, okay!" And I fired off a couple more blind shots into the confusion.

It worked like a charm. Every time we got static on the radio, I cursed and screamed like a good combat animal and fired a few random rockets at the ground and nobody challenged us as we threaded our way south over the combat zone.

Once we were well clear, we went back up to three thousand feet, and the only traffic we saw between Daly City and Palo Alto was a few more gunships heading north into the mess far below who probably didn't even see us.

We landed inside the Sutcliffe compound right in front of the administration building and sat there with our rotor whumping as company rent-a-cops poured raggedly out of the building and finally managed to get us surrounded.

"Stay here, and fer chrissakes keep the engine running," I told Linda and the pilot. And climbed out of the chopper to make like a modern major general.

"National Emergency!" I barked at the bozo in charge of the rent-a-cops. "Direct orders from Walter T. Bigelow, director of the Federal Quarantine Agency. He wants Harlow Prinz and Warren Feinstein in his headquarters half an hour ago, and we're here to get 'em!"

"Hey, I got no orders to—"

"Argue with Bigelow if you want to!" I snapped. I gave the

sucker a comradely shrug. "But I don't advise it. I mean, there's already been some kind of screw-up over this with all the heat going on, and he ain't exactly being reasonable just now, if you get me."

"I don't take my orders from the SP!"

"Your funeral, pal," I told him, nodding toward the chopper. "I got orders to blow the shit out of this place if I meet any resistance, and there's five more gunships orbiting just over the ridgeline in case you got any dumb notions . . ."

"Hey, hey, don't get your balls in an uproar," the head rent-a-cop soothed much more politely, and trotted off into the building.

I waited there outside the chopper surrounded by rent-a-cops for what seemed like ten thousand sweaty years but couldn't have been more than ten minutes by the clock.

Finally the head rent-a-cop appeared with two middle-aged bozos. One of them seemed to be staggering toward me in a daze, but the other was the sort of arrogant in-charge son of a bitch you want to kill on sight.

"What's the meaning of this?" he screamed in my face. "I'm Harlow Prinz, I'm the president of this company, and I don't—"

"And I'm just Walter Bigelow's errand boy, but I don't take shit either," I told him. "Except of course from the boss man, and I got enough of that for being late already! So do us both a big favor and get into this chopper." I waved my miniauto. " 'Cause if you don't, shit is about to flow downhill, if you get my meaning."

The wimpy type, who had to be Warren Feinstein, started to climb aboard, but that murdering meatfucker Prinz stood there with his hands on his hips looking suspicious. He took a good long look at my badly fitting uniform. "Let's see your papers," he said.

I brought up the muzzle of my piece and pointed it at his belly button. "You're lookin' right at 'em," I said.

"Harlow, for chrissakes, he *means* it!" Feinstein said, and hustled his ass into the copter.

Prinz moved slowly past me to the door and reluctantly started to board the chopper, but he must've spotted Linda when he peered inside and put it all together.

'Cause he suddenly aimed a sloppy kick at my nuts that missed the target but knocked me off balance, yelled, "Shoot! Shoot!" at his rent-a-cops, and broke and ran.

Furious as I was, I didn't blow my combat cool.

I leaped through the door, scattering the rent-a-cops with a long fanning burst as our pilot lifted the chopper, and flipped myself into the copilot's seat.

By this time we were about a hundred feet in the air, and heading straight up into the wild blue yonder.

"Hold it right here a minute!" I told the pilot.

The rent-a-cops were scattering for cover. Only a few of 'em had the balls to fire a few useless shots up over their shoulders and they plinked harmlessly off the chopper's armored belly.

Prinz was running for the administration building. I smiled. I lined the bastard up in my sights and savored it just for a moment. This, after all, was the son of a bitch who was willing to let the Plague take us all to line his own pockets. I had wasted more citizens than I could count, but this was going to be special. This was going to be primo.

"Thanks ever so much for making my day," I told Harlow Prinz as he reached the stairs leading up to the entrance. And I fired a single rocket.

A perfect shot. It hit him right in the base of the spine and blew him to dogmeat.

I went aft, where Feinstein was cowering against a bulkhead. I grabbed him by the neck with my left hand, squeezed his jaws open, and jammed the muzzle of my piece down his throat.

"You saw what I did to your buddy," I told him. "And knowing what I know about you sons of bitches and what you've done, you better believe I enjoyed it just as much as I'll enjoy wasting *you* if you don't do exactly what you're told. Get the message, meatfucker?"

Feinstein nodded and I pulled the gun barrel out of his mouth. And when I tossed his worthless ass onto the deck, he just lay there blubbering. "I *told* Harlow he was going too far, it's not my fault, it wasn't my idea, Bigelow will believe me, won't he, I swear I'll tell him the truth, I never thought, I never knew. . . ."

"He *better* believe you, meatfucker, or a lot of asses are gonna be grass," I told him. "And *you* better believe that you're gonna go first!"

*   *   *

WALTER T. BIGELOW

The station was in an uproar. The situation was growing graver by the minute. The mob had bridged the gap in the Golden Gate and fighting was raging on the Marin side of the span. Our gunboats were sinking scores of small craft loaded to the gunwales with black-carders, but all was chaos on the Bay; they couldn't establish or hold a line. The landward Quarantine Line was crumbling under human wave onslaughts.

There was no alternative. When I got the president on the line I was going to have to ask him to authorize an immediate nuclear strike against San Francisco.

But while I was waiting for my call to the White House to get through, there was a commotion in my outer office, and a moment later an SP captain burst inside.

"Warren Feinstein's outside, Mr. Director," he stammered. "There's . . . there's a girl with him who says she's Our Lady of Love Reborn . . . and there's a man holding him at gunpoint. Says he's gonna blow his head off if we make a move and—"

There was a further commotion in the outer office and then Feinstein was rudely thrown through the doorway by a man who held the barrel of a miniauto at the back of his neck, followed by a young girl, and half-a-dozen SP men with drawn pistols.

The man with the miniauto was John David, whom I had sent into San Francisco after Richard Bruno. And he was wearing an SP uniform.

"What's the meaning of this?" I demanded. "This isn't Bruno! How did you—"

"No shit!" David snarled, prodding Feinstein with his gun barrel. "Go ahead, tell the man, or I'll blow your worthless head off!"

Tears poured from the eyes of Sutcliffe's chairman as he blubbered out the most incredible and chilling story.

"Harlow *lied* to you, Bruno's virus wasn't an ambient Plague variant, it was a *cure* for all Plague variants, an artificial venereal disease—"

"*A cure?* But then why—"

"—that conferred total immunity—"

"If it was a cure, then why on Earth did you suppress it?" I shouted at him. "Why did you tell me—"

"It's a venereal disease!" Feinstein babbled. "Spreads by

itself, nothing for us to market, it would have bankrupted Sutcliffe, brought on an economic depression, Harlow insisted—''

I could not believe my ears. I could not be hearing this. ''You suppressed a total cure for the Plague to preserve your own profits? My God, Prinz kept trying to get me to nuke San Francisco *just to keep Sutcliffe solvent?''*

Feinstein shook his head. ''By then it was too late, don't you see?'' he moaned. ''The whole thing had gone too far. I warned him, I swear I did, but he insisted that San Francisco *had* to be nuked to cover up what we'd done. . . .''

Feinstein seemed to pull himself together with an enormous effort. ''But you can't do that now,'' he said much more coherently. ''You won't do that now. I'm willing to take my medicine, even if it means spending the rest of my life in jail. Harlow was wrong, monstrously wrong, and I was weak, horribly weak. You can't nuke San Francisco. You can't kill millions of people. You can't destroy the dreadnaught virus.''

Was this the truth, or was it Satan's greatest lie? Feinstein was, after all, speaking with a gun at his throat. And he was a self-admitted liar.

If this was the Devil speaking through him, and I believed Satan's greatest lie, I would infect the nation with a deadly new Plague variant that might destroy all human life.

But if God had chosen this unlikely instrument to reveal His truth at the eleventh hour and I *didn't* believe it, I would not only be responsible for the deaths of a million people, I would be responsible for destroying God's own cure for the Plague.

What was I to do? What could I believe? *Whatever* the truth was, Satan could not have devised for me a more perfect moral dilemma.

''The president on the line . . .'' said a voice on my intercom.

No man should be forced to make such a decision. But I was. And I had to do it now. But I could not. There was only one thing that I could do.

There, in front of Feinstein, and David, and my own men, and with the president of the United States waiting on the telephone, I sank unashamedly to my knees and prayed aloud.

''Please, Jesus, I know that this cup cannot pass from me,'' I prayed. ''But grant me at least one mercy. Send me a Sign. Show me Your Countenance.''

And God, in His infinite wisdom, answered my prayer, through the most unlikely of instruments.

The young girl stepped forward. ''Let me help you,'' she

said softly. She took my hand in hers and raised me to my feet
"Let me be your Sign," she said.

"*You*? You're—"

"Our Lady of Love Reborn—"

"—the blasphemous mouthpiece of Satan!"

"No, I'm not. Nothing speaks through me but the truth in an
ordinary girl's heart, and I'm very much afraid," she said with
the strangest gentleness. "But I know that this man is speaking
the truth, and there's no one else. So I *have* to be your Sign, now
don't I? In the only way I can."

"How?" I asked softly, wanting very much, in that moment,
to believe. In Jesus. In God's Grace. In anything that would
show me the truth.

Even in she whom I had believed to be my nemesis, even in
Our Lady of Love Reborn, if she could make me.

"By placing my life in your hands," she said.

I locked eyes with Our Lady of Love Reborn. They were
young and they were fearful, but there was a strength in them too
that seemed timeless. She smiled the Madonna's smile at me. Or
was this only what I was longing to see?

"There's a helicopter waiting outside. I'm going to go to it
and fly back to San Francisco. If the city dies at your hand, so
will I. Would Satan's mouthpiece do that, Walter Bigelow?"

"The president on the line . . ."

"You would do that?" I said. "You'd really do that?"

She nibbled nervously at her bottom lip. She nodded de-
murely. "You'll have to kill me right now to stop me," she
said, letting go of my hand, and turning to confront the men
blocking the doorway. "Will you tell these men to shoot me,
Mr. Bigelow? Or will you let me pass?"

JOHN DAVID
■■■■■■■■

"Hey, Linda, you can't do that, we're safe here, don't be
crazy!" I said, grabbing her by the arm.

The SP guards trained their pistols on us, looking to Bigelow
for orders. I brought up my miniauto, flipped it to full rock and
roll as conspicuously as I could, just daring the mothers to try it.

"I can, John, I must," Linda told me, and took two steps forward with me hanging on to her.

I turned to confront Bigelow. I could see that he *wanted* to believe. Wouldn't you?

What can I tell you, brothers and sisters? Maybe I figured Bigelow needed a final push. Anyway, how could I let her do this thing all alone? A short life, but a happy one, as we say in the Army of the Living Dead.

"Not without me, you don't," I said, taking her hand.

"The president on the line . . ."

I whipped the miniauto around and pointed it right at Bigelow's head. "I could blow you away right now," I told him. "And don't think I wouldn't enjoy it, meatfucker!"

Walter T. Bigelow looked straight into my eyes and didn't flinch. The bastard had balls, you had to give him that.

"But I won't," I told him. " 'Cause this old zombie believes her. And you've gotta believe her too."

"Make me," Walter T. Bigelow said softly. "I truly pray that you can."

"Then try *this*," I said. I smiled, I shrugged, and I threw the miniauto on the floor in front of him. "We're gonna walk out of here to that helicopter, and we're gonna fly back to San Francisco. You can clock us on radar."

I turned to face the pistols of the SPs. "Or you can have these bozos fill us fill of holes—your choice, Bigelow," I said over my shoulder. "Of course then you'll never know, now will you?"

And hand in hand we walked toward the armed men blocking the doorway.

The guards' fingers tightened against their triggers.

The moment hung in the air.

"Let them pass," Walter T. Bigelow said behind us. "Praise the mysterious workings of the Lord."

WALTER T. BIGELOW

And the two of them walked out of the room hand in hand toward the helicopter, toward San Francisco, toward their faith in the wisdom and mercy of God, which no true Christian, in that moment, could justly deny.

In all my life, no one had placed greater trust in me than this young girl and this savage young man.

A nimbus of clear white light seemed to surround them as they walked out the door, and there were tears in my eyes as I watched them go.

God could not have granted me a clearer Sign.

I sank once more to my knees and gave thanks for His infinite wisdom, His infinite mercy, for His presence in that room, in that moment, in my heart, for the Sign He had granted me in my ultimate hour of need.

The rest is, as they say, history, and this is the end of the story of my part in it.

I did not ask the president for a nuclear strike. Instead I told him what Feinstein had told me. And I issued an order for my troops to cease firing, to let those seeking to leave San Francisco pass as well.

There was much confusion afterward as hundreds of thousands of people poured out of the San Francisco Quarantine Zone. Congress called for my impeachment. I offered up my resignation. It was refused. Proceedings began in the House.

But as the hearings began, hundreds of escapees from San Francisco were rounded up, and all of them tested out blue. And the dreadnaught virus was found in all of their bodies.

So did the Plague Years end. And so too my public life. I became a national hero once more, and though there was no further need for a Federal Quarantine Agency or its director, I could no doubt have been elected to any office in the land.

But I chose instead to retire. And write this memoir. And go off on a long retreat into the desert with my family to try to understand the mysterious ways of God. And to reconcile with my wife.

And God granted us an easy reconciliation, for Satan had gone from her, if he had every really possessed her, and she believed in me again.

"It was a true Christian act, Walter, and a brave one," she told me the night she took me once more into her arms. "God works in mysterious ways."

So He does. And perhaps the true wisdom is that that is all we can ever really know of the workings of His Will.

Did Satan send the Plague to torment us? Or did God send the Plague to chastise and test us?

If so, it was a terrible chastisement and a cruel testing. But so was the Great Flood, and the Ten Plagues, and the Forty Years in the Wilderness, and of course Jesus's own martyrdom on the Cross.

"Love thy neighbor as thyself," Jesus told us, and was crucified for it.

How could that be the Will of a God of Love?

How could the Plague Years be the Will of God either?

I don't know. I don't think I ever will.

And yet my faith is still strong. For God spoke to me in my greatest hour of need through the unlikely instrumentalities of a young girl whom I had believed to be Satan's daughter and a vicious creature who had certainly spent most of his life doing the Devil's work on Earth.

Such a God I will never understand.

In such a God I can only believe.

Such a God I can only love.

ABOUT THE EDITORS

Lou Aronica is the Publisher of Bantam Spectra Books, a publishing imprint he founded. He lives in Manhattan with his wife, Barbara Cohen.

Shawna McCarthy is a Senior Editor at Bantam Books. She has edited several previous anthologies and edited *Isaac Asimov's Science Fiction Magazine* for several years. She won the Hugo Award for Best Professional Editor in 1984. She lives in Manhattan with her husband, Wayne Barlowe, and their infant daughter Cayley.